Crabgrass

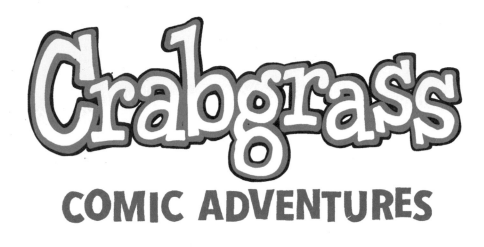

COMIC ADVENTURES

Crabgrass
COMIC ADVENTURES

TAUHID BONDIA

Andrews McMeel
PUBLISHING®

ONCE UPON A TIME (NOT LONG AGO), PHONES WERE CONNECTED DIRECTLY TO THE WALL AND NEVER RAN OUT OF BATTERY. TELEVISIONS WERE DEEPER THAN THEY WERE WIDE, AND HAVING MORE THAN 35 CHANNELS MEANT YOU WERE RICH. YES, THINGS WERE VERY DIFFERENT IN THIS GOLDEN, BYGONE ERA, BUT NOT ALL THINGS. BACK THEN, JUST LIKE NOW, A COUPLE OF KIDS COULD MEET, HAVE AN AWESOME ADVENTURE AND FORGE A LIFELONG PACT OF FRIENDSHIP IN THE MATTER OF A FEW HOURS. SOMETIMES THOSE KIDS ARE NAMED KEVIN AND MILES. AND WHEN THAT'S THE CASE, WELL, YOU MAKE A BOOK ABOUT THEM, DON'T YOU?

THIS IS THAT BOOK. IT'S ALSO ABOUT KEVIN AND MILES' FAMILIES AND FRIENDS, BUT IT'S MOSTLY ABOUT THE FRIENDSHIPS WE FIND OURSELVES A PART OF AS KIDS AND HOW THEY SHAPE WHO WE ARE. KEVIN AND MILES ARE ME AND MY BEST FRIEND GROWING UP. THEY ARE EVERY KID I KNEW IN MY CHILDHOOD. THEY ARE MY DAUGHTER, MY SON, MY NIECES AND NEPHEWS, AND RANDOM CHILDREN I COME ACROSS IN THE WILD. IN FACT, ONE (OR BOTH) OF THEM IS PROBABLY YOU! ISN'T THAT NICE?

THIS BOOK IS FOR HAILEY. EVERYTHING I DO IS FOR HAILEY.

TAUHID BONDIA

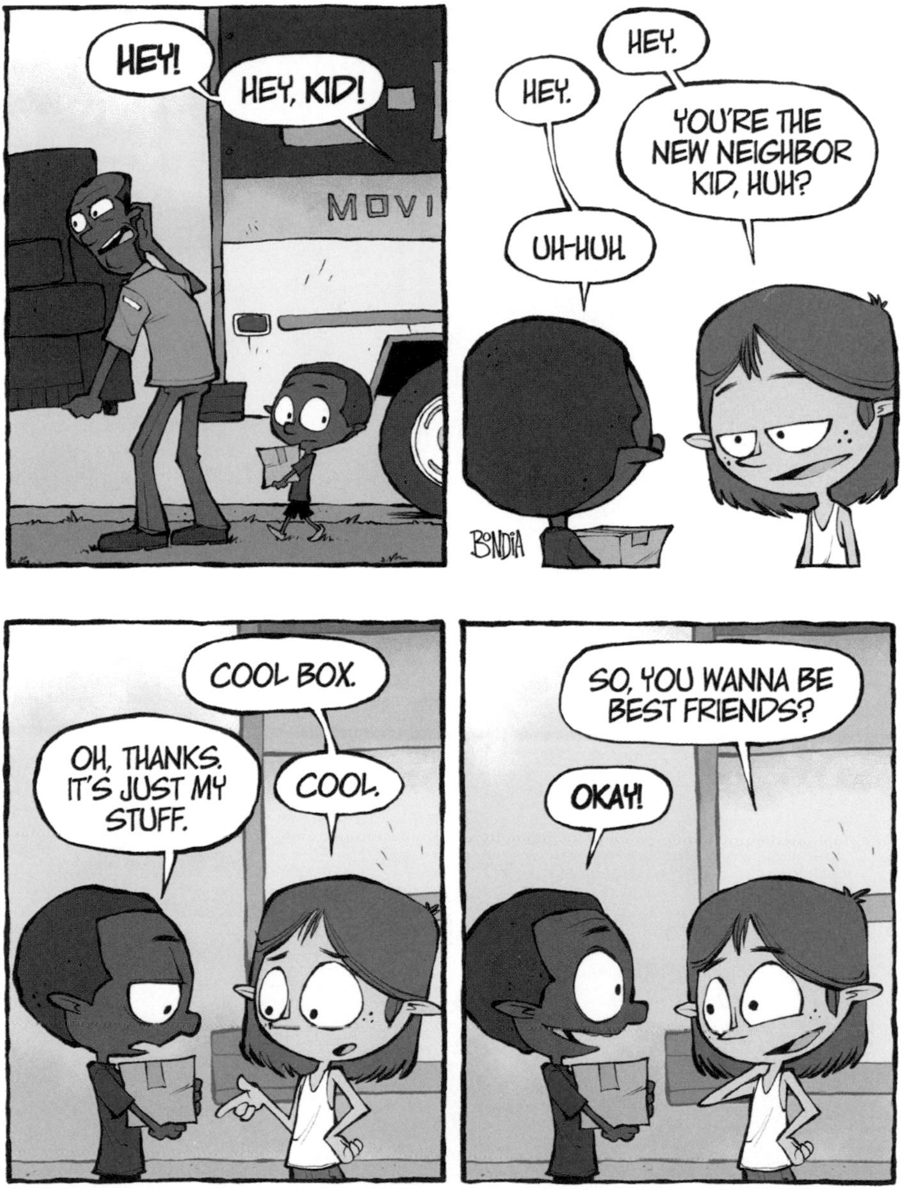
HEY!
HEY, KID!
MOVI
HEY.
HEY.
UH-HUH.
YOU'RE THE NEW NEIGHBOR KID, HUH?
BONDIA
COOL BOX.
OH, THANKS. IT'S JUST MY STUFF.
COOL.
SO, YOU WANNA BE BEST FRIENDS?
OKAY!

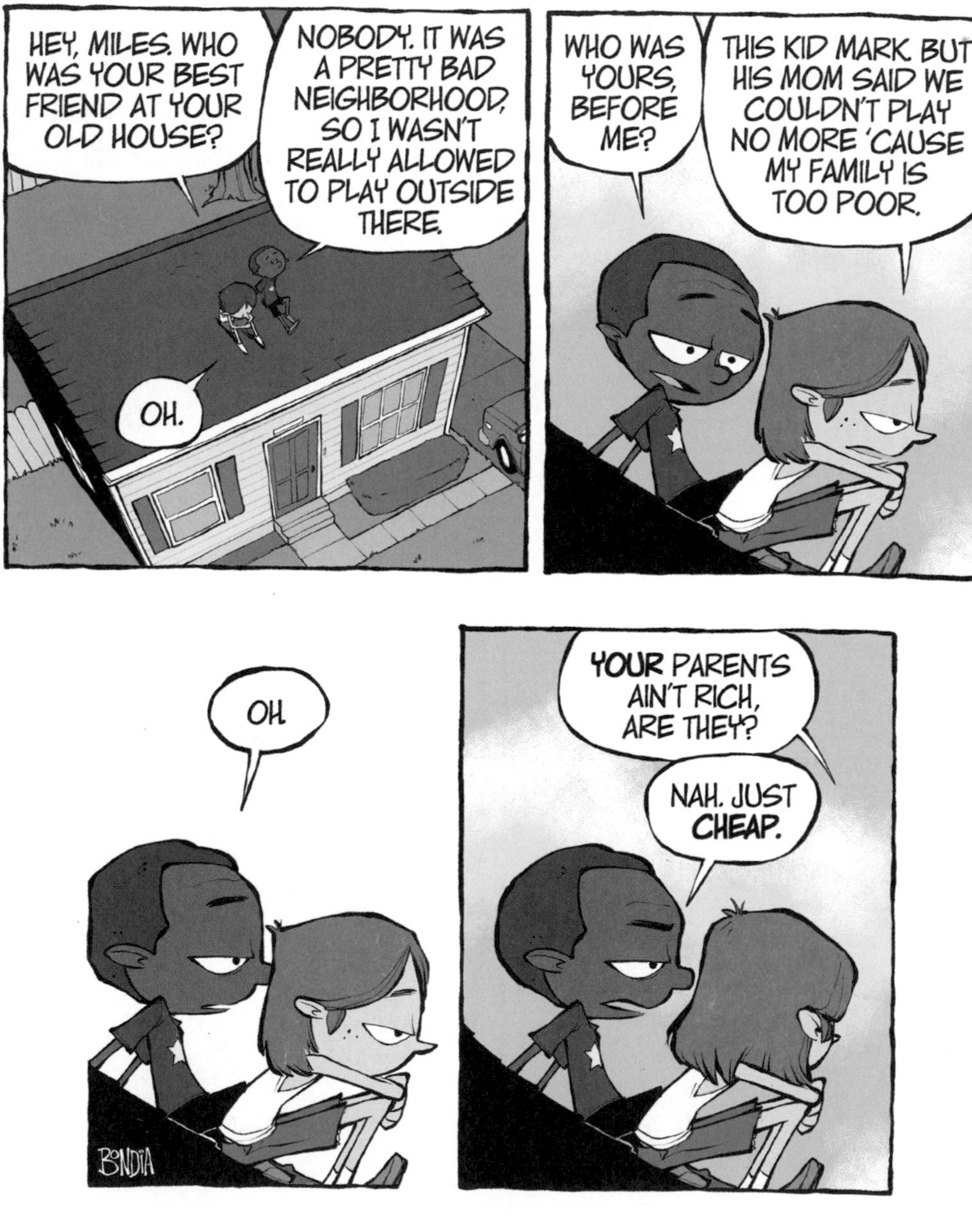
HEY, MILES. WHO WAS YOUR BEST FRIEND AT YOUR OLD HOUSE?
NOBODY. IT WAS A PRETTY BAD NEIGHBORHOOD, SO I WASN'T REALLY ALLOWED TO PLAY OUTSIDE THERE.
OH.
WHO WAS YOURS, BEFORE ME?
THIS KID MARK. BUT HIS MOM SAID WE COULDN'T PLAY NO MORE 'CAUSE MY FAMILY IS TOO POOR.
OH.
BONDIA
YOUR PARENTS AIN'T RICH, ARE THEY?
NAH. JUST **CHEAP.**

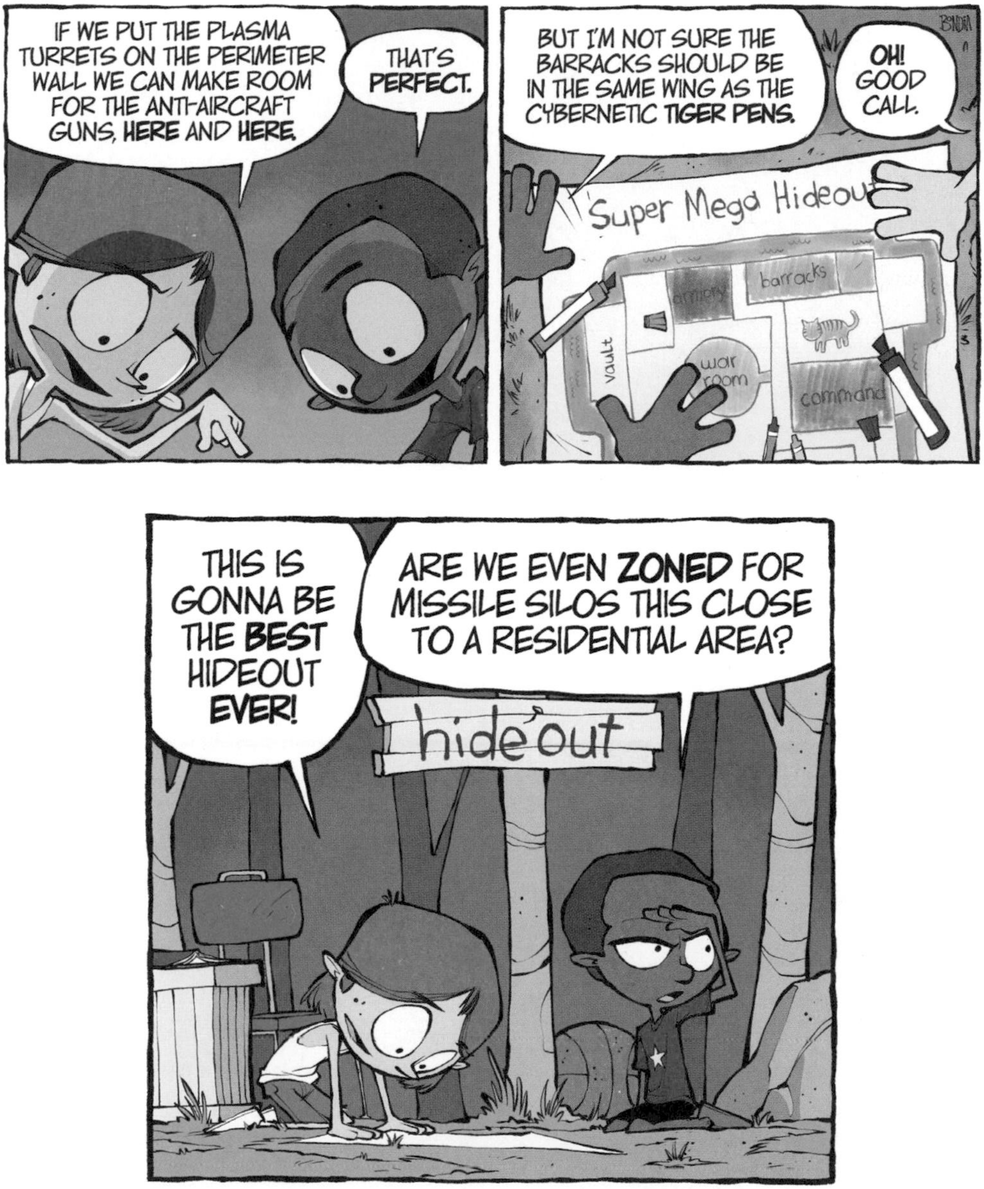
IF WE PUT THE PLASMA TURRETS ON THE PERIMETER WALL WE CAN MAKE ROOM FOR THE ANTI-AIRCRAFT GUNS, **HERE** AND **HERE**.
THAT'S **PERFECT**.
BUT I'M NOT SURE THE BARRACKS SHOULD BE IN THE SAME WING AS THE CYBERNETIC **TIGER PENS**.
OH! GOOD CALL.
Super Mega Hideout
armory
barracks
vault
war room
command
THIS IS GONNA BE THE **BEST** HIDEOUT **EVER**!
ARE WE EVEN **ZONED** FOR MISSILE SILOS THIS CLOSE TO A RESIDENTIAL AREA?
hide'out

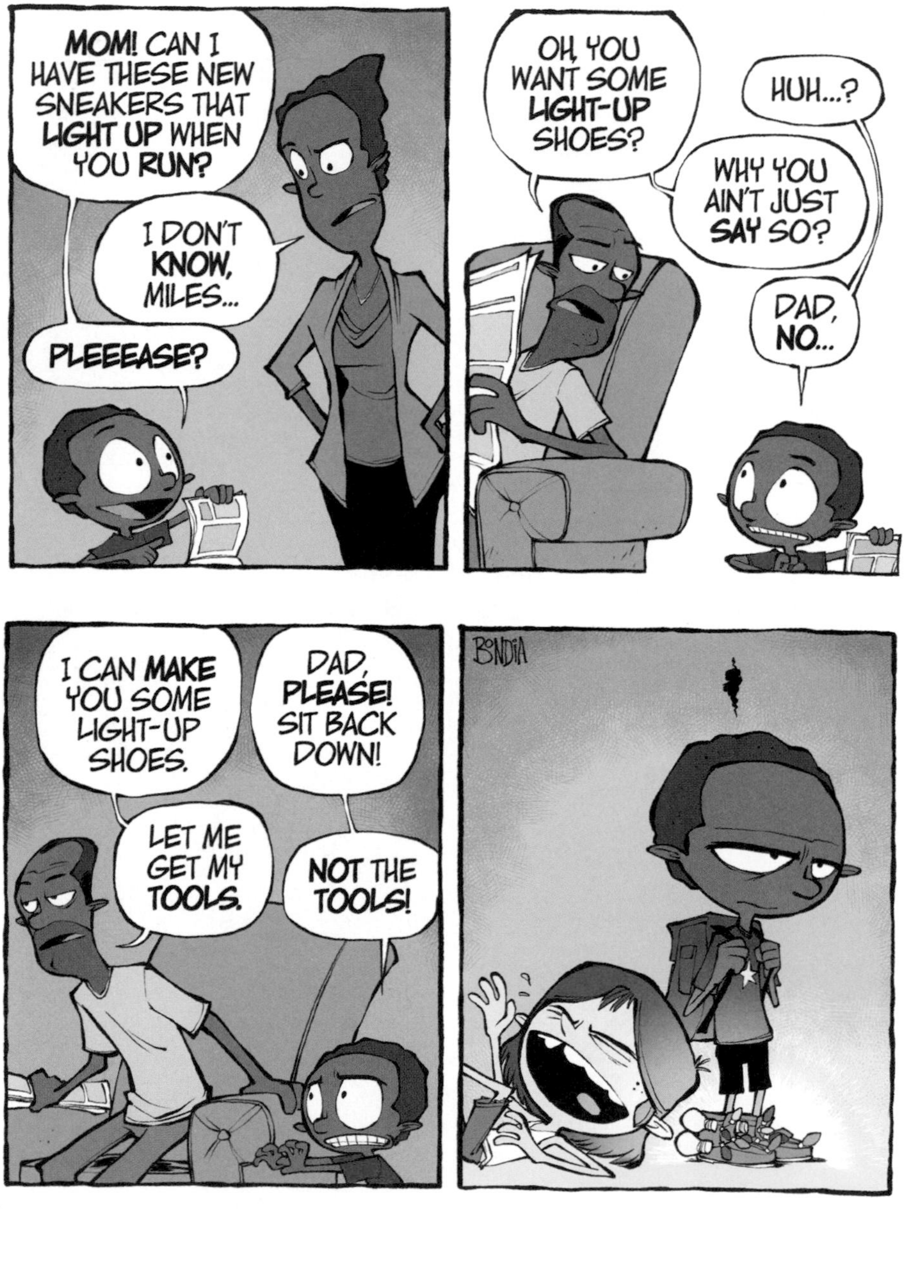
MOM! CAN I HAVE THESE NEW SNEAKERS THAT LIGHT UP WHEN YOU RUN?
I DON'T KNOW, MILES...
PLEEEASE?
OH, YOU WANT SOME LIGHT-UP SHOES?
HUH...?
WHY YOU AIN'T JUST SAY SO?
DAD, NO...
I CAN MAKE YOU SOME LIGHT-UP SHOES.
LET ME GET MY TOOLS.
DAD, PLEASE! SIT BACK DOWN!
NOT THE TOOLS!
BONDIA

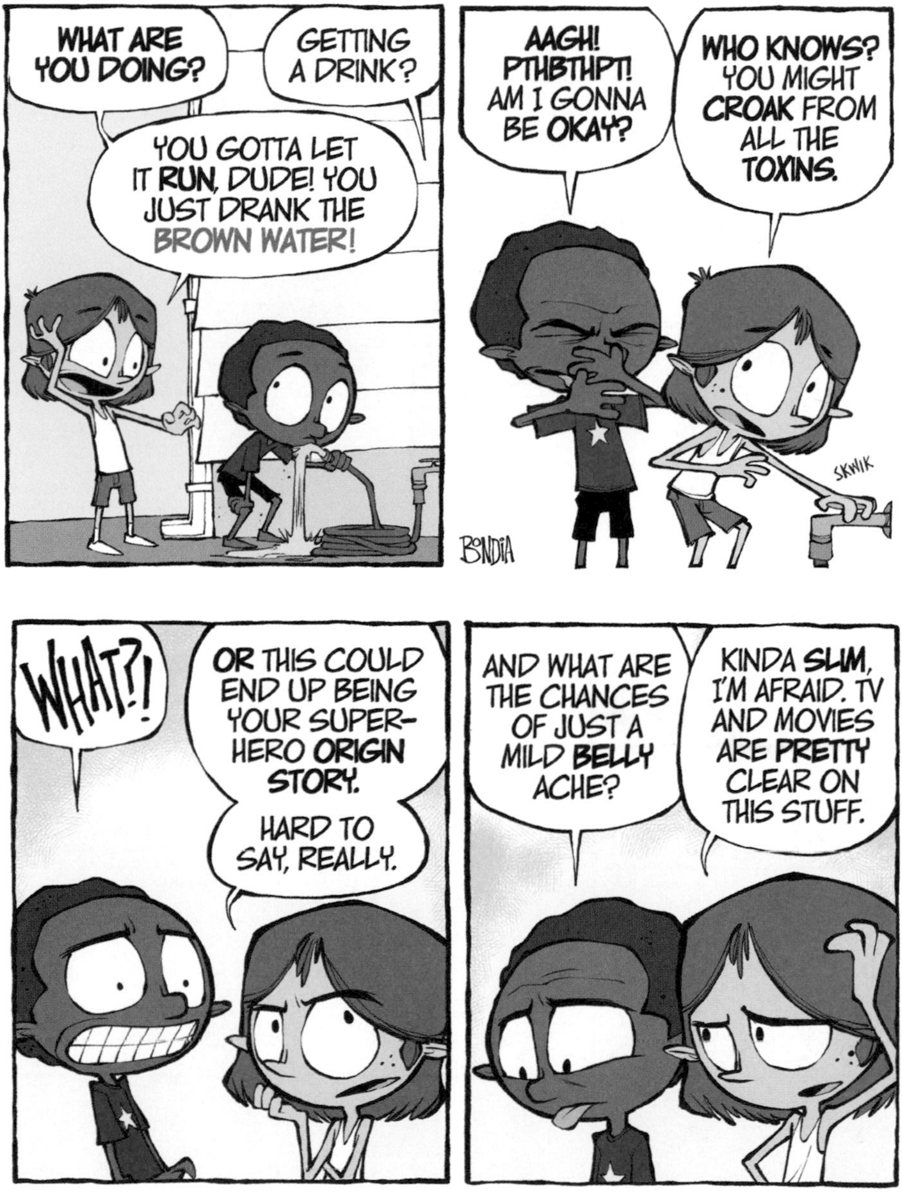
WHAT ARE YOU DOING?
GETTING A DRINK?
YOU GOTTA LET IT RUN, DUDE! YOU JUST DRANK THE BROWN WATER!
AAGH! PTHBTHPT! AM I GONNA BE OKAY?
WHO KNOWS? YOU MIGHT CROAK FROM ALL THE TOXINS.
SKWIK
BONDIA
WHAT?!
OR THIS COULD END UP BEING YOUR SUPER-HERO ORIGIN STORY.
HARD TO SAY, REALLY.
AND WHAT ARE THE CHANCES OF JUST A MILD BELLY ACHE?
KINDA SLIM, I'M AFRAID. TV AND MOVIES ARE PRETTY CLEAR ON THIS STUFF.

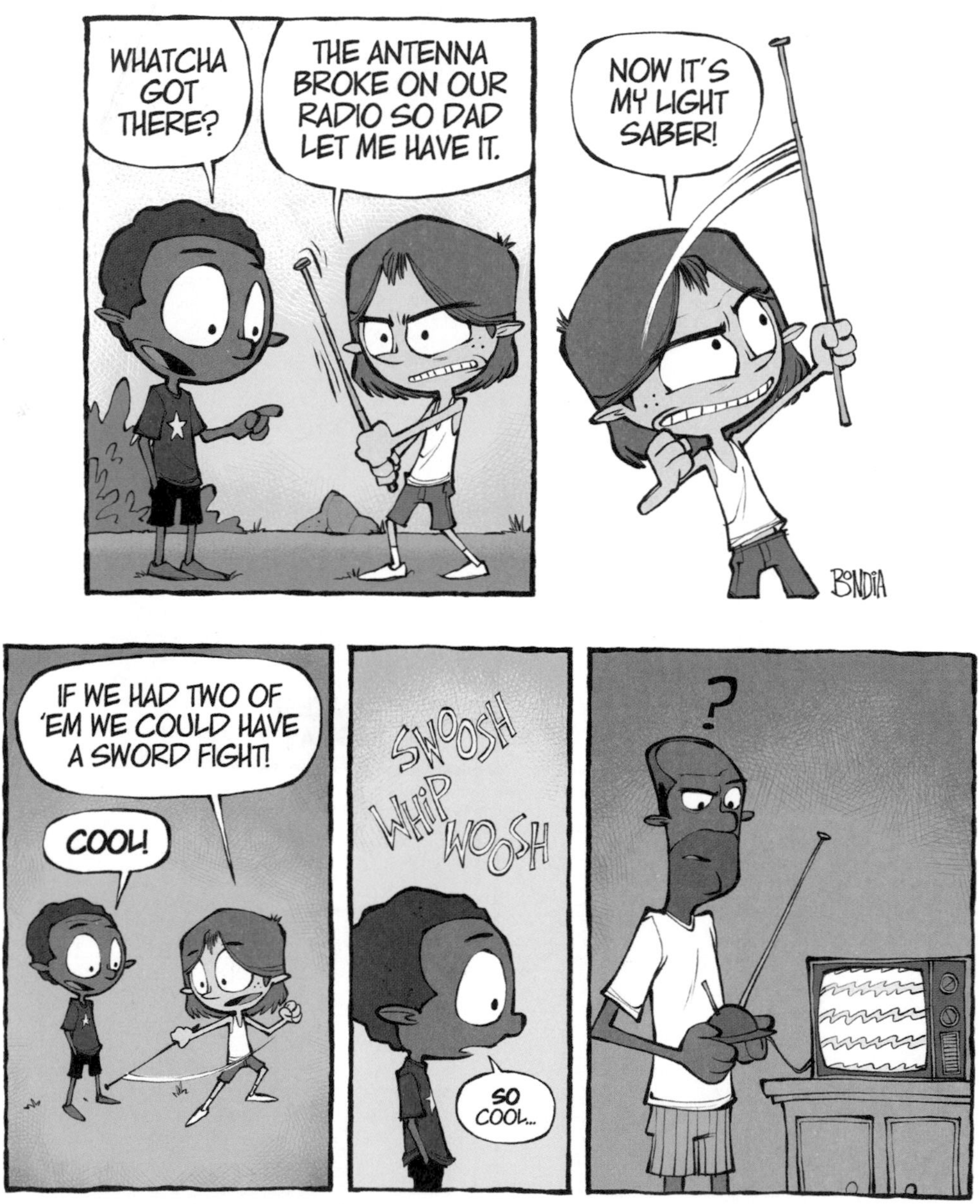
WHATCHA GOT THERE?
THE ANTENNA BROKE ON OUR RADIO SO DAD LET ME HAVE IT.
NOW IT'S MY LIGHT SABER!
BONDIA
IF WE HAD TWO OF 'EM WE COULD HAVE A SWORD FIGHT!
COOL!
SWOOSH
WHIP
WOOSH
SO COOL...
?

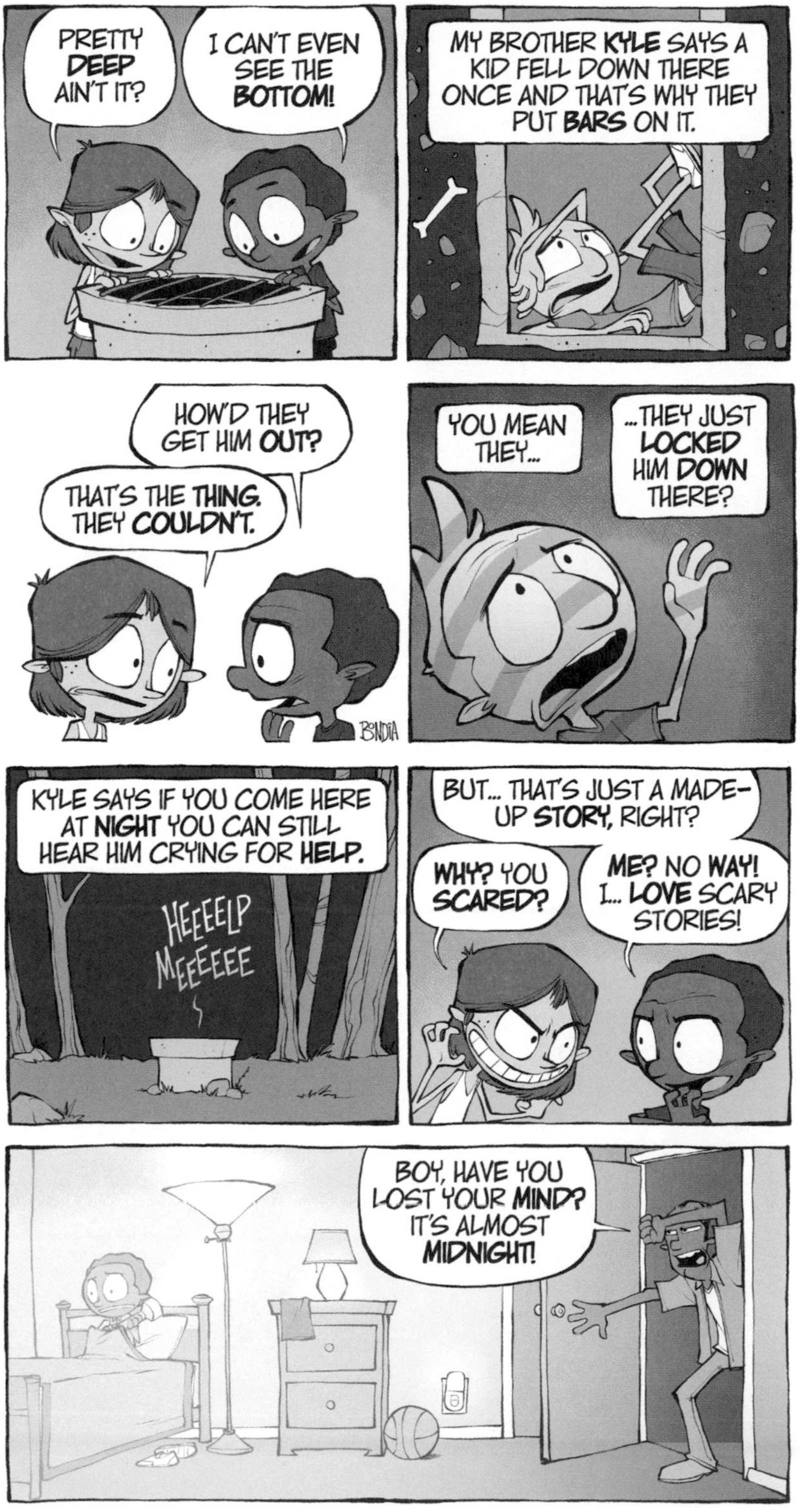
PRETTY DEEP AIN'T IT?
I CAN'T EVEN SEE THE BOTTOM!
MY BROTHER KYLE SAYS A KID FELL DOWN THERE ONCE AND THAT'S WHY THEY PUT BARS ON IT.
HOW'D THEY GET HIM OUT?
THAT'S THE THING. THEY COULDN'T.
BONDIA
YOU MEAN THEY...
...THEY JUST LOCKED HIM DOWN THERE?
KYLE SAYS IF YOU COME HERE AT NIGHT YOU CAN STILL HEAR HIM CRYING FOR HELP.
HEEEELP MEEEEEE
BUT... THAT'S JUST A MADE-UP STORY, RIGHT?
WHY? YOU SCARED?
ME? NO WAY! I... LOVE SCARY STORIES!
BOY, HAVE YOU LOST YOUR MIND? IT'S ALMOST MIDNIGHT!

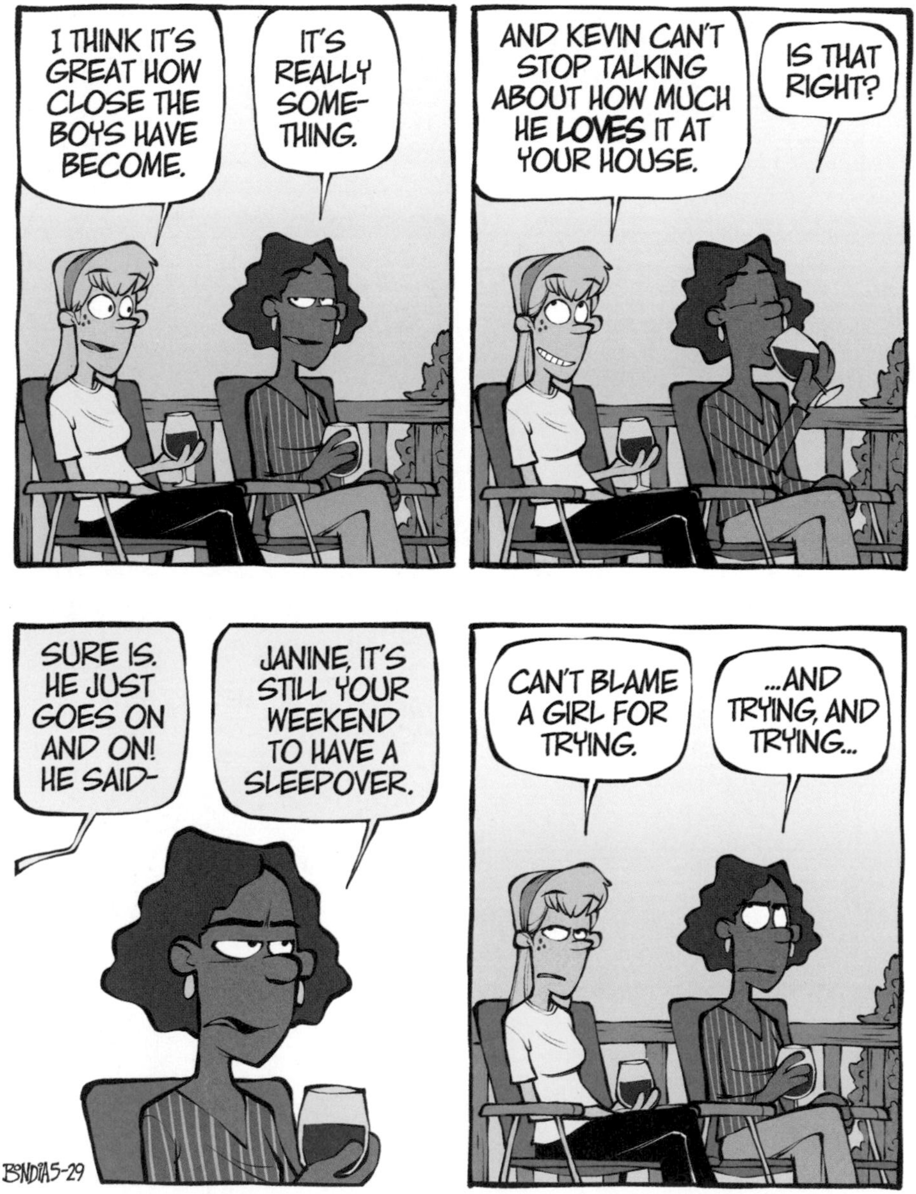
I THINK IT'S GREAT HOW CLOSE THE BOYS HAVE BECOME.
IT'S REALLY SOME-THING.
AND KEVIN CAN'T STOP TALKING ABOUT HOW MUCH HE **LOVES** IT AT YOUR HOUSE.
IS THAT RIGHT?
SURE IS. HE JUST GOES ON AND ON! HE SAID-
JANINE, IT'S STILL YOUR WEEKEND TO HAVE A SLEEPOVER.
CAN'T BLAME A GIRL FOR TRYING.
...AND TRYING, AND TRYING...
BSNDIA5-29

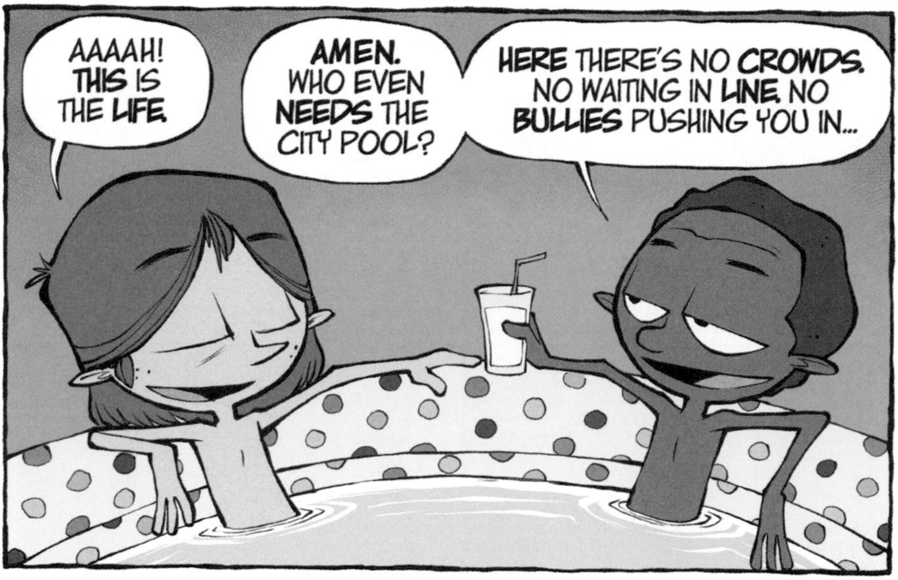
AAAAH! THIS IS THE LIFE.
AMEN. WHO EVEN NEEDS THE CITY POOL?
HERE THERE'S NO CROWDS. NO WAITING IN LINE. NO BULLIES PUSHING YOU IN...

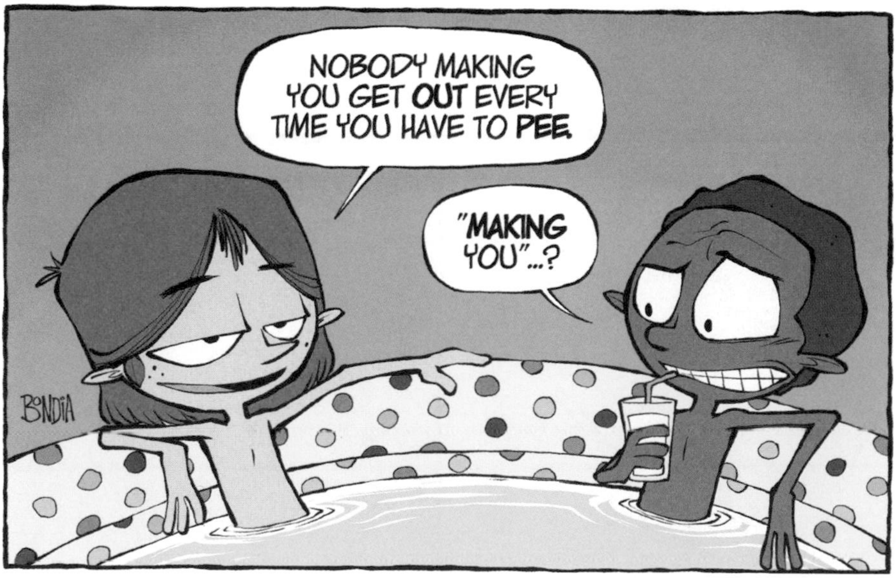
NOBODY MAKING YOU GET OUT EVERY TIME YOU HAVE TO PEE.
"MAKING YOU"...?
BONDIA

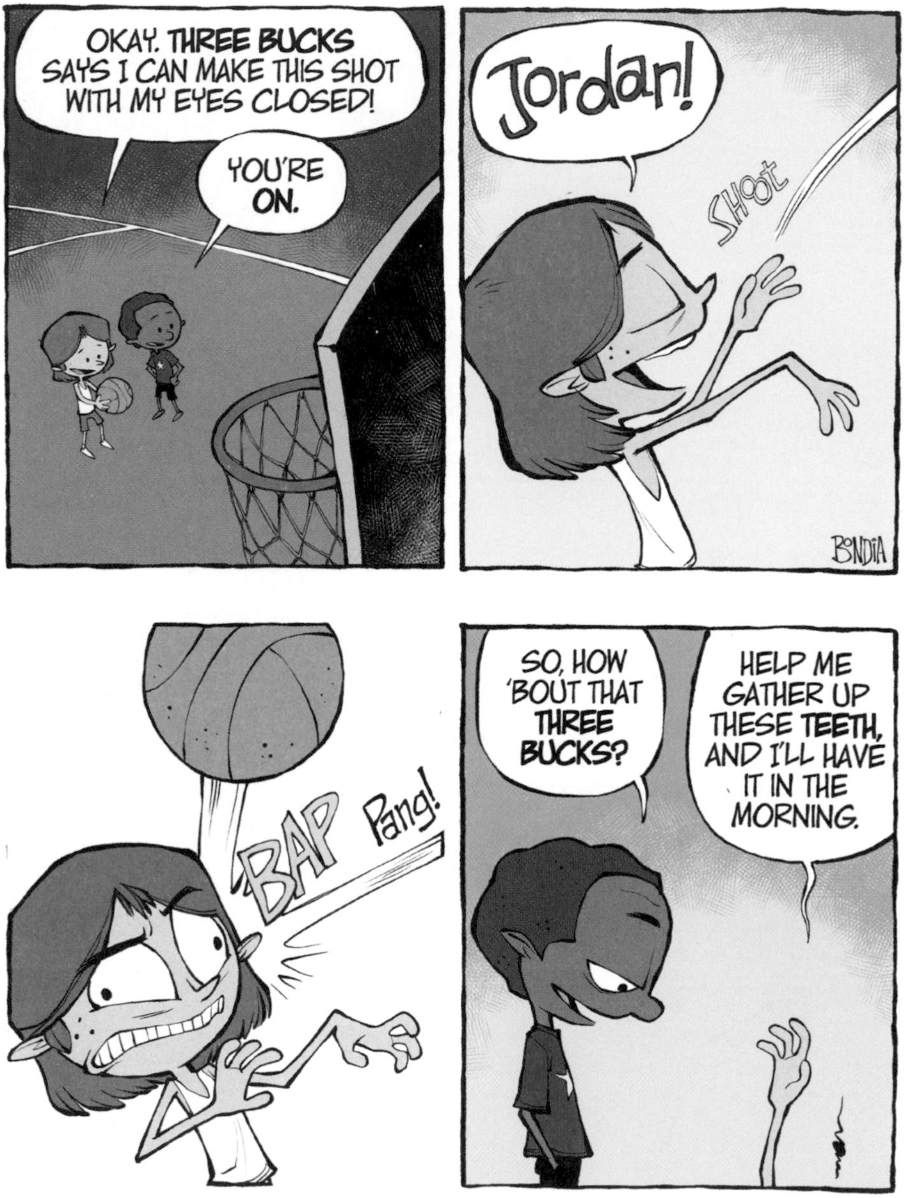
OKAY. THREE BUCKS SAYS I CAN MAKE THIS SHOT WITH MY EYES CLOSED!
YOU'RE ON.
Jordan!
SHOOT
BONDIA
BAP
Pang!
SO, HOW 'BOUT THAT THREE BUCKS?
HELP ME GATHER UP THESE TEETH, AND I'LL HAVE IT IN THE MORNING.

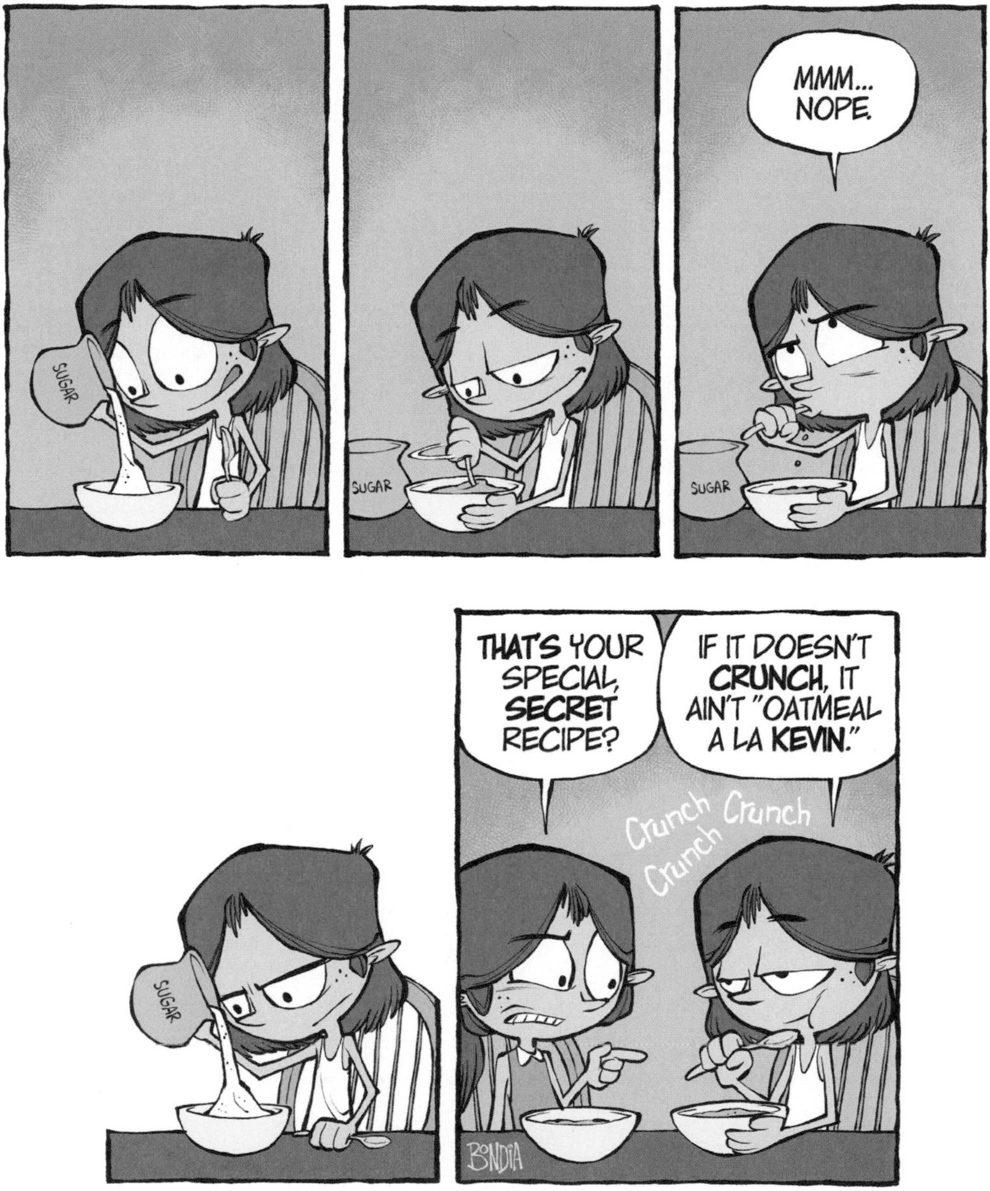
SUGAR
SUGAR
SUGAR
MMM... NOPE.
SUGAR
THAT'S YOUR SPECIAL, SECRET RECIPE?
IF IT DOESN'T CRUNCH, IT AIN'T "OATMEAL A LA KEVIN."
Crunch Crunch Crunch
BONDIA

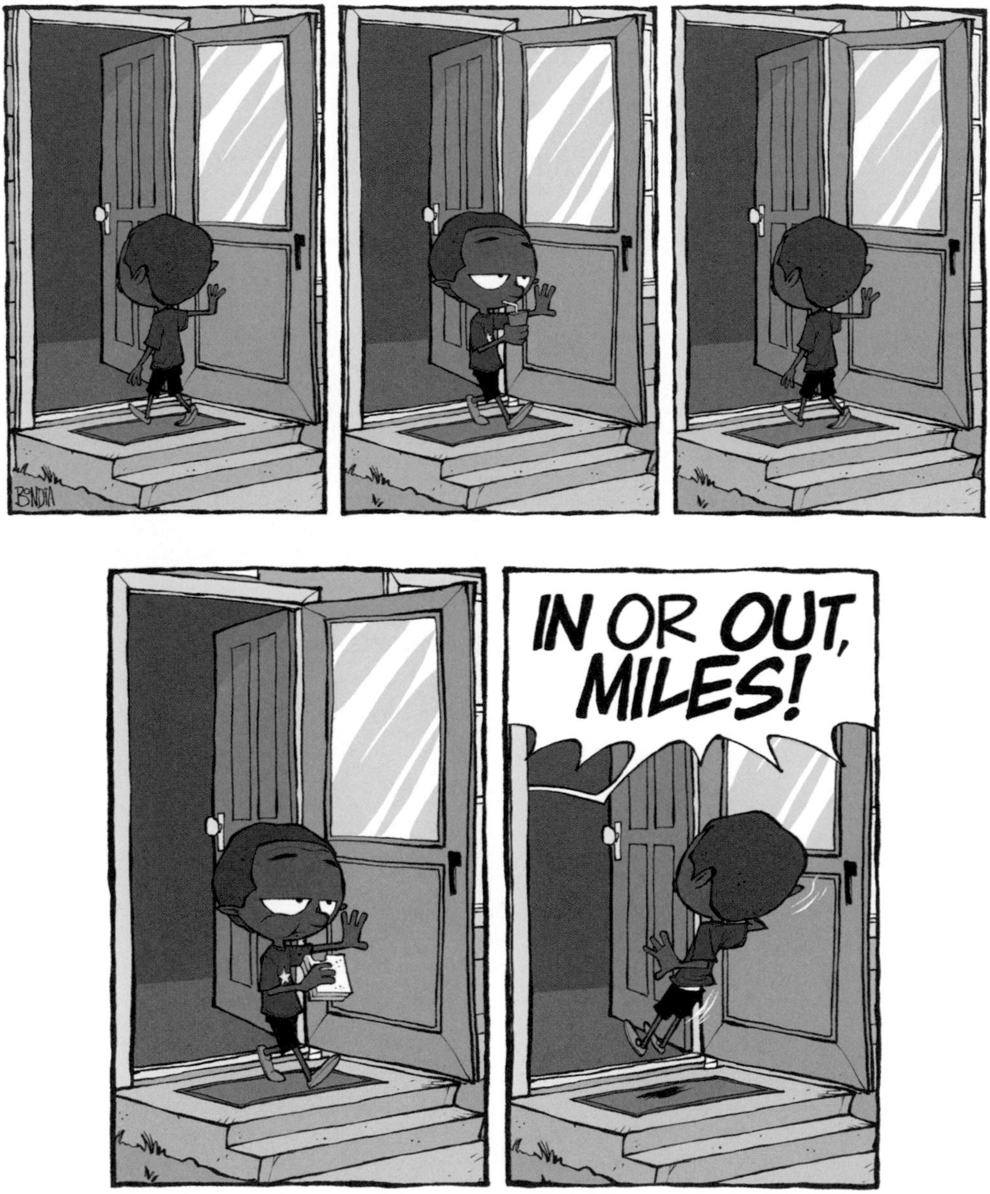
BONDIA
IN OR OUT, MILES!

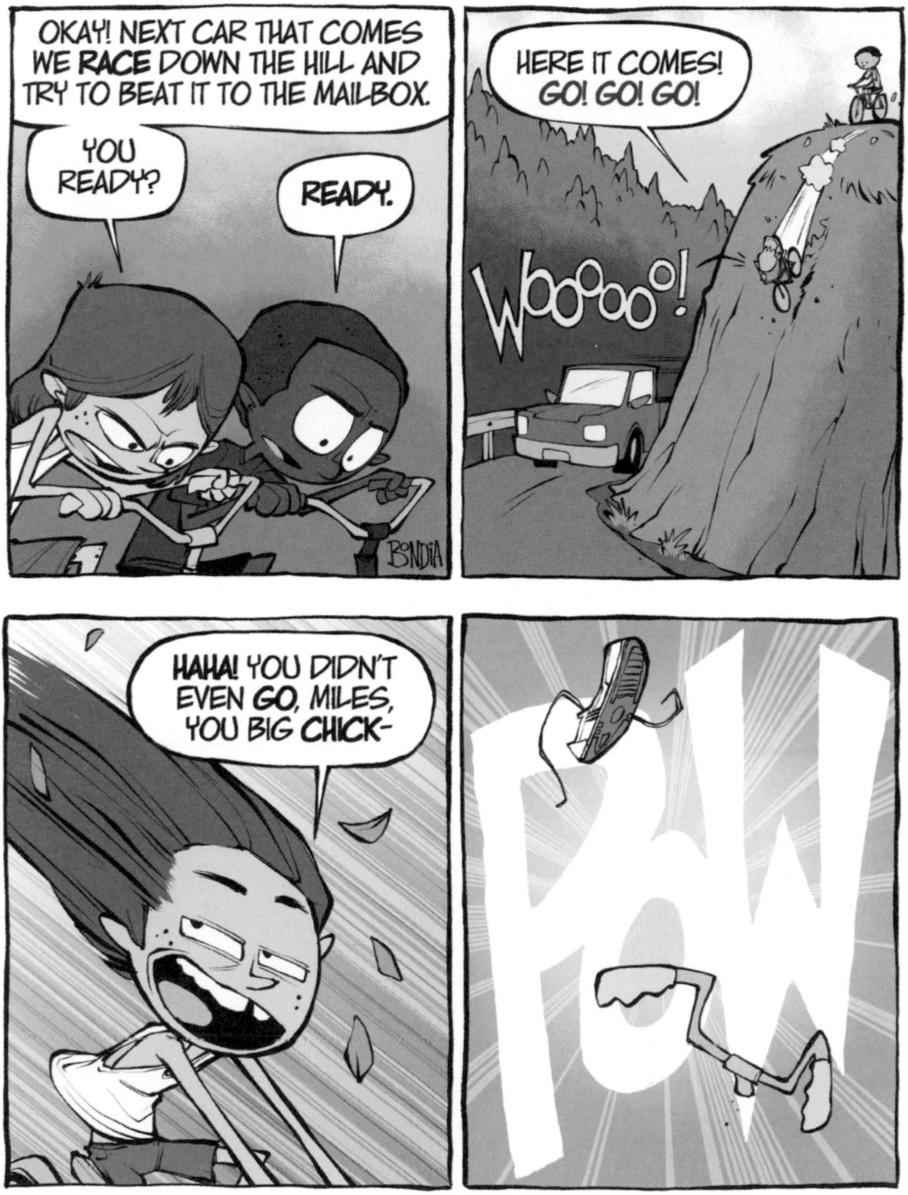
OKAY! NEXT CAR THAT COMES WE **RACE** DOWN THE HILL AND TRY TO BEAT IT TO THE MAILBOX.
YOU READY?
READY.
BSNDIA
HERE IT COMES! **GO! GO! GO!**
WOOOOOO!
HAHA! YOU DIDN'T EVEN **GO**, MILES, YOU BIG **CHICK-**
POW

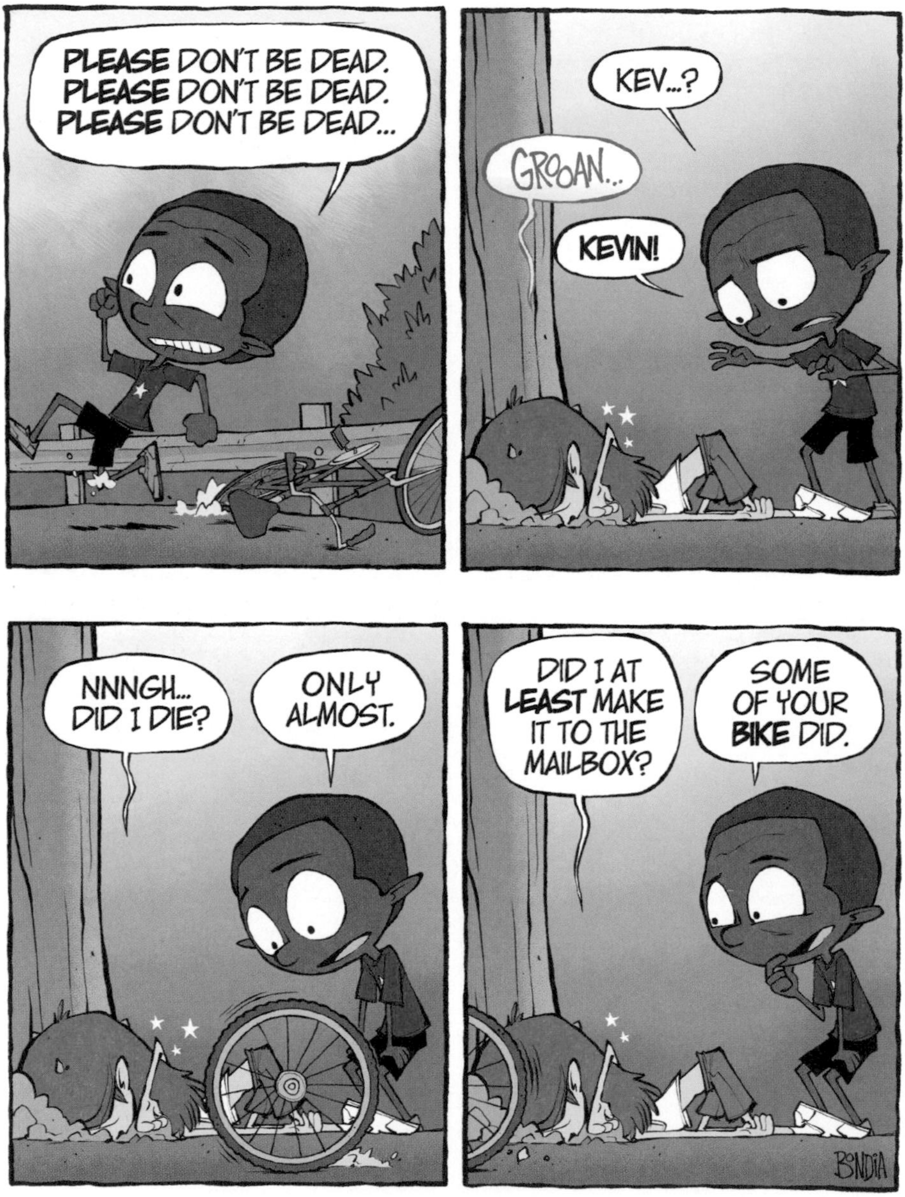
PLEASE DON'T BE DEAD. PLEASE DON'T BE DEAD. PLEASE DON'T BE DEAD...
KEV...?
GROOAN...
KEVIN!
NNNGH... DID I DIE?
ONLY ALMOST.
DID I AT LEAST MAKE IT TO THE MAILBOX?
SOME OF YOUR BIKE DID.
BONDIA

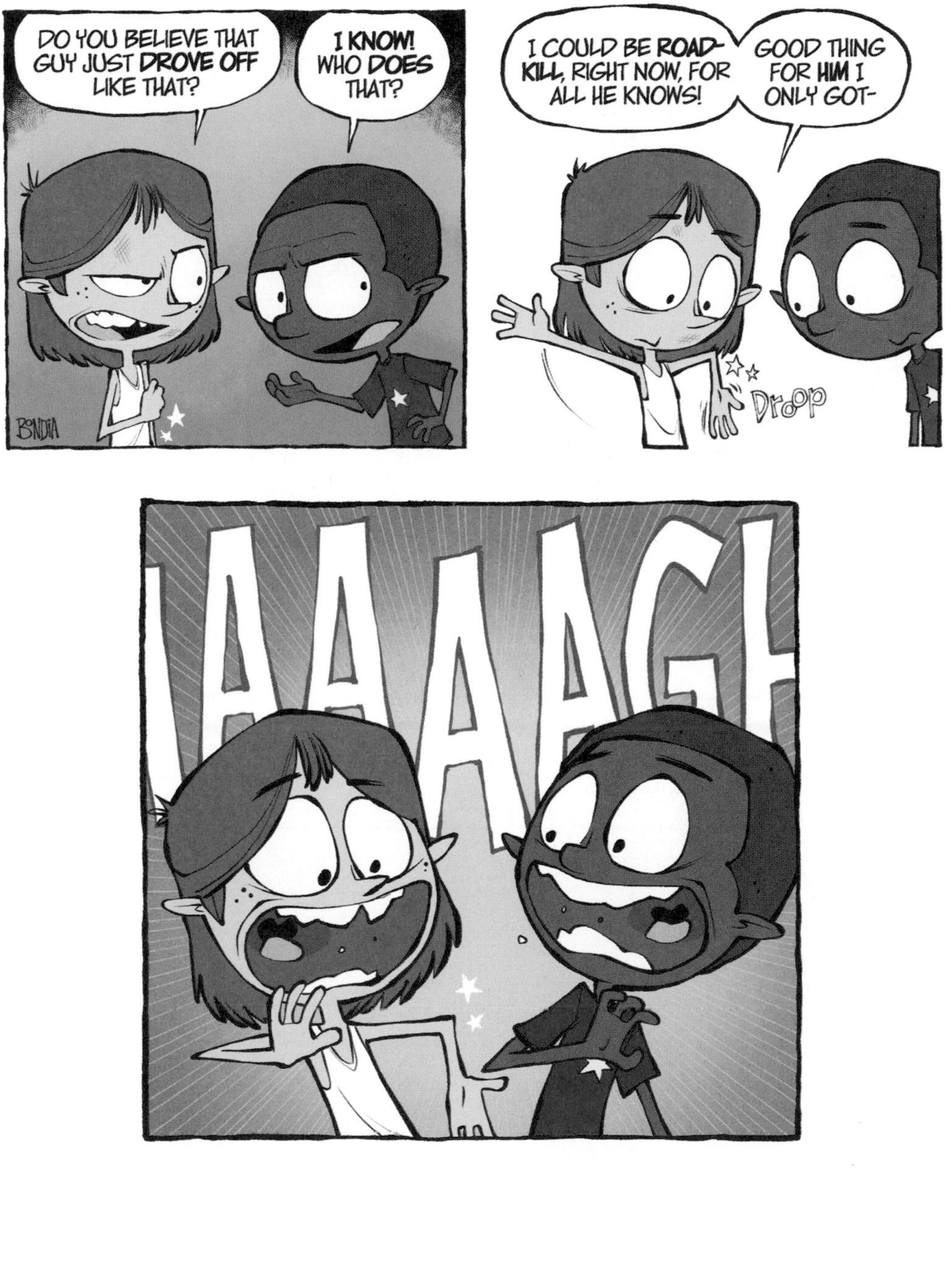

DO YOU BELIEVE THAT GUY JUST **DROVE OFF** LIKE THAT?
I KNOW! WHO **DOES** THAT?
I COULD BE **ROAD-KILL**, RIGHT NOW, FOR ALL HE KNOWS!
GOOD THING FOR **HIM** I ONLY GOT-
Droop
AAAAG

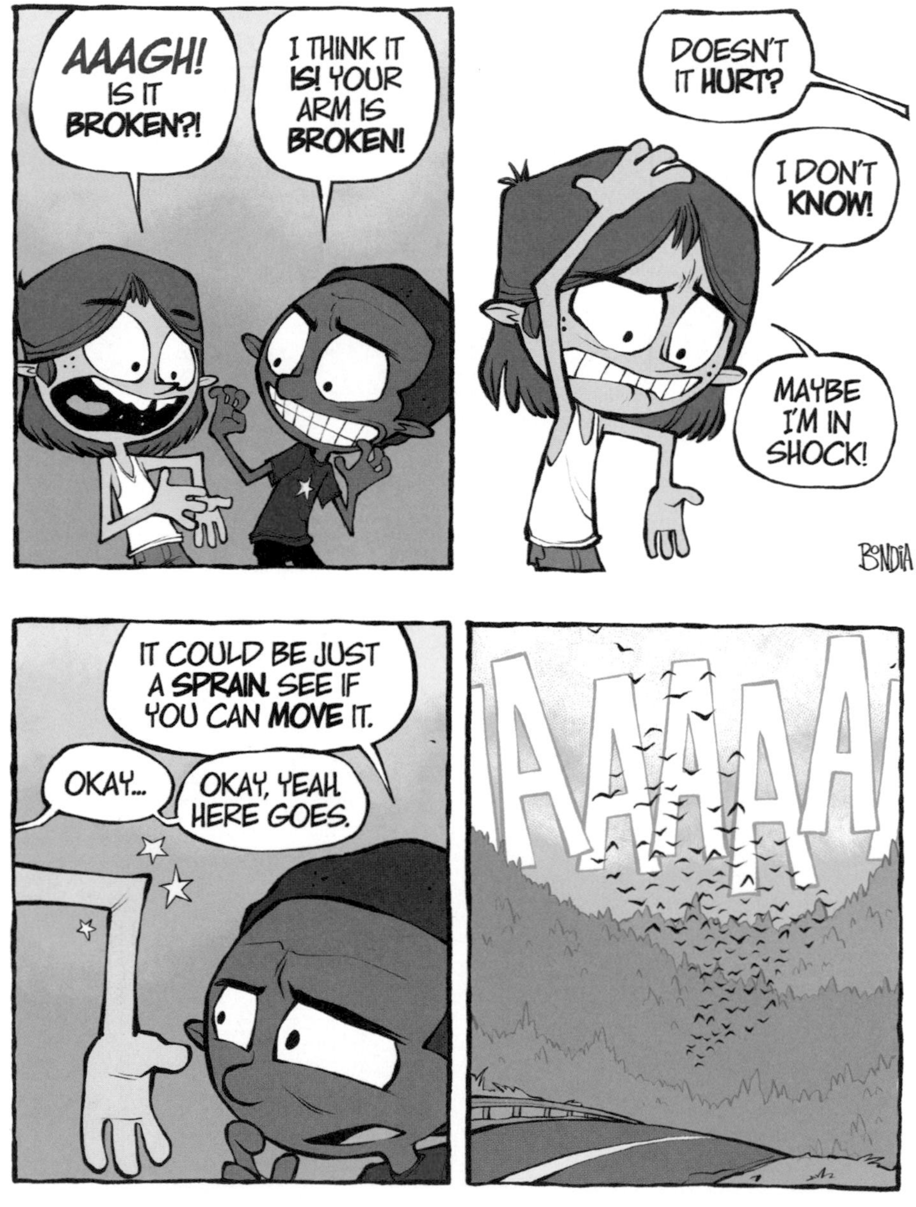
AAAGH! IS IT BROKEN?!
I THINK IT IS! YOUR ARM IS BROKEN!
DOESN'T IT HURT?
I DON'T KNOW!
MAYBE I'M IN SHOCK!
BONDIA
IT COULD BE JUST A SPRAIN. SEE IF YOU CAN MOVE IT.
OKAY...
OKAY, YEAH. HERE GOES.
AAAAA

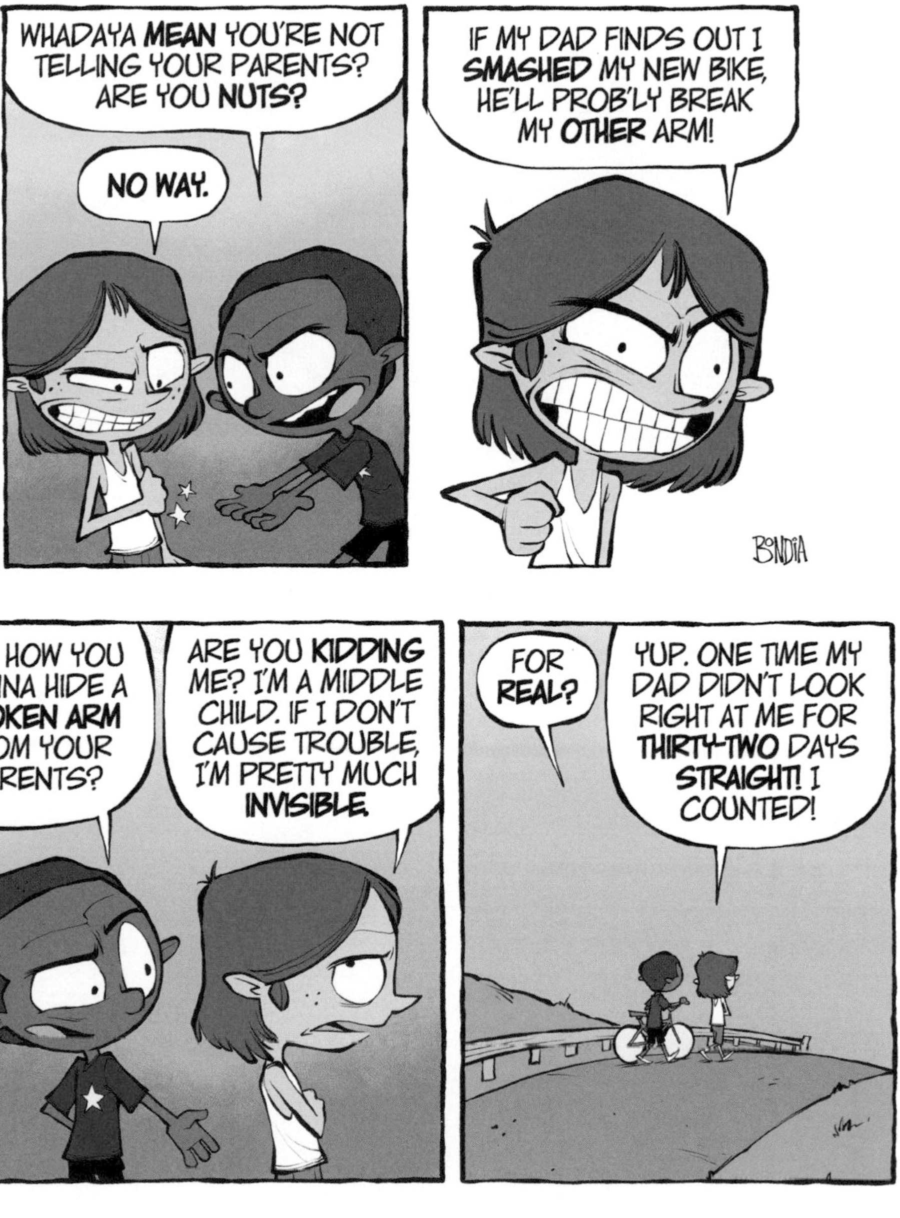
WHADAYA MEAN YOU'RE NOT TELLING YOUR PARENTS? ARE YOU NUTS?
NO WAY.
IF MY DAD FINDS OUT I SMASHED MY NEW BIKE, HE'LL PROB'LY BREAK MY OTHER ARM!
BONDIA
BUT, HOW YOU GONNA HIDE A BROKEN ARM FROM YOUR PARENTS?
ARE YOU KIDDING ME? I'M A MIDDLE CHILD. IF I DON'T CAUSE TROUBLE, I'M PRETTY MUCH INVISIBLE.
FOR REAL?
YUP. ONE TIME MY DAD DIDN'T LOOK RIGHT AT ME FOR THIRTY-TWO DAYS STRAIGHT! I COUNTED!

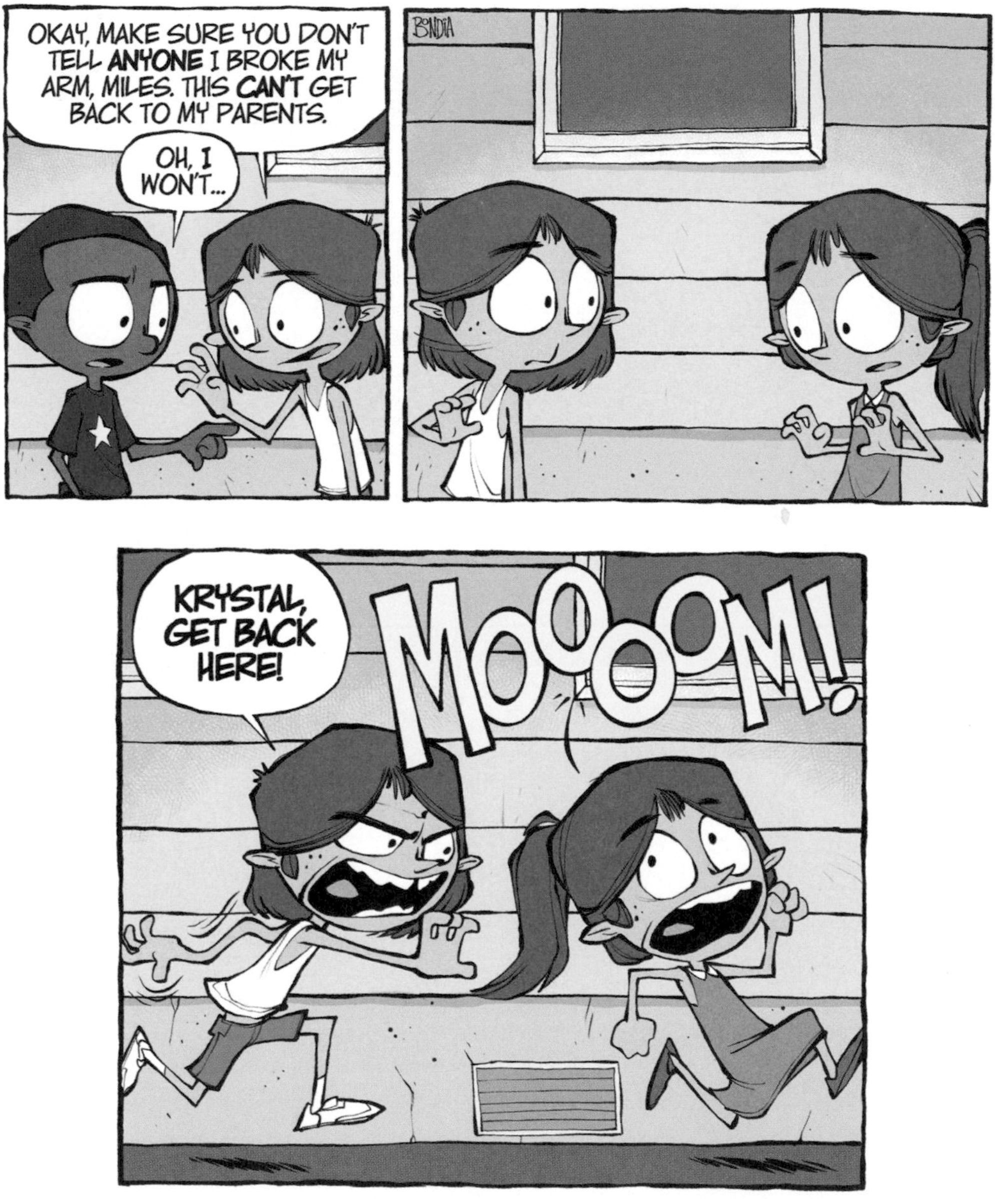
OKAY, MAKE SURE YOU DON'T TELL **ANYONE** I BROKE MY ARM, MILES. THIS **CAN'T** GET BACK TO MY PARENTS.
OH, I WON'T...
BONDIA
KRYSTAL, GET BACK HERE!
MOOOOM!

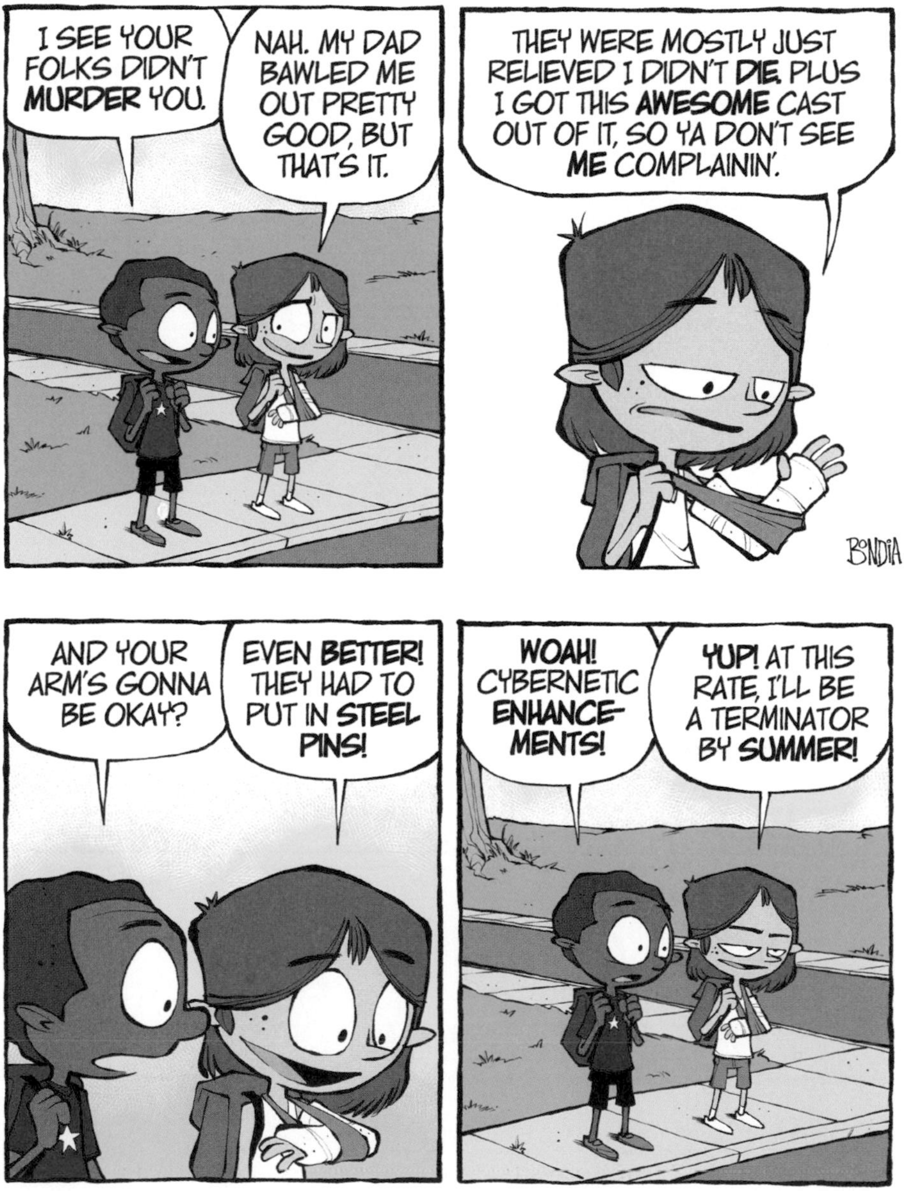
I SEE YOUR FOLKS DIDN'T **MURDER** YOU.
NAH. MY DAD BAWLED ME OUT PRETTY GOOD, BUT THAT'S IT.
THEY WERE MOSTLY JUST RELIEVED I DIDN'T **DIE**. PLUS I GOT THIS **AWESOME** CAST OUT OF IT, SO YA DON'T SEE **ME** COMPLAININ'.
BONDIA
AND YOUR ARM'S GONNA BE OKAY?
EVEN **BETTER!** THEY HAD TO PUT IN **STEEL PINS!**
WOAH! CYBERNETIC **ENHANCEMENTS!**
YUP! AT THIS RATE, I'LL BE A TERMINATOR BY **SUMMER!**

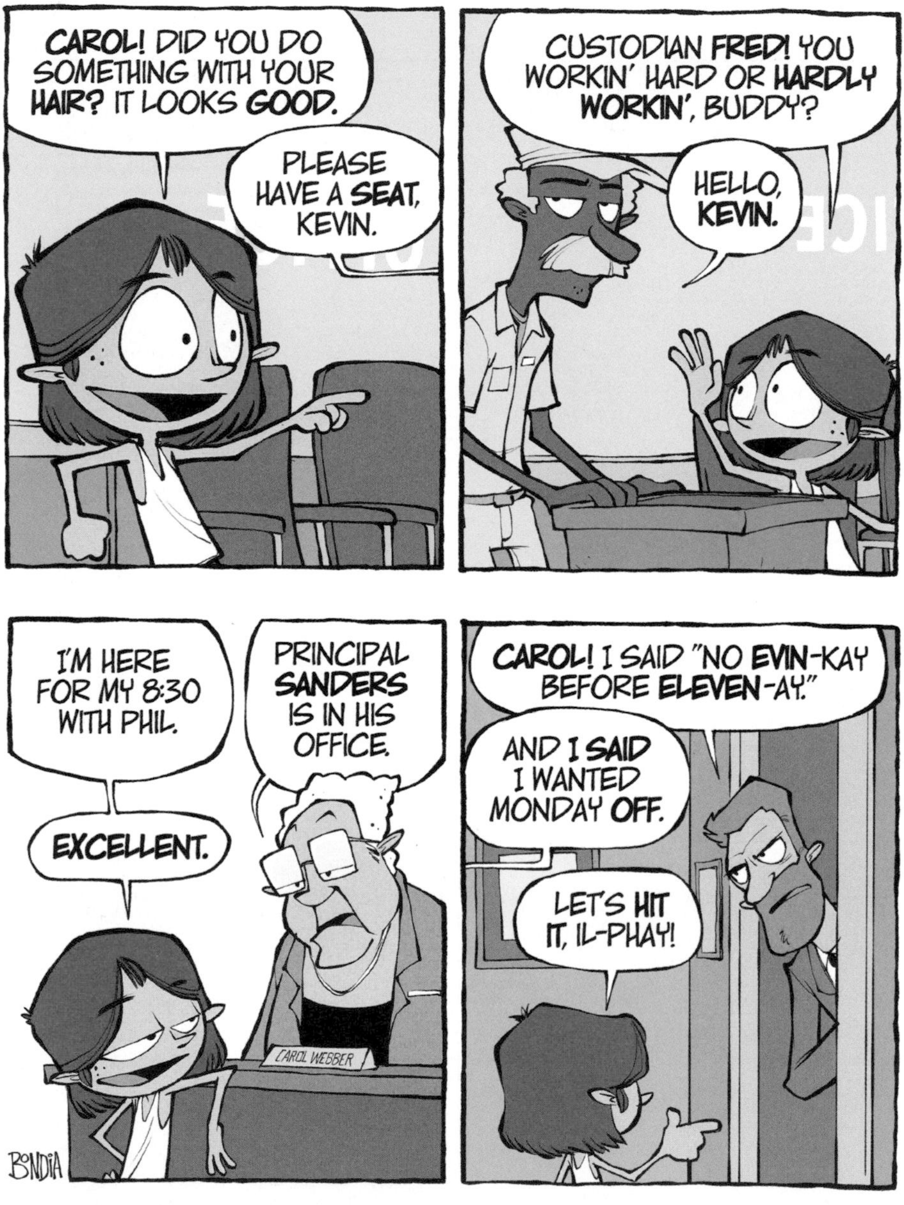
CAROL! DID YOU DO SOMETHING WITH YOUR HAIR? IT LOOKS GOOD.
PLEASE HAVE A SEAT, KEVIN.
CUSTODIAN FRED! YOU WORKIN' HARD OR HARDLY WORKIN', BUDDY?
HELLO, KEVIN.
I'M HERE FOR MY 8:30 WITH PHIL.
PRINCIPAL SANDERS IS IN HIS OFFICE.
EXCELLENT.
CAROL WEBBER
BONDIA
CAROL! I SAID "NO EVIN-KAY BEFORE ELEVEN-AY."
AND I SAID I WANTED MONDAY OFF.
LET'S HIT IT, IL-PHAY!

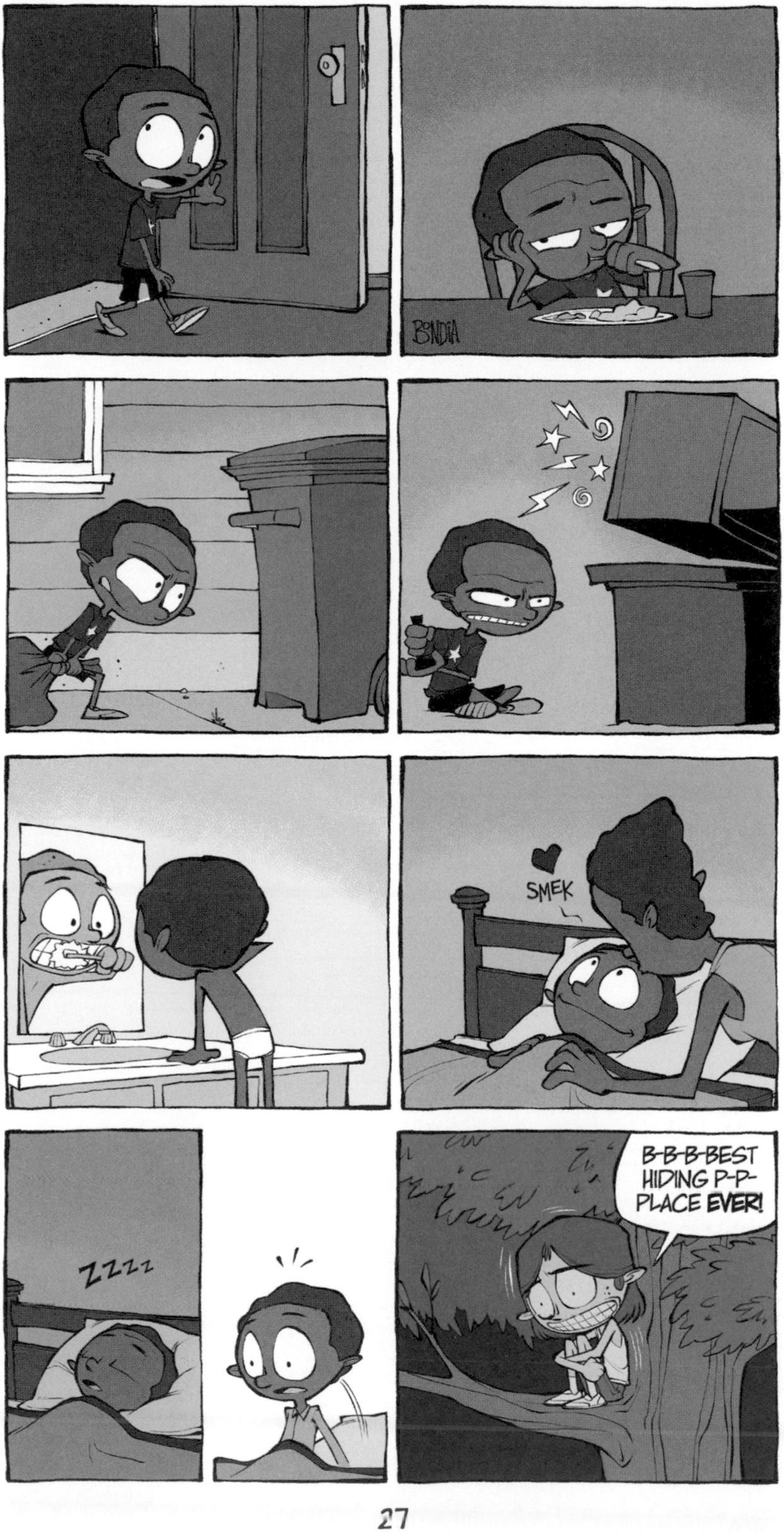
BONDIA
SMEK
ZZZZ
B-B-B-BEST HIDING P-P-PLACE EVER!

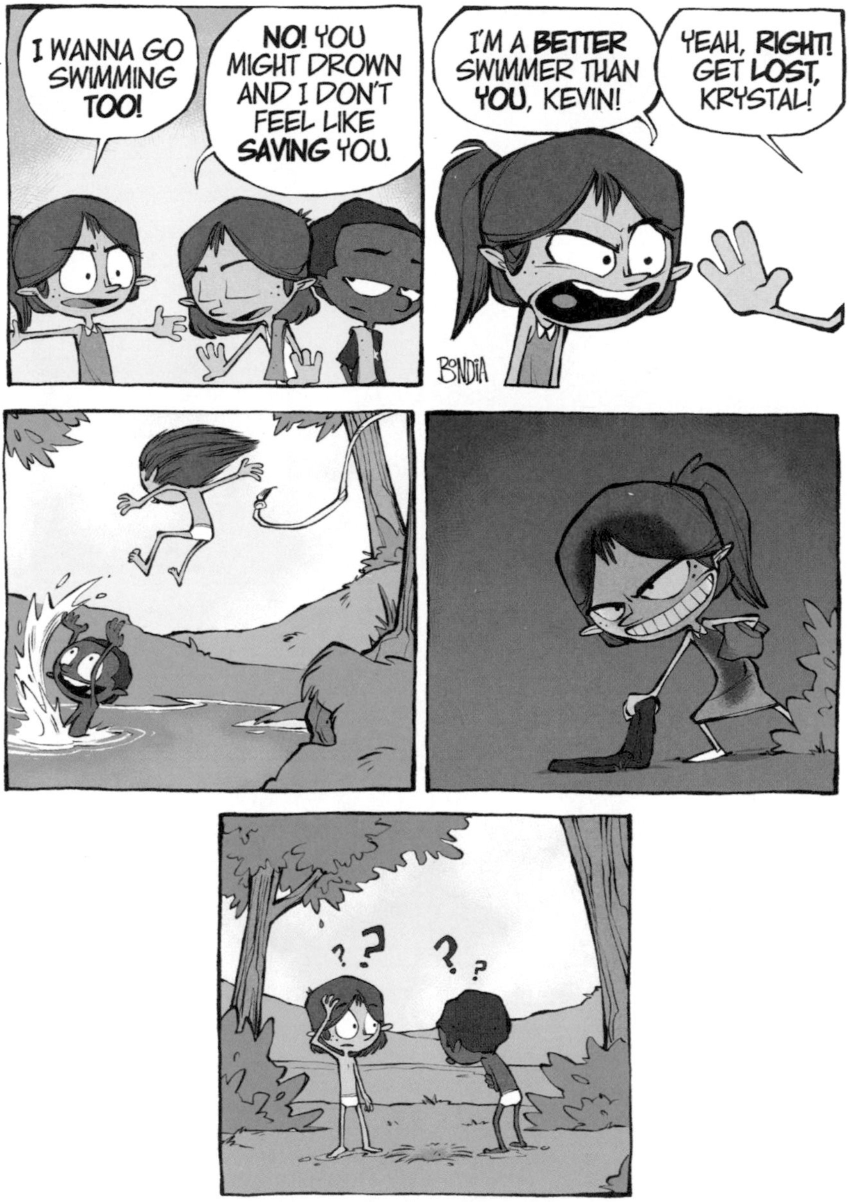
I WANNA GO SWIMMING TOO!
NO! YOU MIGHT DROWN AND I DON'T FEEL LIKE SAVING YOU.
I'M A BETTER SWIMMER THAN YOU, KEVIN!
YEAH, RIGHT! GET LOST, KRYSTAL!
BONDIA
? ? ? ?

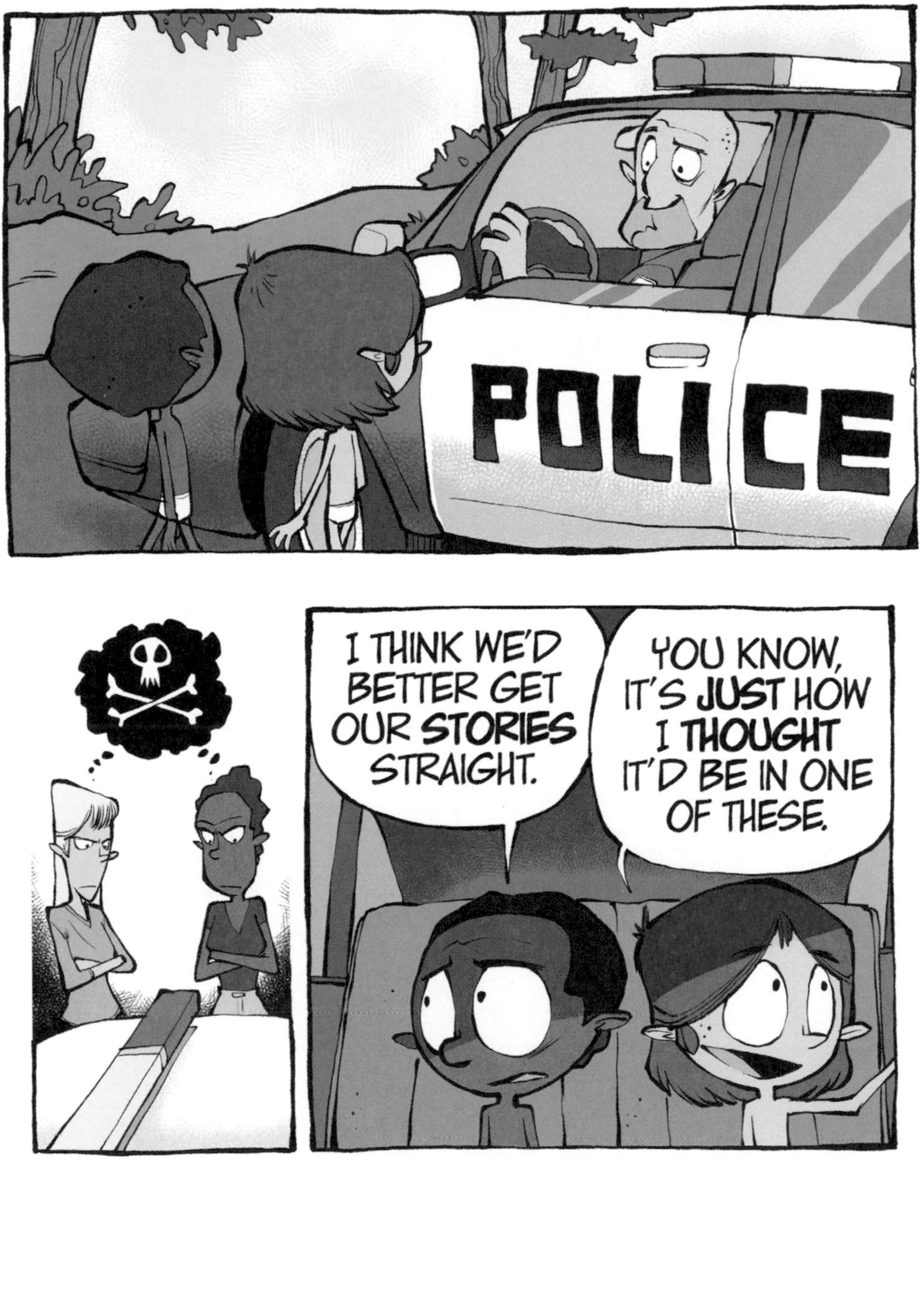
POLICE
I THINK WE'D BETTER GET OUR **STORIES** STRAIGHT.
YOU KNOW, IT'S **JUST** HOW I **THOUGHT** IT'D BE IN ONE OF THESE.

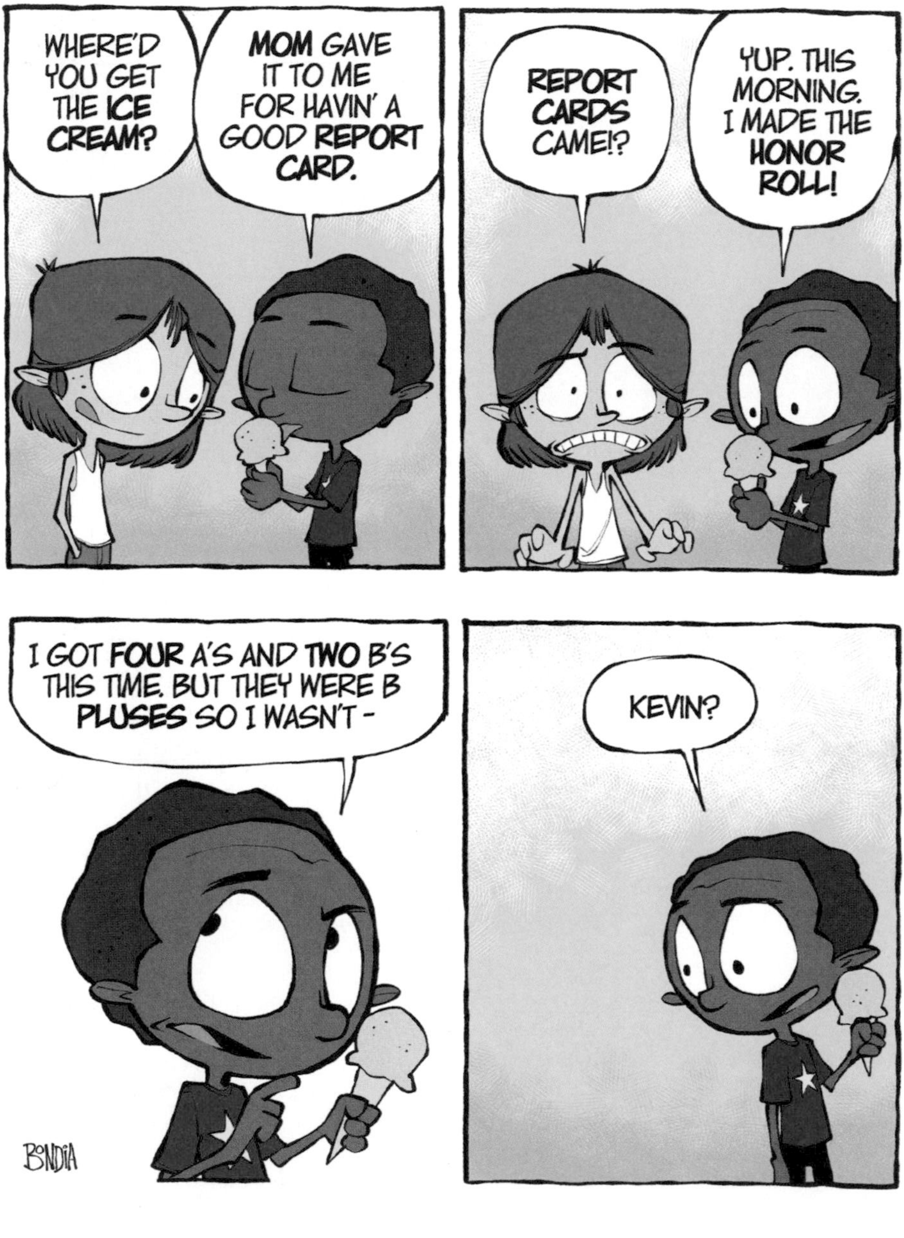
WHERE'D YOU GET THE ICE CREAM?
MOM GAVE IT TO ME FOR HAVIN' A GOOD REPORT CARD.
REPORT CARDS CAME!?
YUP. THIS MORNING. I MADE THE HONOR ROLL!
I GOT FOUR A'S AND TWO B'S THIS TIME. BUT THEY WERE B PLUSES SO I WASN'T -
BONDIA
KEVIN?

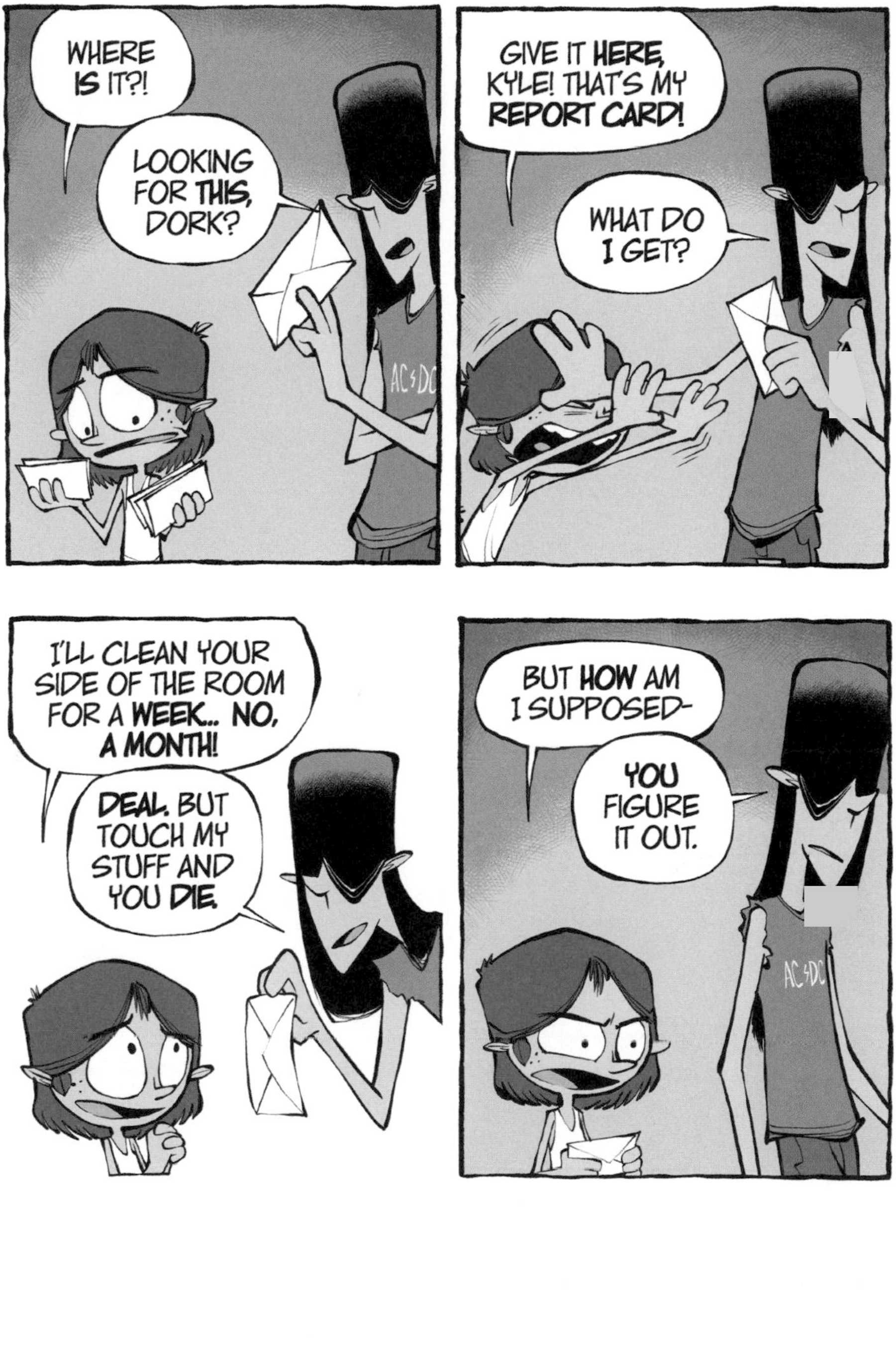
WHERE IS IT?!
LOOKING FOR THIS, DORK?
GIVE IT HERE, KYLE! THAT'S MY REPORT CARD!
WHAT DO I GET?
I'LL CLEAN YOUR SIDE OF THE ROOM FOR A WEEK... NO, A MONTH!
DEAL. BUT TOUCH MY STUFF AND YOU DIE.
BUT HOW AM I SUPPOSED-
YOU FIGURE IT OUT.
AC/DC

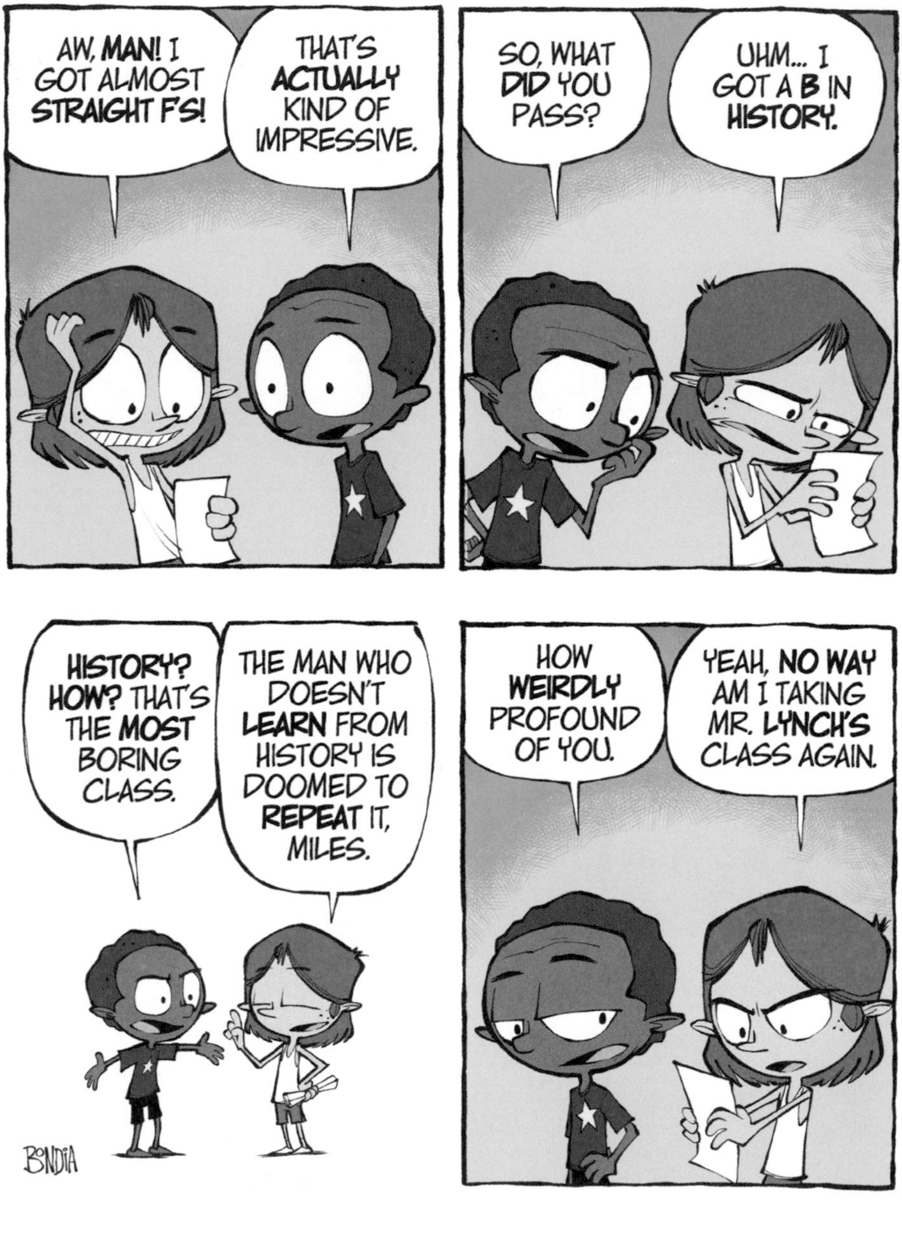
AW, MAN! I GOT ALMOST STRAIGHT F'S!
THAT'S ACTUALLY KIND OF IMPRESSIVE.
SO, WHAT DID YOU PASS?
UHM... I GOT A B IN HISTORY.
HISTORY? HOW? THAT'S THE MOST BORING CLASS.
THE MAN WHO DOESN'T LEARN FROM HISTORY IS DOOMED TO REPEAT IT, MILES.
HOW WEIRDLY PROFOUND OF YOU.
YEAH, NO WAY AM I TAKING MR. LYNCH'S CLASS AGAIN.
BONDIA

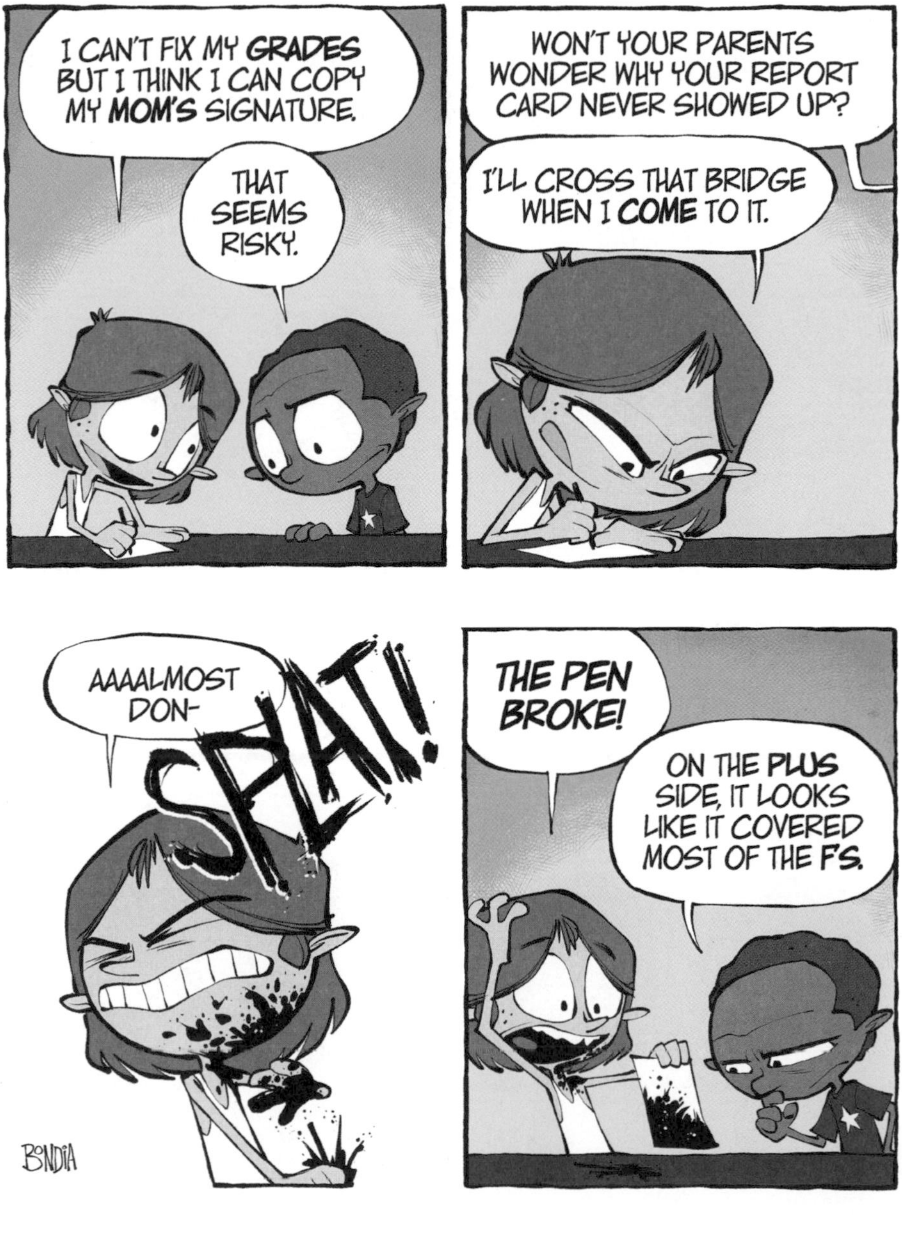
I CAN'T FIX MY GRADES BUT I THINK I CAN COPY MY MOM'S SIGNATURE.
THAT SEEMS RISKY.
WON'T YOUR PARENTS WONDER WHY YOUR REPORT CARD NEVER SHOWED UP?
I'LL CROSS THAT BRIDGE WHEN I COME TO IT.
AAAALMOST DON-
SPLAT!!
THE PEN BROKE!
ON THE PLUS SIDE, IT LOOKS LIKE IT COVERED MOST OF THE F'S.
BONDIA

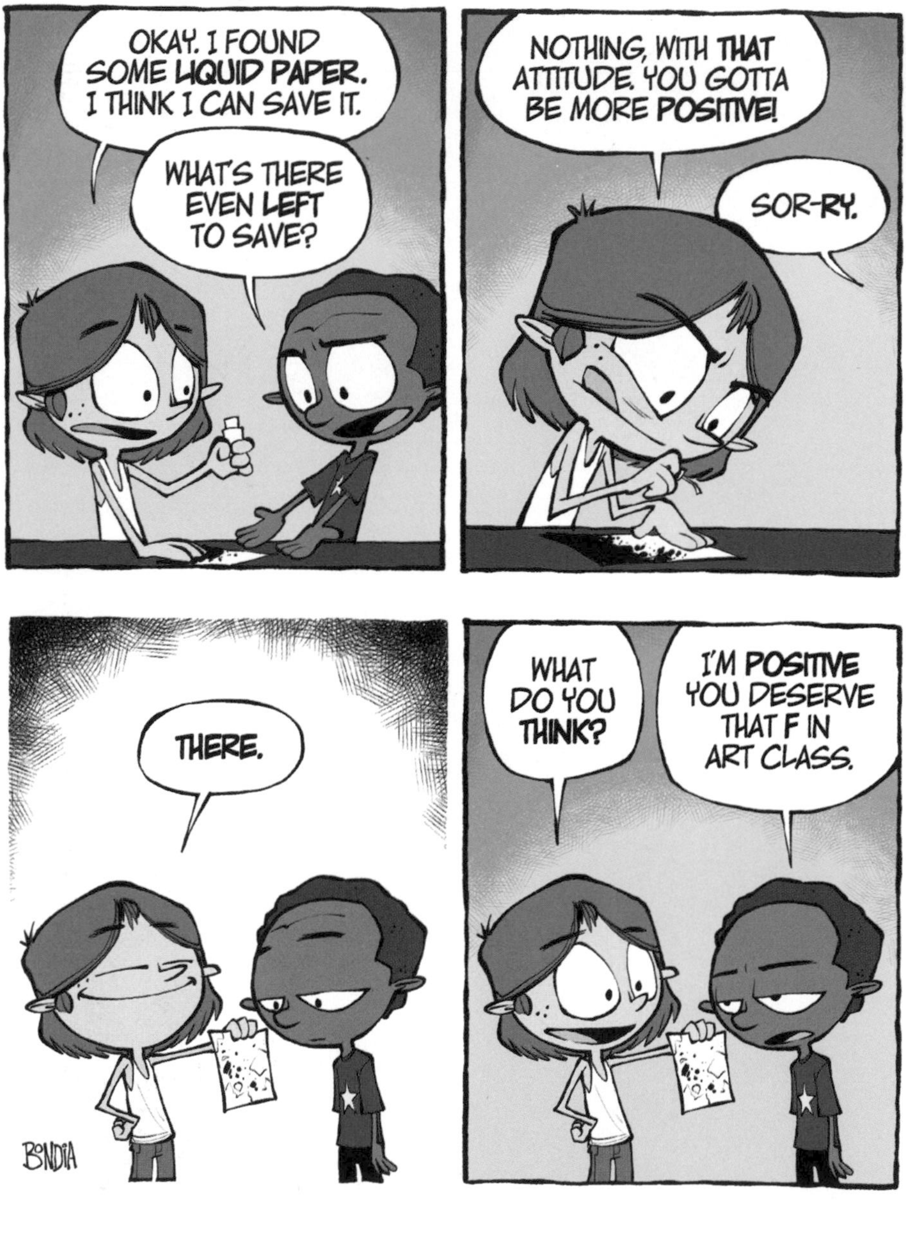
OKAY. I FOUND SOME LIQUID PAPER. I THINK I CAN SAVE IT.
WHAT'S THERE EVEN LEFT TO SAVE?
NOTHING, WITH THAT ATTITUDE. YOU GOTTA BE MORE POSITIVE!
SOR-RY.
THERE.
BONDIA
WHAT DO YOU THINK?
I'M POSITIVE YOU DESERVE THAT F IN ART CLASS.

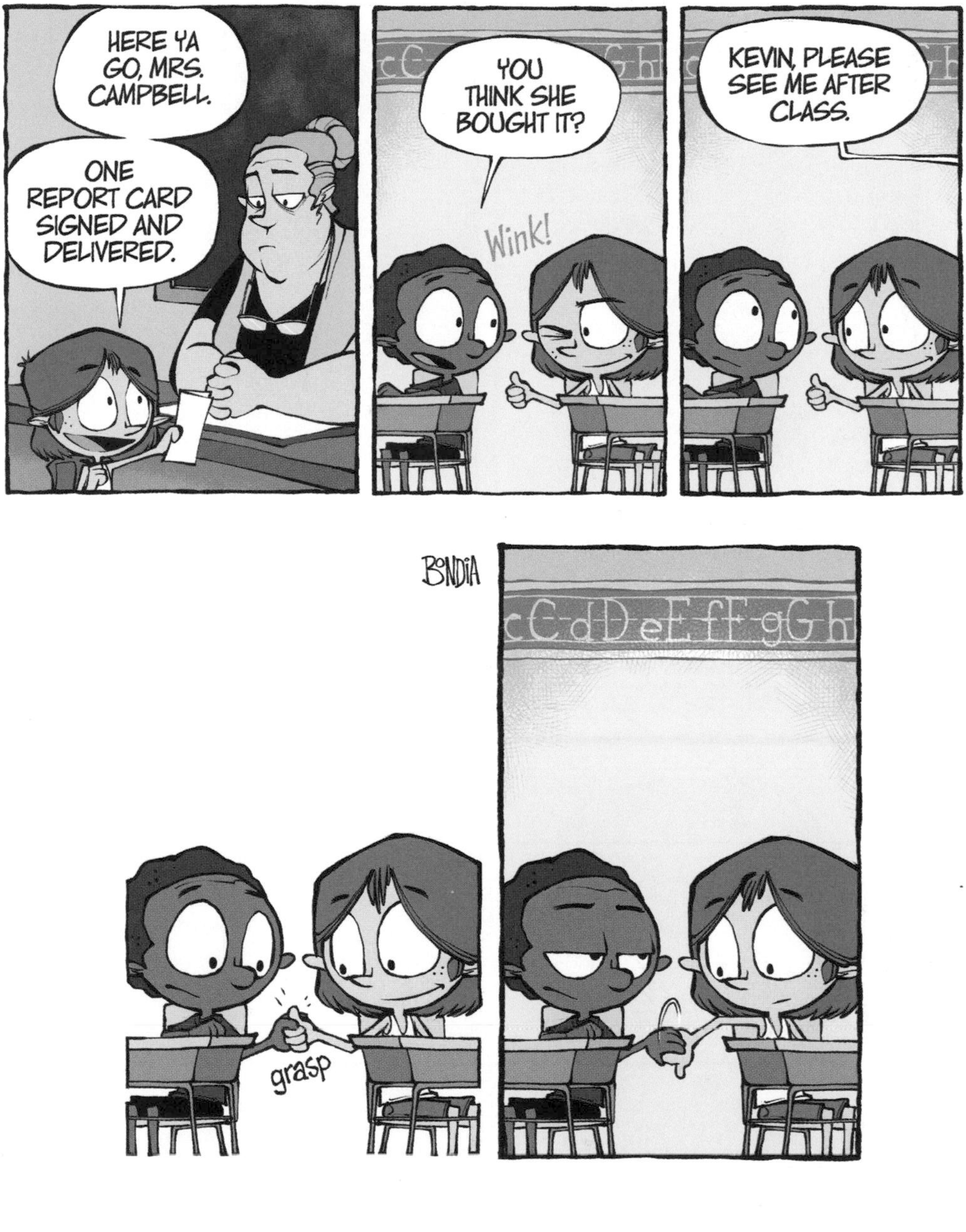
HERE YA GO, MRS. CAMPBELL.
ONE REPORT CARD SIGNED AND DELIVERED.
YOU THINK SHE BOUGHT IT?
Wink!
KEVIN, PLEASE SEE ME AFTER CLASS.
BONDIA
grasp

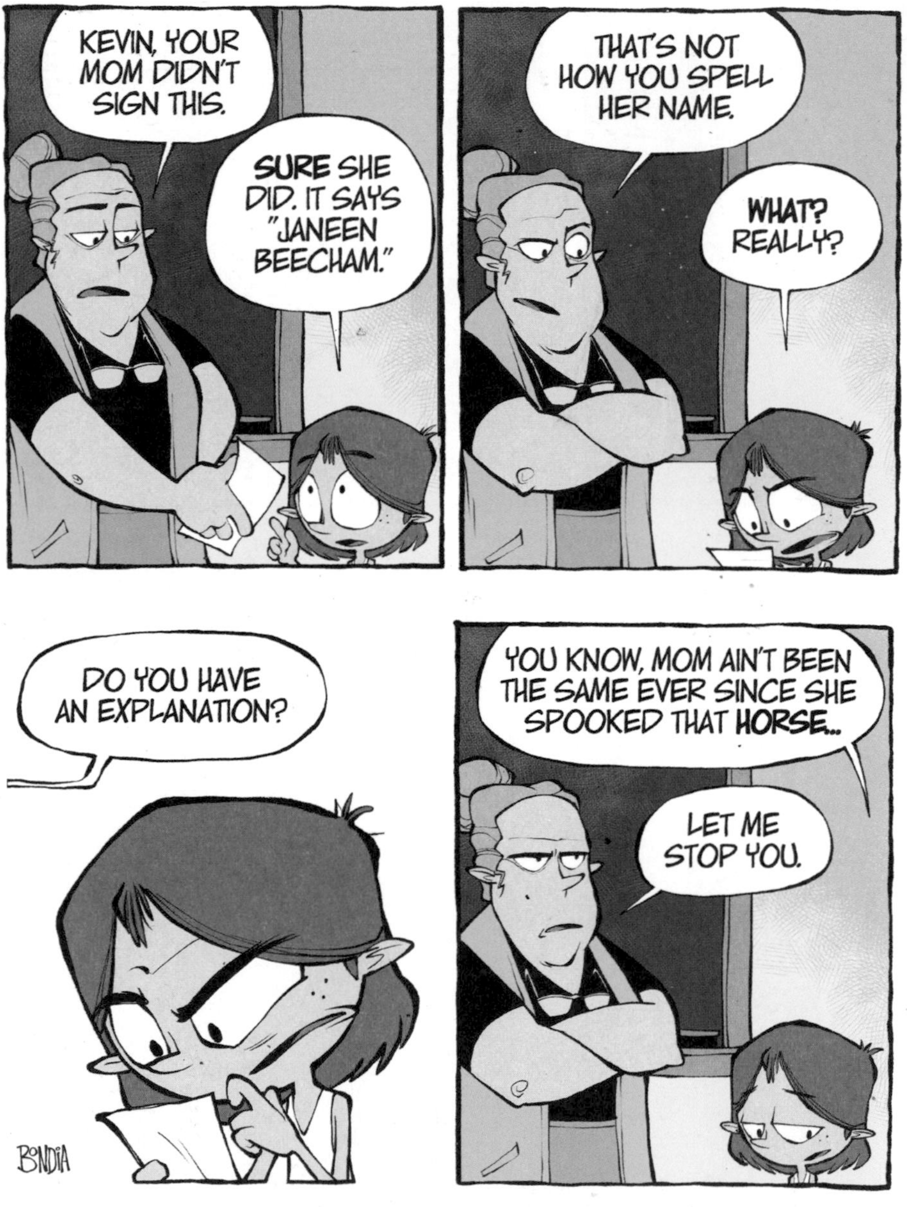
KEVIN, YOUR MOM DIDN'T SIGN THIS.
SURE SHE DID. IT SAYS "JANEEN BEECHAM."
THAT'S NOT HOW YOU SPELL HER NAME.
WHAT? REALLY?
DO YOU HAVE AN EXPLANATION?
YOU KNOW, MOM AIN'T BEEN THE SAME EVER SINCE SHE SPOOKED THAT **HORSE...**
LET ME STOP YOU.
BONDIA

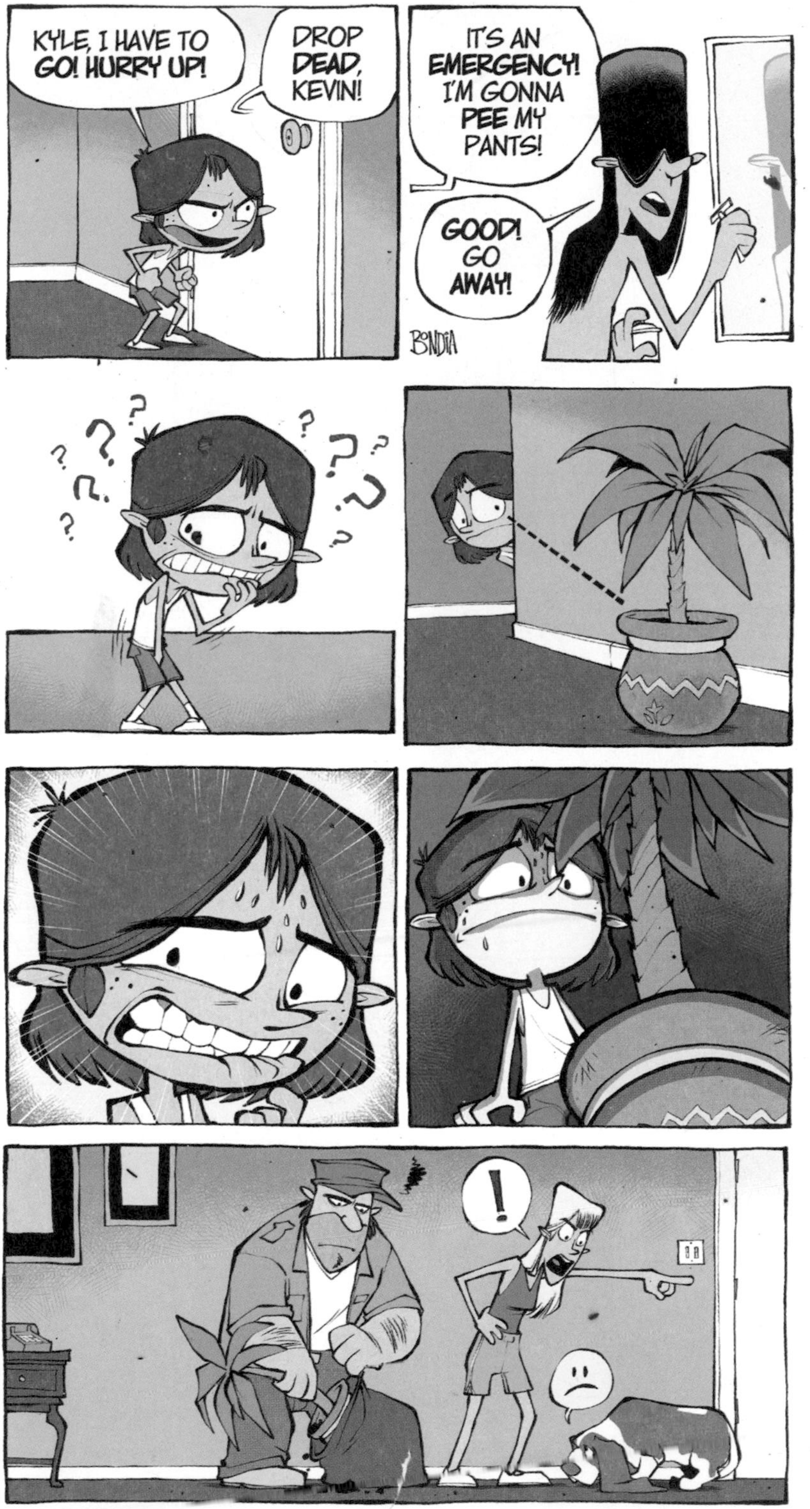
KYLE, I HAVE TO GO! HURRY UP!
DROP DEAD, KEVIN!
IT'S AN EMERGENCY! I'M GONNA PEE MY PANTS!
GOOD! GO AWAY!
BONDIA
!

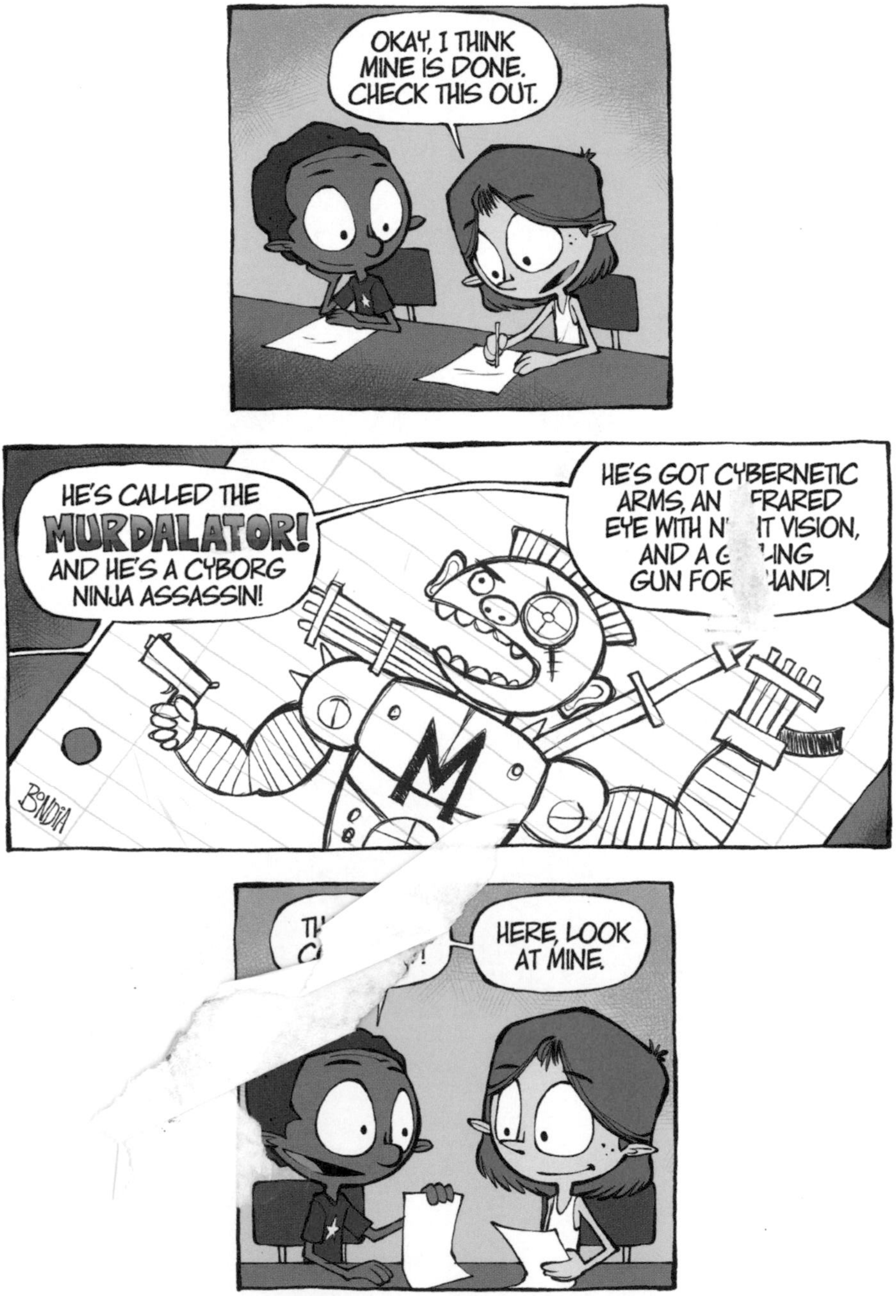
OKAY, I THINK MINE IS DONE. CHECK THIS OUT.
HE'S CALLED THE MURDALATOR! AND HE'S A CYBORG NINJA ASSASSIN!
HE'S GOT CYBERNETIC ARMS, AN FRARED EYE WITH N IT VISION, AND A G LING GUN FOR HAND!
BONDIA
HERE, LOOK AT MINE.

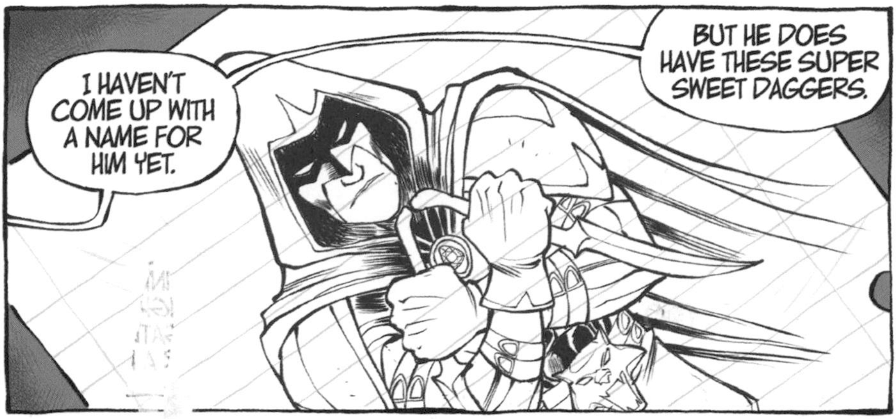
I HAVEN'T COME UP WITH A NAME FOR HIM YET.
BUT HE DOES HAVE THESE SUPER SWEET DAGGERS.

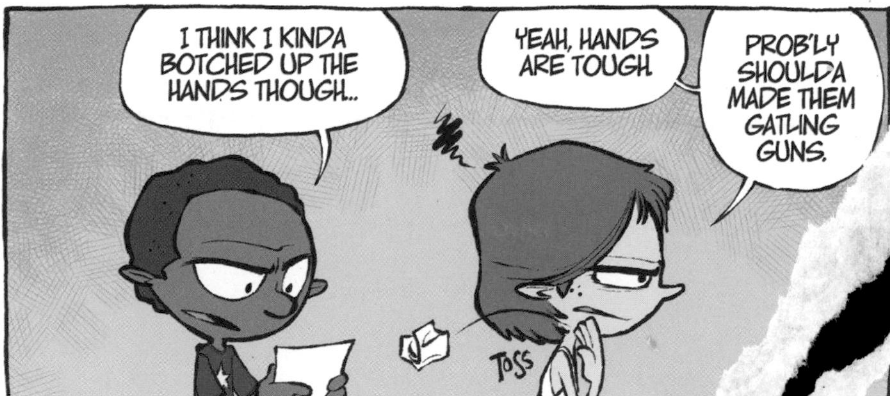
I THINK I KINDA BOTCHED UP THE HANDS THOUGH..
YEAH, HANDS ARE TOUGH.
PROB'LY SHOULDA MADE THEM GATLING GUNS.
TOSS

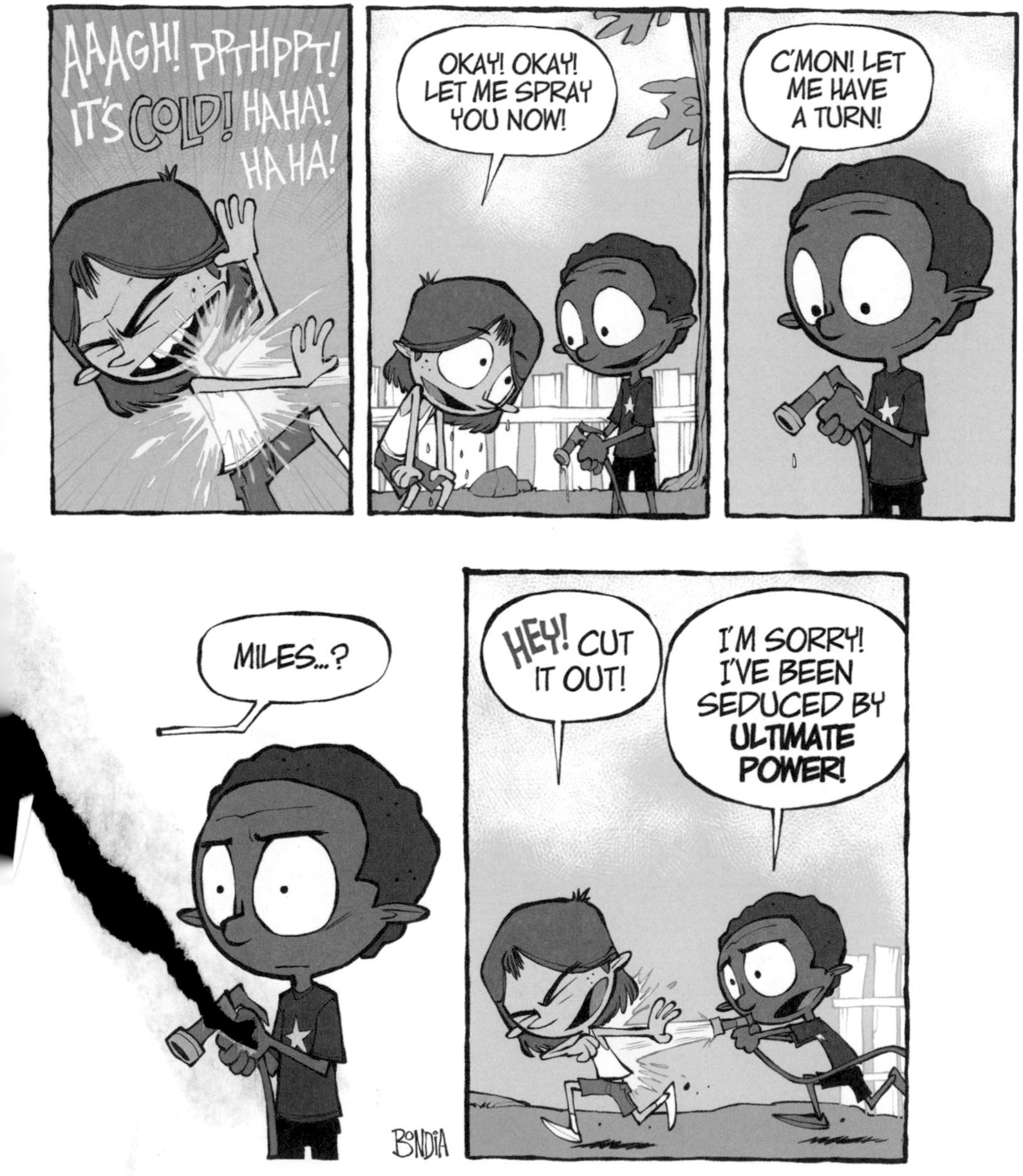
AAAGH! PPTHPPT! IT'S COLD! HAHA! HA HA!
OKAY! OKAY! LET ME SPRAY YOU NOW!
C'MON! LET ME HAVE A TURN!
MILES...?
HEY! CUT IT OUT!
I'M SORRY! I'VE BEEN SEDUCED BY ULTIMATE POWER!
BONDIA

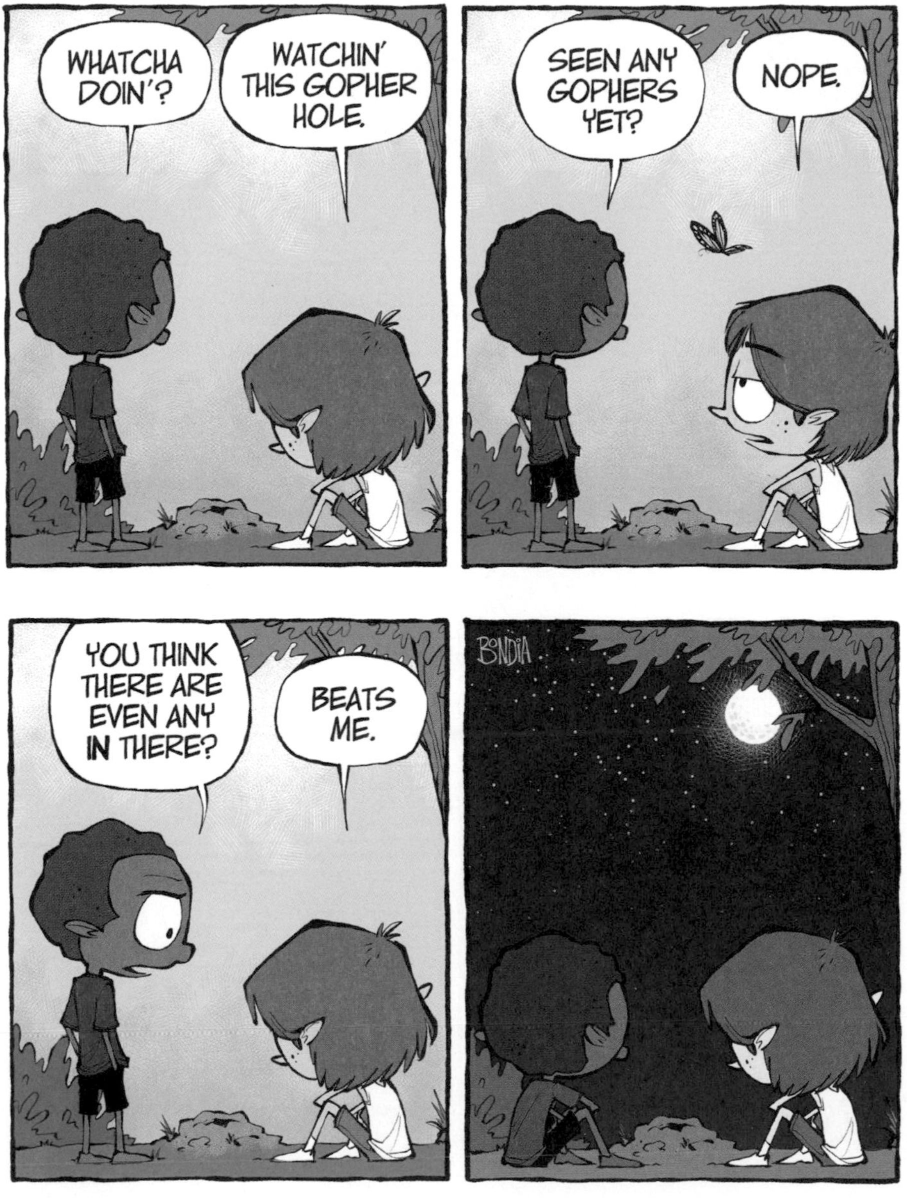
WHATCHA DOIN'?
WATCHIN' THIS GOPHER HOLE.
SEEN ANY GOPHERS YET?
NOPE.
YOU THINK THERE ARE EVEN ANY **IN** THERE?
BEATS ME.
BONDIA

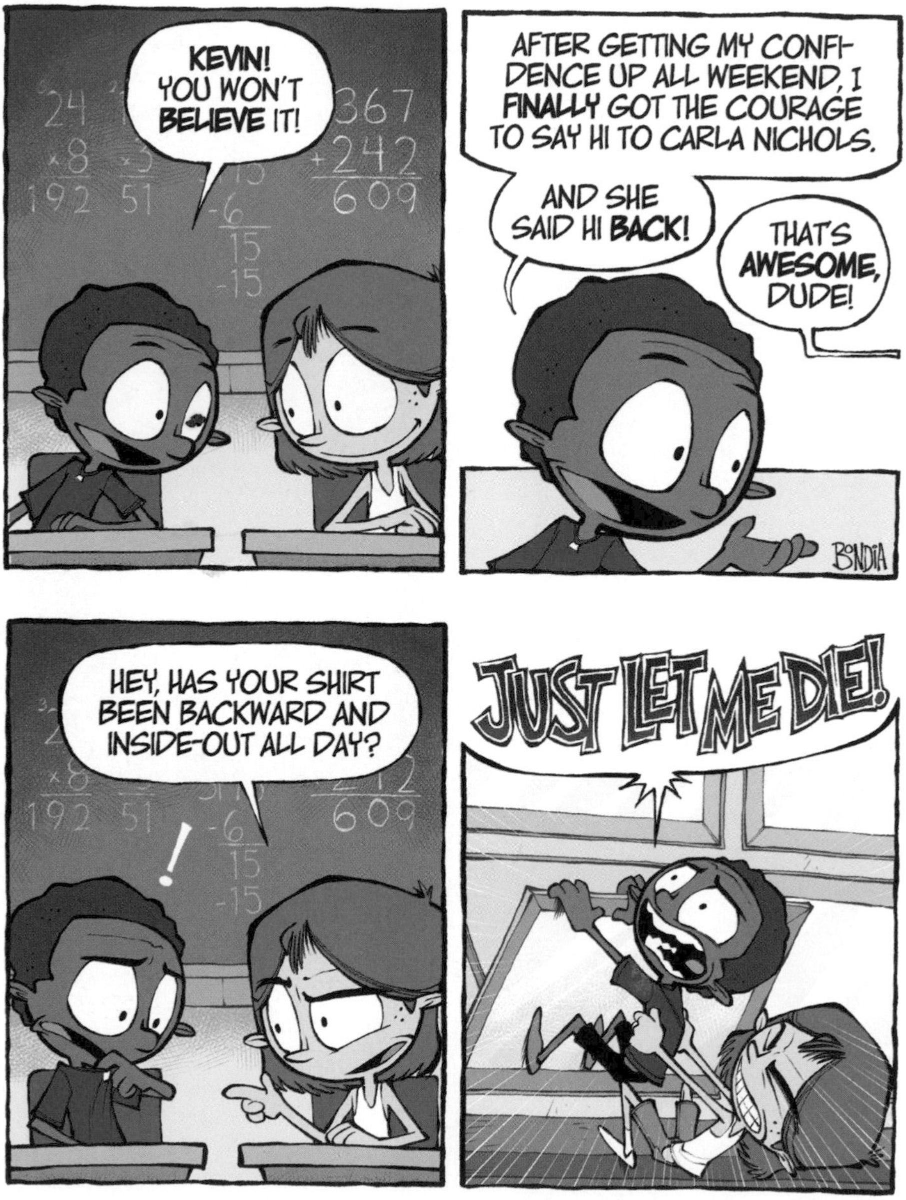
KEVIN! YOU WON'T BELIEVE IT!
AFTER GETTING MY CONFIDENCE UP ALL WEEKEND, I FINALLY GOT THE COURAGE TO SAY HI TO CARLA NICHOLS.
AND SHE SAID HI BACK!
THAT'S AWESOME, DUDE!
BONDIA
HEY, HAS YOUR SHIRT BEEN BACKWARD AND INSIDE-OUT ALL DAY?
!
JUST LET ME DIE!

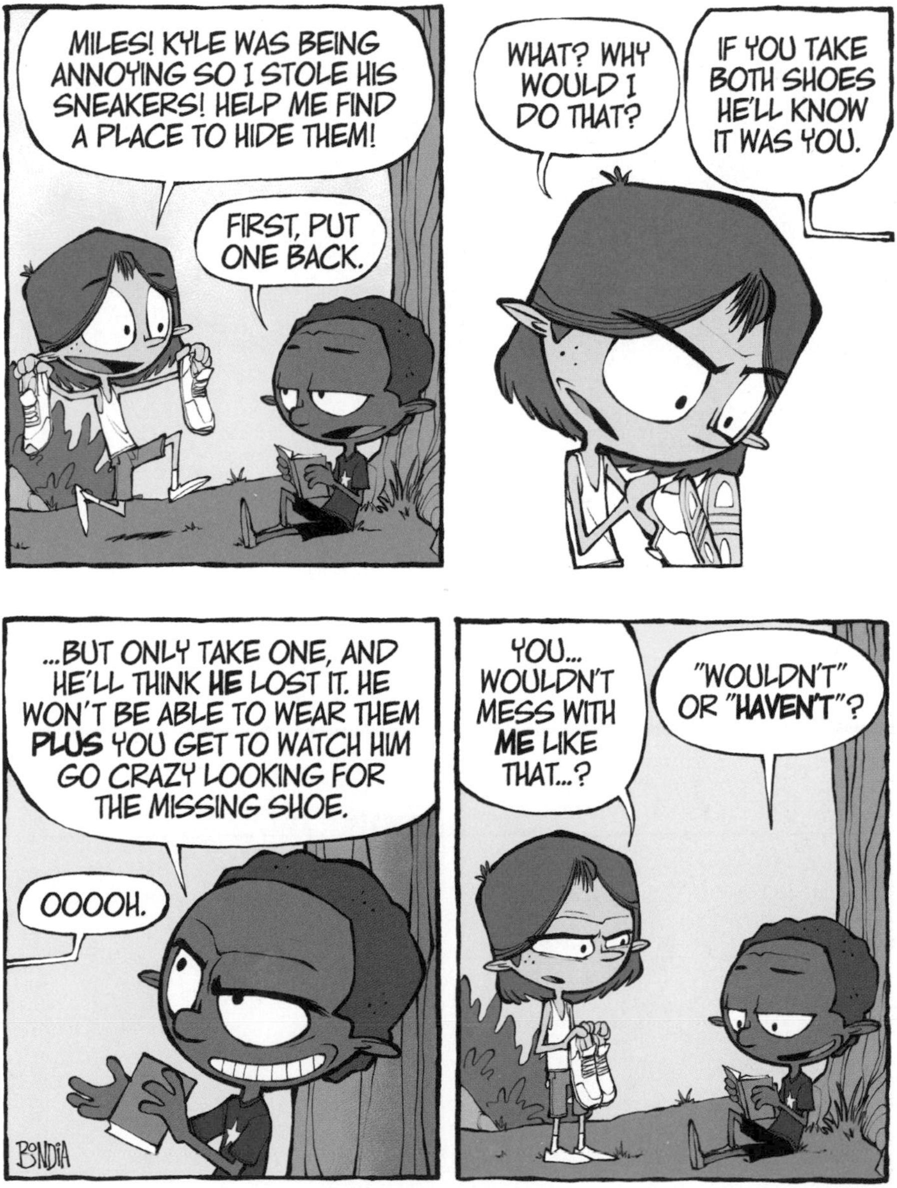
MILES! KYLE WAS BEING ANNOYING SO I STOLE HIS SNEAKERS! HELP ME FIND A PLACE TO HIDE THEM!
FIRST, PUT ONE BACK.
WHAT? WHY WOULD I DO THAT?
IF YOU TAKE BOTH SHOES HE'LL KNOW IT WAS YOU.
...BUT ONLY TAKE ONE, AND HE'LL THINK **HE** LOST IT. HE WON'T BE ABLE TO WEAR THEM **PLUS** YOU GET TO WATCH HIM GO CRAZY LOOKING FOR THE MISSING SHOE.
OOOOH.
BONDIA
YOU... WOULDN'T MESS WITH **ME** LIKE THAT...?
"WOULDN'T" OR "**HAVEN'T**"?

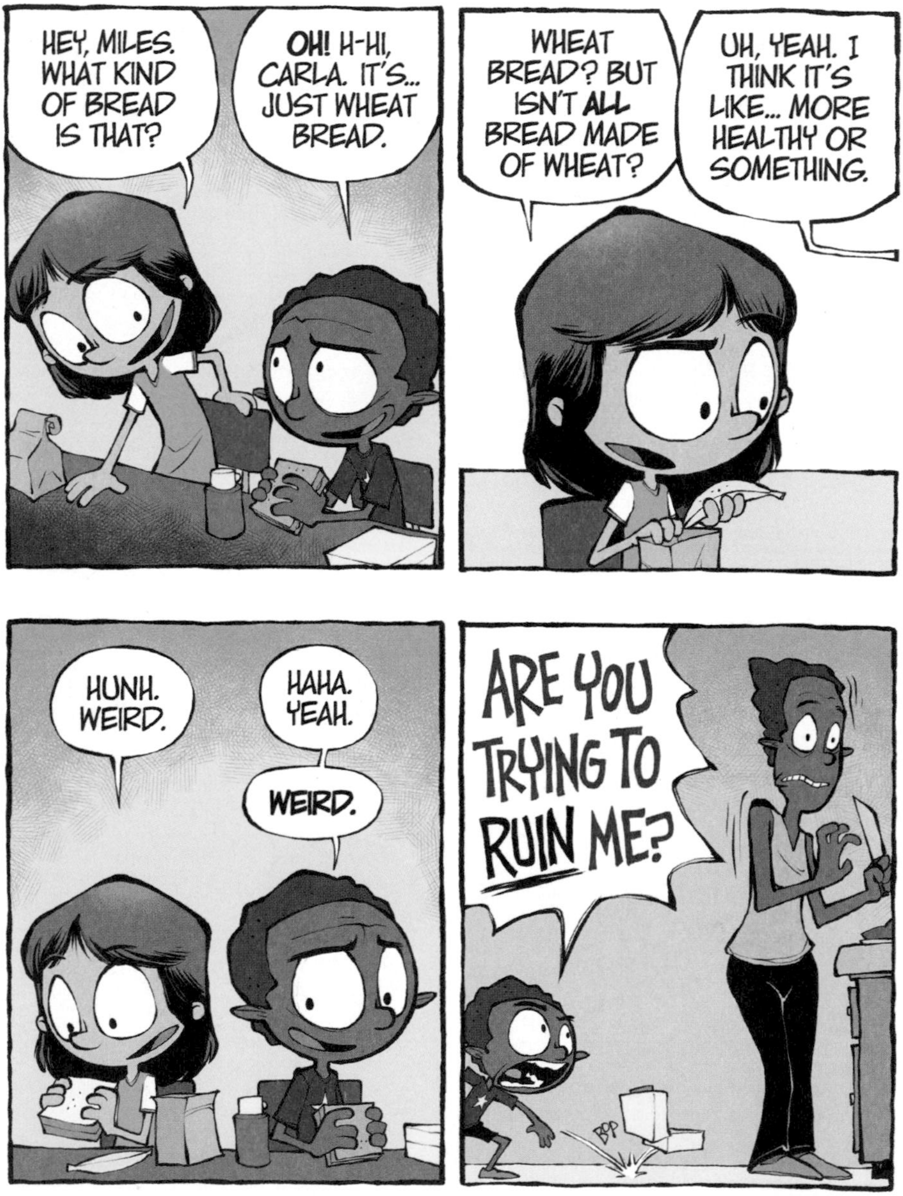
HEY, MILES. WHAT KIND OF BREAD IS THAT?
OH! H-HI, CARLA. IT'S... JUST WHEAT BREAD.
WHEAT BREAD? BUT ISN'T ALL BREAD MADE OF WHEAT?
UH, YEAH. I THINK IT'S LIKE... MORE HEALTHY OR SOMETHING.
HUNH. WEIRD.
HAHA. YEAH.
WEIRD.
ARE YOU TRYING TO RUIN ME?
BOP

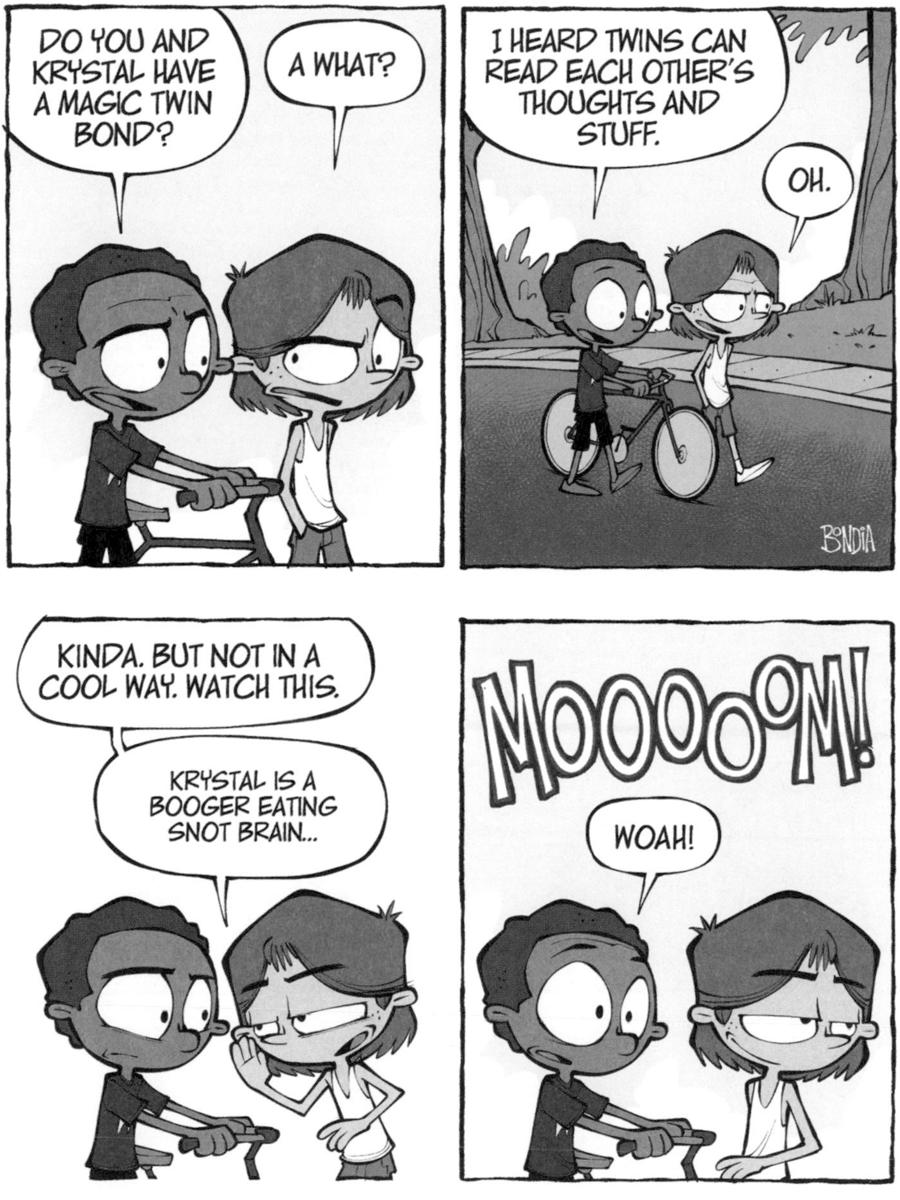
DO YOU AND KRYSTAL HAVE A MAGIC TWIN BOND?
A WHAT?
I HEARD TWINS CAN READ EACH OTHER'S THOUGHTS AND STUFF.
OH.
BONDIA
KINDA. BUT NOT IN A COOL WAY. WATCH THIS.
KRYSTAL IS A BOOGER EATING SNOT BRAIN...
MOOOOOM!
WOAH!

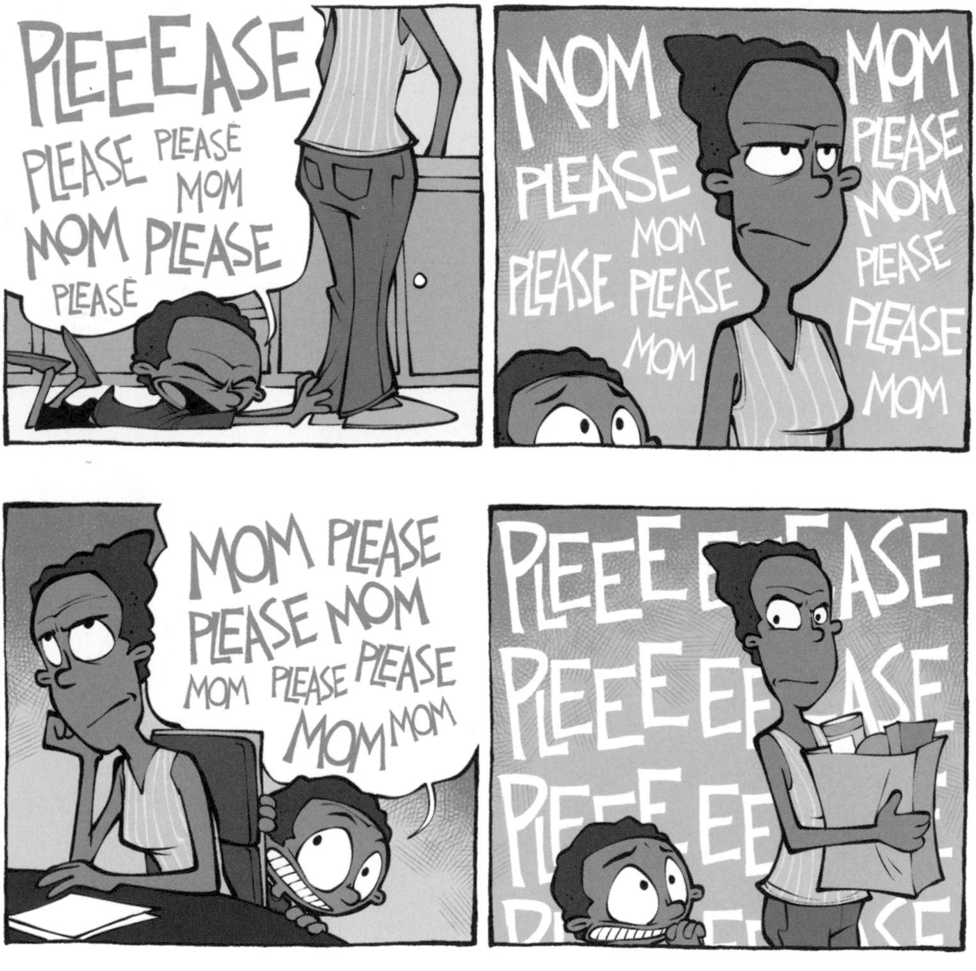
PLEEEASE
PLEASE PLEASE
MOM
MOM PLEASE
PLEASE
MOM
PLEASE
MOM
PLEASE MOM PLEASE
MOM
MOM
PLEASE
MOM
PLEASE
PLEASE
MOM
MOM PLEASE
PLEASE MOM
MOM PLEASE PLEASE
MOM MOM

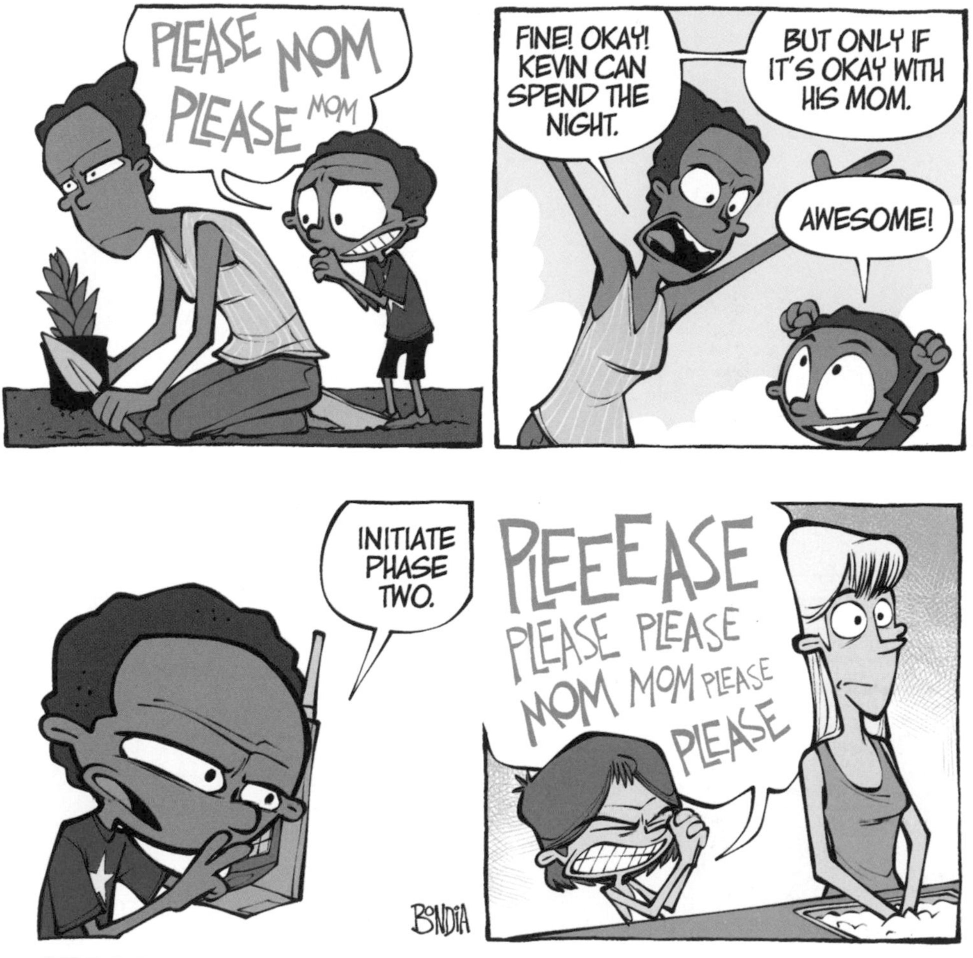
PLEASE MOM PLEASE MOM
FINE! OKAY! KEVIN CAN SPEND THE NIGHT.
BUT ONLY IF IT'S OKAY WITH HIS MOM.
AWESOME!
INITIATE PHASE TWO.
PLEEEASE PLEASE PLEASE MOM MOM PLEASE PLEASE
BONDIA

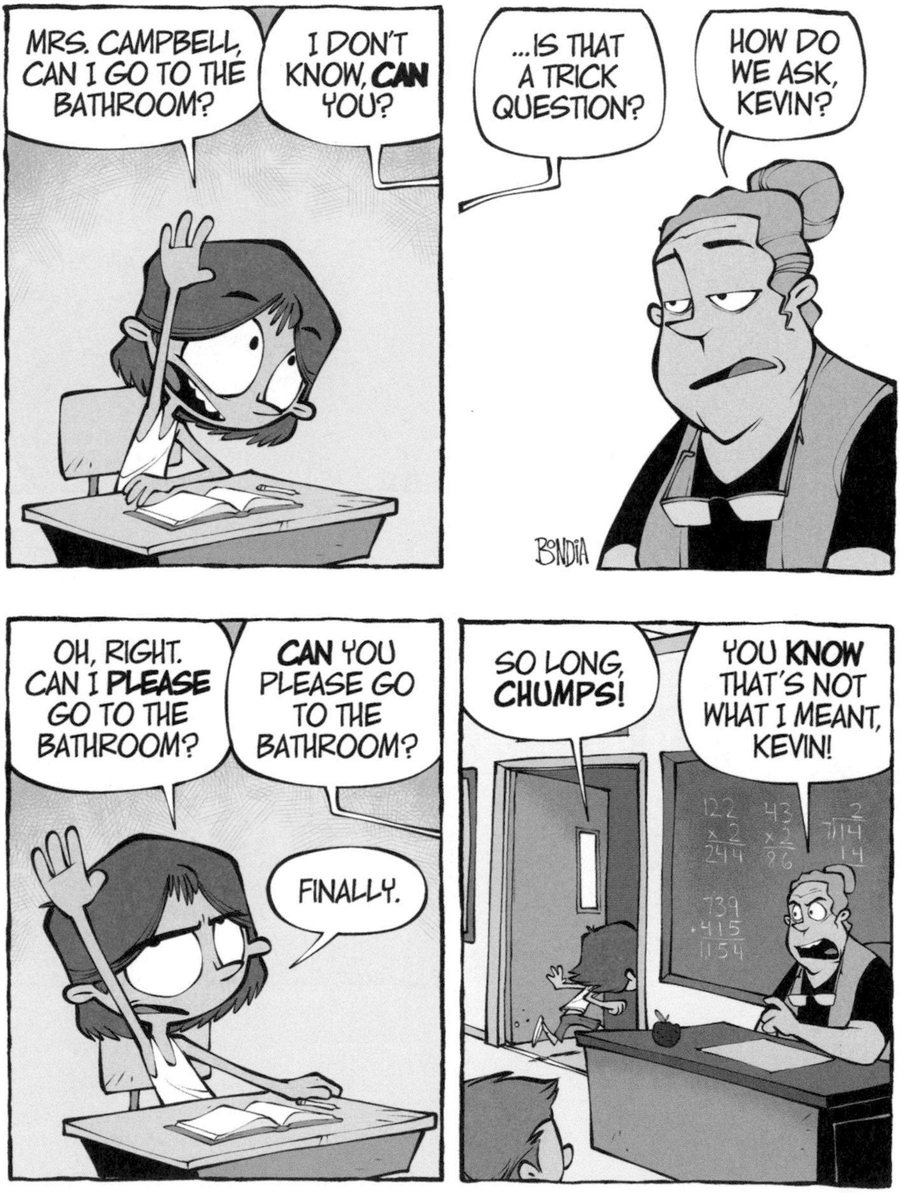
MRS. CAMPBELL, CAN I GO TO THE BATHROOM?
I DON'T KNOW, CAN YOU?
...IS THAT A TRICK QUESTION?
HOW DO WE ASK, KEVIN?
BONDIA
OH, RIGHT. CAN I PLEASE GO TO THE BATHROOM?
CAN YOU PLEASE GO TO THE BATHROOM?
FINALLY.
SO LONG, CHUMPS!
YOU KNOW THAT'S NOT WHAT I MEANT, KEVIN!

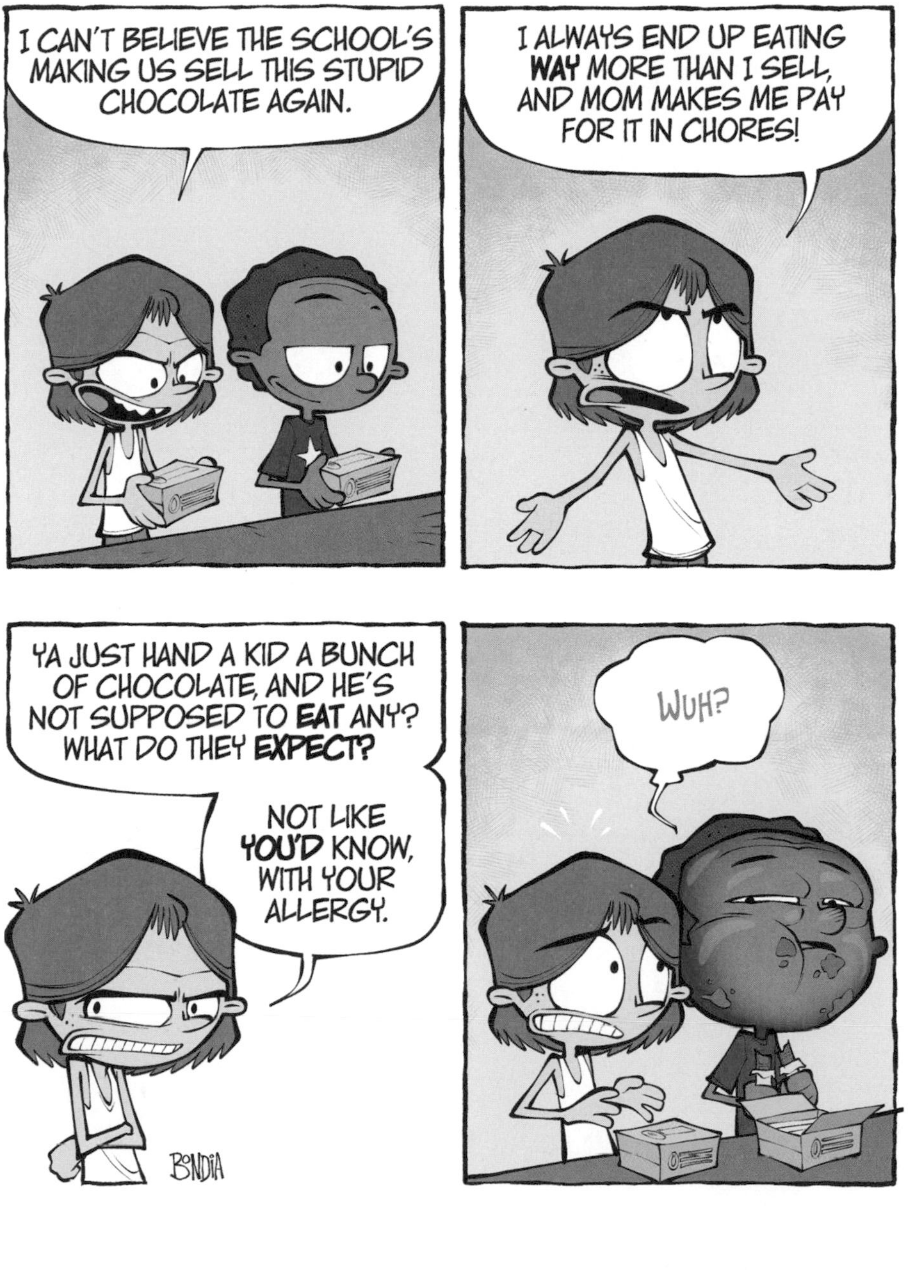
I CAN'T BELIEVE THE SCHOOL'S MAKING US SELL THIS STUPID CHOCOLATE AGAIN.
I ALWAYS END UP EATING **WAY** MORE THAN I SELL, AND MOM MAKES ME PAY FOR IT IN CHORES!
YA JUST HAND A KID A BUNCH OF CHOCOLATE, AND HE'S NOT SUPPOSED TO **EAT** ANY? WHAT DO THEY **EXPECT?**
NOT LIKE **YOU'D** KNOW, WITH YOUR ALLERGY.
BONDIA
WUH?

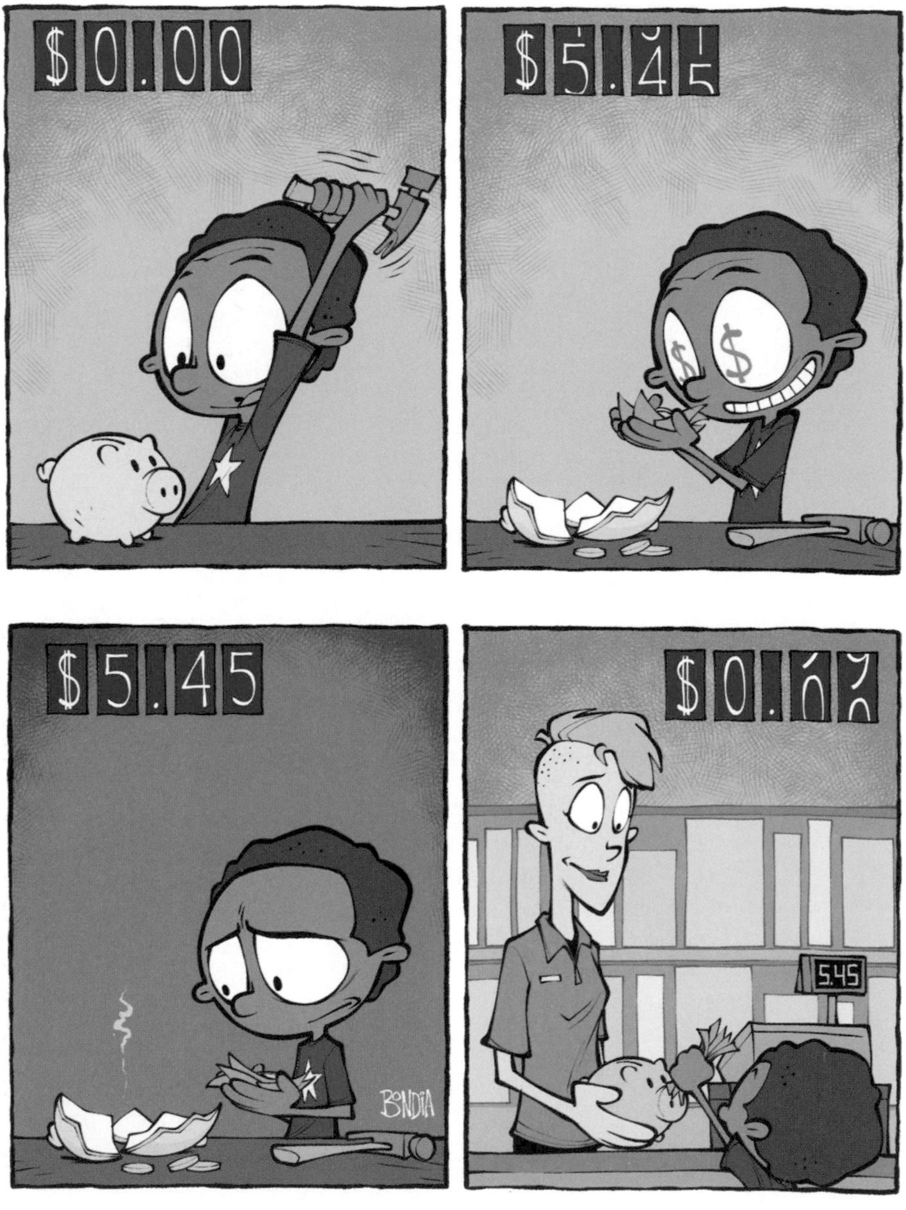
$0.00
$5.45
BONDIA
5.45

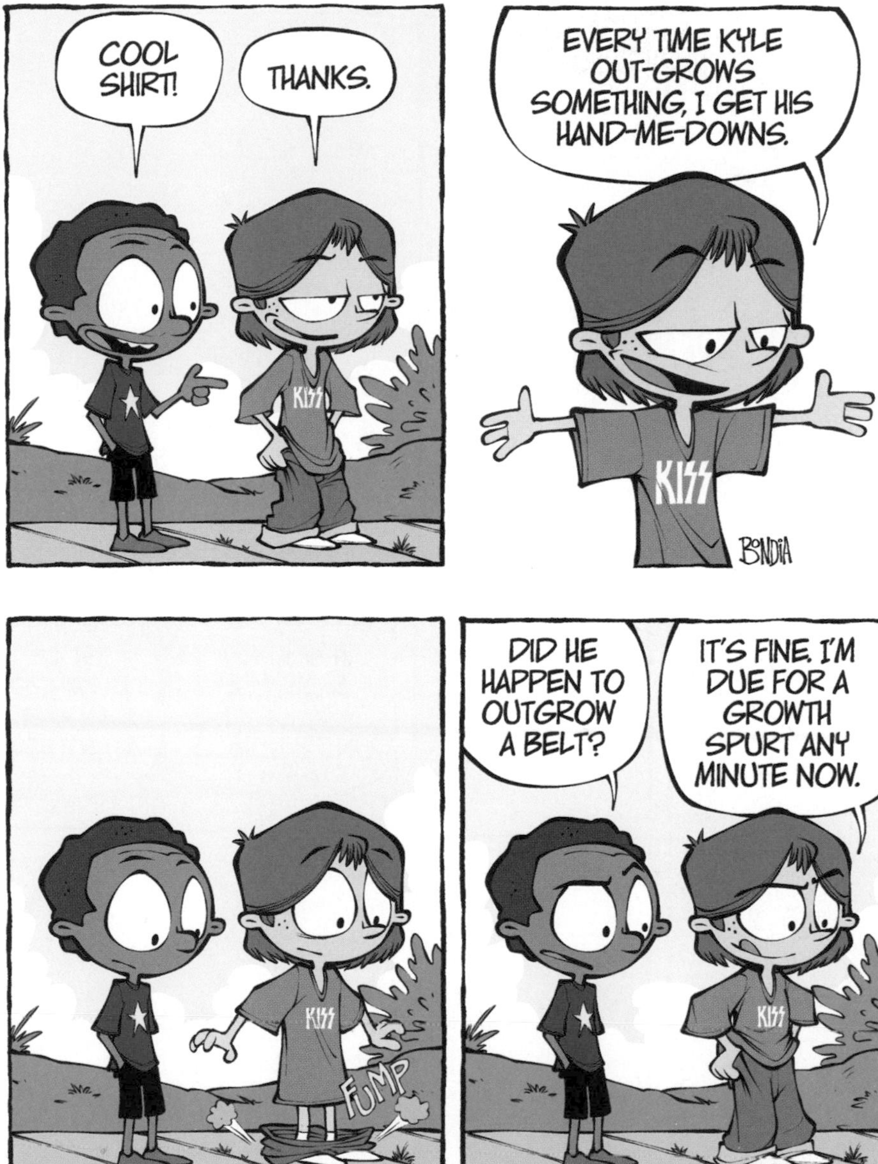
COOL SHIRT!
THANKS.
EVERY TIME KYLE OUT-GROWS SOMETHING, I GET HIS HAND-ME-DOWNS.
KISS
BONDIA
FUMP
DID HE HAPPEN TO OUTGROW A BELT?
IT'S FINE. I'M DUE FOR A GROWTH SPURT ANY MINUTE NOW.

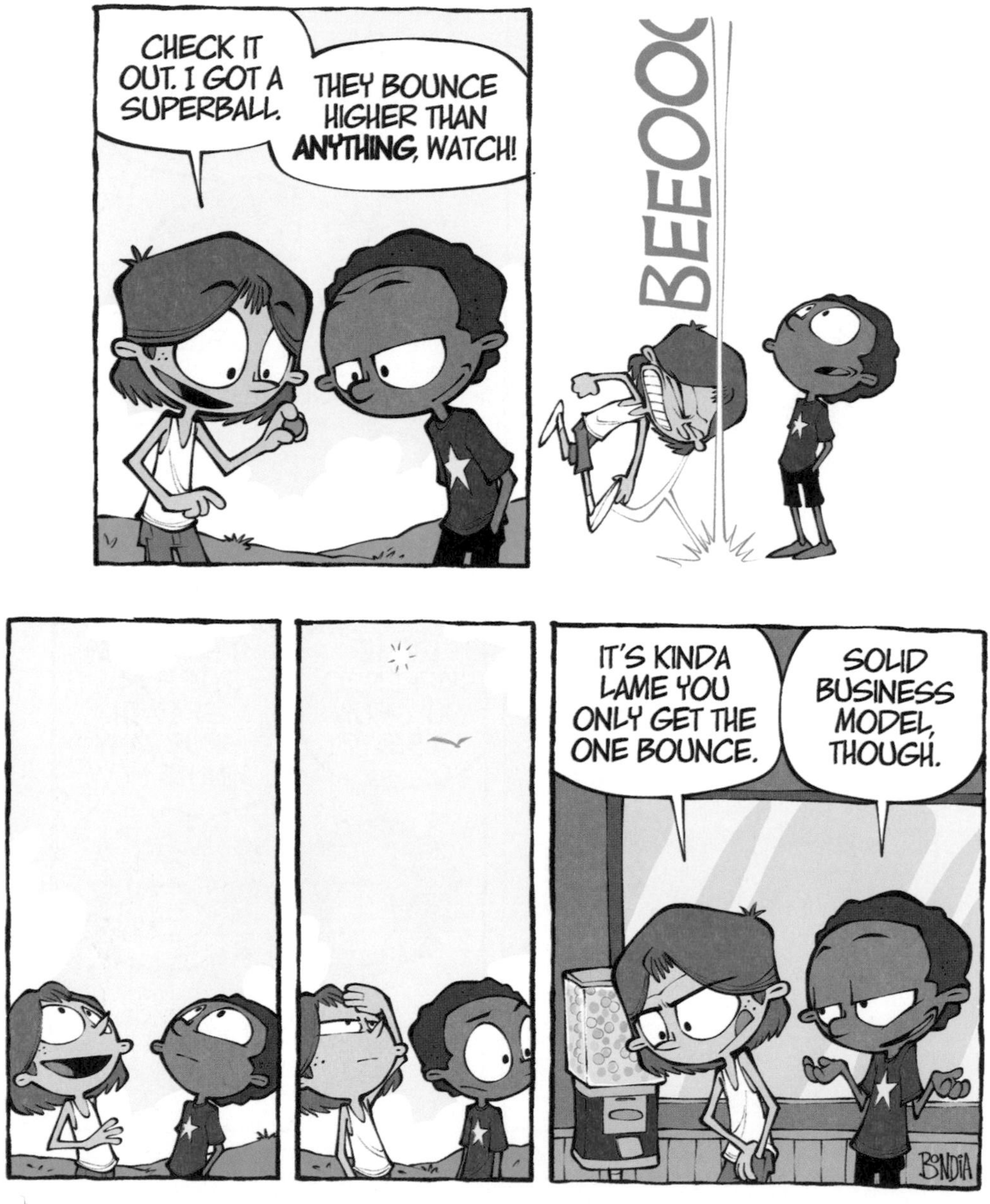
CHECK IT OUT. I GOT A SUPERBALL.
THEY BOUNCE HIGHER THAN ANYTHING, WATCH!
BEEOOO
IT'S KINDA LAME YOU ONLY GET THE ONE BOUNCE.
SOLID BUSINESS MODEL, THOUGH.
BONDIA

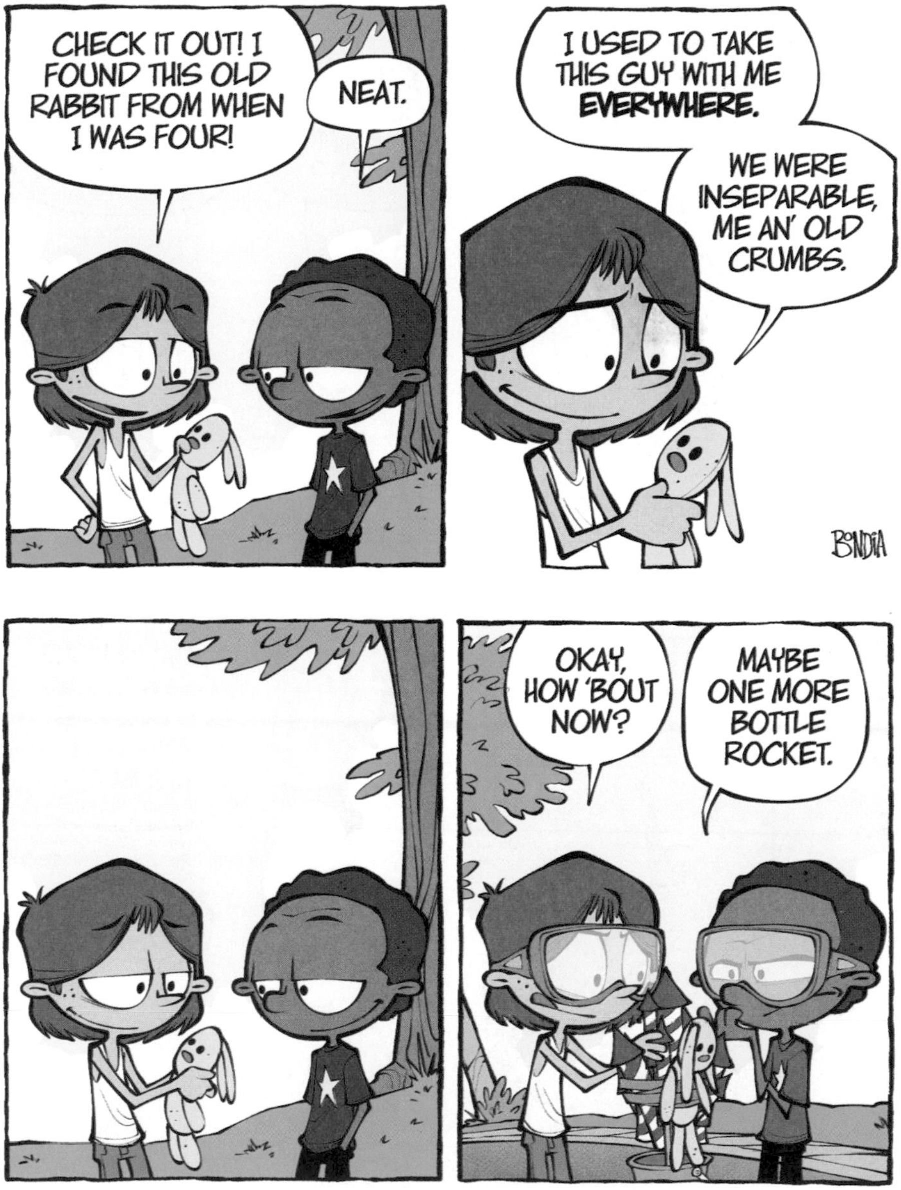
CHECK IT OUT! I FOUND THIS OLD RABBIT FROM WHEN I WAS FOUR!
NEAT.
I USED TO TAKE THIS GUY WITH ME **EVERYWHERE.**
WE WERE INSEPARABLE, ME AN' OLD CRUMBS.
BONDIA
OKAY, HOW 'BOUT NOW?
MAYBE ONE MORE BOTTLE ROCKET.

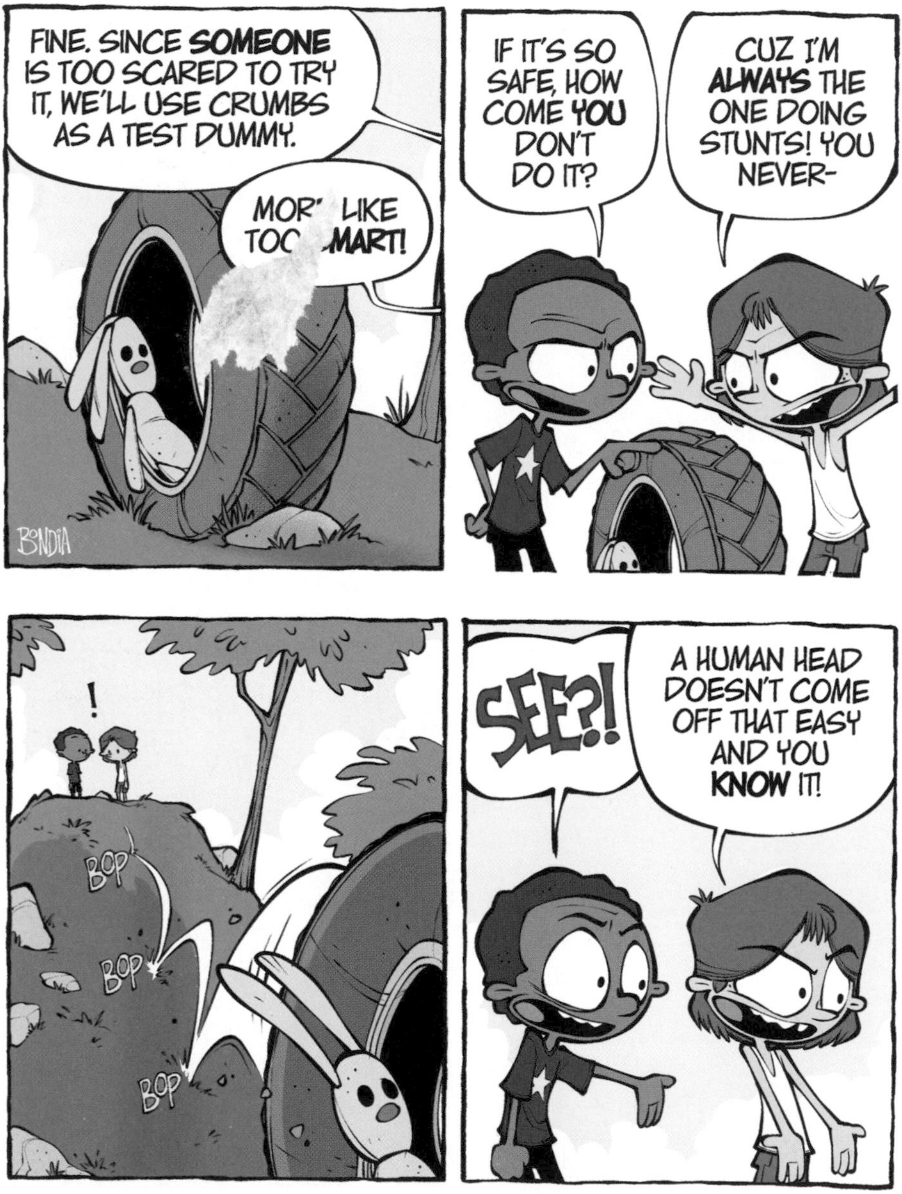
FINE. SINCE **SOMEONE** IS TOO SCARED TO TRY IT, WE'LL USE CRUMBS AS A TEST DUMMY.
MOR' LIKE TOC MART!
BONDIA
IF IT'S SO SAFE, HOW COME **YOU** DON'T DO IT?
CUZ I'M **ALWAYS** THE ONE DOING STUNTS! YOU NEVER-
!
BOP
BOP
BOP
SEE?!
A HUMAN HEAD DOESN'T COME OFF THAT EASY AND YOU **KNOW** IT!

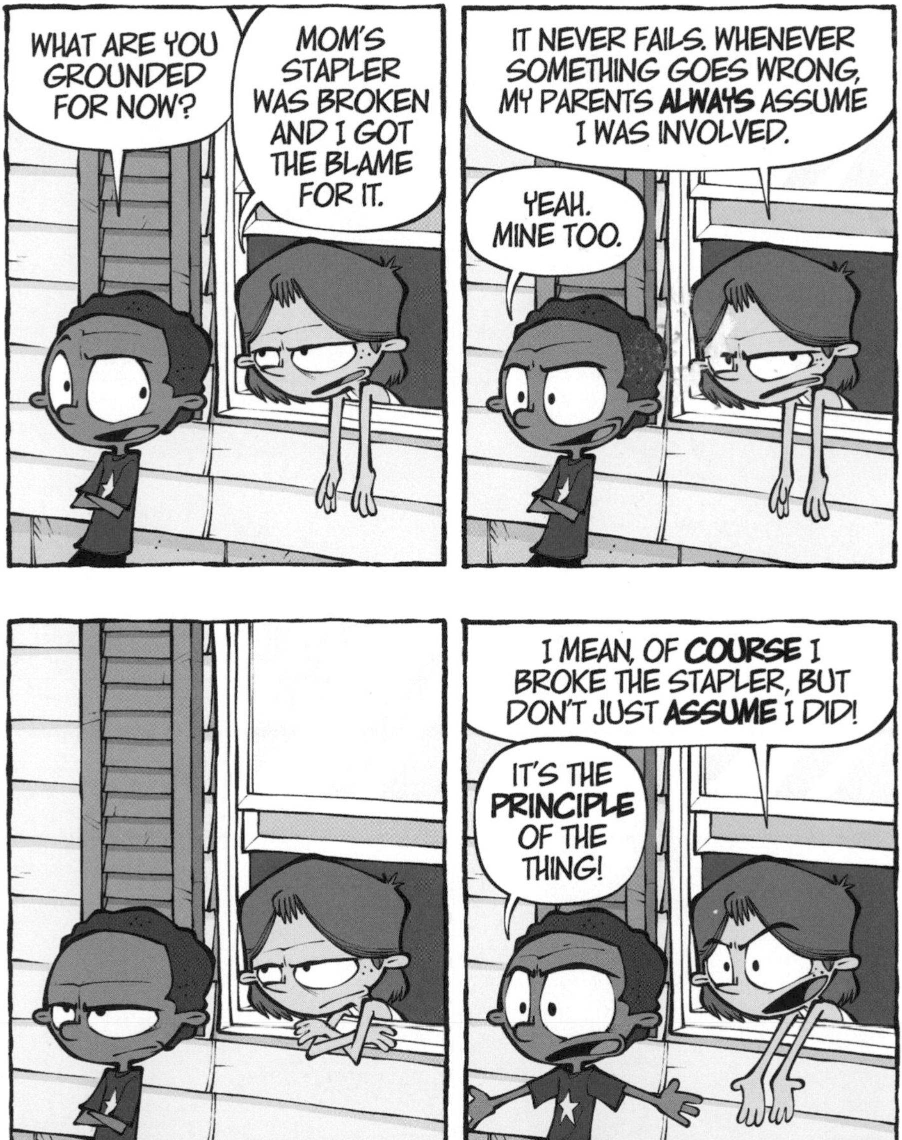
WHAT ARE YOU GROUNDED FOR NOW?
MOM'S STAPLER WAS BROKEN AND I GOT THE BLAME FOR IT.
IT NEVER FAILS. WHENEVER SOMETHING GOES WRONG, MY PARENTS **ALWAYS** ASSUME I WAS INVOLVED.
YEAH. MINE TOO.
I MEAN, OF **COURSE** I BROKE THE STAPLER, BUT DON'T JUST **ASSUME** I DID!
IT'S THE **PRINCIPLE** OF THE THING!
BONDIA

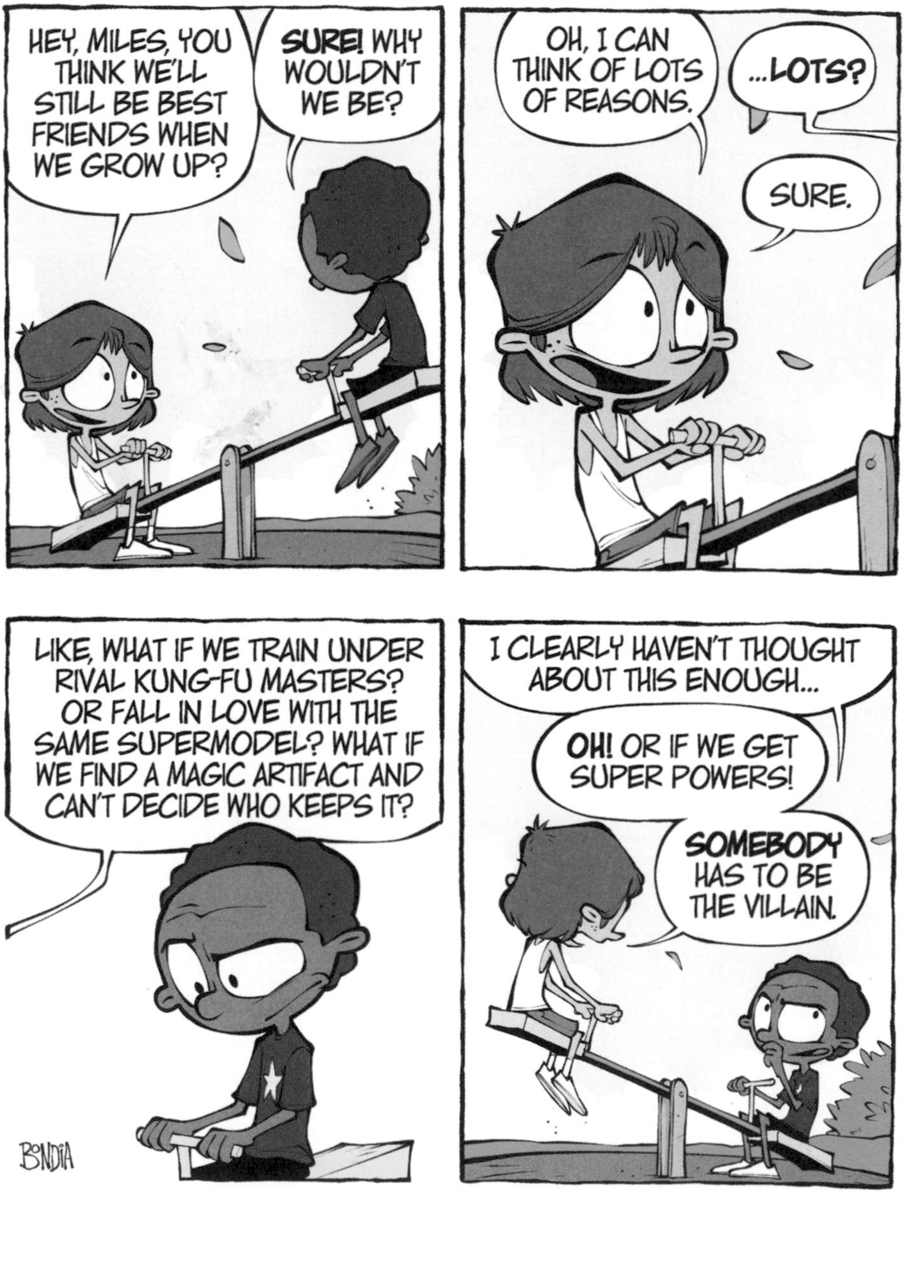
HEY, MILES, YOU THINK WE'LL STILL BE BEST FRIENDS WHEN WE GROW UP?
SURE! WHY WOULDN'T WE BE?
OH, I CAN THINK OF LOTS OF REASONS.
...LOTS?
SURE.
LIKE, WHAT IF WE TRAIN UNDER RIVAL KUNG-FU MASTERS? OR FALL IN LOVE WITH THE SAME SUPERMODEL? WHAT IF WE FIND A MAGIC ARTIFACT AND CAN'T DECIDE WHO KEEPS IT?
I CLEARLY HAVEN'T THOUGHT ABOUT THIS ENOUGH...
OH! OR IF WE GET SUPER POWERS!
SOMEBODY HAS TO BE THE VILLAIN.
BONDIA

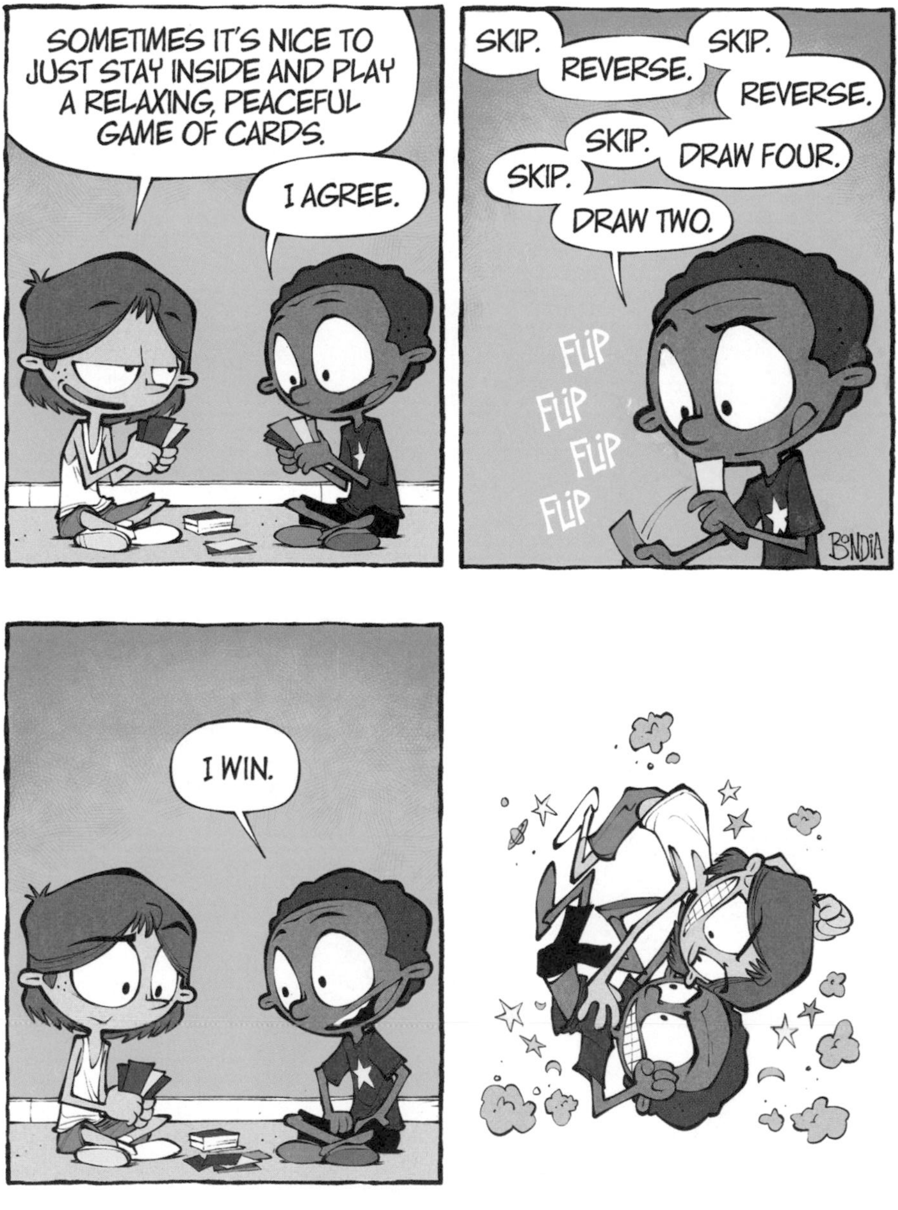

SOMETIMES IT'S NICE TO JUST STAY INSIDE AND PLAY A RELAXING, PEACEFUL GAME OF CARDS.
I AGREE.
SKIP.
REVERSE.
SKIP.
REVERSE.
SKIP.
DRAW FOUR.
SKIP.
DRAW TWO.
FLIP
FLIP
FLIP
FLIP
BONDIA
I WIN.

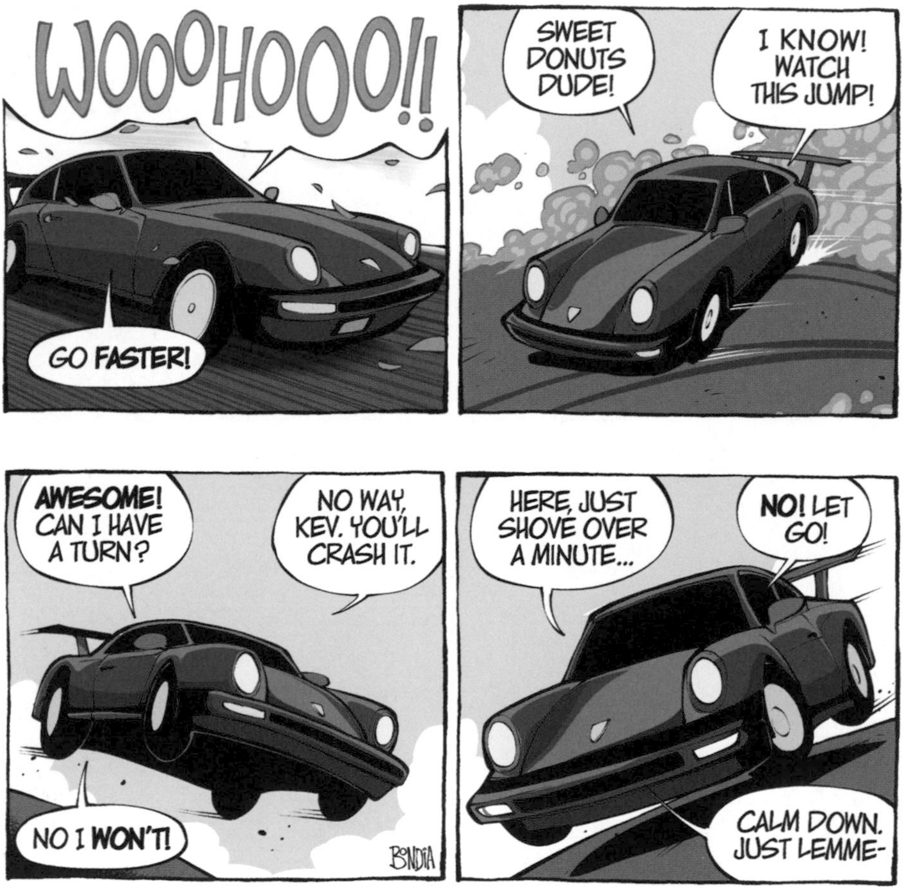
WOOOHOOO!!
GO FASTER!
SWEET DONUTS DUDE!
I KNOW! WATCH THIS JUMP!
AWESOME! CAN I HAVE A TURN?
NO WAY, KEV. YOU'LL CRASH IT.
NO I WON'T!
BONDIA
HERE, JUST SHOVE OVER A MINUTE...
NO! LET GO!
CALM DOWN. JUST LEMME-

WATCH OUT!!
CRUNCH
IT WAS AN ACCIDENT!
I'LL SHOW YOU AN ACCIDENT!

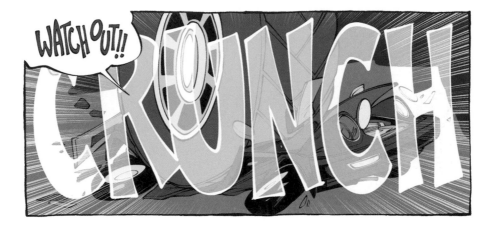

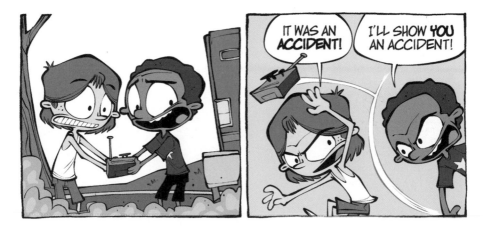

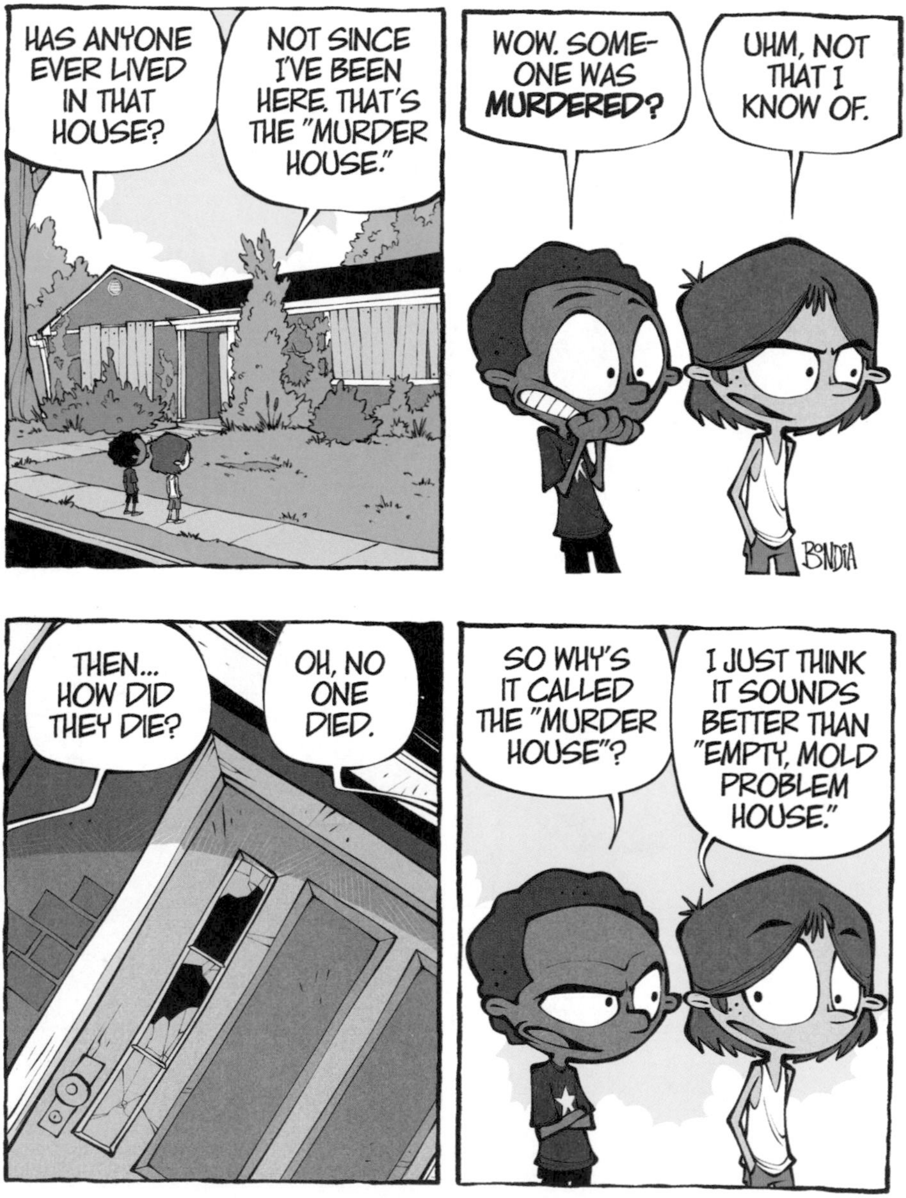
HAS ANYONE EVER LIVED IN THAT HOUSE?
NOT SINCE I'VE BEEN HERE. THAT'S THE "MURDER HOUSE."
WOW. SOME-ONE WAS **MURDERED?**
UHM, NOT THAT I KNOW OF.
BONDIA
THEN... HOW DID THEY DIE?
OH, NO ONE DIED.
SO WHY'S IT CALLED THE "MURDER HOUSE"?
I JUST THINK IT SOUNDS BETTER THAN "EMPTY, MOLD PROBLEM HOUSE."

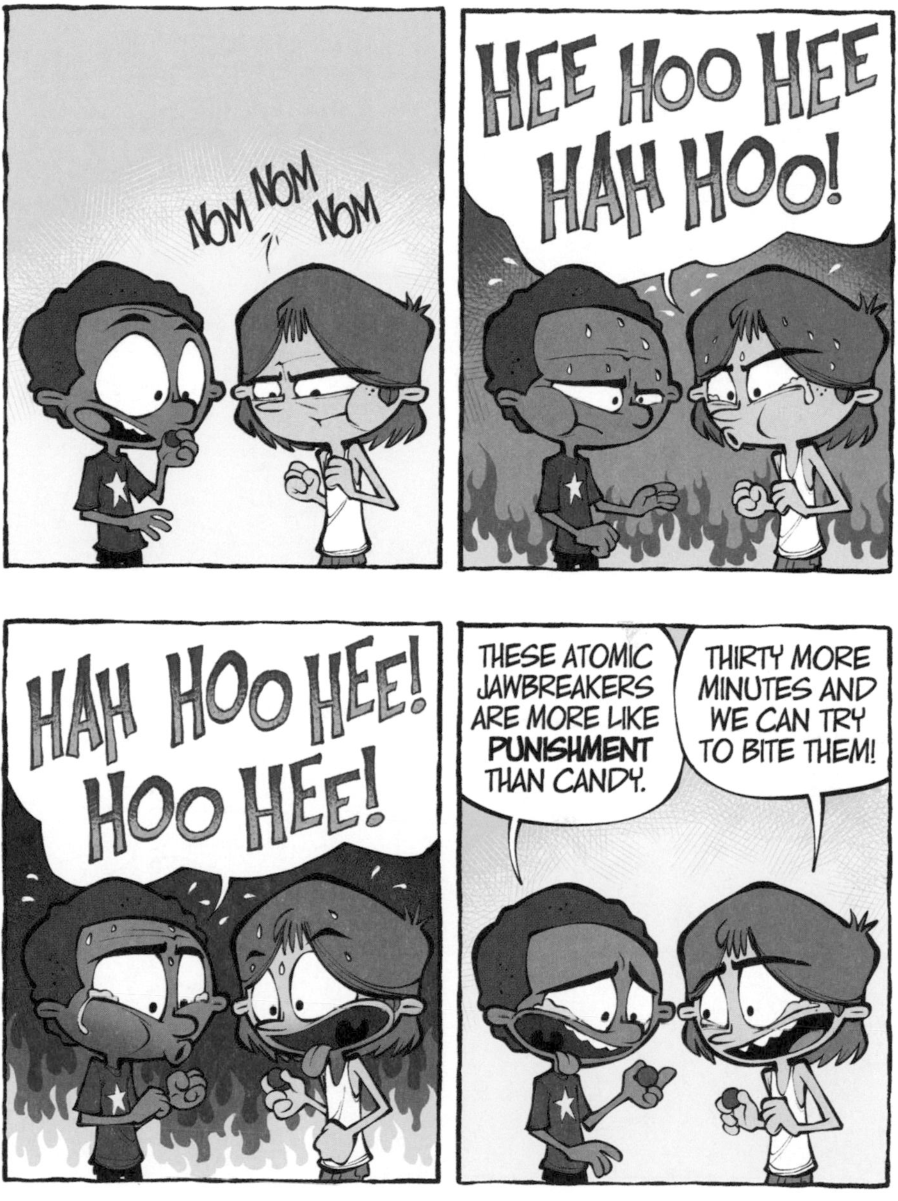
NOM NOM NOM
HEE HOO HEE HAH HOO!
HAH HOO HEE! HOO HEE!
THESE ATOMIC JAWBREAKERS ARE MORE LIKE **PUNISHMENT** THAN CANDY.
THIRTY MORE MINUTES AND WE CAN TRY TO BITE THEM!

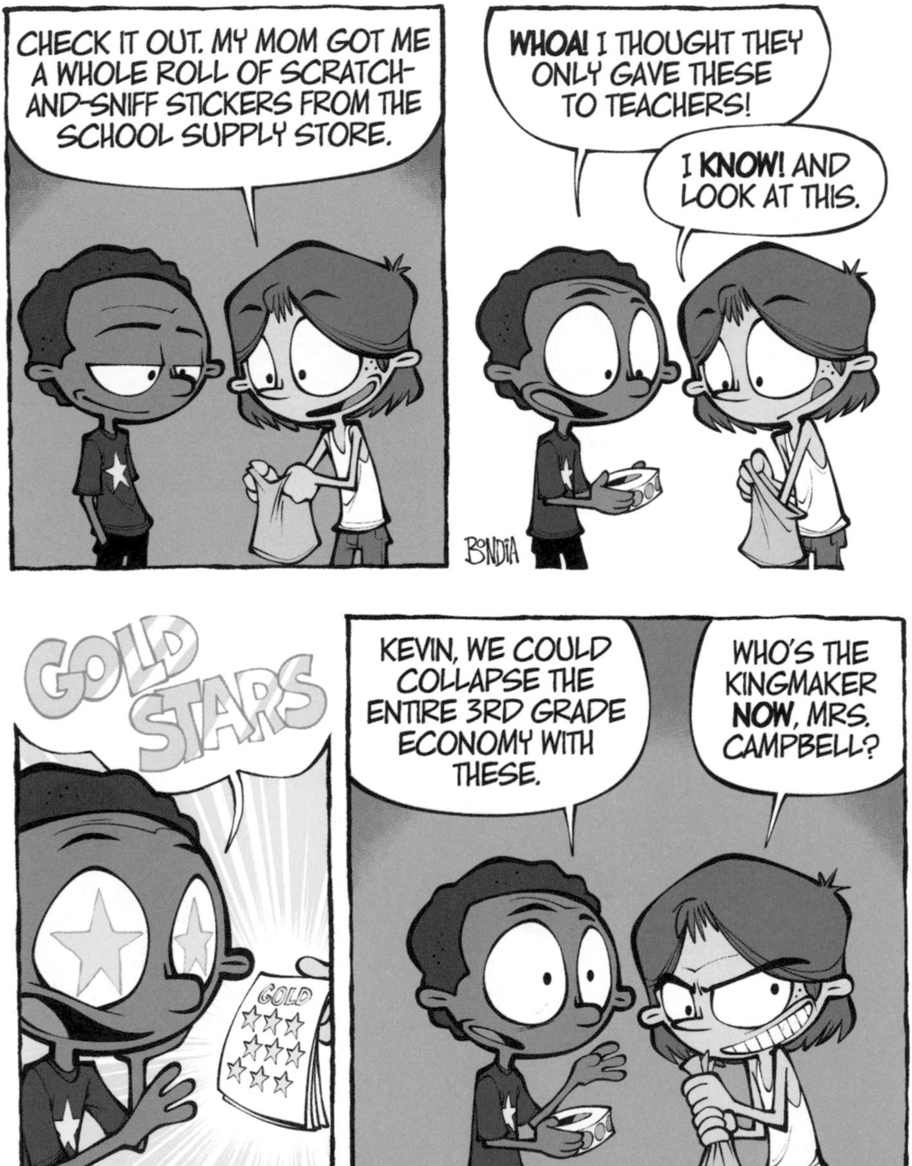
CHECK IT OUT. MY MOM GOT ME A WHOLE ROLL OF SCRATCH-AND-SNIFF STICKERS FROM THE SCHOOL SUPPLY STORE.
WHOA! I THOUGHT THEY ONLY GAVE THESE TO TEACHERS!
I KNOW! AND LOOK AT THIS.
BONDIA
GOLD STARS
GOLD
KEVIN, WE COULD COLLAPSE THE ENTIRE 3RD GRADE ECONOMY WITH THESE.
WHO'S THE KINGMAKER NOW, MRS. CAMPBELL?

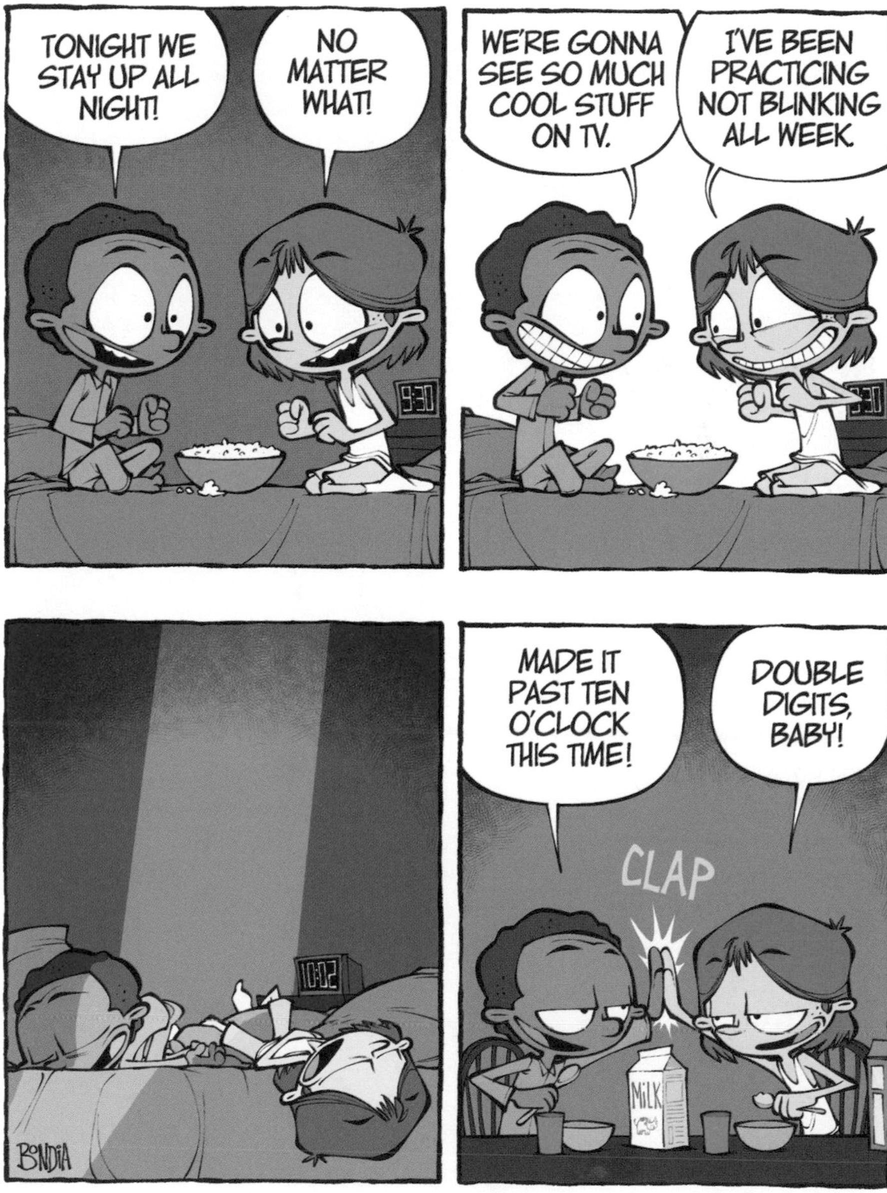
TONIGHT WE STAY UP ALL NIGHT!
NO MATTER WHAT!
9:30
WE'RE GONNA SEE SO MUCH COOL STUFF ON TV.
I'VE BEEN PRACTICING NOT BLINKING ALL WEEK.
10:02
BONDIA
MADE IT PAST TEN O'CLOCK THIS TIME!
DOUBLE DIGITS, BABY!
CLAP
MILK

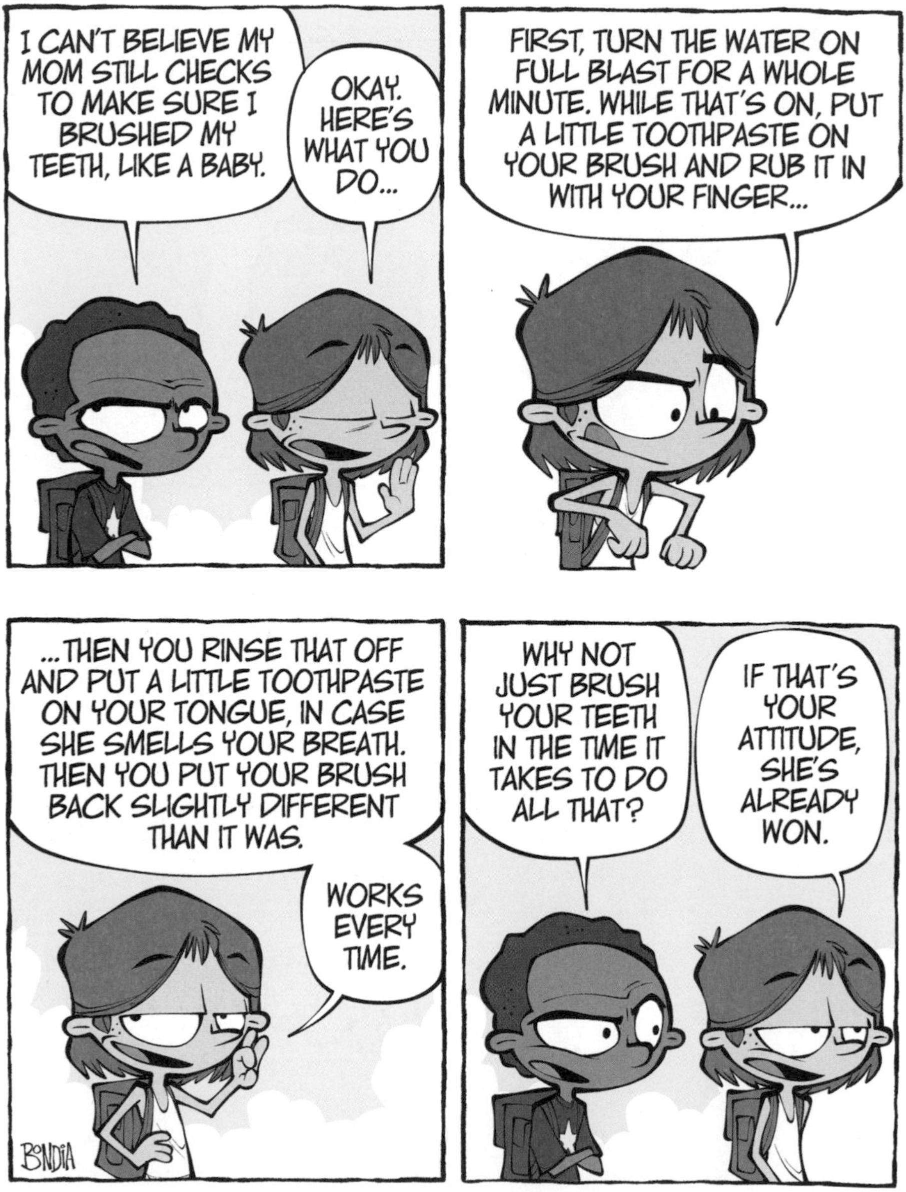
I CAN'T BELIEVE MY MOM STILL CHECKS TO MAKE SURE I BRUSHED MY TEETH, LIKE A BABY.
OKAY. HERE'S WHAT YOU DO...
FIRST, TURN THE WATER ON FULL BLAST FOR A WHOLE MINUTE. WHILE THAT'S ON, PUT A LITTLE TOOTHPASTE ON YOUR BRUSH AND RUB IT IN WITH YOUR FINGER...
...THEN YOU RINSE THAT OFF AND PUT A LITTLE TOOTHPASTE ON YOUR TONGUE, IN CASE SHE SMELLS YOUR BREATH. THEN YOU PUT YOUR BRUSH BACK SLIGHTLY DIFFERENT THAN IT WAS.
WORKS EVERY TIME.
BONDIA
WHY NOT JUST BRUSH YOUR TEETH IN THE TIME IT TAKES TO DO ALL THAT?
IF THAT'S YOUR ATTITUDE, SHE'S ALREADY WON.

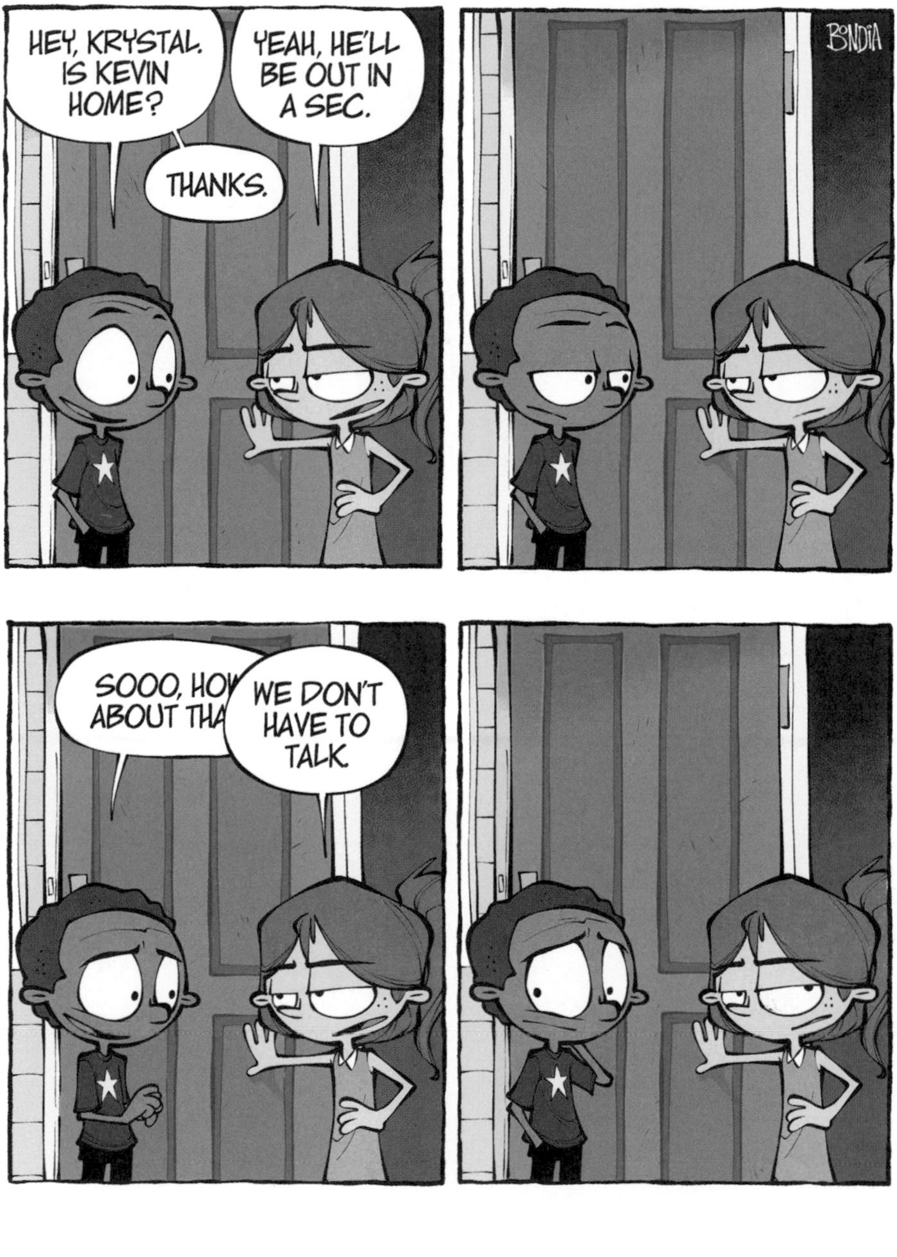
HEY, KRYSTAL. IS KEVIN HOME?
YEAH, HE'LL BE OUT IN A SEC.
THANKS.
BONDIA
SOOO, HOW ABOUT THA
WE DON'T HAVE TO TALK.

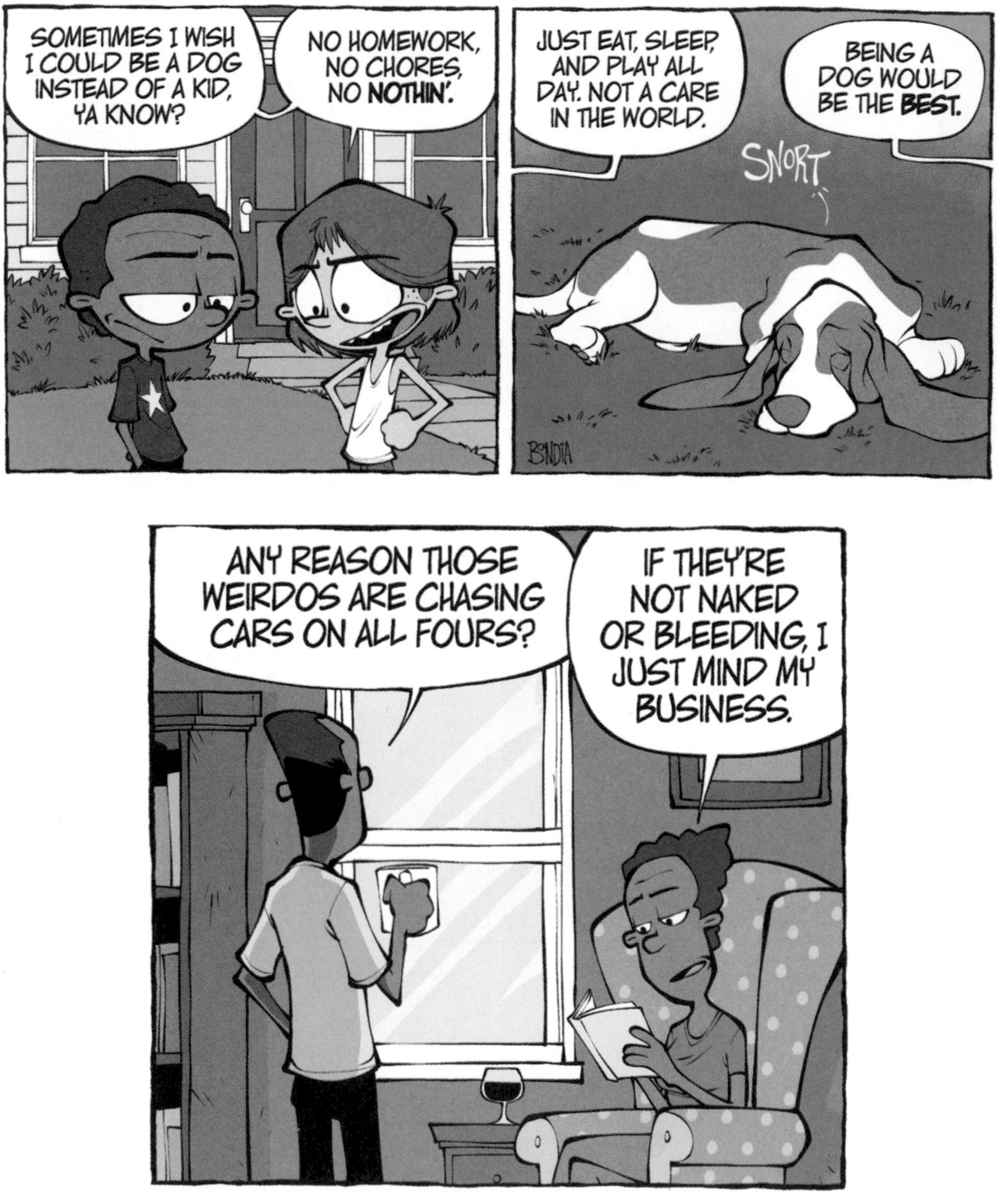
SOMETIMES I WISH I COULD BE A DOG INSTEAD OF A KID, YA KNOW?
NO HOMEWORK, NO CHORES, NO NOTHIN'.
JUST EAT, SLEEP, AND PLAY ALL DAY. NOT A CARE IN THE WORLD.
BEING A DOG WOULD BE THE BEST.
SNORT
BONDIA
ANY REASON THOSE WEIRDOS ARE CHASING CARS ON ALL FOURS?
IF THEY'RE NOT NAKED OR BLEEDING, I JUST MIND MY BUSINESS.

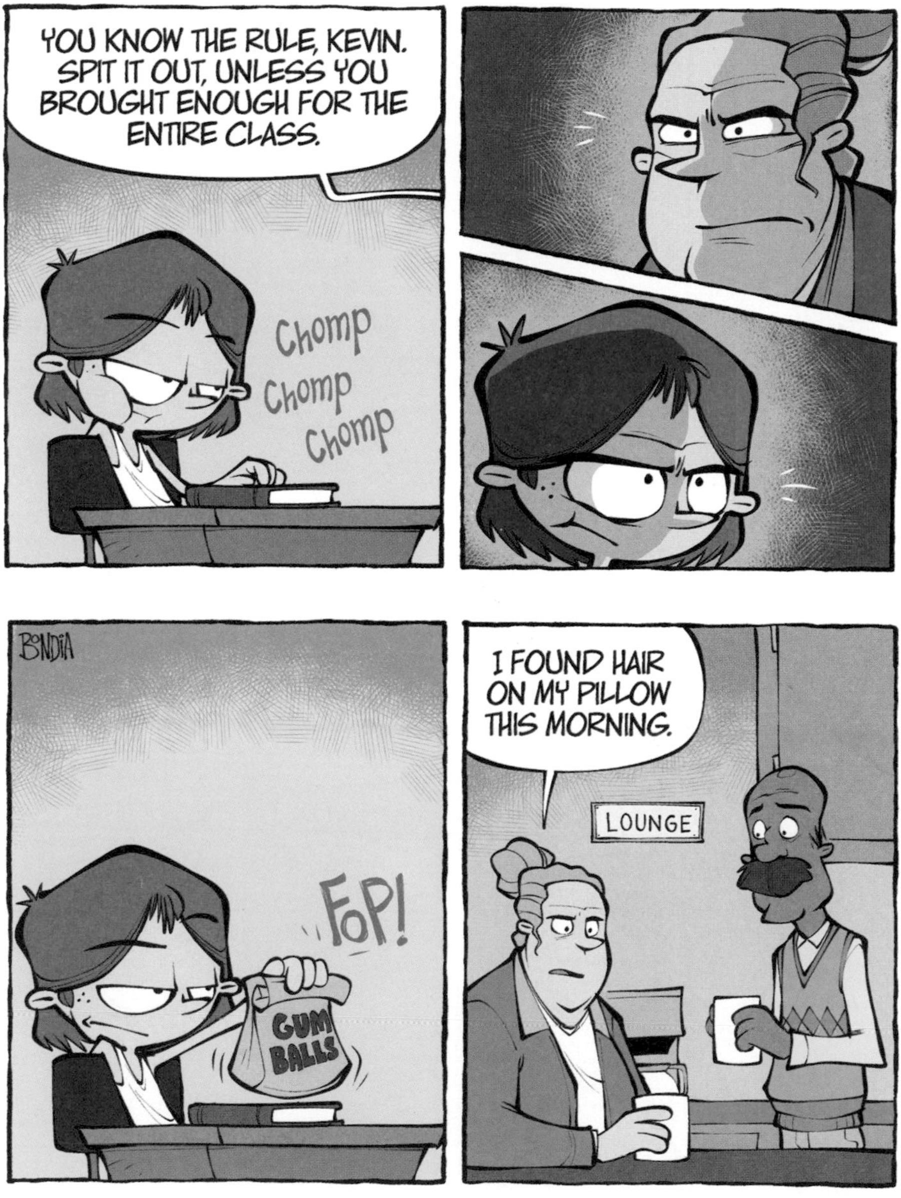

YOU KNOW THE RULE, KEVIN. SPIT IT OUT, UNLESS YOU BROUGHT ENOUGH FOR THE ENTIRE CLASS.
Chomp
Chomp
Chomp
BONDIA
FOP!
GUM BALLS
I FOUND HAIR ON MY PILLOW THIS MORNING.
LOUNGE

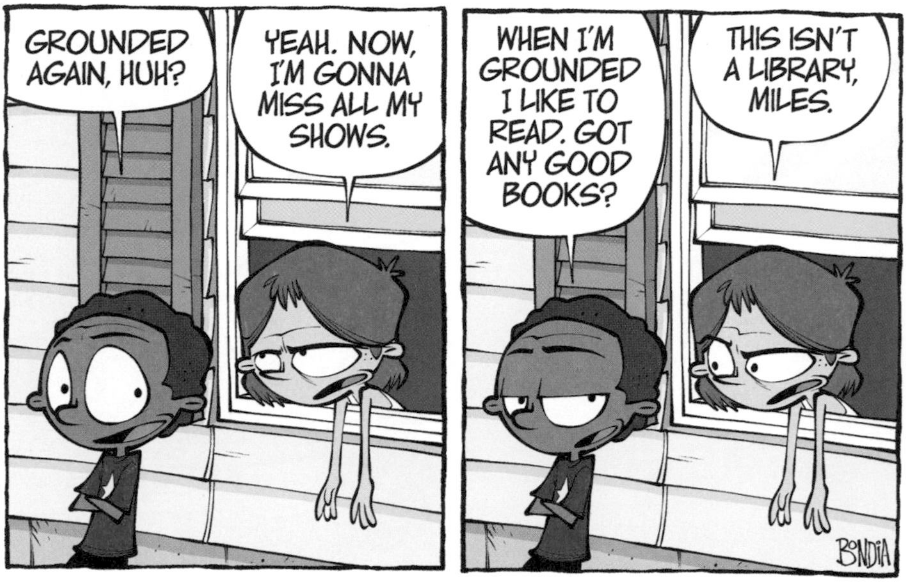
GROUNDED AGAIN, HUH?
YEAH. NOW, I'M GONNA MISS ALL MY SHOWS.
WHEN I'M GROUNDED I LIKE TO READ. GOT ANY GOOD BOOKS?
THIS ISN'T A LIBRARY, MILES.
BONDIA

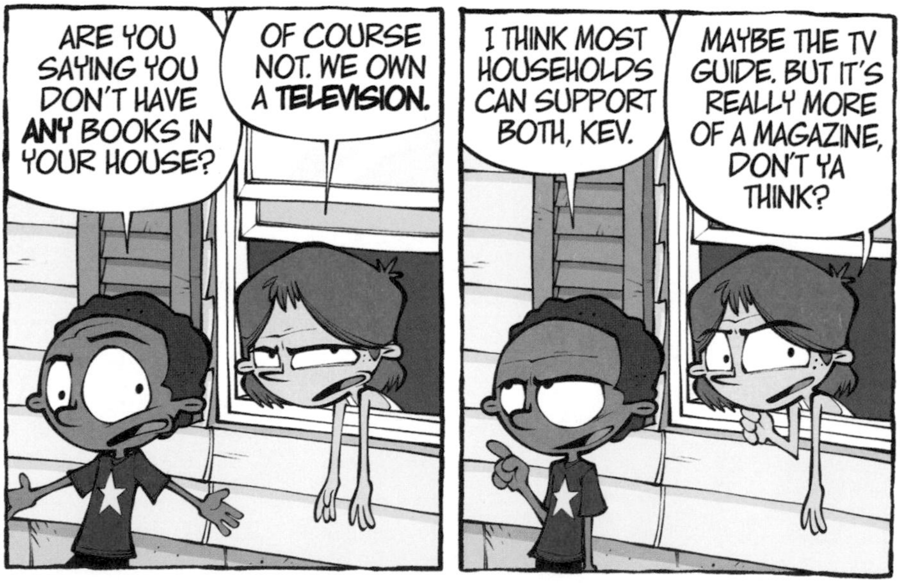
ARE YOU SAYING YOU DON'T HAVE ANY BOOKS IN YOUR HOUSE?
OF COURSE NOT. WE OWN A TELEVISION.
I THINK MOST HOUSEHOLDS CAN SUPPORT BOTH, KEV.
MAYBE THE TV GUIDE. BUT IT'S REALLY MORE OF A MAGAZINE, DON'T YA THINK?

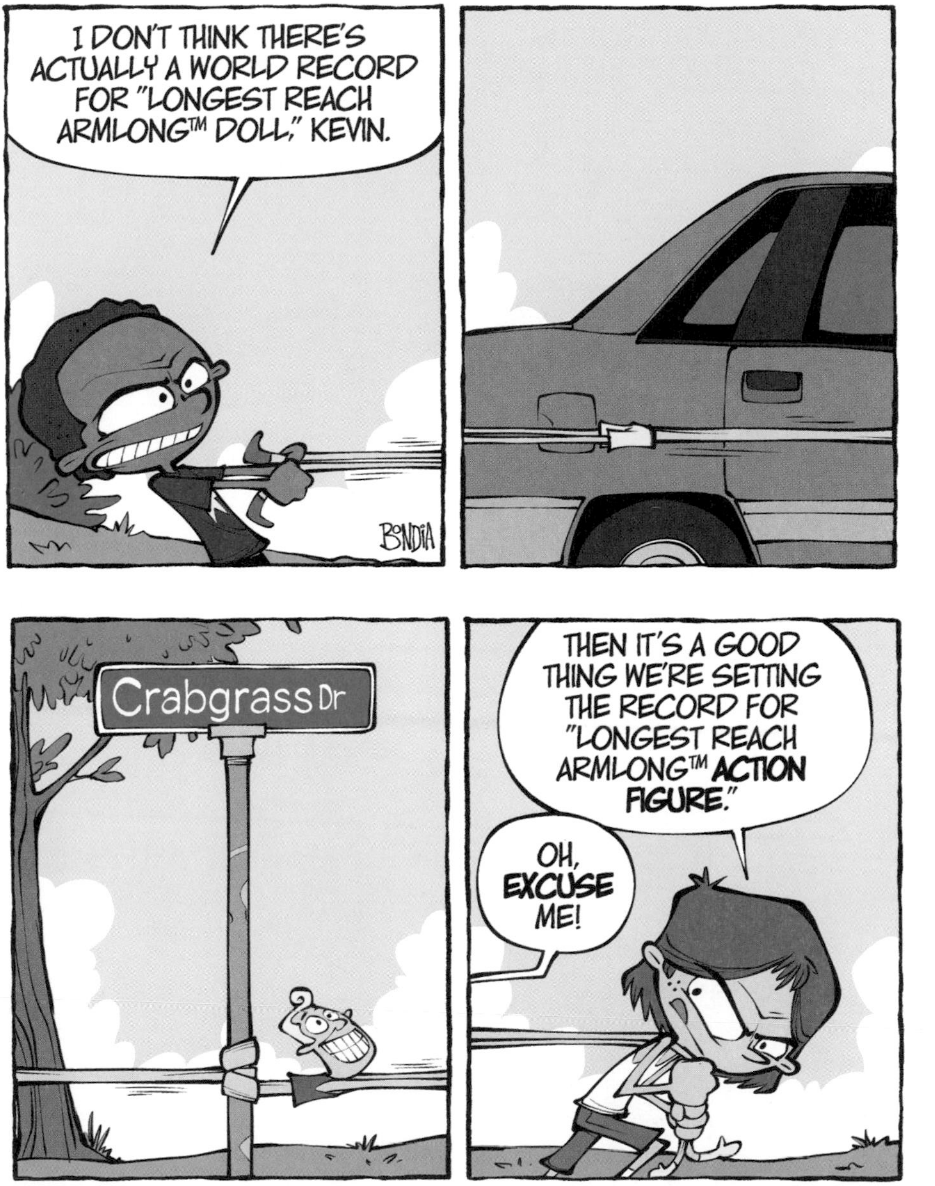
I DON'T THINK THERE'S ACTUALLY A WORLD RECORD FOR "LONGEST REACH ARMLONG™ DOLL," KEVIN.
BONDIA
Crabgrass Dr
THEN IT'S A GOOD THING WE'RE SETTING THE RECORD FOR "LONGEST REACH ARMLONG™ **ACTION FIGURE**."
OH, **EXCUSE** ME!

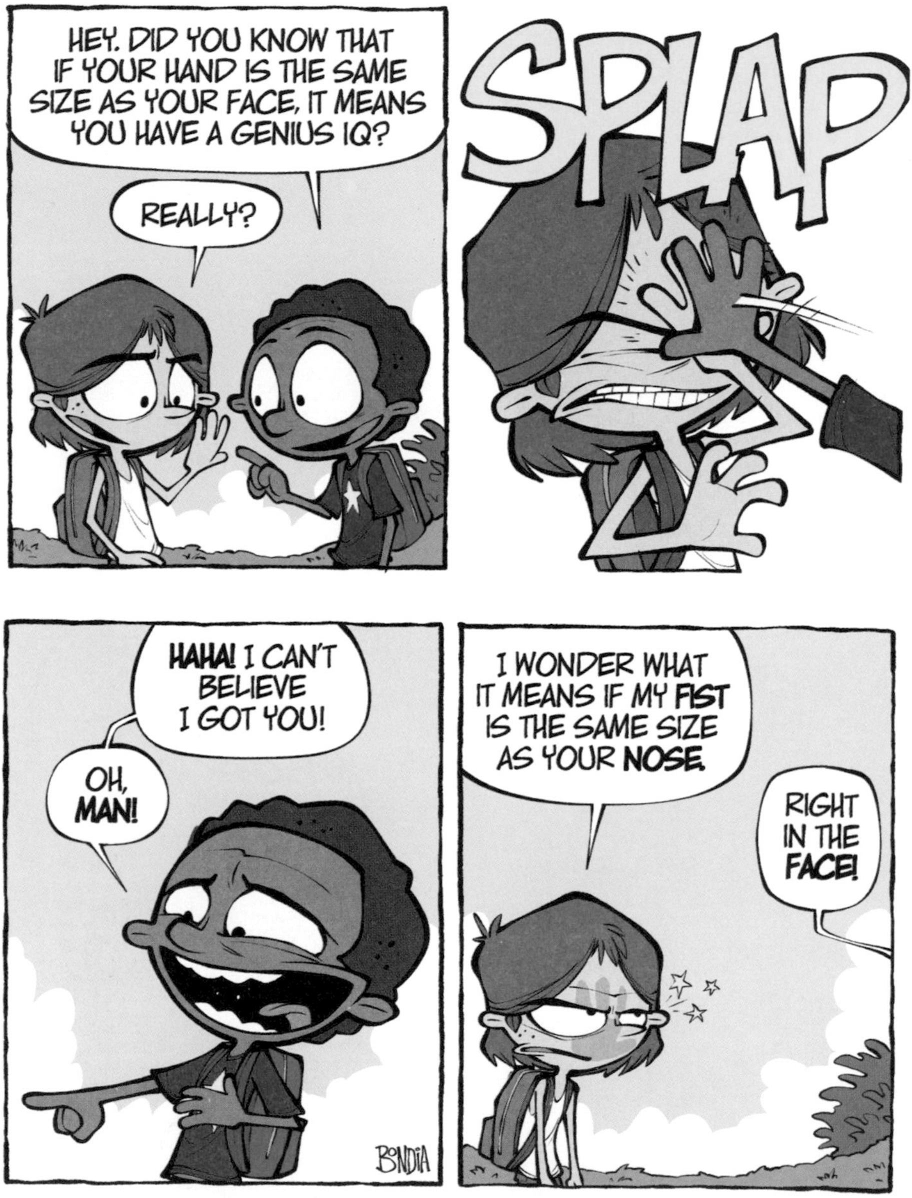
HEY. DID YOU KNOW THAT IF YOUR HAND IS THE SAME SIZE AS YOUR FACE, IT MEANS YOU HAVE A GENIUS IQ?
REALLY?
SPLAP
HAHA! I CAN'T BELIEVE I GOT YOU!
OH, MAN!
BONDIA
I WONDER WHAT IT MEANS IF MY FIST IS THE SAME SIZE AS YOUR NOSE.
RIGHT IN THE FACE!

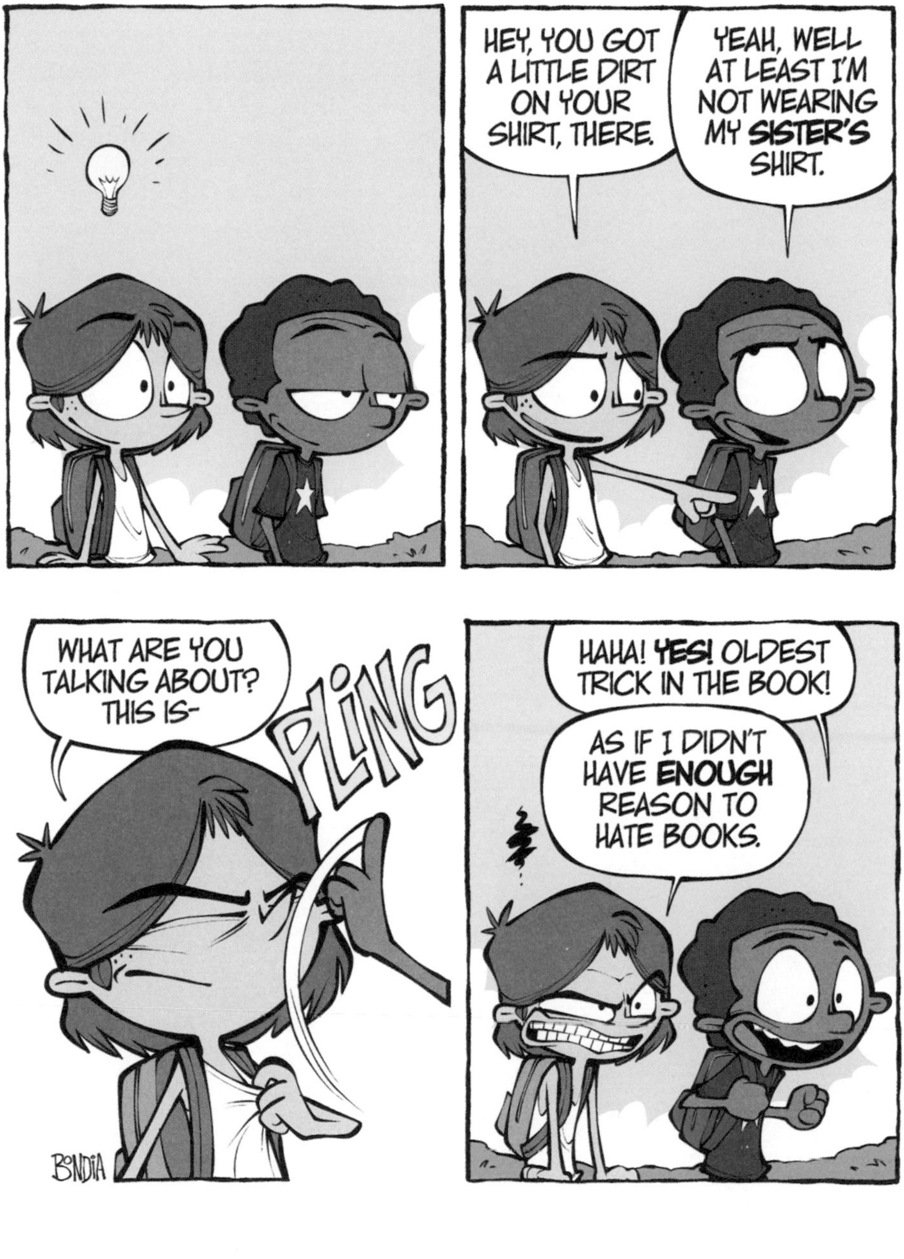

HEY, YOU GOT A LITTLE DIRT ON YOUR SHIRT, THERE.
YEAH, WELL AT LEAST I'M NOT WEARING MY **SISTER'S** SHIRT.
WHAT ARE YOU TALKING ABOUT? THIS IS-
PLING
HAHA! **YES!** OLDEST TRICK IN THE BOOK!
AS IF I DIDN'T HAVE **ENOUGH** REASON TO HATE BOOKS.
BONDIA

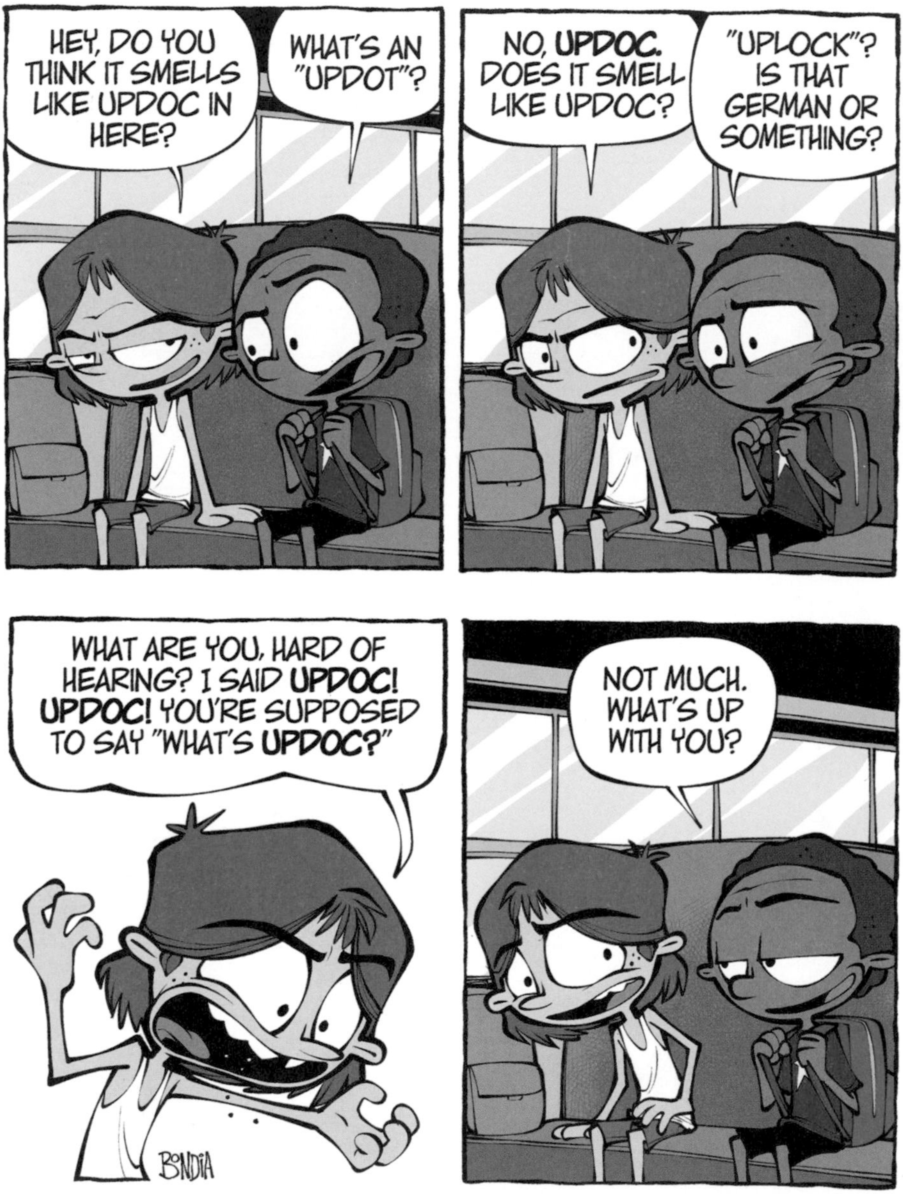
HEY, DO YOU THINK IT SMELLS LIKE UPDOC IN HERE?
WHAT'S AN "UPDOT"?
NO, **UPDOC.** DOES IT SMELL LIKE UPDOC?
"UPLOCK"? IS THAT GERMAN OR SOMETHING?
WHAT ARE YOU, HARD OF HEARING? I SAID **UPDOC! UPDOC!** YOU'RE SUPPOSED TO SAY "WHAT'S **UPDOC?**"
BONDIA
NOT MUCH. WHAT'S UP WITH YOU?

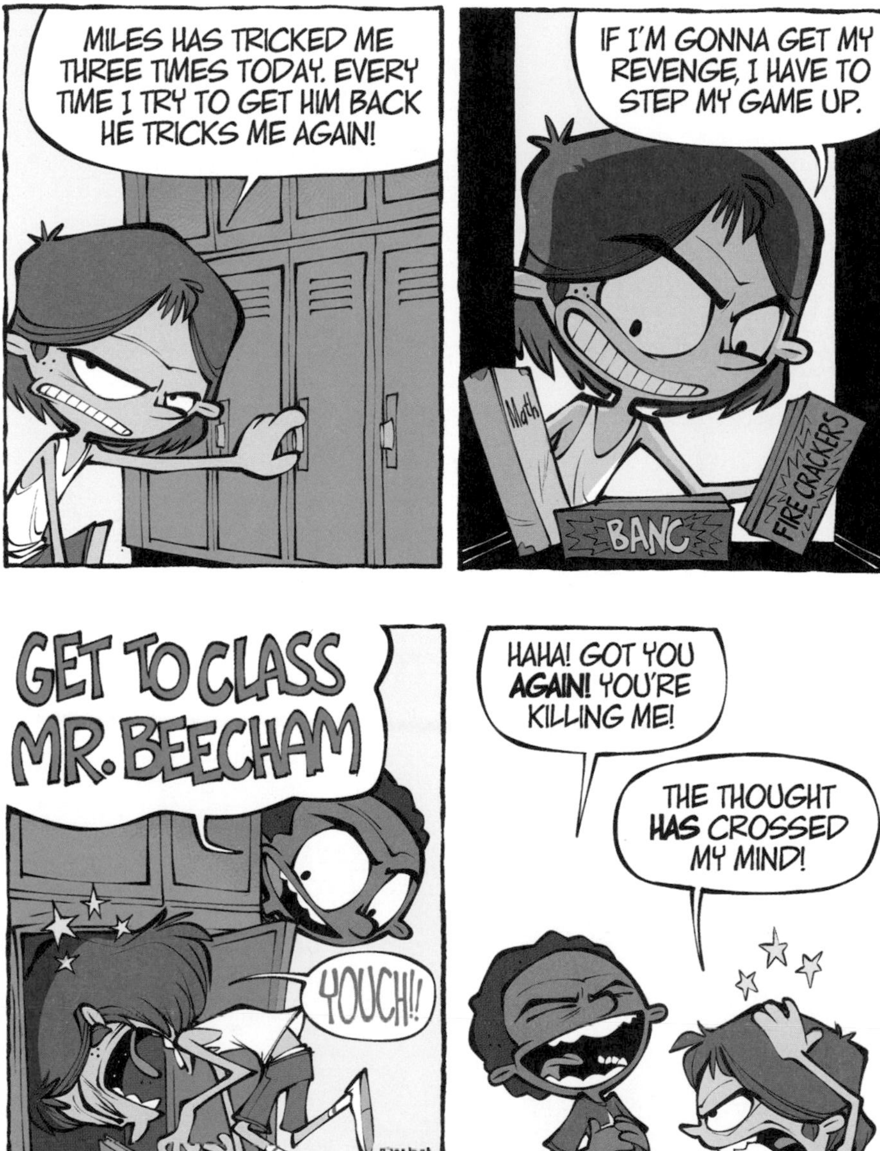
MILES HAS TRICKED ME THREE TIMES TODAY. EVERY TIME I TRY TO GET HIM BACK HE TRICKS ME AGAIN!
IF I'M GONNA GET MY REVENGE, I HAVE TO STEP MY GAME UP.
Math
BANG
FIRE CRACKERS
GET TO CLASS MR. BEECHAM
YOUCH!!
BONDIA
HAHA! GOT YOU AGAIN! YOU'RE KILLING ME!
THE THOUGHT HAS CROSSED MY MIND!

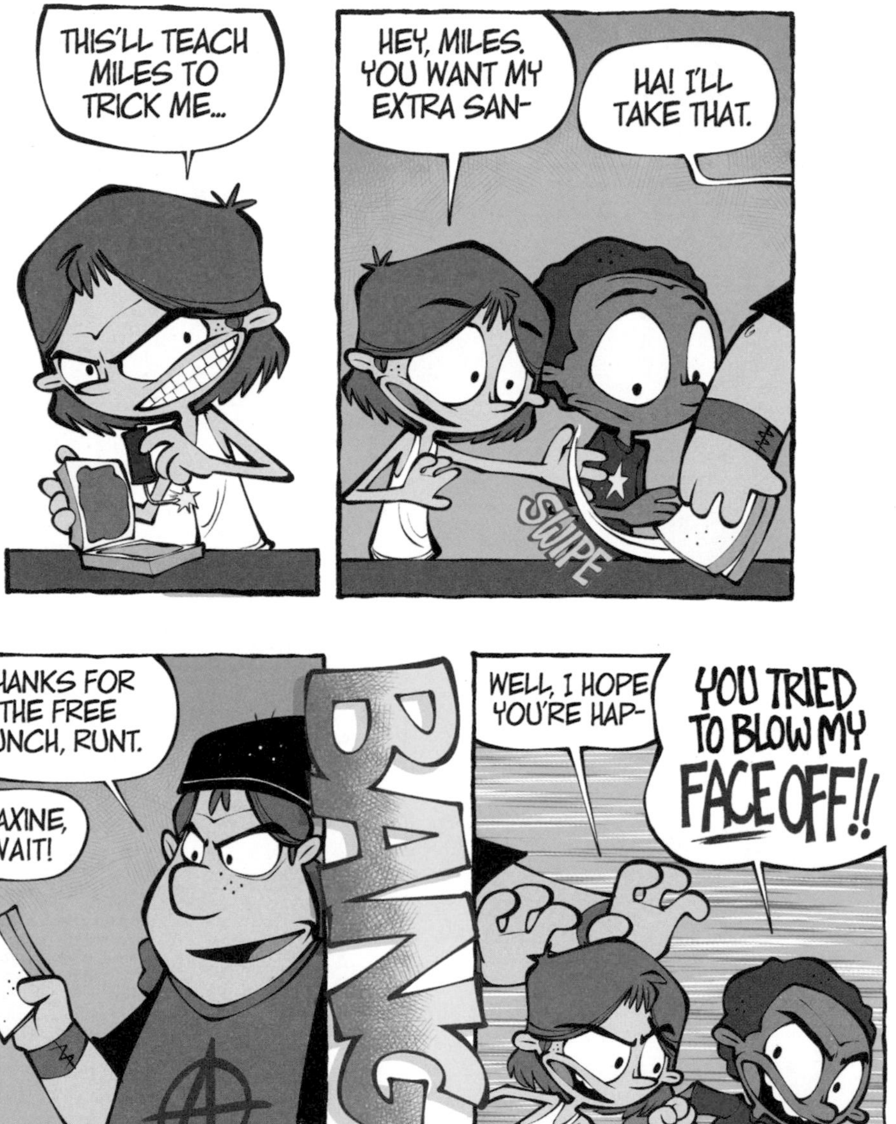
THIS'LL TEACH MILES TO TRICK ME...
HEY, MILES. YOU WANT MY EXTRA SAN-
HA! I'LL TAKE THAT.
SWIPE
THANKS FOR THE FREE LUNCH, RUNT.
MAXINE, WAIT!
BONDIA
BANG!
WELL, I HOPE YOU'RE HAP-
YOU TRIED TO BLOW MY FACE OFF!!

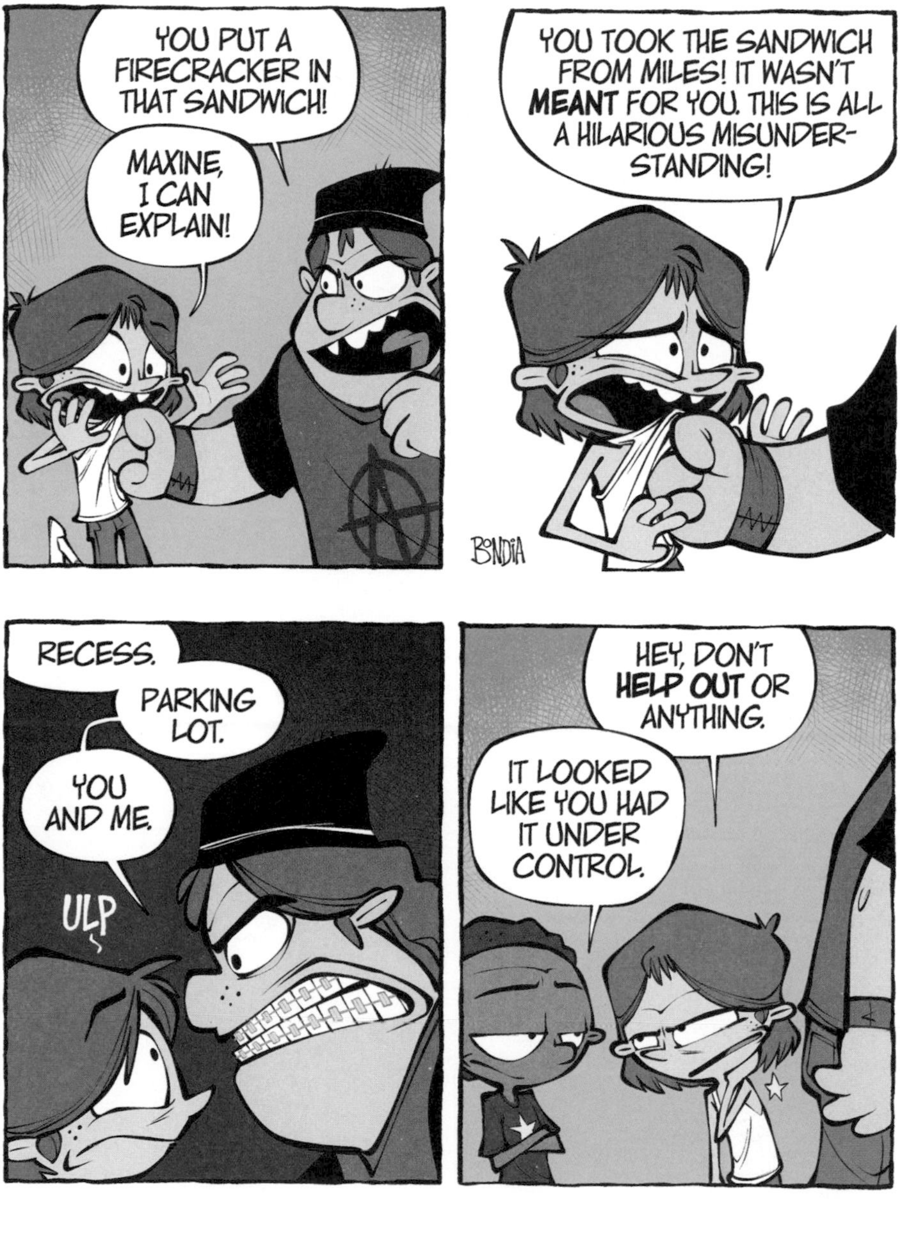
YOU PUT A FIRECRACKER IN THAT SANDWICH!
MAXINE, I CAN EXPLAIN!
YOU TOOK THE SANDWICH FROM MILES! IT WASN'T **MEANT** FOR YOU. THIS IS ALL A HILARIOUS MISUNDER-STANDING!
BONDIA
RECESS.
PARKING LOT.
YOU AND ME.
ULP
HEY, DON'T **HELP OUT** OR ANYTHING.
IT LOOKED LIKE YOU HAD IT UNDER CONTROL.

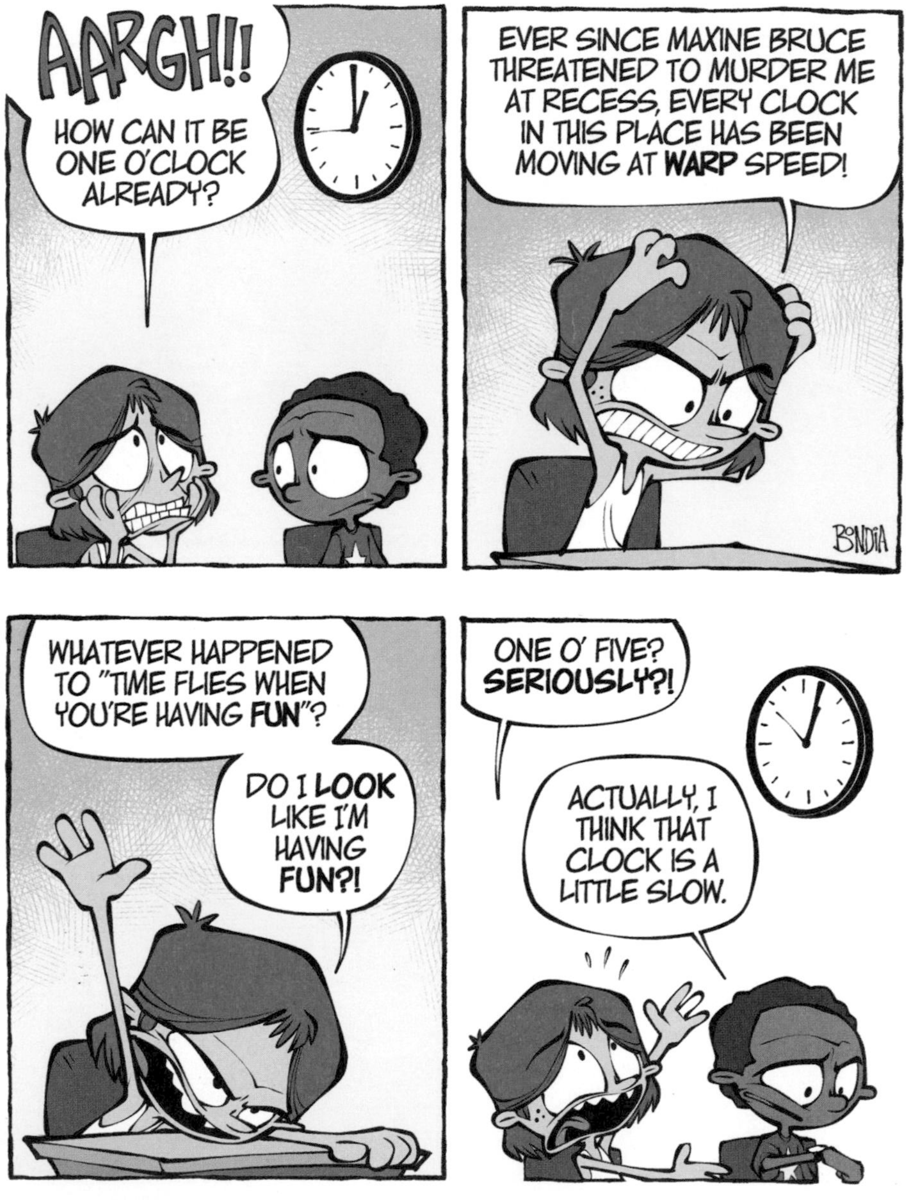
AARGH!!
HOW CAN IT BE ONE O'CLOCK ALREADY?
EVER SINCE MAXINE BRUCE THREATENED TO MURDER ME AT RECESS, EVERY CLOCK IN THIS PLACE HAS BEEN MOVING AT WARP SPEED!
BONDIA
WHATEVER HAPPENED TO "TIME FLIES WHEN YOU'RE HAVING FUN"?
DO I LOOK LIKE I'M HAVING FUN?!
ONE O' FIVE? SERIOUSLY?!
ACTUALLY, I THINK THAT CLOCK IS A LITTLE SLOW.

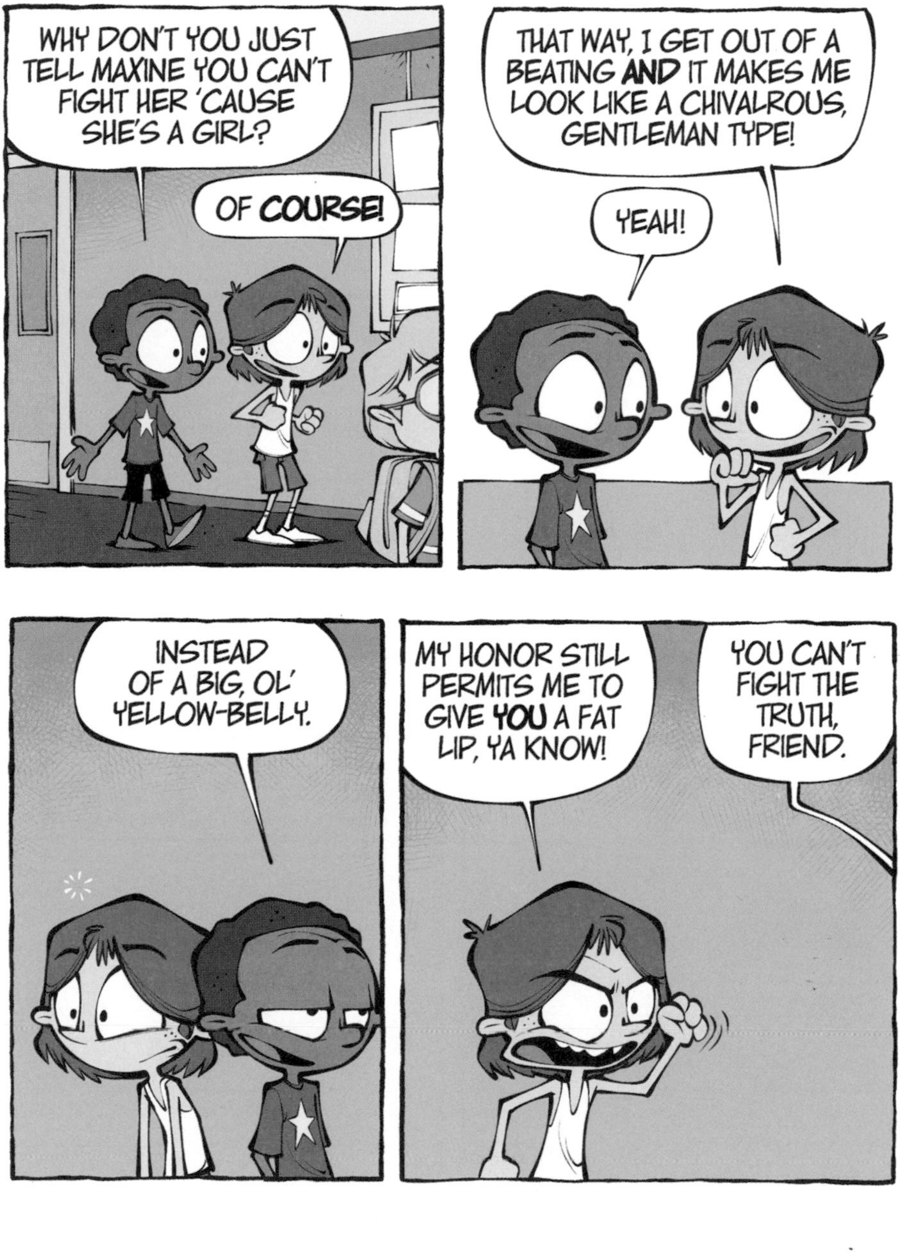
WHY DON'T YOU JUST TELL MAXINE YOU CAN'T FIGHT HER 'CAUSE SHE'S A GIRL?
OF COURSE!
THAT WAY, I GET OUT OF A BEATING AND IT MAKES ME LOOK LIKE A CHIVALROUS, GENTLEMAN TYPE!
YEAH!
INSTEAD OF A BIG, OL' YELLOW-BELLY.
MY HONOR STILL PERMITS ME TO GIVE YOU A FAT LIP, YA KNOW!
YOU CAN'T FIGHT THE TRUTH, FRIEND.

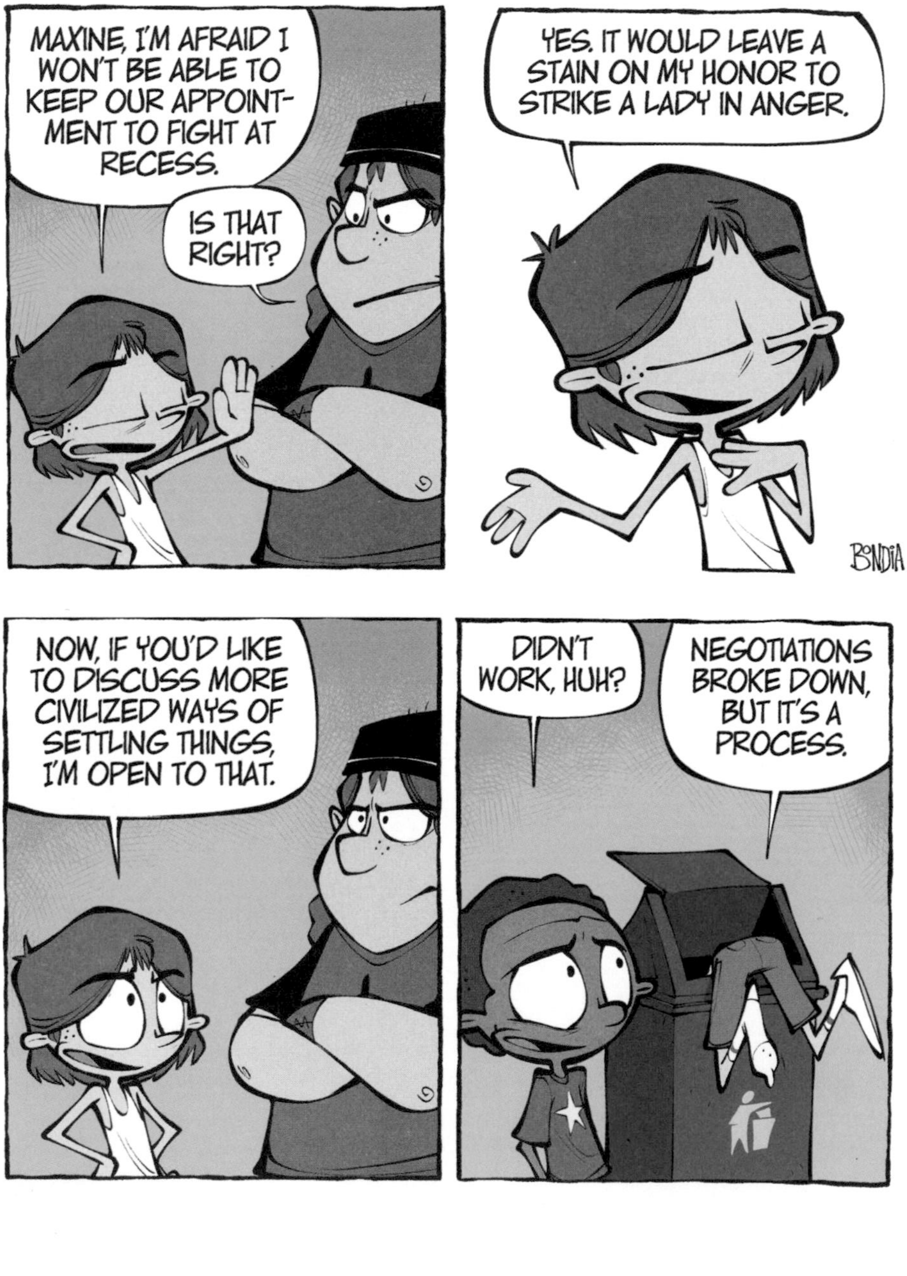
MAXINE, I'M AFRAID I WON'T BE ABLE TO KEEP OUR APPOINTMENT TO FIGHT AT RECESS.
IS THAT RIGHT?
YES. IT WOULD LEAVE A STAIN ON MY HONOR TO STRIKE A LADY IN ANGER.
BONDIA
NOW, IF YOU'D LIKE TO DISCUSS MORE CIVILIZED WAYS OF SETTLING THINGS, I'M OPEN TO THAT.
DIDN'T WORK, HUH?
NEGOTIATIONS BROKE DOWN, BUT IT'S A PROCESS.

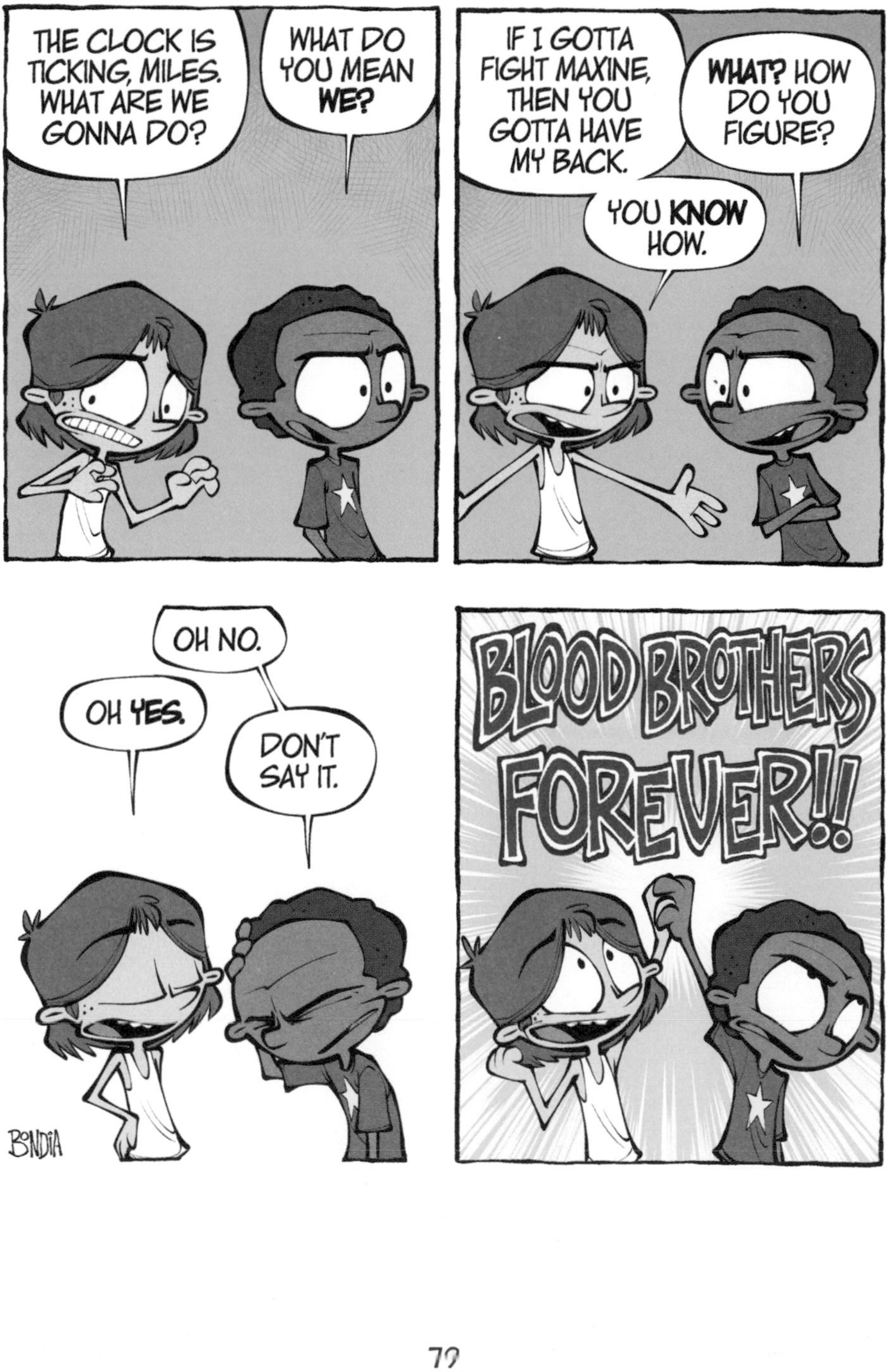
THE CLOCK IS TICKING, MILES. WHAT ARE WE GONNA DO?
WHAT DO YOU MEAN **WE?**
IF I GOTTA FIGHT MAXINE, THEN YOU GOTTA HAVE MY BACK.
WHAT? HOW DO YOU FIGURE?
YOU **KNOW** HOW.
OH NO.
OH **YES.**
DON'T SAY IT.
BONDIA
BLOOD BROTHERS FOREVER!!

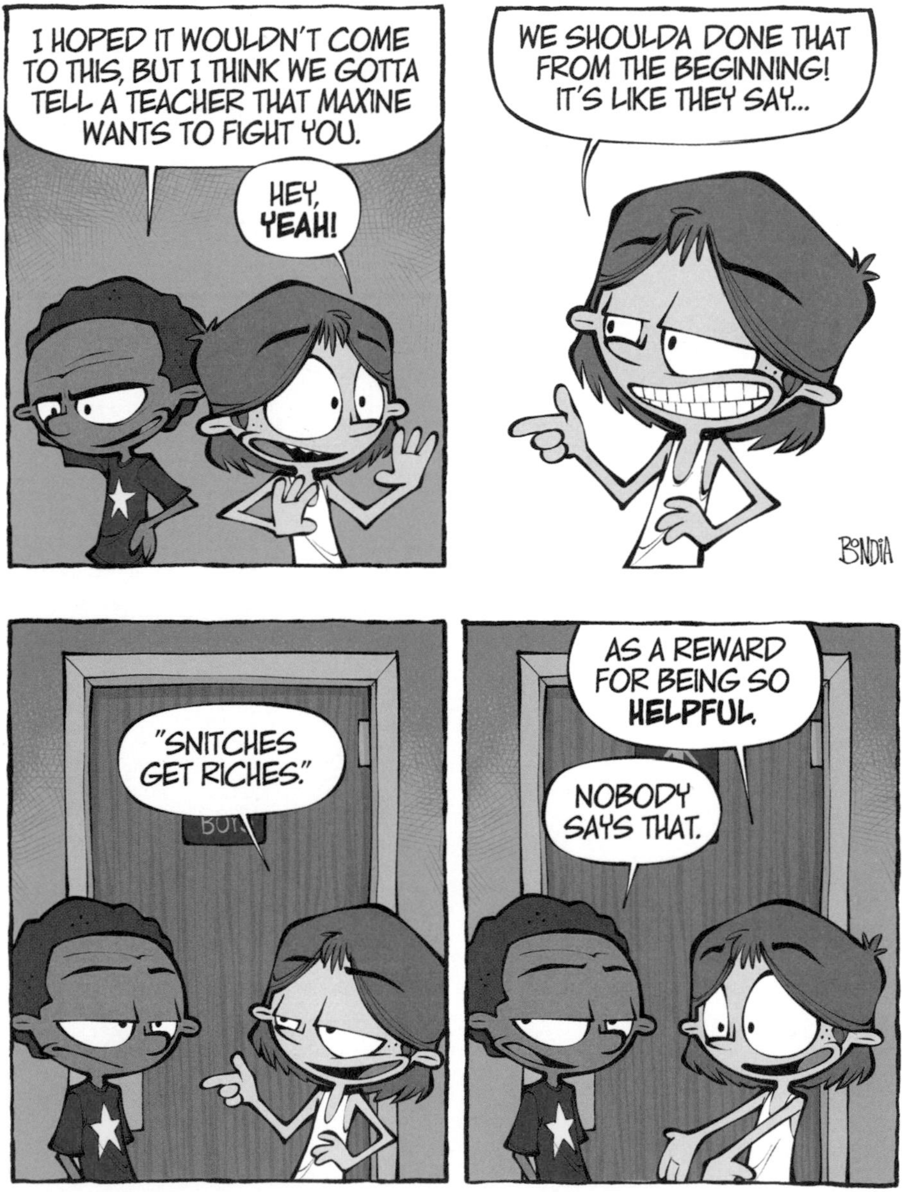
I HOPED IT WOULDN'T COME TO THIS, BUT I THINK WE GOTTA TELL A TEACHER THAT MAXINE WANTS TO FIGHT YOU.
HEY, **YEAH!**
WE SHOULDA DONE THAT FROM THE BEGINNING! IT'S LIKE THEY SAY...
BONDIA
"SNITCHES GET RICHES."
AS A REWARD FOR BEING SO **HELPFUL.**
NOBODY SAYS THAT.

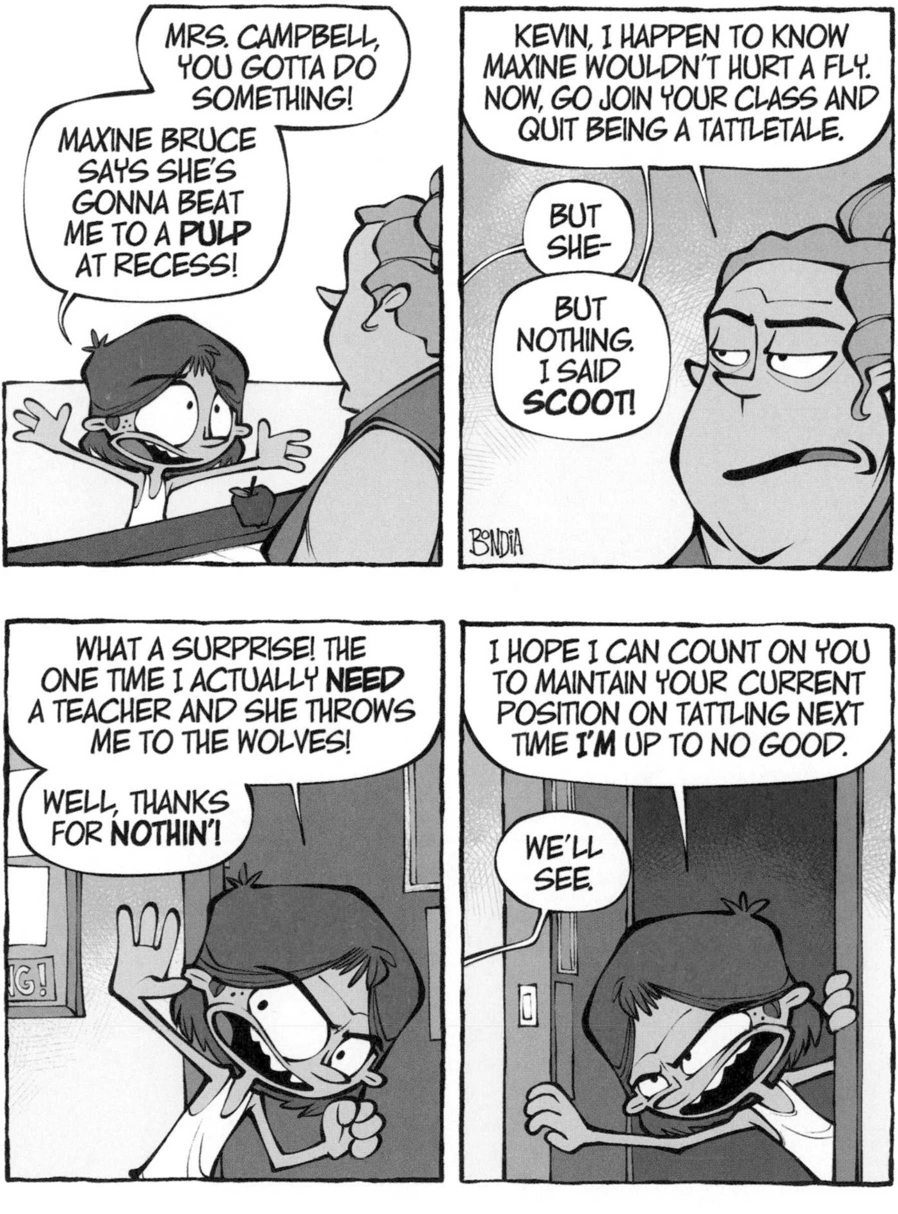
MRS. CAMPBELL, YOU GOTTA DO SOMETHING!
MAXINE BRUCE SAYS SHE'S GONNA BEAT ME TO A **PULP** AT RECESS!
KEVIN, I HAPPEN TO KNOW MAXINE WOULDN'T HURT A FLY. NOW, GO JOIN YOUR CLASS AND QUIT BEING A TATTLETALE.
BUT SHE-
BUT NOTHING. I SAID **SCOOT**!
BONDIA
WHAT A SURPRISE! THE ONE TIME I ACTUALLY **NEED** A TEACHER AND SHE THROWS ME TO THE WOLVES!
WELL, THANKS FOR **NOTHIN'**!
I HOPE I CAN COUNT ON YOU TO MAINTAIN YOUR CURRENT POSITION ON TATTLING NEXT TIME **I'M** UP TO NO GOOD.
WE'LL SEE.

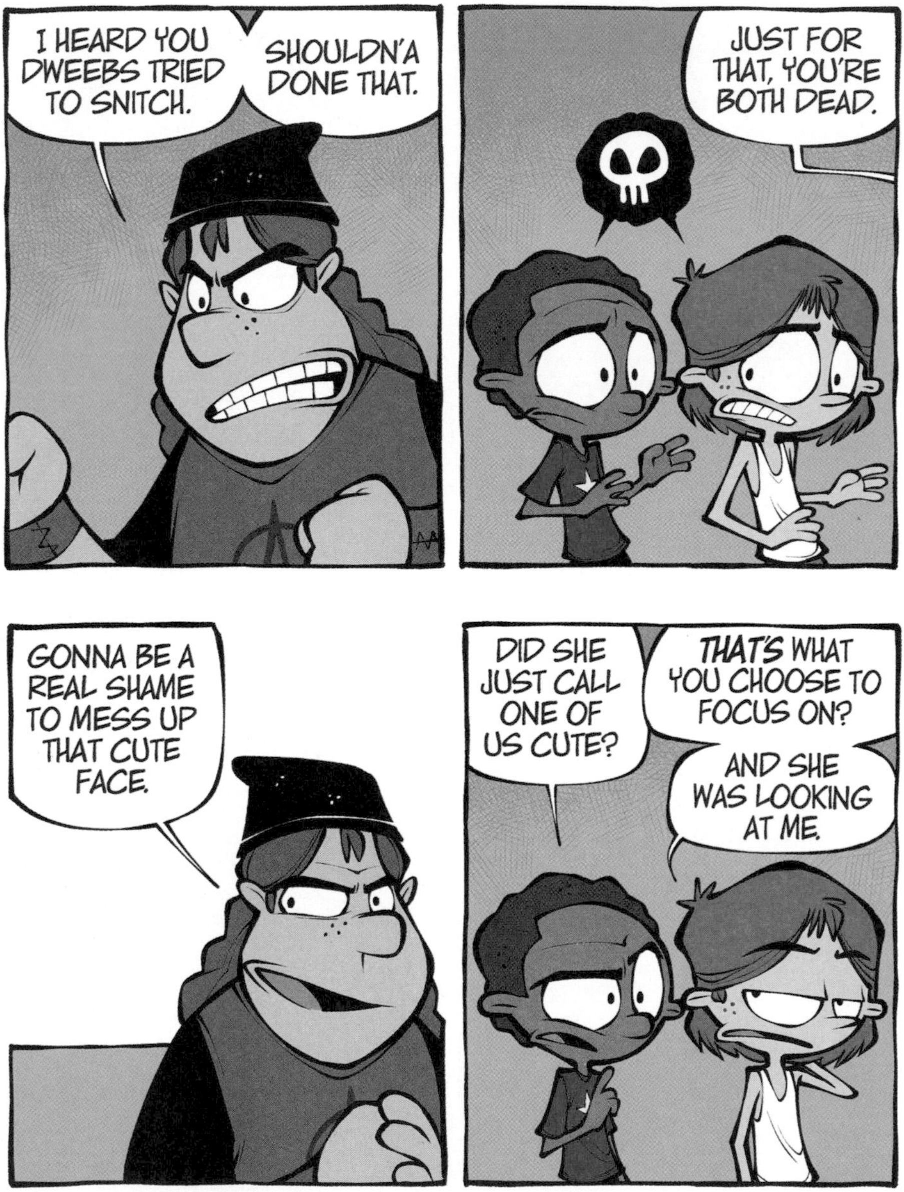
I HEARD YOU DWEEBS TRIED TO SNITCH.
SHOULDN'A DONE THAT.
JUST FOR THAT, YOU'RE BOTH DEAD.
GONNA BE A REAL SHAME TO MESS UP THAT CUTE FACE.
DID SHE JUST CALL ONE OF US CUTE?
THAT'S WHAT YOU CHOOSE TO FOCUS ON?
AND SHE WAS LOOKING AT ME.

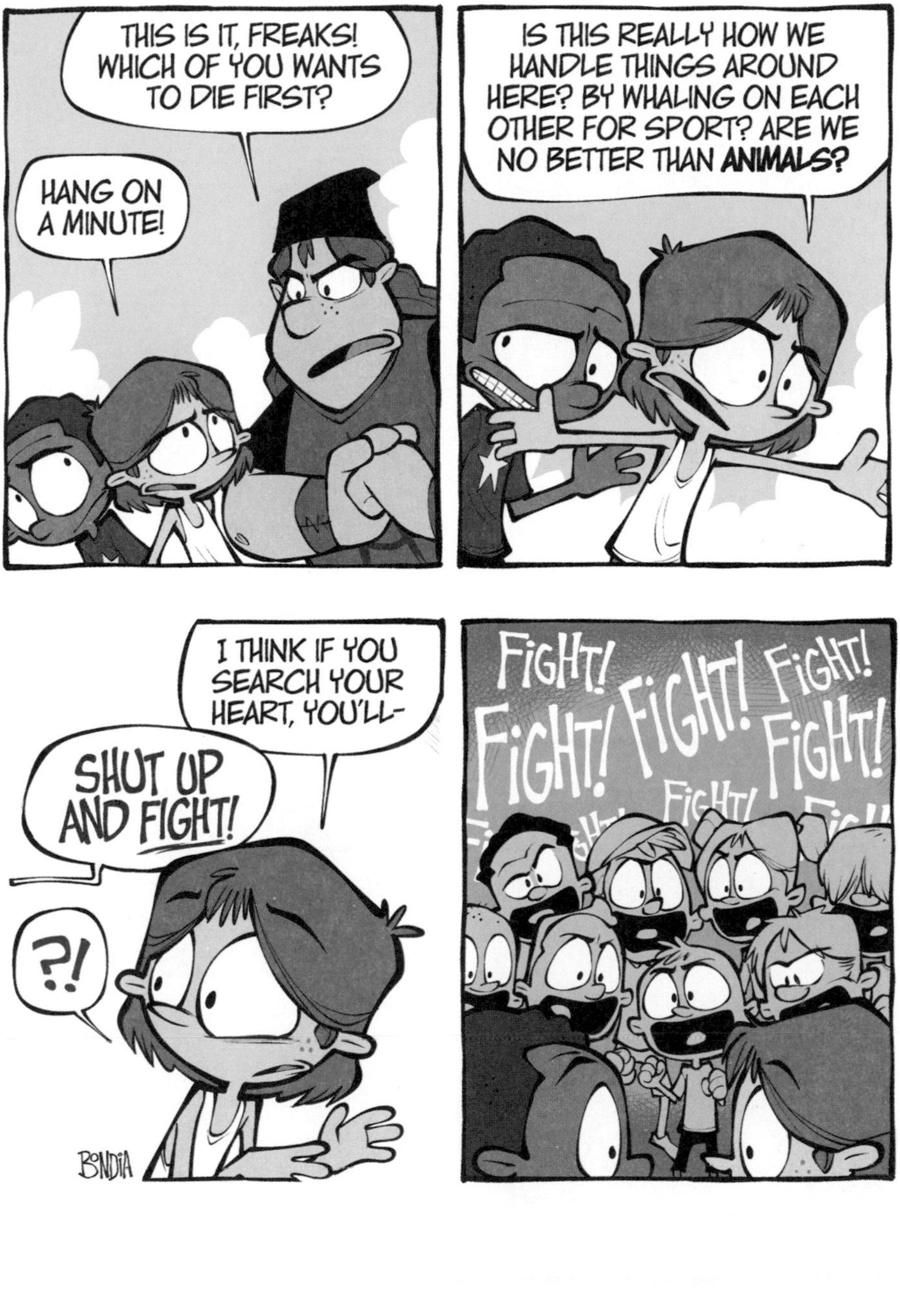
THIS IS IT, FREAKS! WHICH OF YOU WANTS TO DIE FIRST?
HANG ON A MINUTE!
IS THIS REALLY HOW WE HANDLE THINGS AROUND HERE? BY WHALING ON EACH OTHER FOR SPORT? ARE WE NO BETTER THAN **ANIMALS?**
I THINK IF YOU SEARCH YOUR HEART, YOU'LL-
SHUT UP AND FIGHT!
?!
BONDIA
FIGHT! FIGHT! FIGHT! FIGHT! FIGHT! FIGHT! FIGHT!

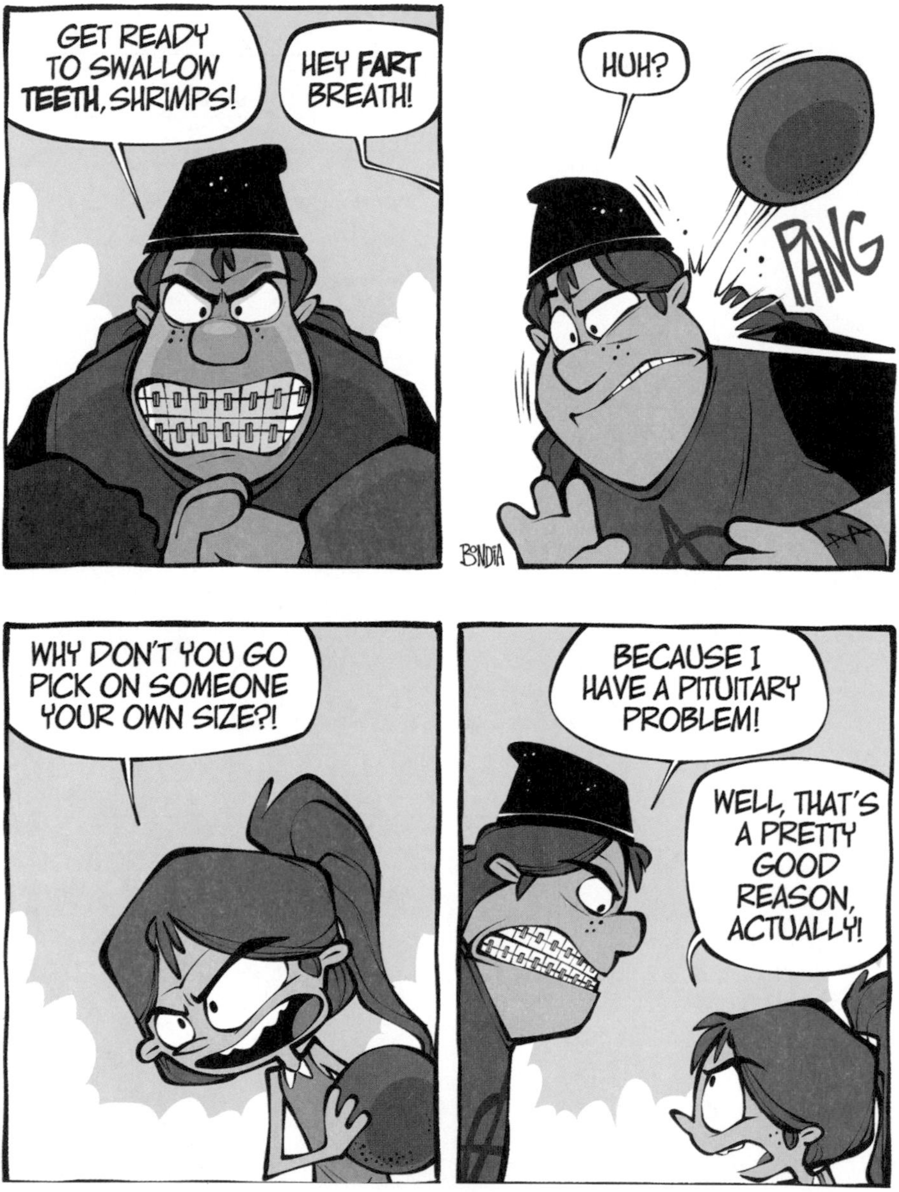
GET READY TO SWALLOW TEETH, SHRIMPS!
HEY FART BREATH!
HUH?
PANG
BONDIA
WHY DON'T YOU GO PICK ON SOMEONE YOUR OWN SIZE?!
BECAUSE I HAVE A PITUITARY PROBLEM!
WELL, THAT'S A PRETTY GOOD REASON, ACTUALLY!

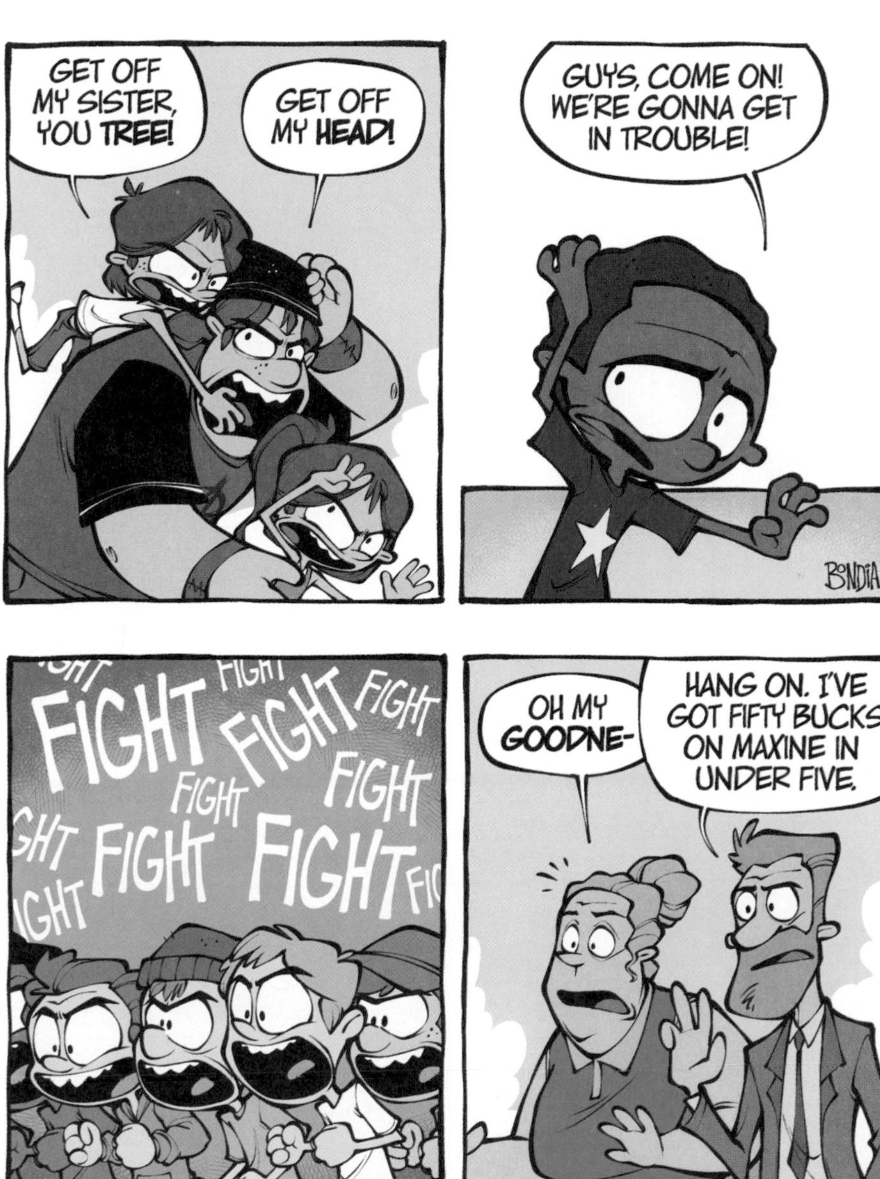
GET OFF MY SISTER, YOU **TREE!**
GET OFF MY **HEAD!**
GUYS, COME ON! WE'RE GONNA GET IN TROUBLE!
BONDIA
FIGHT FIGHT FIGHT FIGHT FIGHT FIGHT FIGHT FIGHT
OH MY **GOODNE-**
HANG ON. I'VE GOT FIFTY BUCKS ON MAXINE IN UNDER FIVE.

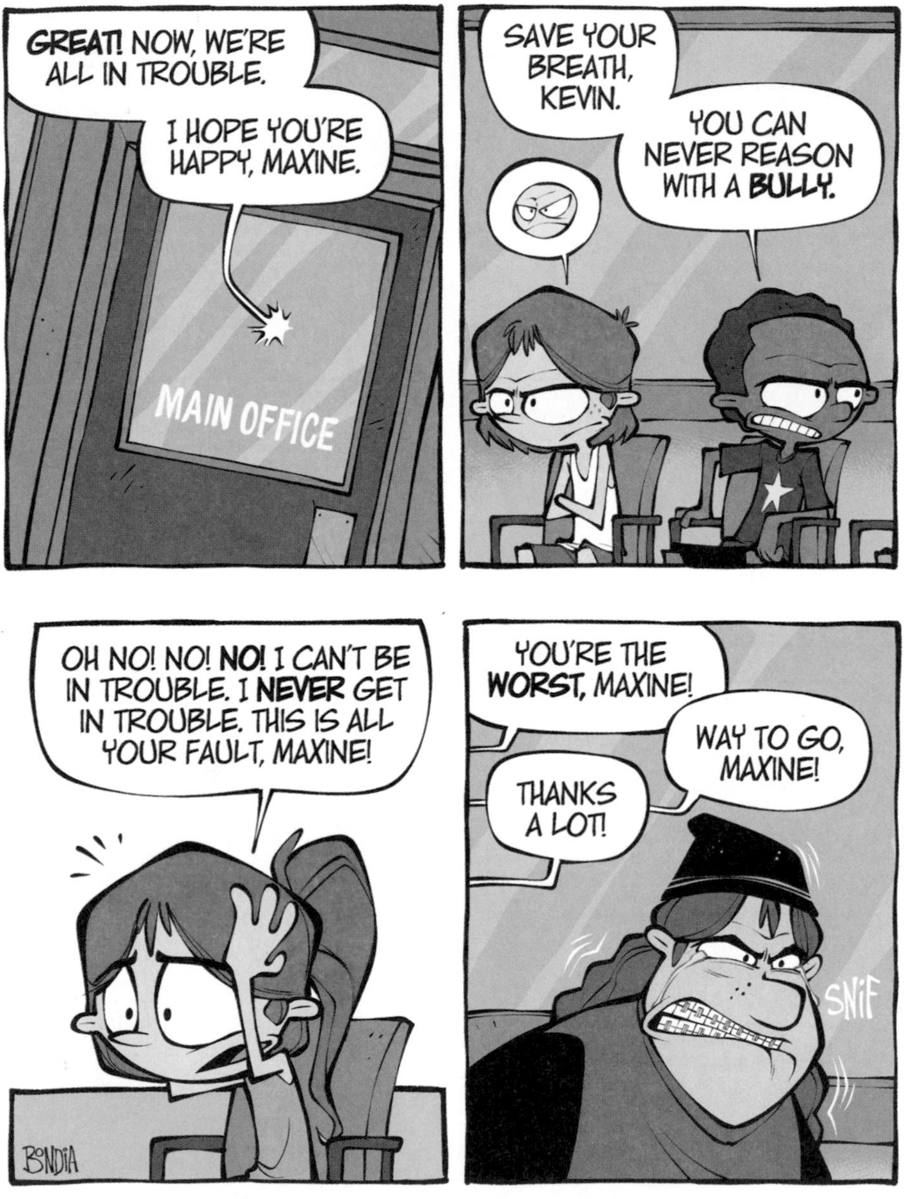
GREAT! NOW, WE'RE ALL IN TROUBLE.
I HOPE YOU'RE HAPPY, MAXINE.
MAIN OFFICE
SAVE YOUR BREATH, KEVIN.
YOU CAN NEVER REASON WITH A BULLY.
OH NO! NO! NO! I CAN'T BE IN TROUBLE. I NEVER GET IN TROUBLE. THIS IS ALL YOUR FAULT, MAXINE!
BONDIA
YOU'RE THE WORST, MAXINE!
WAY TO GO, MAXINE!
THANKS A LOT!
SNIF

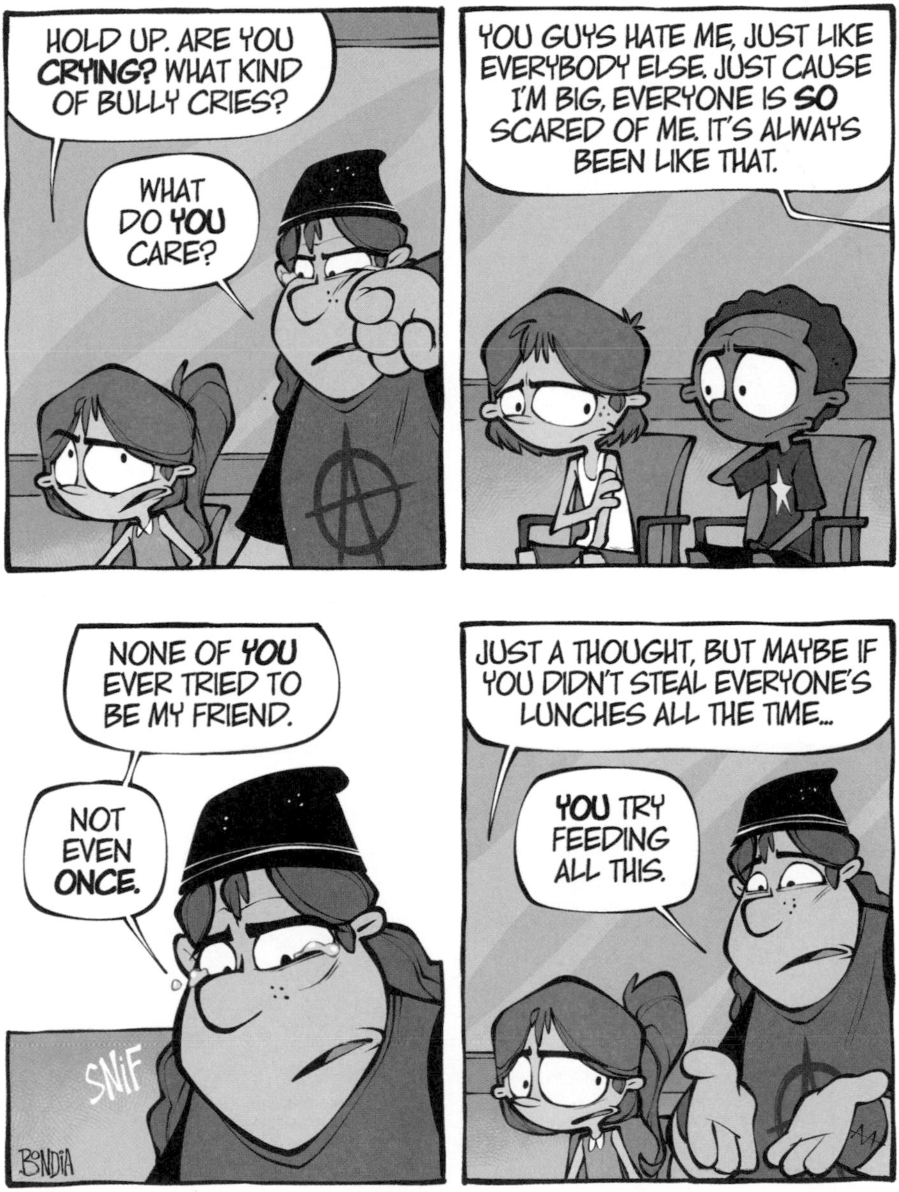
HOLD UP. ARE YOU CRYING? WHAT KIND OF BULLY CRIES?
WHAT DO YOU CARE?
YOU GUYS HATE ME, JUST LIKE EVERYBODY ELSE. JUST CAUSE I'M BIG, EVERYONE IS SO SCARED OF ME. IT'S ALWAYS BEEN LIKE THAT.
NONE OF YOU EVER TRIED TO BE MY FRIEND.
NOT EVEN ONCE.
SNIF
BONDIA
JUST A THOUGHT, BUT MAYBE IF YOU DIDN'T STEAL EVERYONE'S LUNCHES ALL THE TIME...
YOU TRY FEEDING ALL THIS.

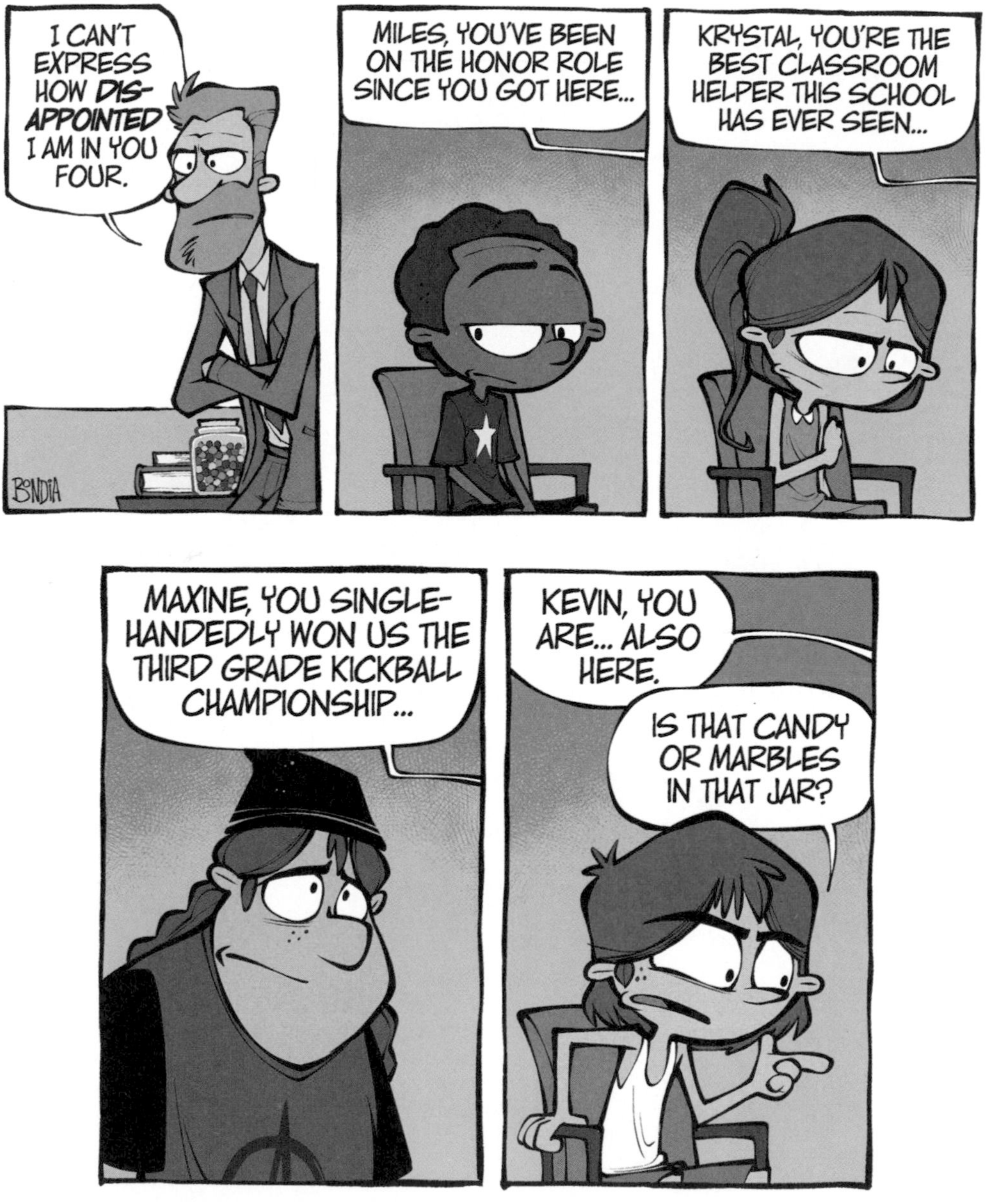
I CAN'T EXPRESS HOW **DIS-APPOINTED** I AM IN YOU FOUR.
MILES, YOU'VE BEEN ON THE HONOR ROLE SINCE YOU GOT HERE...
KRYSTAL, YOU'RE THE BEST CLASSROOM HELPER THIS SCHOOL HAS EVER SEEN...
MAXINE, YOU SINGLE-HANDEDLY WON US THE THIRD GRADE KICKBALL CHAMPIONSHIP...
KEVIN, YOU ARE... ALSO HERE.
IS THAT CANDY OR MARBLES IN THAT JAR?
BONDIA

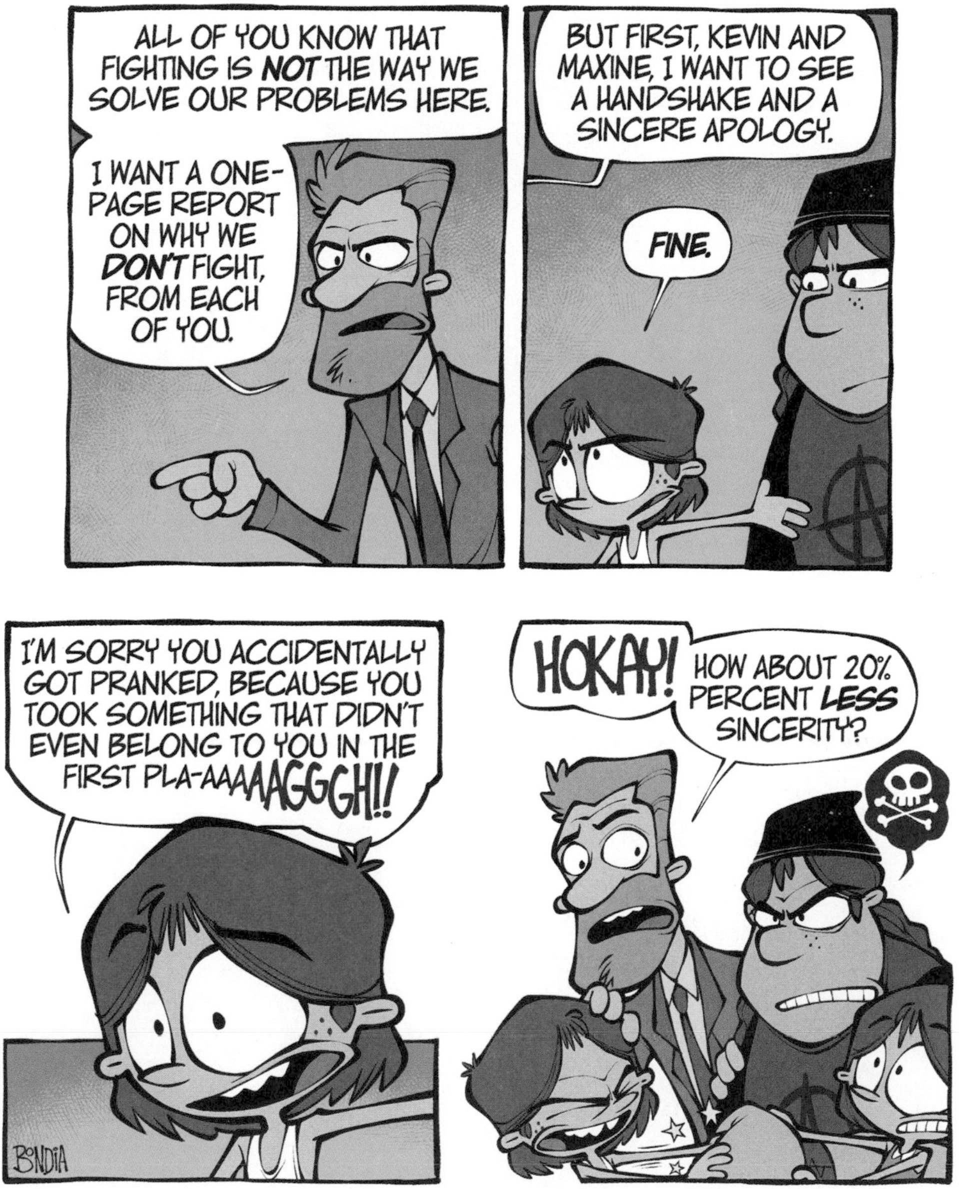
ALL OF YOU KNOW THAT FIGHTING IS **NOT** THE WAY WE SOLVE OUR PROBLEMS HERE.
I WANT A ONE-PAGE REPORT ON WHY WE **DON'T** FIGHT, FROM EACH OF YOU.
BUT FIRST, KEVIN AND MAXINE, I WANT TO SEE A HANDSHAKE AND A SINCERE APOLOGY.
FINE.
I'M SORRY YOU ACCIDENTALLY GOT PRANKED, BECAUSE YOU TOOK SOMETHING THAT DIDN'T EVEN BELONG TO YOU IN THE FIRST PLA-AAAAAGGGH!!
BONDIA
HOKAY!
HOW ABOUT 20% PERCENT **LESS** SINCERITY?

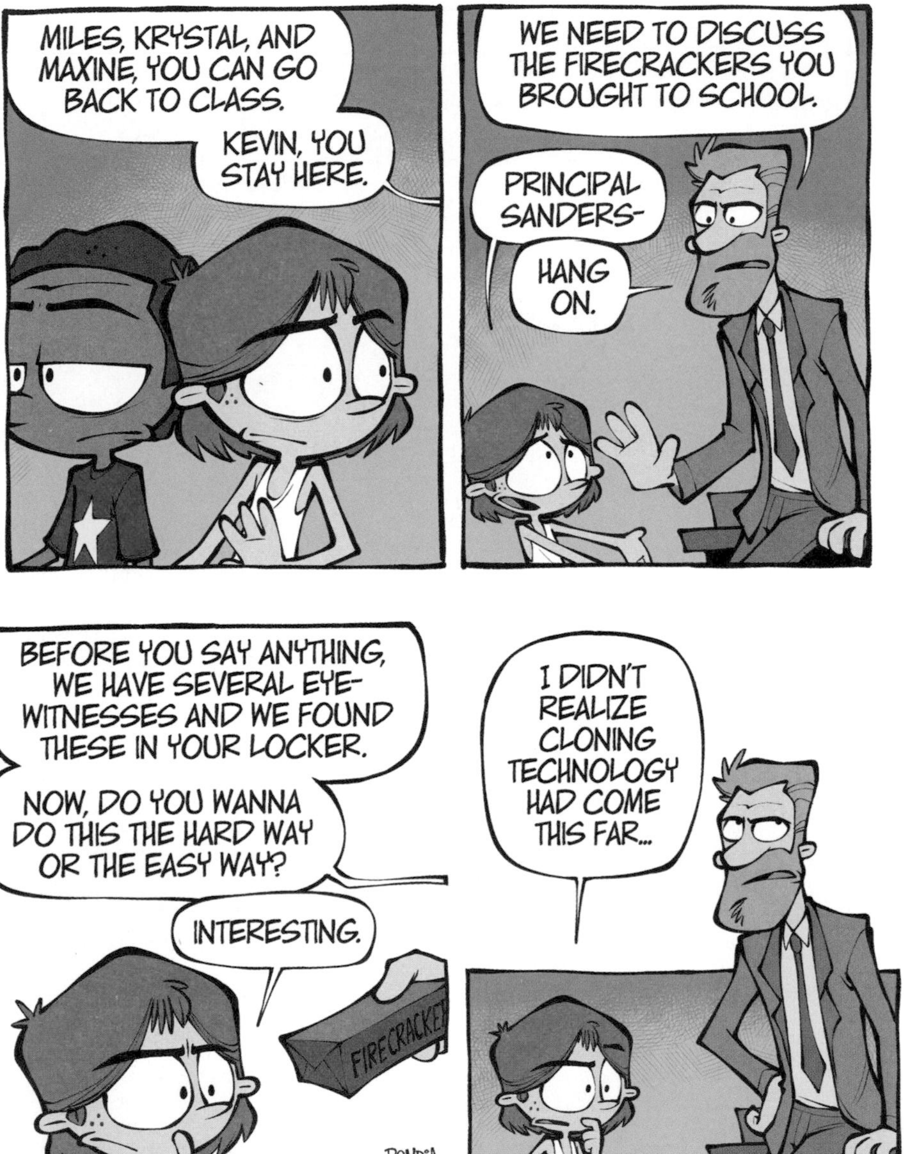
MILES, KRYSTAL, AND MAXINE, YOU CAN GO BACK TO CLASS.
KEVIN, YOU STAY HERE.
WE NEED TO DISCUSS THE FIRECRACKERS YOU BROUGHT TO SCHOOL.
PRINCIPAL SANDERS-
HANG ON.
BEFORE YOU SAY ANYTHING, WE HAVE SEVERAL EYE-WITNESSES AND WE FOUND THESE IN YOUR LOCKER.
NOW, DO YOU WANNA DO THIS THE HARD WAY OR THE EASY WAY?
INTERESTING.
FIRECRACKER
BONDIA
I DIDN'T REALIZE CLONING TECHNOLOGY HAD COME THIS FAR...

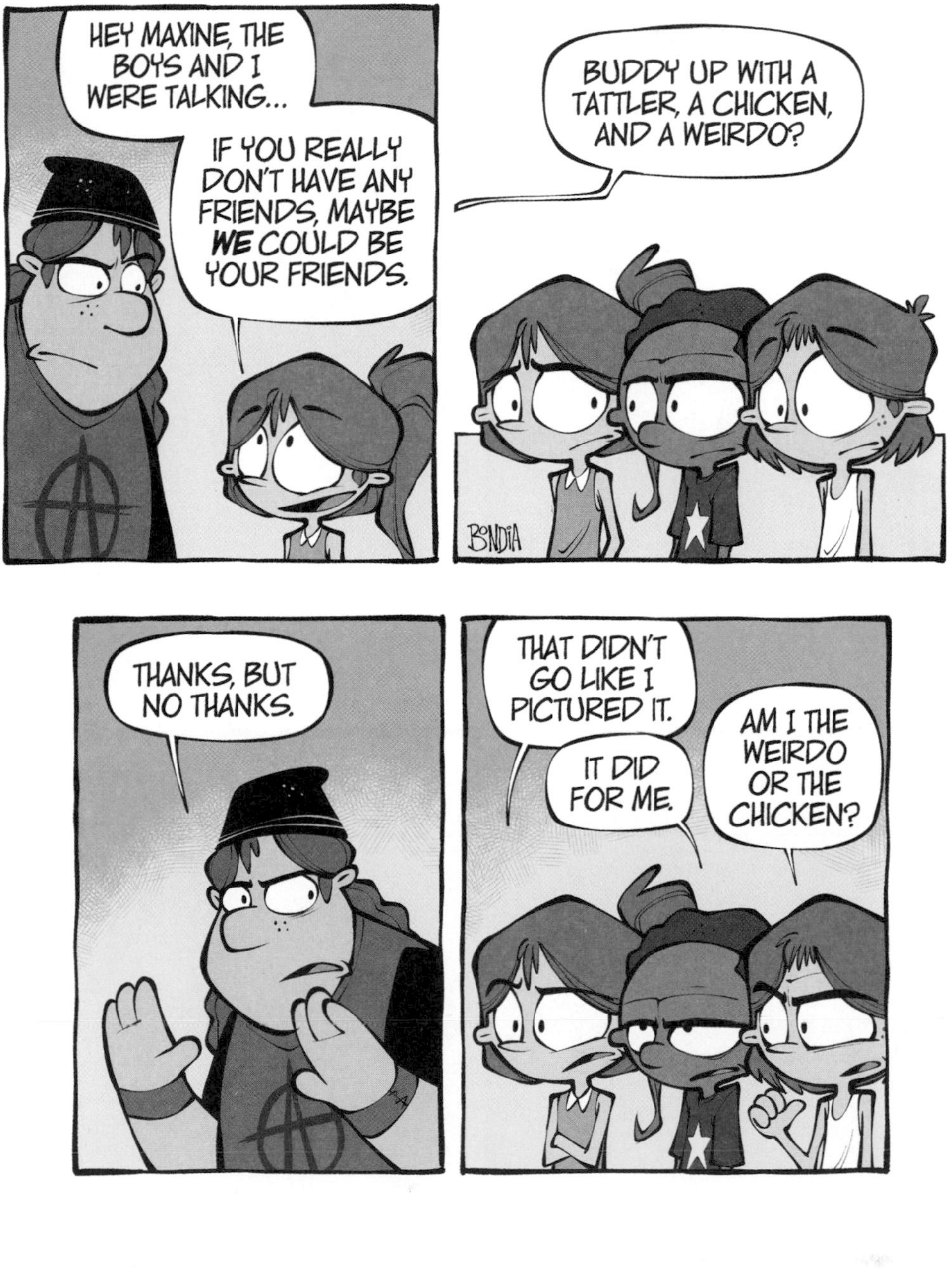
HEY MAXINE, THE BOYS AND I WERE TALKING...
IF YOU REALLY DON'T HAVE ANY FRIENDS, MAYBE **WE** COULD BE YOUR FRIENDS.
BUDDY UP WITH A TATTLER, A CHICKEN, AND A WEIRDO?
BONDIA
THANKS, BUT NO THANKS.
THAT DIDN'T GO LIKE I PICTURED IT.
IT DID FOR ME.
AM I THE WEIRDO OR THE CHICKEN?

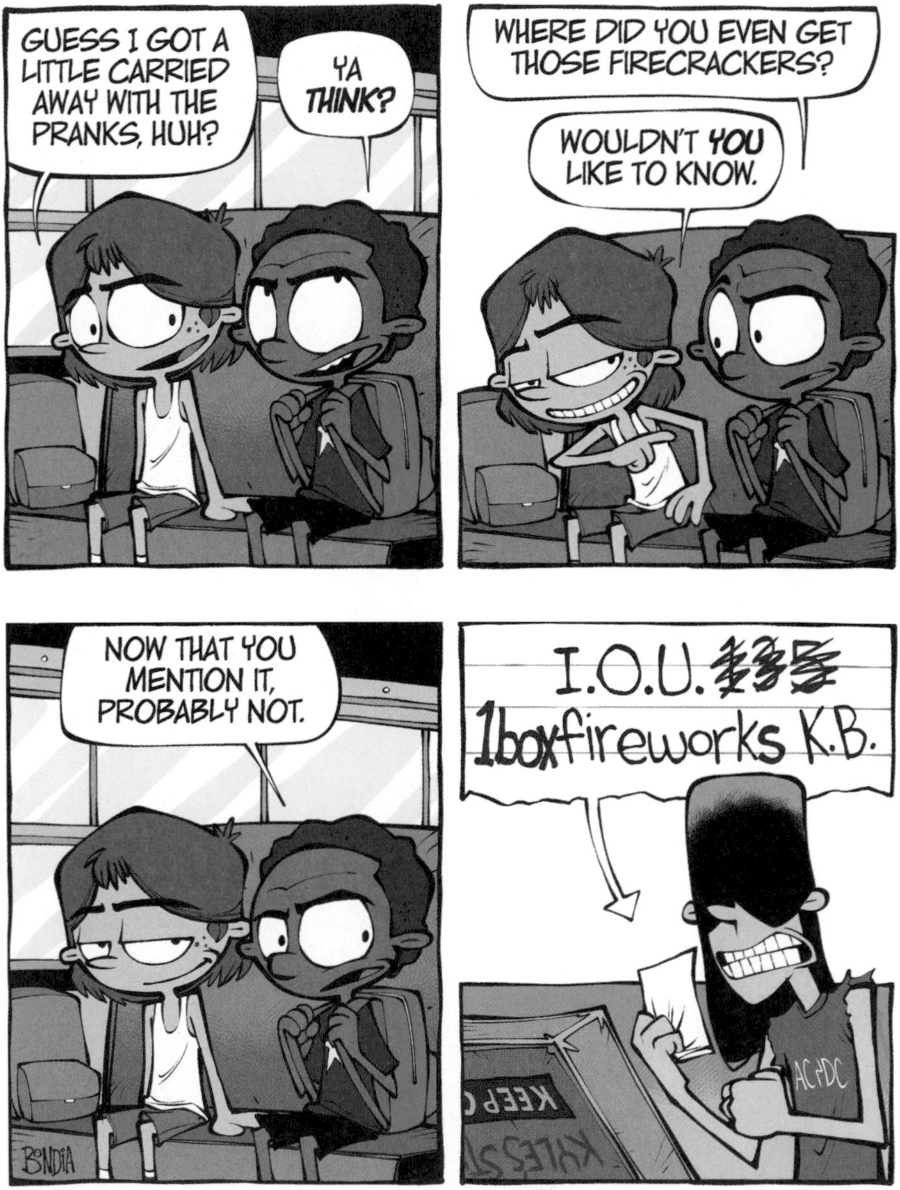
GUESS I GOT A LITTLE CARRIED AWAY WITH THE PRANKS, HUH?
YA THINK?
WHERE DID YOU EVEN GET THOSE FIRECRACKERS?
WOULDN'T YOU LIKE TO KNOW.
NOW THAT YOU MENTION IT, PROBABLY NOT.
I.O.U.
1boxfireworks K.B.
AC/DC

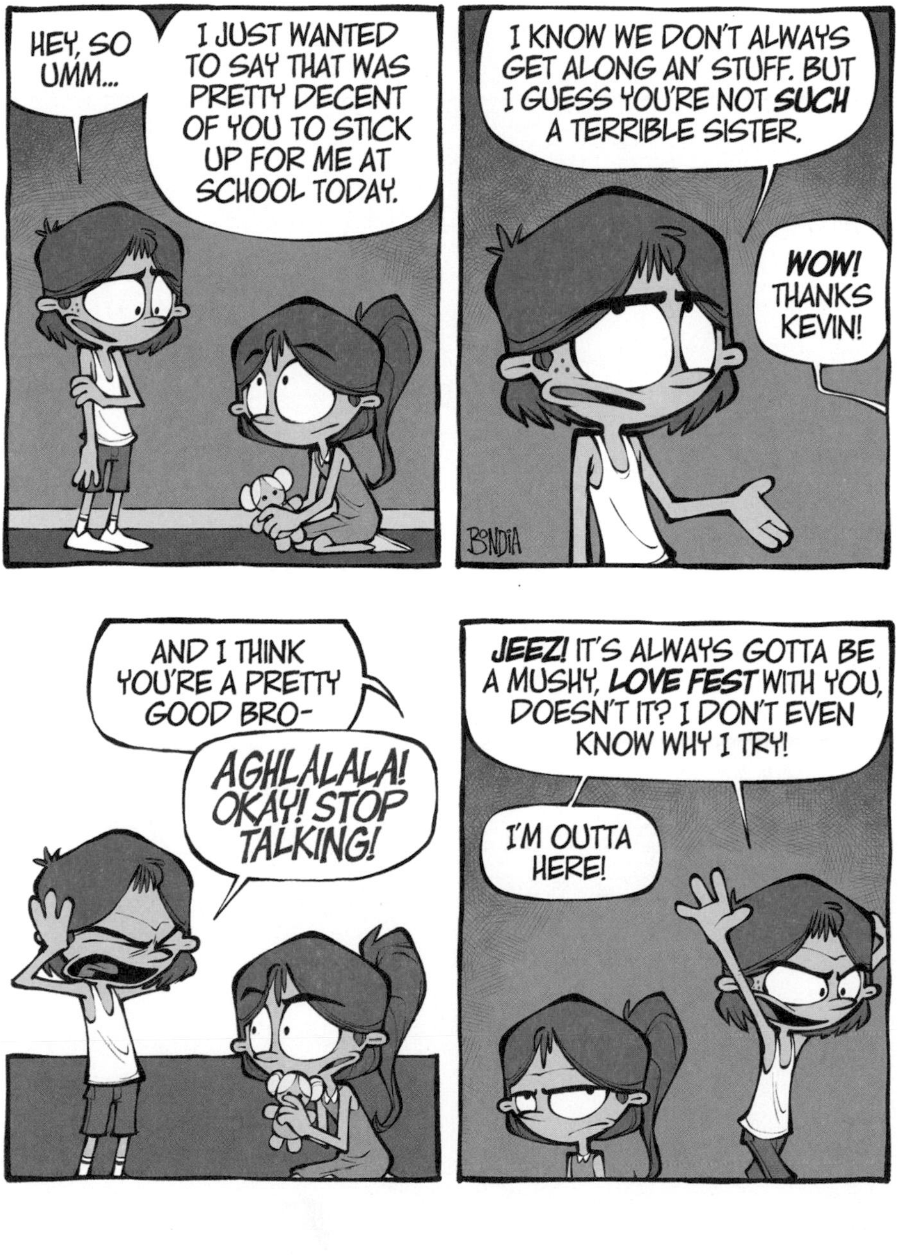
HEY, SO UMM...
I JUST WANTED TO SAY THAT WAS PRETTY DECENT OF YOU TO STICK UP FOR ME AT SCHOOL TODAY.
I KNOW WE DON'T ALWAYS GET ALONG AN' STUFF. BUT I GUESS YOU'RE NOT SUCH A TERRIBLE SISTER.
WOW! THANKS KEVIN!
BONDIA
AND I THINK YOU'RE A PRETTY GOOD BRO-
AGHLALALA! OKAY! STOP TALKING!
JEEZ! IT'S ALWAYS GOTTA BE A MUSHY, LOVE FEST WITH YOU, DOESN'T IT? I DON'T EVEN KNOW WHY I TRY!
I'M OUTTA HERE!

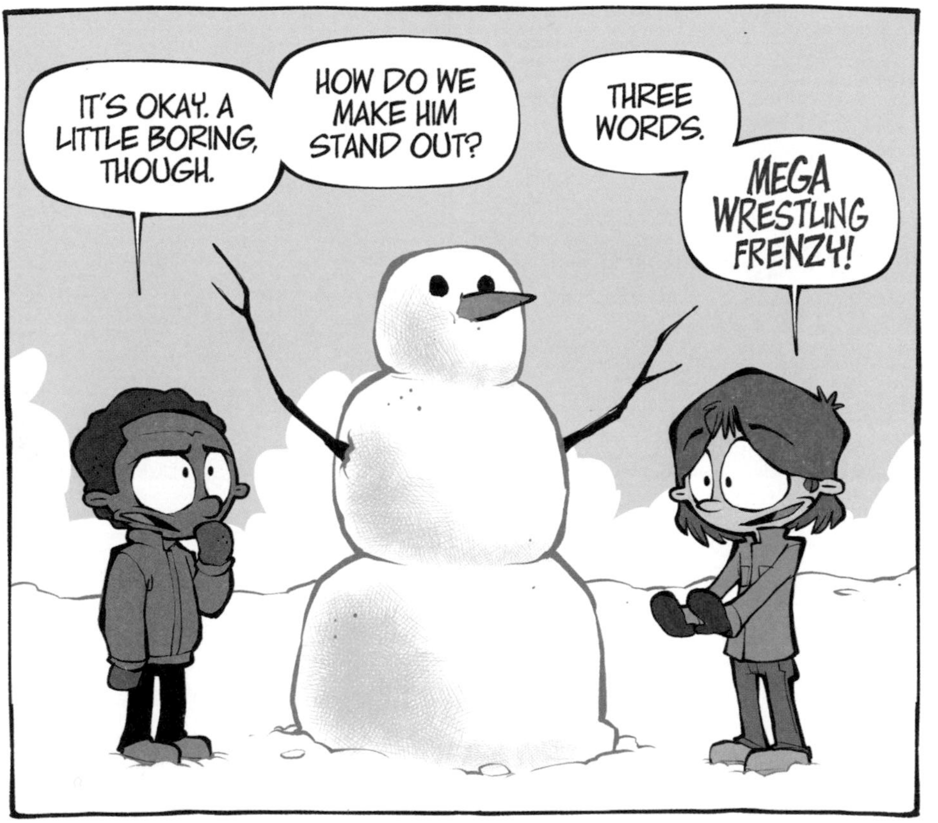
IT'S OKAY. A LITTLE BORING, THOUGH.
HOW DO WE MAKE HIM STAND OUT?
THREE WORDS.
MEGA WRESTLING FRENZY!

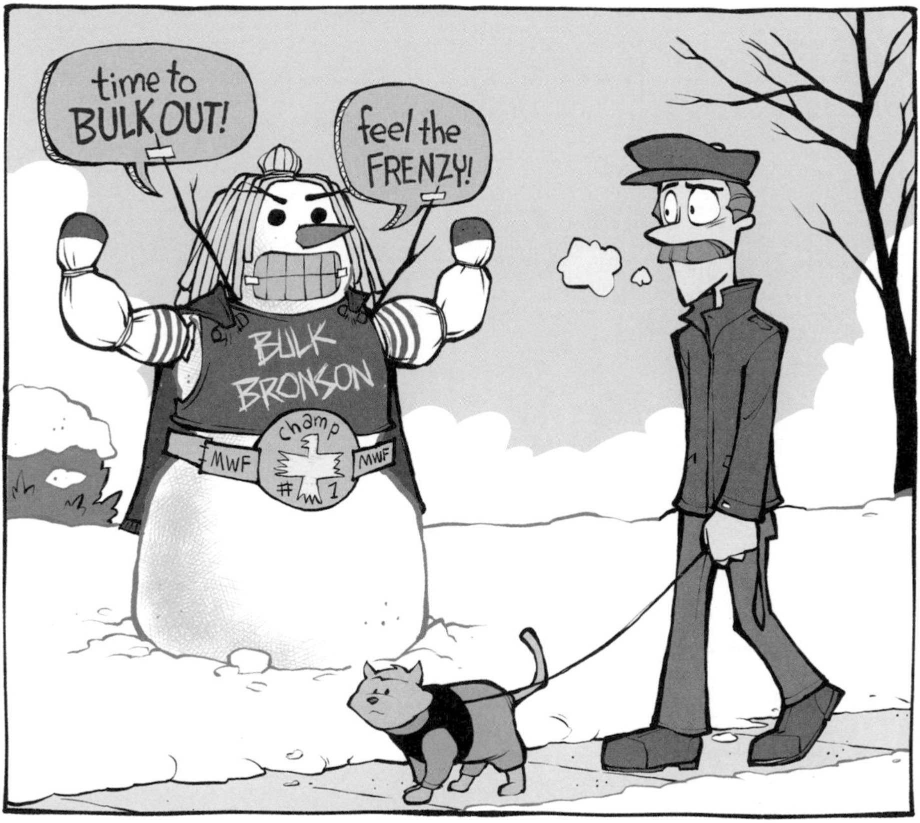
time to BULK OUT!
feel the FRENZY!
BULK BRONSON
champ
MWF
MWF
#1

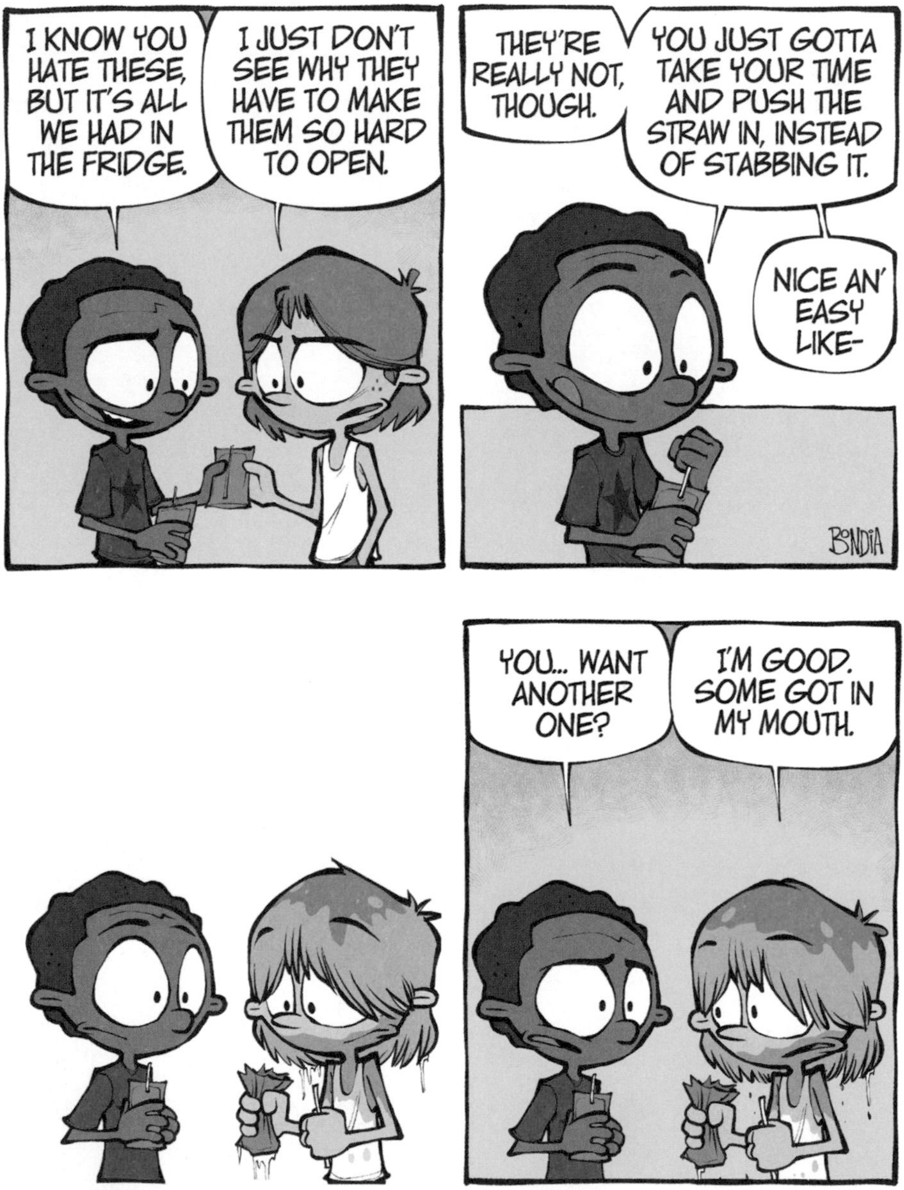
I KNOW YOU HATE THESE, BUT IT'S ALL WE HAD IN THE FRIDGE.
I JUST DON'T SEE WHY THEY HAVE TO MAKE THEM SO HARD TO OPEN.
THEY'RE REALLY NOT, THOUGH.
YOU JUST GOTTA TAKE YOUR TIME AND PUSH THE STRAW IN, INSTEAD OF STABBING IT.
NICE AN' EASY LIKE-
BONDIA
YOU... WANT ANOTHER ONE?
I'M GOOD. SOME GOT IN MY MOUTH.

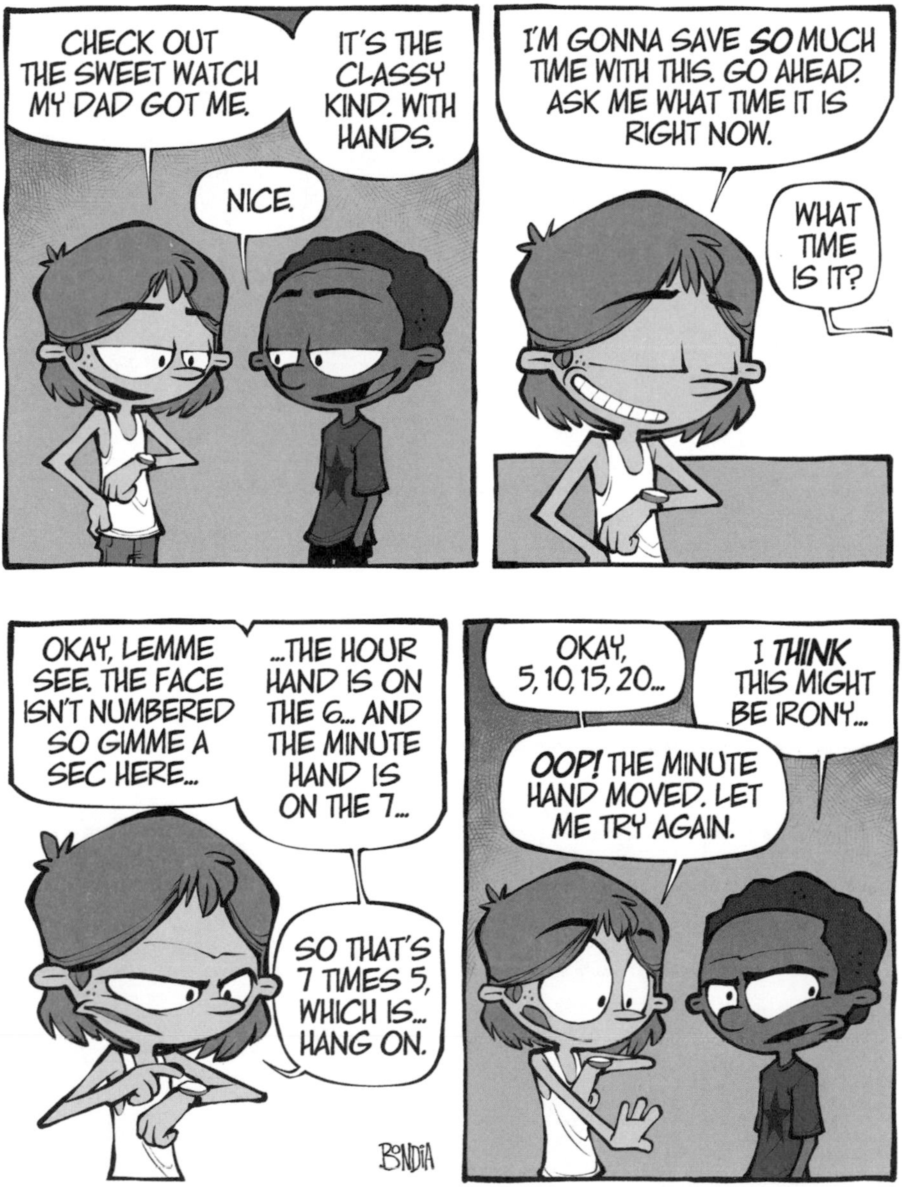
CHECK OUT THE SWEET WATCH MY DAD GOT ME.
IT'S THE CLASSY KIND. WITH HANDS.
NICE.
I'M GONNA SAVE **SO** MUCH TIME WITH THIS. GO AHEAD. ASK ME WHAT TIME IT IS RIGHT NOW.
WHAT TIME IS IT?
OKAY, LEMME SEE. THE FACE ISN'T NUMBERED SO GIMME A SEC HERE...
...THE HOUR HAND IS ON THE 6... AND THE MINUTE HAND IS ON THE 7...
SO THAT'S 7 TIMES 5, WHICH IS... HANG ON.
BONDIA
OKAY, 5, 10, 15, 20...
OOP! THE MINUTE HAND MOVED. LET ME TRY AGAIN.
I **THINK** THIS MIGHT BE IRONY...

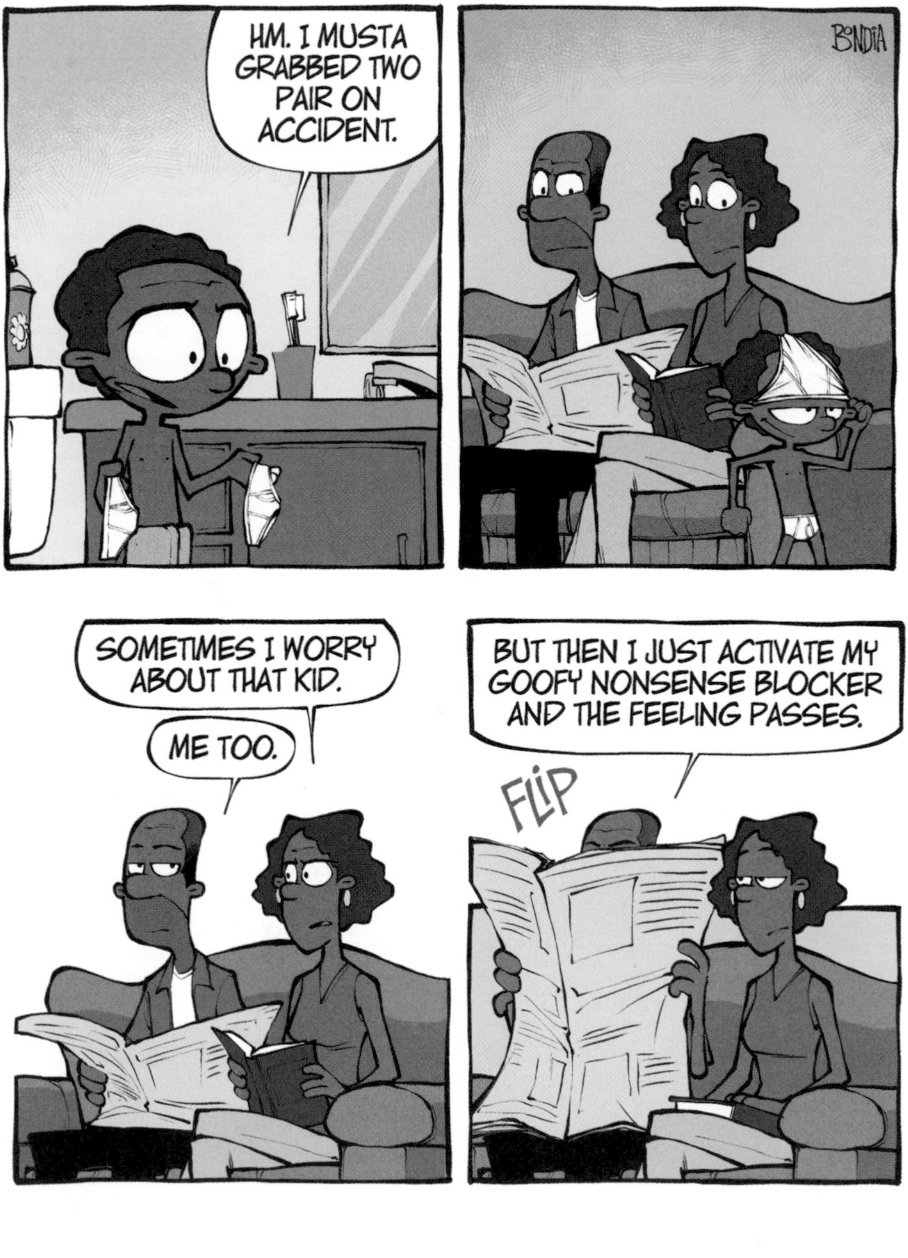
HM. I MUSTA GRABBED TWO PAIR ON ACCIDENT.
BONDIA
SOMETIMES I WORRY ABOUT THAT KID.
ME TOO.
BUT THEN I JUST ACTIVATE MY GOOFY NONSENSE BLOCKER AND THE FEELING PASSES.
FLIP

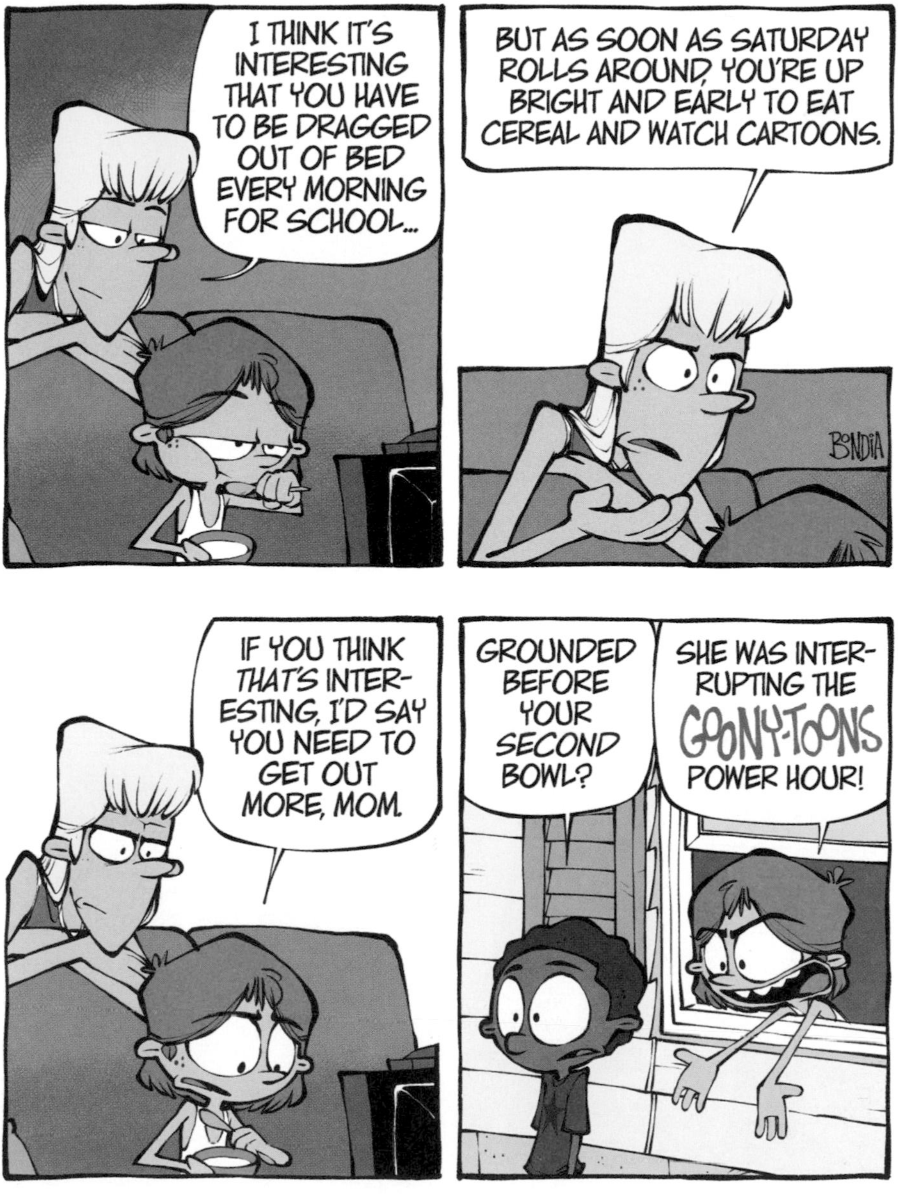
I THINK IT'S INTERESTING THAT YOU HAVE TO BE DRAGGED OUT OF BED EVERY MORNING FOR SCHOOL...
BUT AS SOON AS SATURDAY ROLLS AROUND, YOU'RE UP BRIGHT AND EARLY TO EAT CEREAL AND WATCH CARTOONS.
BONDIA
IF YOU THINK THAT'S INTERESTING, I'D SAY YOU NEED TO GET OUT MORE, MOM.
GROUNDED BEFORE YOUR SECOND BOWL?
SHE WAS INTERRUPTING THE GOONY-TOONS POWER HOUR!

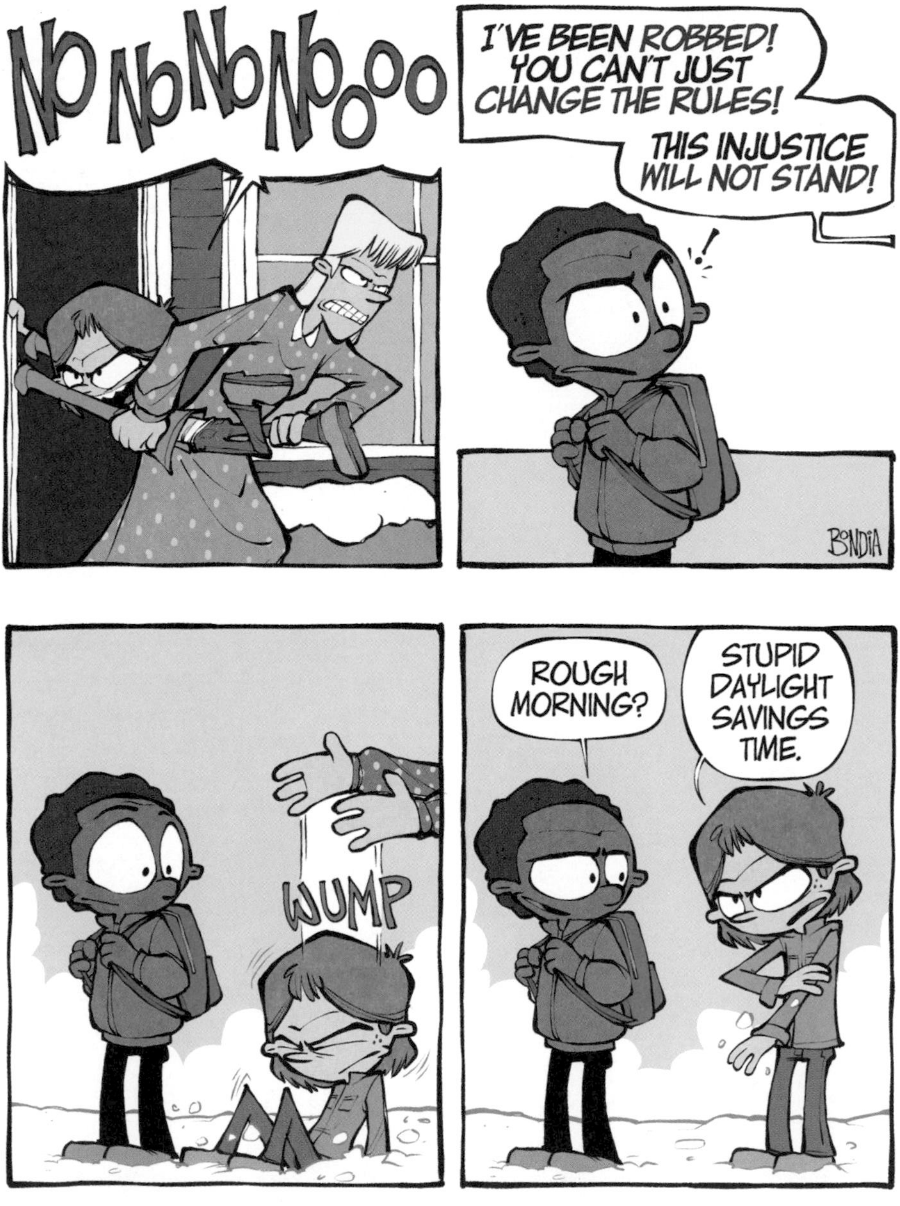
NO NO NO NOOOO
I'VE BEEN ROBBED! YOU CAN'T JUST CHANGE THE RULES!
THIS INJUSTICE WILL NOT STAND!
!
BONDIA
WUMP
ROUGH MORNING?
STUPID DAYLIGHT SAVINGS TIME.

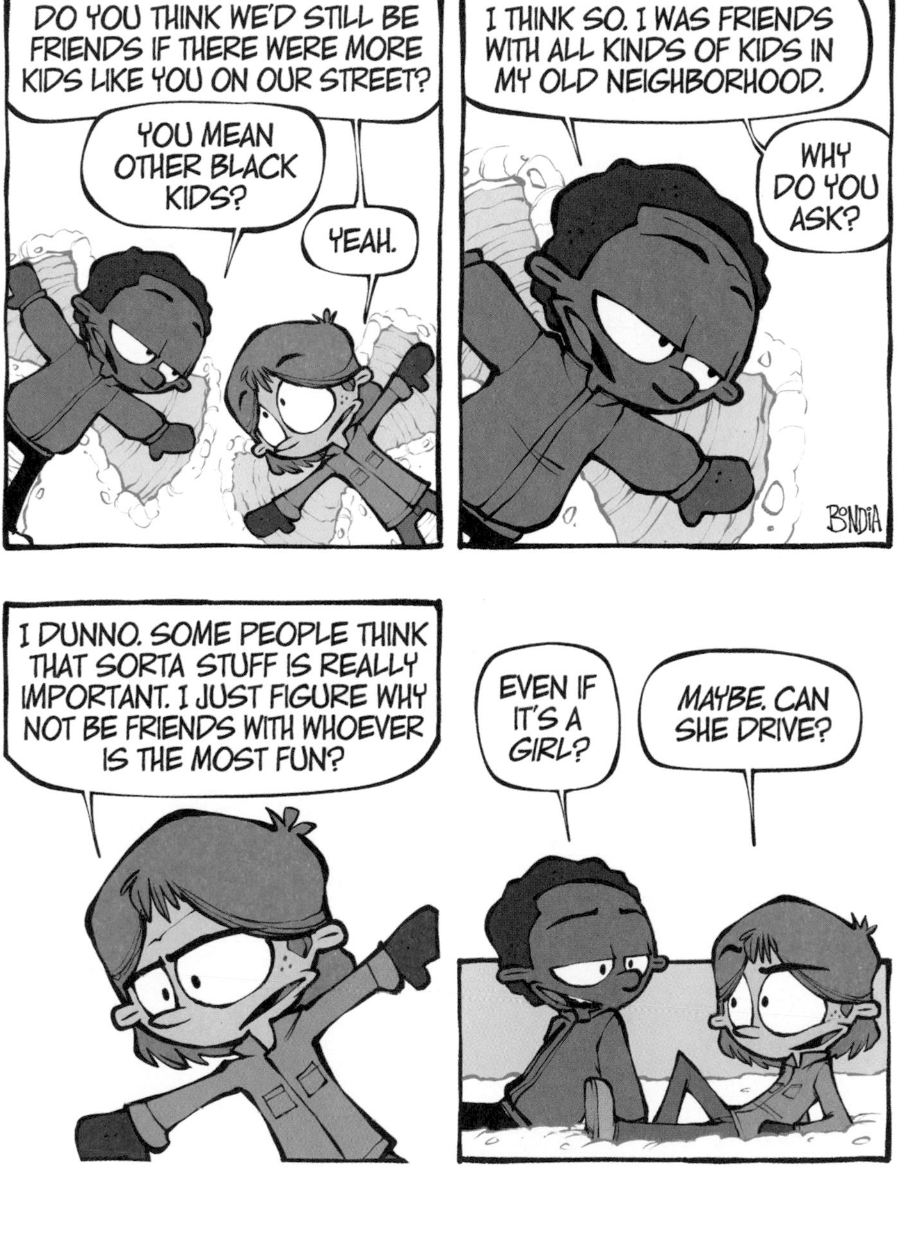
DO YOU THINK WE'D STILL BE FRIENDS IF THERE WERE MORE KIDS LIKE YOU ON OUR STREET?
YOU MEAN OTHER BLACK KIDS?
YEAH.
I THINK SO. I WAS FRIENDS WITH ALL KINDS OF KIDS IN MY OLD NEIGHBORHOOD.
WHY DO YOU ASK?
BONDIA
I DUNNO. SOME PEOPLE THINK THAT SORTA STUFF IS REALLY IMPORTANT. I JUST FIGURE WHY NOT BE FRIENDS WITH WHOEVER IS THE MOST FUN?
EVEN IF IT'S A GIRL?
MAYBE. CAN SHE DRIVE?

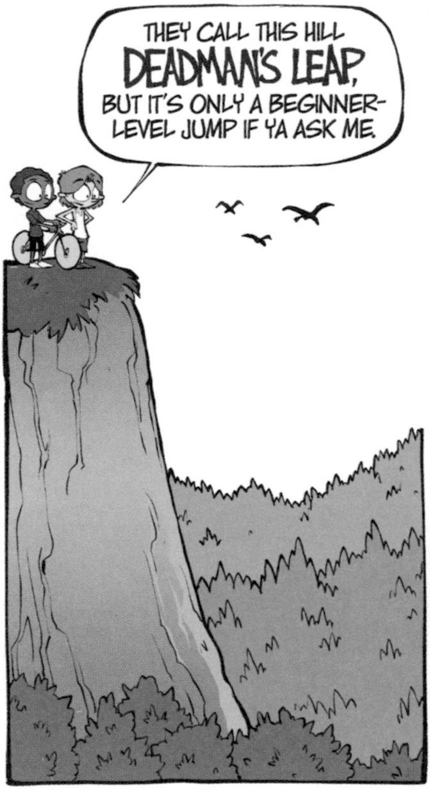
THEY CALL THIS HILL DEADMAN'S LEAP, BUT IT'S ONLY A BEGINNER-LEVEL JUMP IF YA ASK ME.

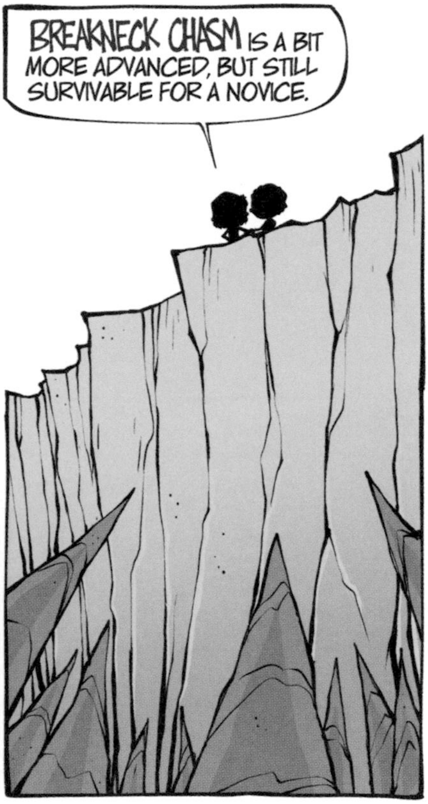
BREAKNECK CHASM IS A BIT MORE ADVANCED, BUT STILL SURVIVABLE FOR A NOVICE.

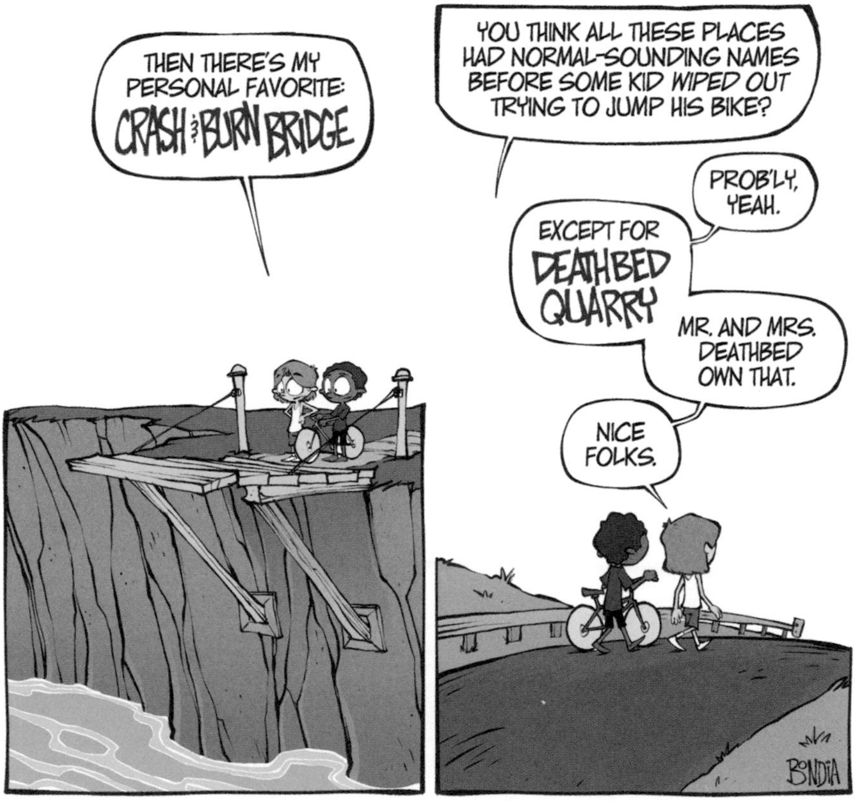
THEN THERE'S MY PERSONAL FAVORITE: CRASH & BURN BRIDGE
YOU THINK ALL THESE PLACES HAD NORMAL-SOUNDING NAMES BEFORE SOME KID WIPED OUT TRYING TO JUMP HIS BIKE?
PROB'LY, YEAH.
EXCEPT FOR DEATHBED QUARRY
MR. AND MRS. DEATHBED OWN THAT.
NICE FOLKS.
BONDIA

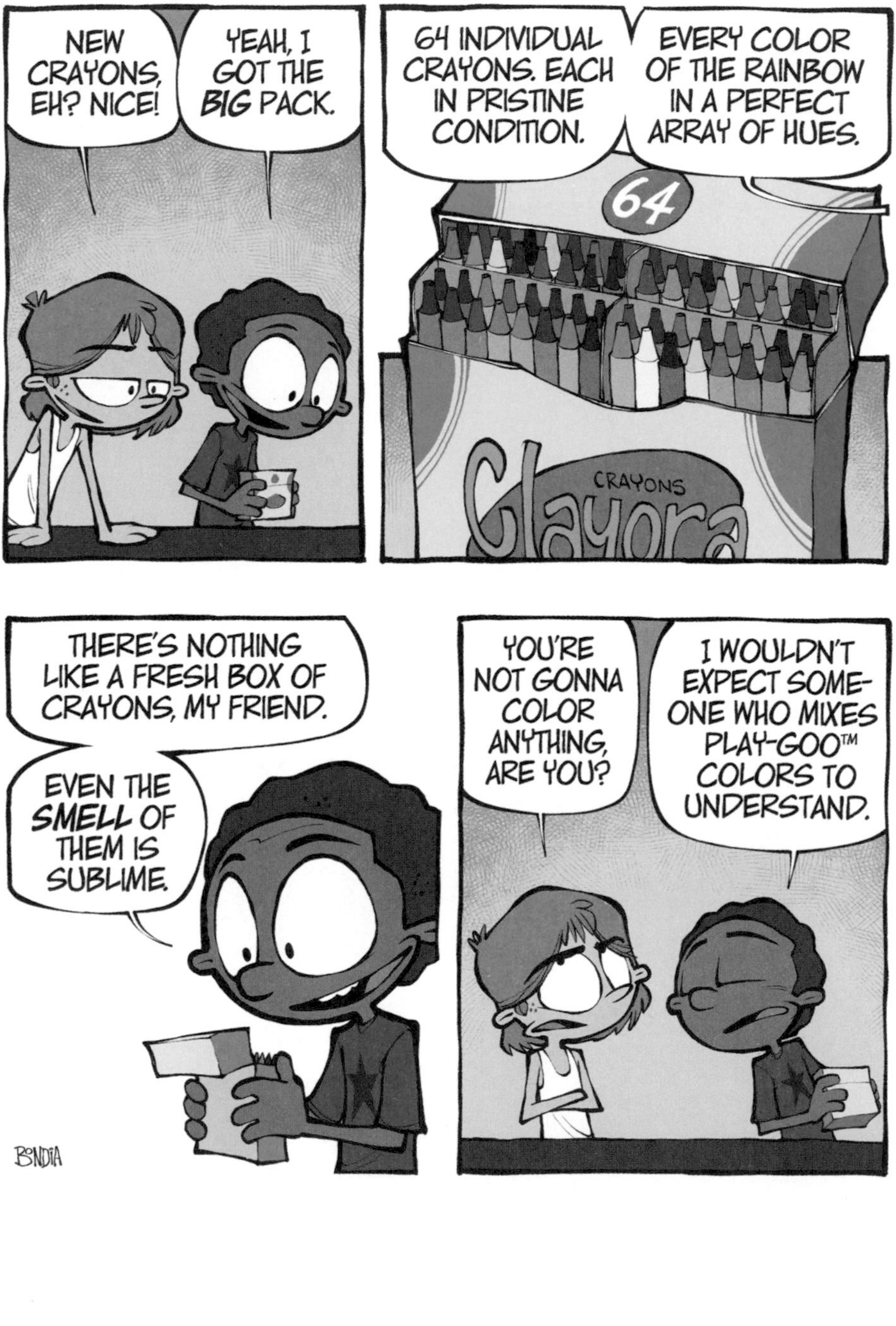
NEW CRAYONS, EH? NICE!
YEAH, I GOT THE BIG PACK.
64 INDIVIDUAL CRAYONS. EACH IN PRISTINE CONDITION.
EVERY COLOR OF THE RAINBOW IN A PERFECT ARRAY OF HUES.
64
CRAYONS
Clayora
THERE'S NOTHING LIKE A FRESH BOX OF CRAYONS, MY FRIEND.
EVEN THE SMELL OF THEM IS SUBLIME.
YOU'RE NOT GONNA COLOR ANYTHING, ARE YOU?
I WOULDN'T EXPECT SOME-ONE WHO MIXES PLAY-GOO™ COLORS TO UNDERSTAND.
BONDIA

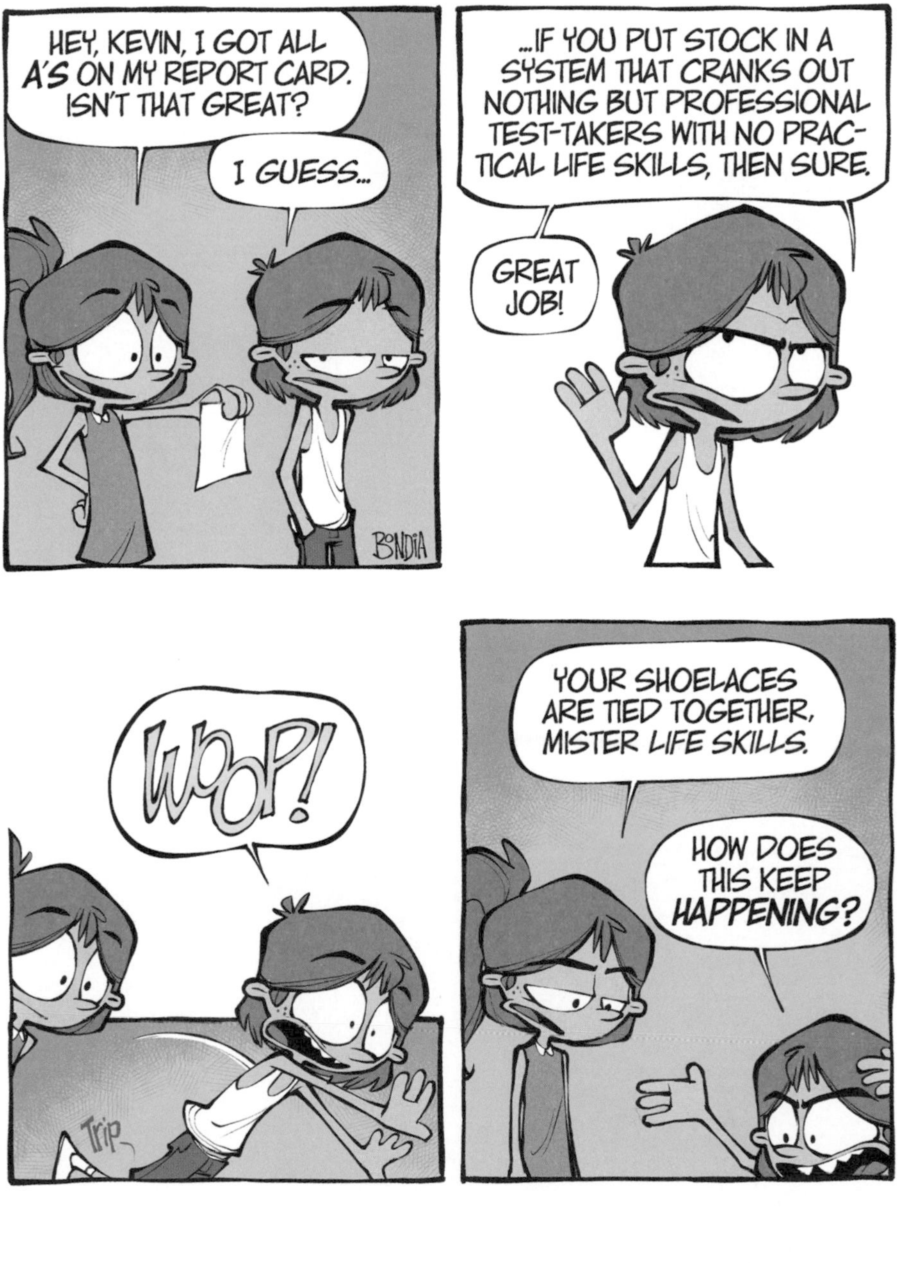
HEY, KEVIN, I GOT ALL A'S ON MY REPORT CARD. ISN'T THAT GREAT?
I GUESS...
BONDIA
...IF YOU PUT STOCK IN A SYSTEM THAT CRANKS OUT NOTHING BUT PROFESSIONAL TEST-TAKERS WITH NO PRACTICAL LIFE SKILLS, THEN SURE.
GREAT JOB!
WOOP!
TRIP
YOUR SHOELACES ARE TIED TOGETHER, MISTER LIFE SKILLS.
HOW DOES THIS KEEP HAPPENING?

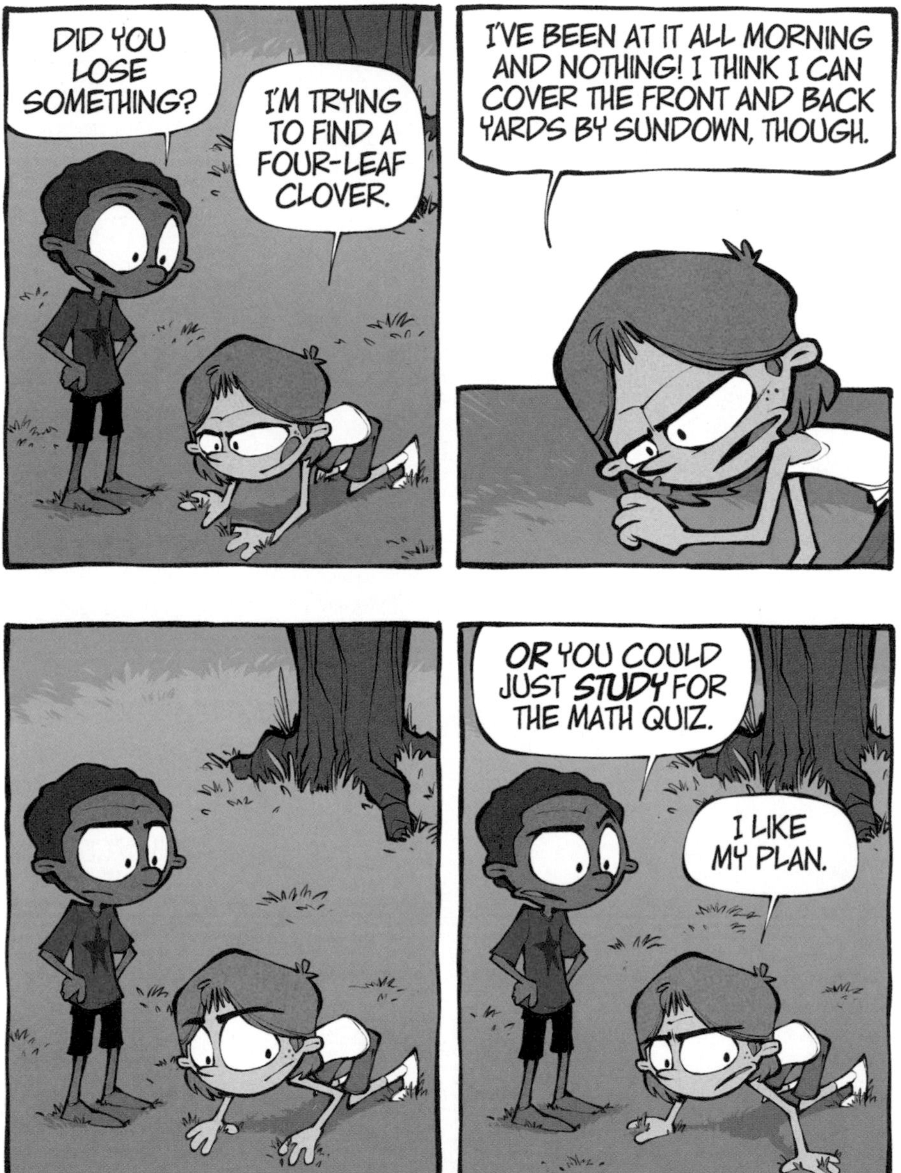
DID YOU LOSE SOMETHING?
I'M TRYING TO FIND A FOUR-LEAF CLOVER.
I'VE BEEN AT IT ALL MORNING AND NOTHING! I THINK I CAN COVER THE FRONT AND BACK YARDS BY SUNDOWN, THOUGH.
OR YOU COULD JUST STUDY FOR THE MATH QUIZ.
I LIKE MY PLAN.

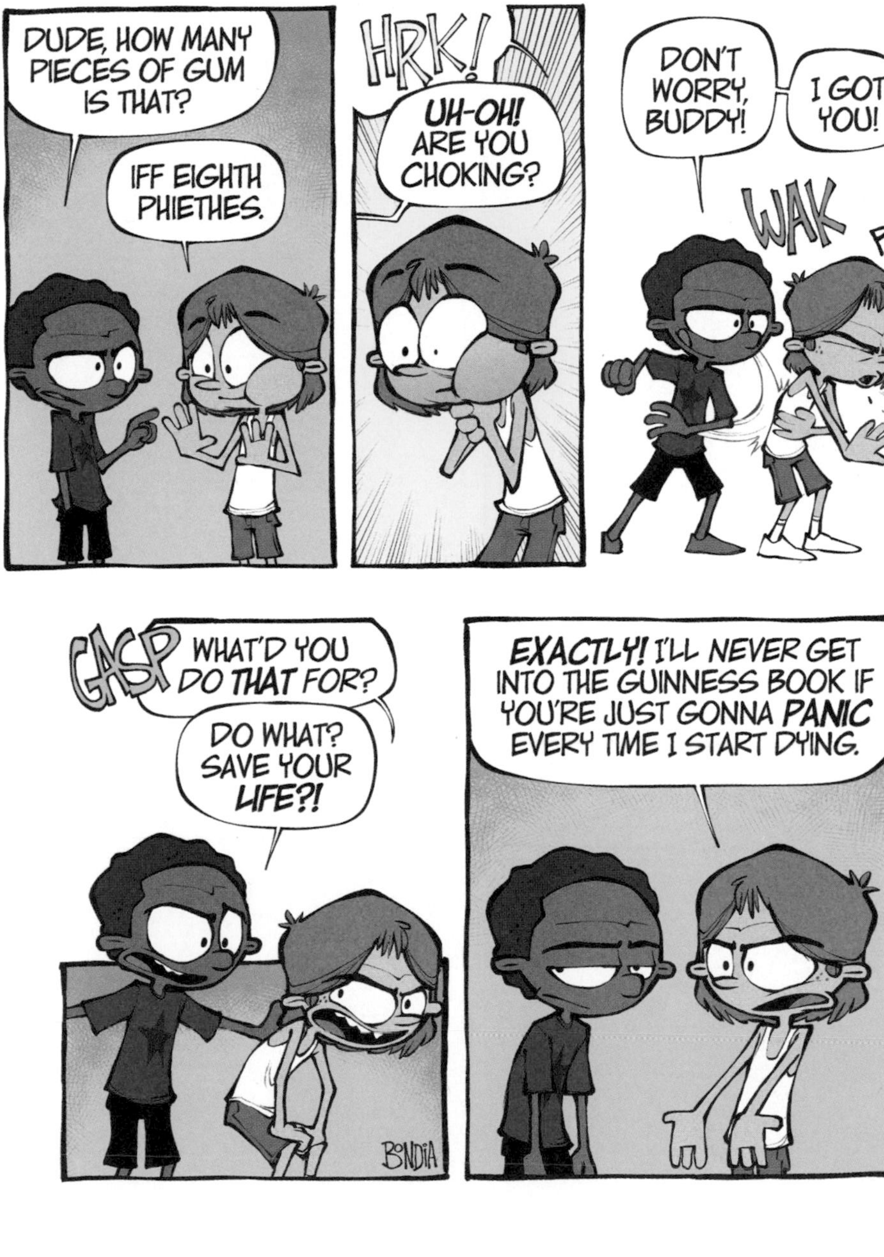
DUDE, HOW MANY PIECES OF GUM IS THAT?
IFF EIGHTH PHIETHES.
HRK!
UH-OH! ARE YOU CHOKING?
DON'T WORRY, BUDDY!
I GOT YOU!
WAK
PTOO
GASP
WHAT'D YOU DO THAT FOR?
DO WHAT? SAVE YOUR LIFE?!
BONDIA
EXACTLY! I'LL NEVER GET INTO THE GUINNESS BOOK IF YOU'RE JUST GONNA PANIC EVERY TIME I START DYING.

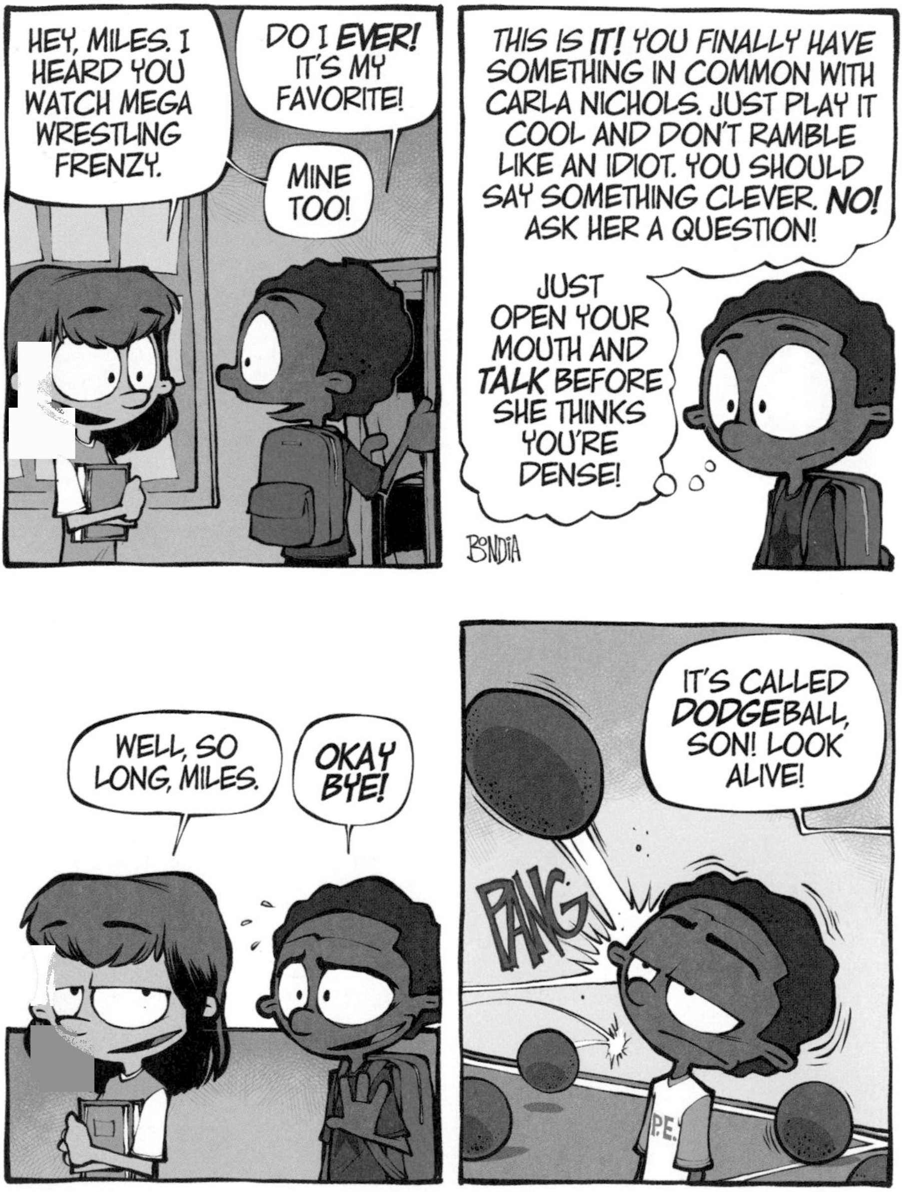
HEY, MILES. I HEARD YOU WATCH MEGA WRESTLING FRENZY.
DO I **EVER!** IT'S MY FAVORITE!
MINE TOO!
THIS IS **IT!** YOU FINALLY HAVE SOMETHING IN COMMON WITH CARLA NICHOLS. JUST PLAY IT COOL AND DON'T RAMBLE LIKE AN IDIOT. YOU SHOULD SAY SOMETHING CLEVER. **NO!** ASK HER A QUESTION!
JUST OPEN YOUR MOUTH AND **TALK** BEFORE SHE THINKS YOU'RE DENSE!
BONDIA
WELL, SO LONG, MILES.
OKAY BYE!
IT'S CALLED **DODGE**BALL, SON! LOOK ALIVE!
BANG
P.E.

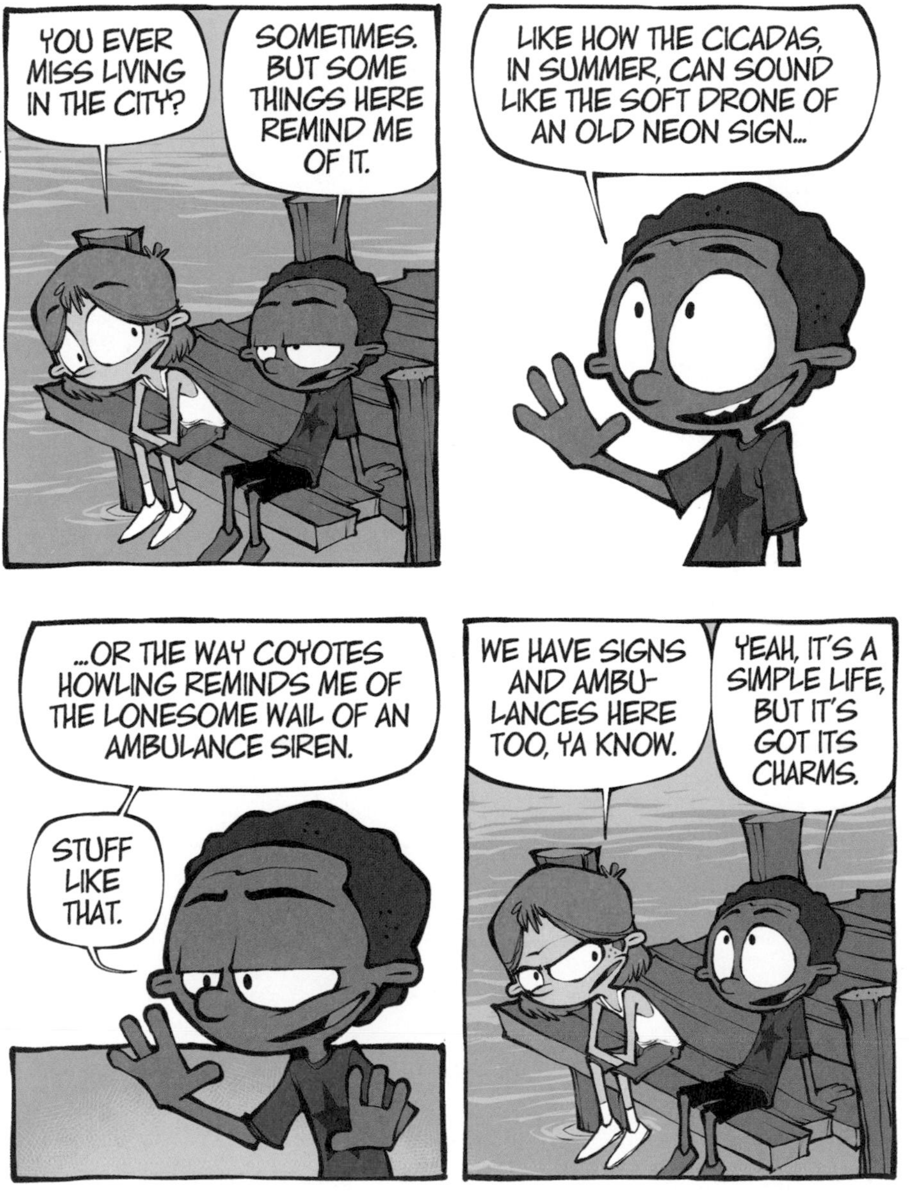
YOU EVER MISS LIVING IN THE CITY?
SOMETIMES. BUT SOME THINGS HERE REMIND ME OF IT.
LIKE HOW THE CICADAS, IN SUMMER, CAN SOUND LIKE THE SOFT DRONE OF AN OLD NEON SIGN...
...OR THE WAY COYOTES HOWLING REMINDS ME OF THE LONESOME WAIL OF AN AMBULANCE SIREN.
STUFF LIKE THAT.
WE HAVE SIGNS AND AMBU-LANCES HERE TOO, YA KNOW.
YEAH, IT'S A SIMPLE LIFE, BUT IT'S GOT ITS CHARMS.

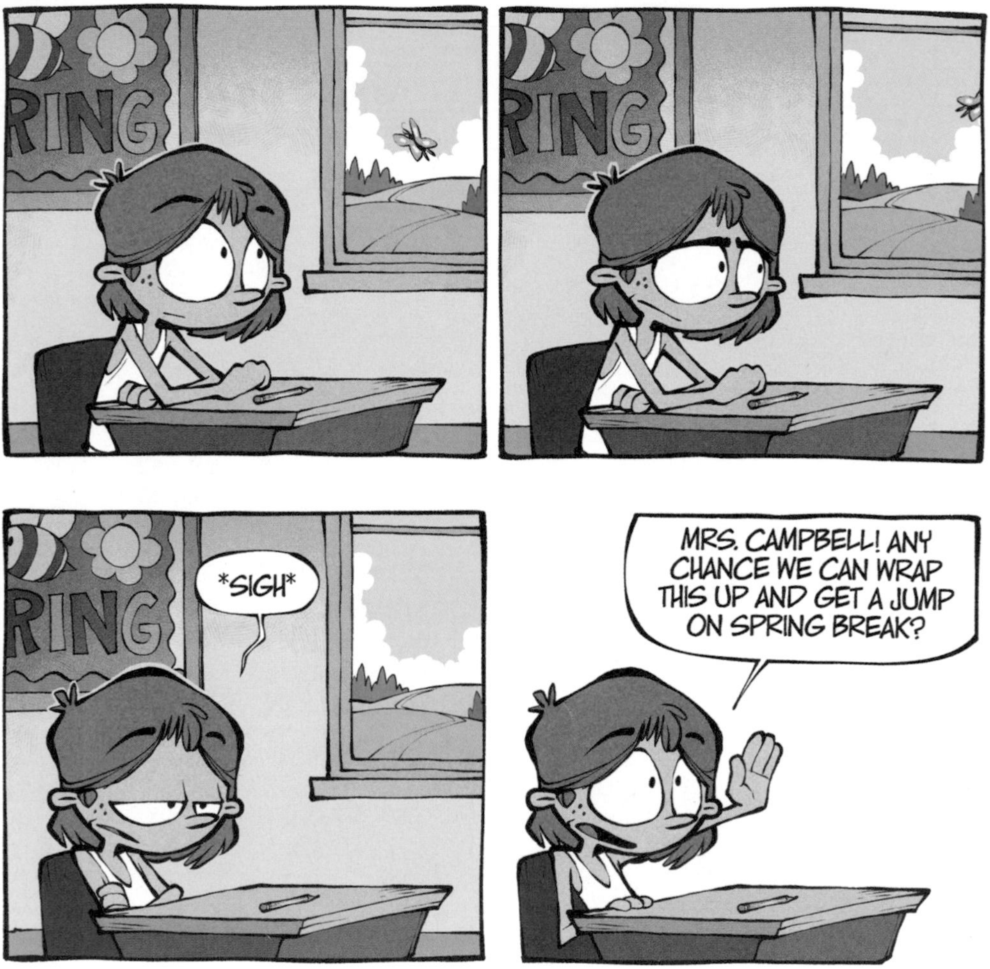
RING
RING
RING
SIGH
MRS. CAMPBELL! ANY CHANCE WE CAN WRAP THIS UP AND GET A JUMP ON SPRING BREAK?

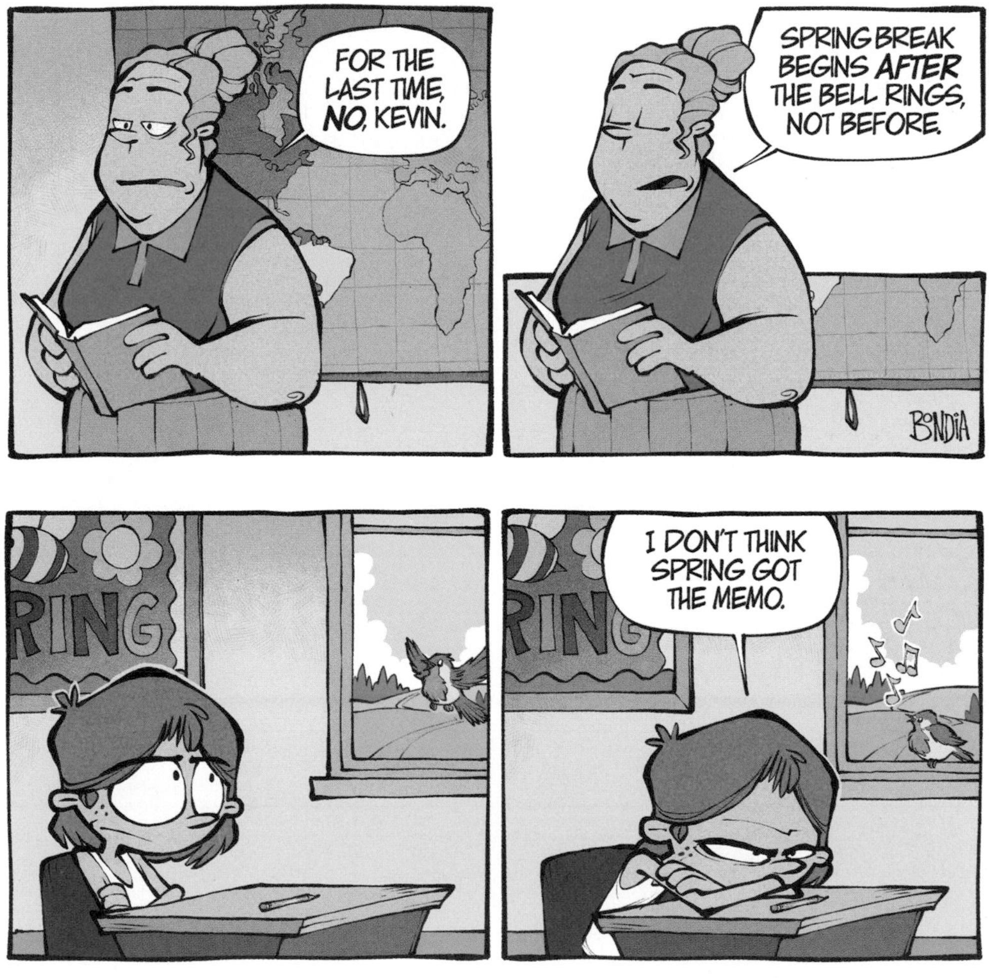
FOR THE LAST TIME, NO, KEVIN.
SPRING BREAK BEGINS AFTER THE BELL RINGS, NOT BEFORE.
BONDIA
RING
RING
I DON'T THINK SPRING GOT THE MEMO.

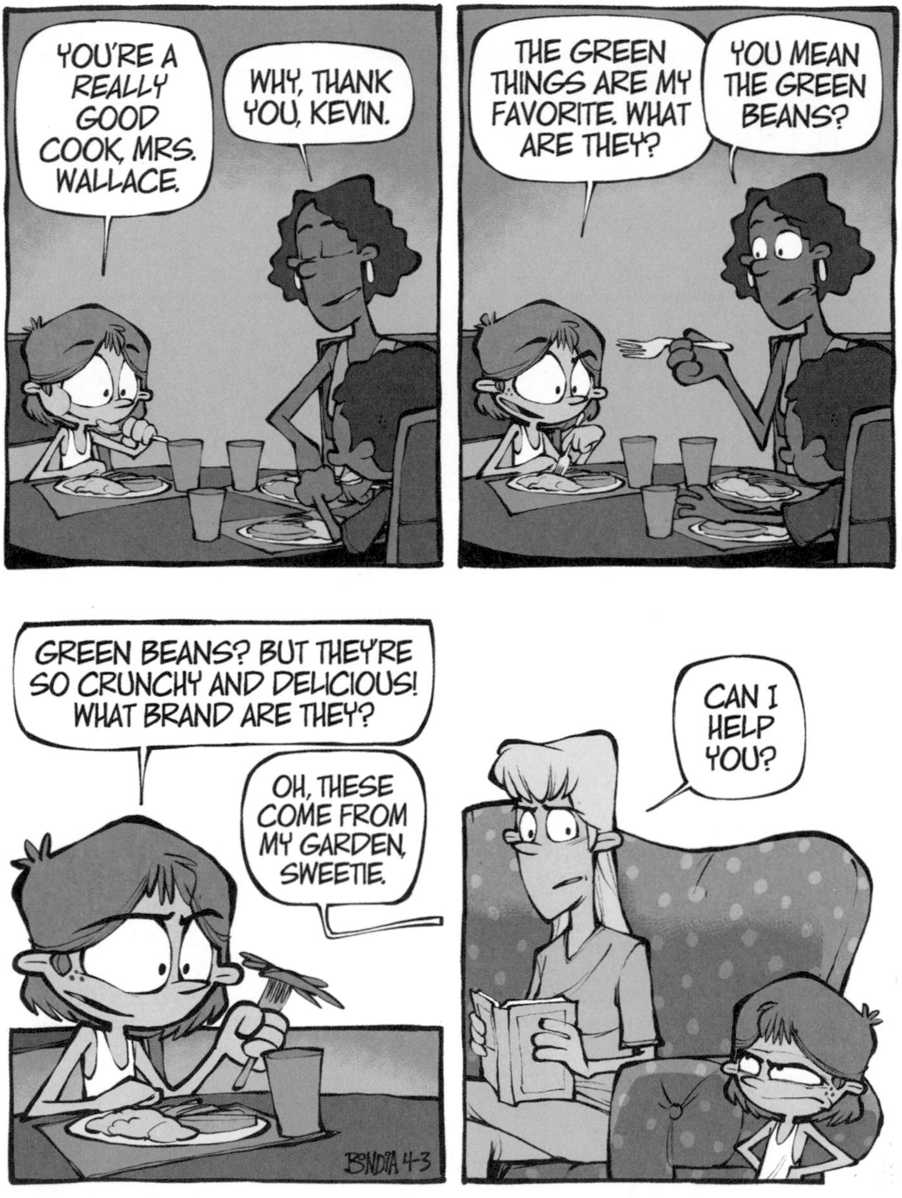
YOU'RE A REALLY GOOD COOK, MRS. WALLACE.
WHY, THANK YOU, KEVIN.
THE GREEN THINGS ARE MY FAVORITE. WHAT ARE THEY?
YOU MEAN THE GREEN BEANS?
GREEN BEANS? BUT THEY'RE SO CRUNCHY AND DELICIOUS! WHAT BRAND ARE THEY?
OH, THESE COME FROM MY GARDEN, SWEETIE.
CAN I HELP YOU?

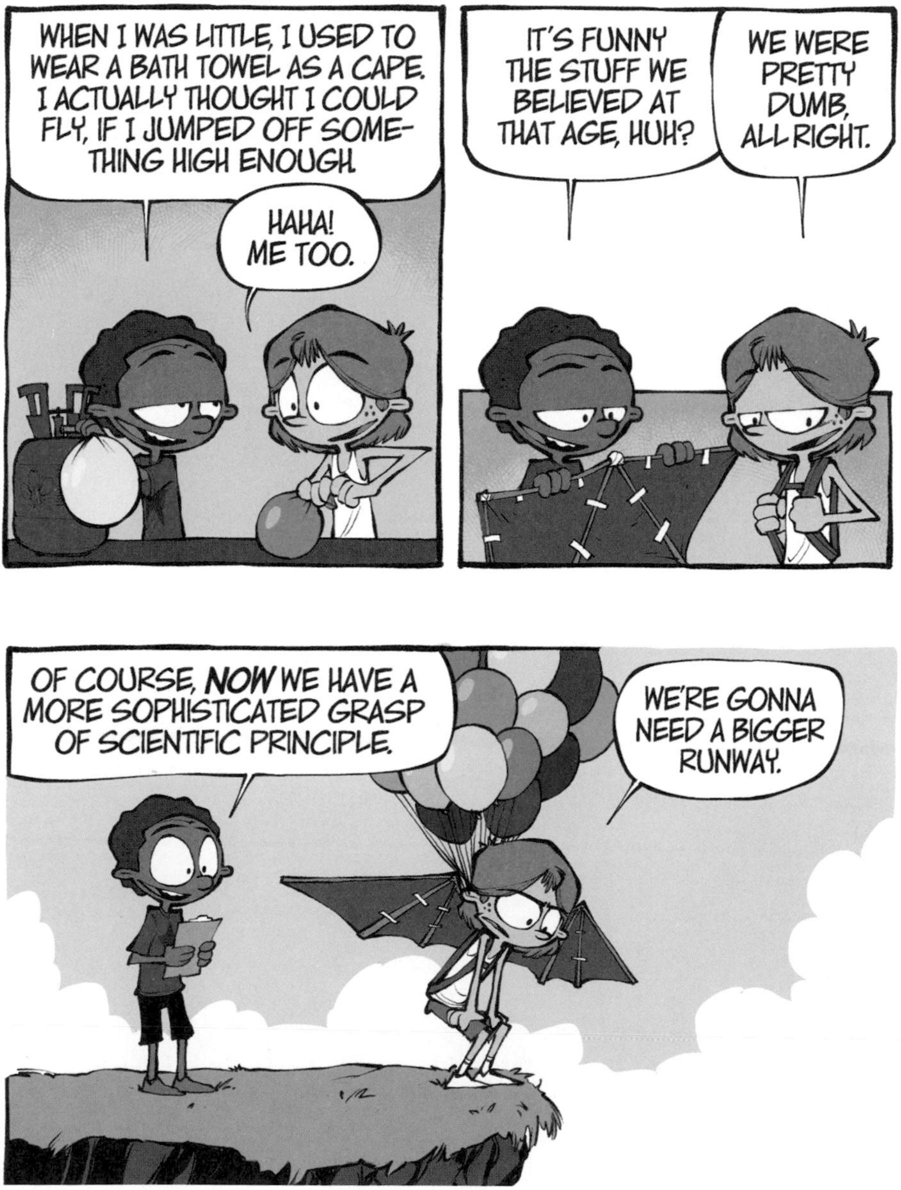
WHEN I WAS LITTLE, I USED TO WEAR A BATH TOWEL AS A CAPE. I ACTUALLY THOUGHT I COULD FLY, IF I JUMPED OFF SOMETHING HIGH ENOUGH.
HAHA! ME TOO.
IT'S FUNNY THE STUFF WE BELIEVED AT THAT AGE, HUH?
WE WERE PRETTY DUMB, ALL RIGHT.
OF COURSE, **NOW** WE HAVE A MORE SOPHISTICATED GRASP OF SCIENTIFIC PRINCIPLE.
WE'RE GONNA NEED A BIGGER RUNWAY.

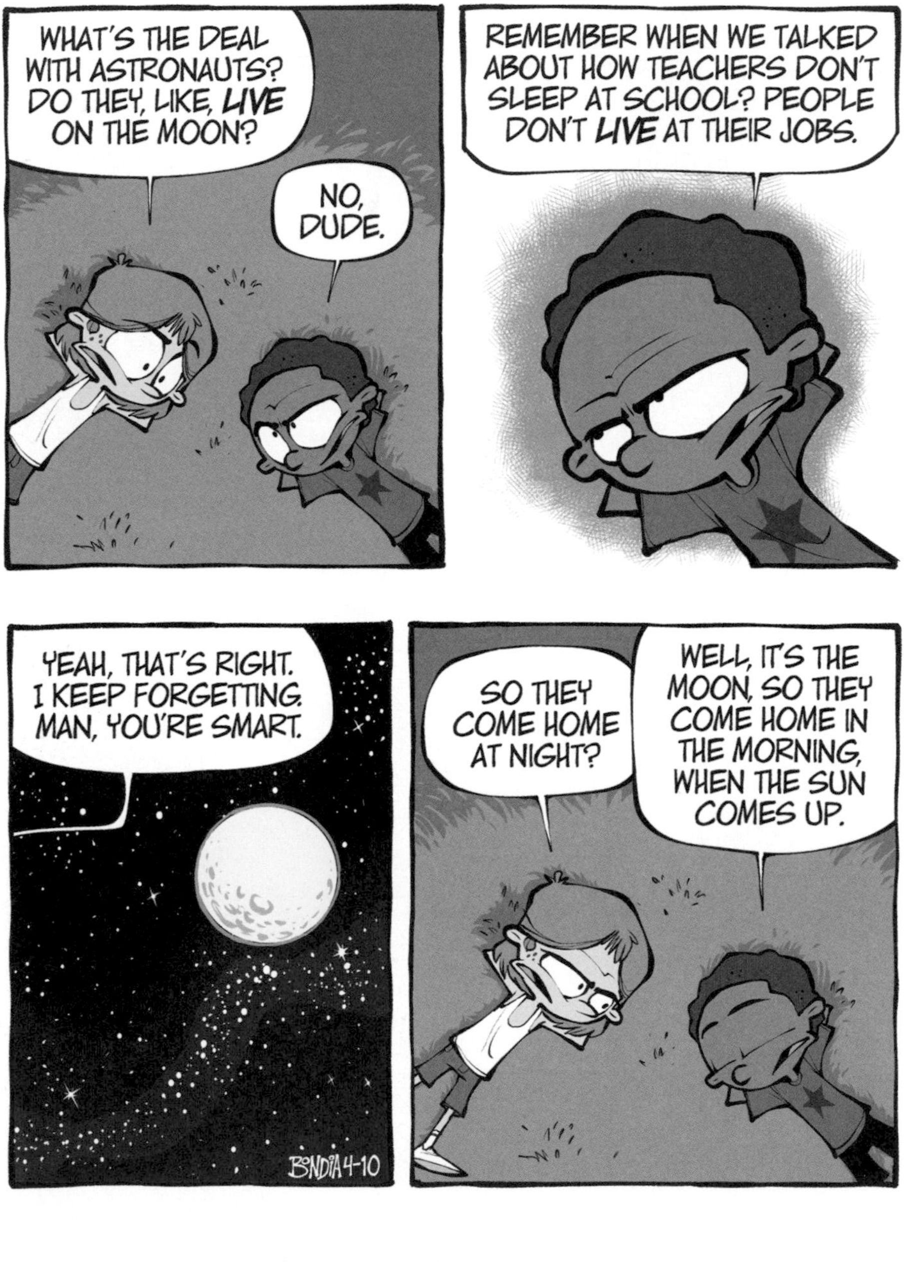
WHAT'S THE DEAL WITH ASTRONAUTS? DO THEY, LIKE, *LIVE* ON THE MOON?
NO, DUDE.
REMEMBER WHEN WE TALKED ABOUT HOW TEACHERS DON'T SLEEP AT SCHOOL? PEOPLE DON'T *LIVE* AT THEIR JOBS.
YEAH, THAT'S RIGHT. I KEEP FORGETTING. MAN, YOU'RE SMART.
BONDIA 4-10
SO THEY COME HOME AT NIGHT?
WELL, IT'S THE MOON, SO THEY COME HOME IN THE MORNING, WHEN THE SUN COMES UP.

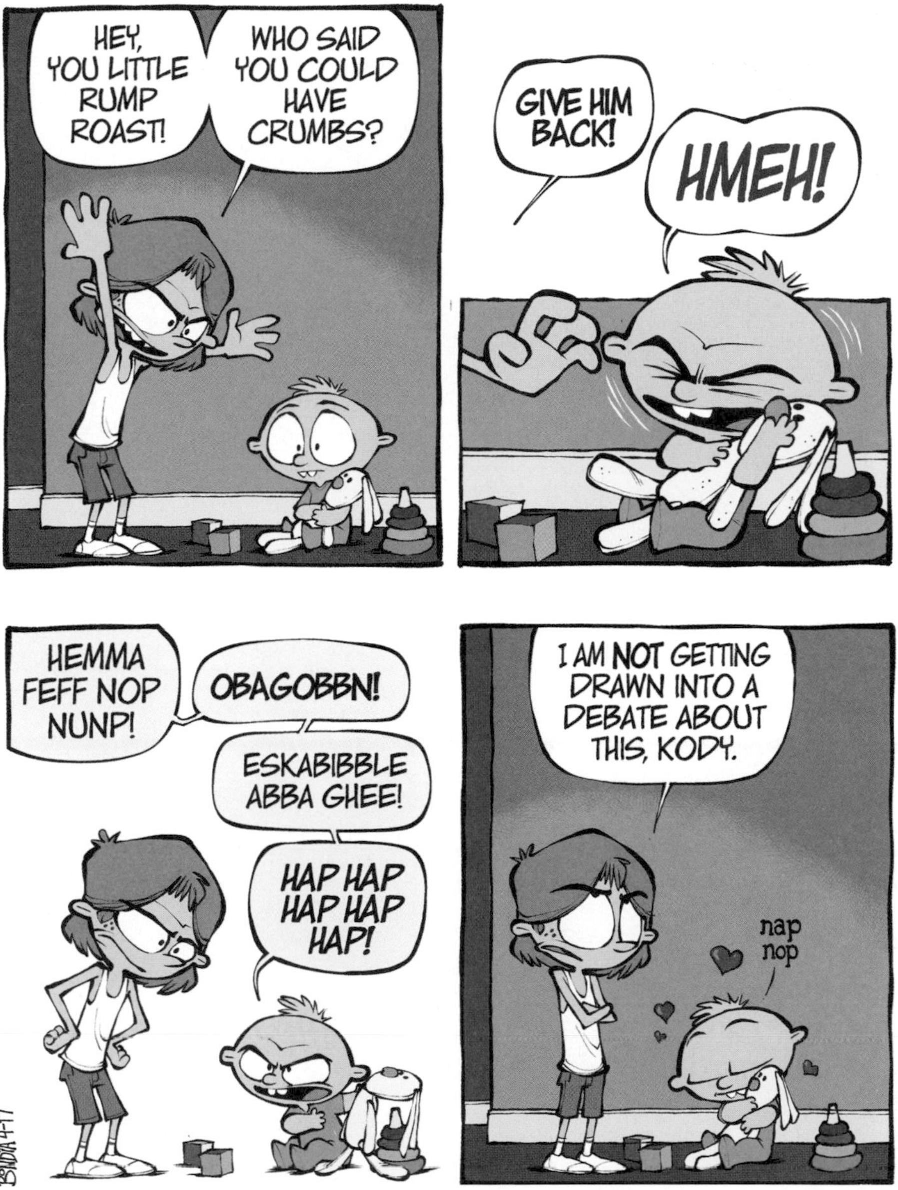
HEY, YOU LITTLE RUMP ROAST!
WHO SAID YOU COULD HAVE CRUMBS?
GIVE HIM BACK!
HMEH!
HEMMA FEFF NOP NUNP!
OBAGOBBN!
ESKABIBBLE ABBA GHEE!
HAP HAP HAP HAP HAP!
BONDRA 4-17
I AM NOT GETTING DRAWN INTO A DEBATE ABOUT THIS, KODY.
nap nop

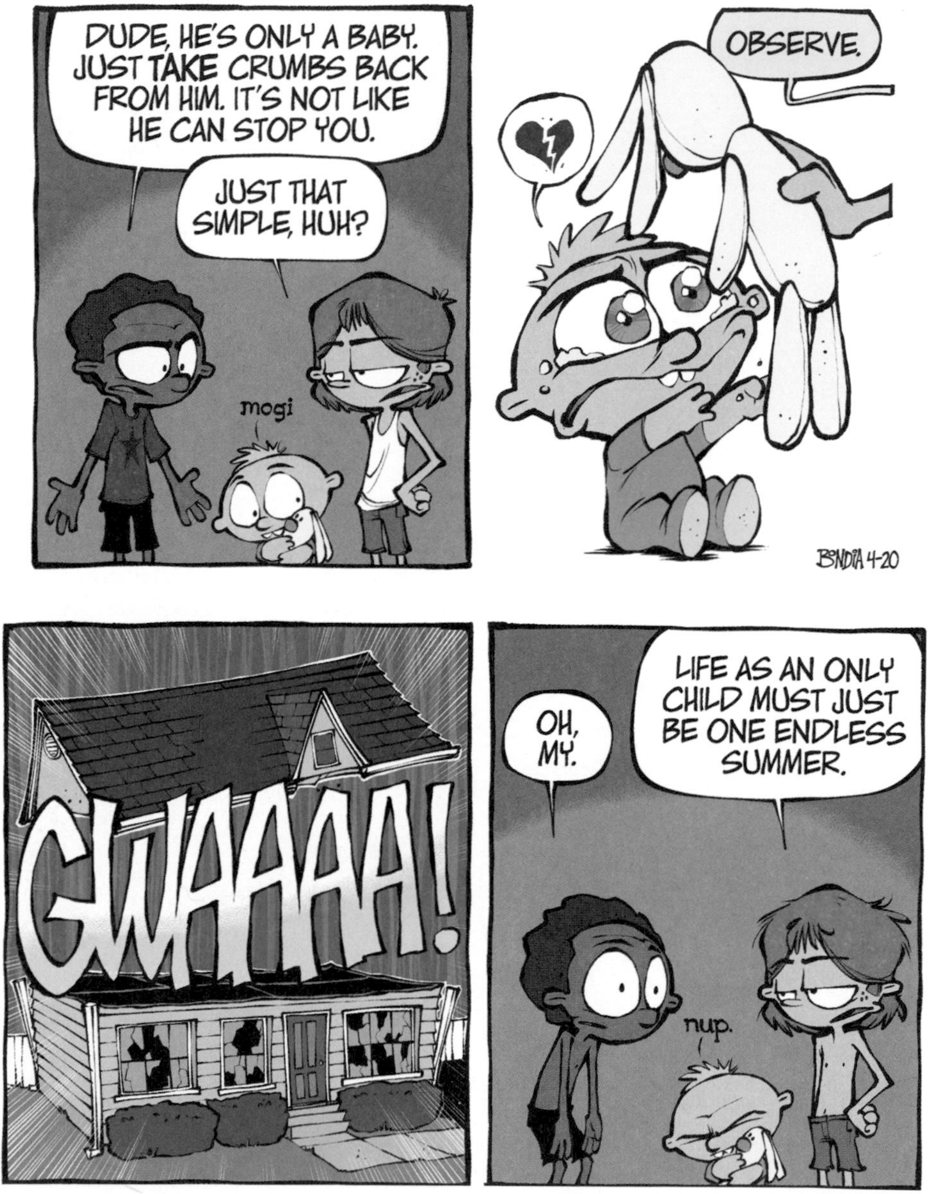
DUDE, HE'S ONLY A BABY. JUST TAKE CRUMBS BACK FROM HIM. IT'S NOT LIKE HE CAN STOP YOU.
JUST THAT SIMPLE, HUH?
mogi
OBSERVE.
BONDIA 4-20
GWAAAAA!
OH, MY.
LIFE AS AN ONLY CHILD MUST JUST BE ONE ENDLESS SUMMER.
nup.

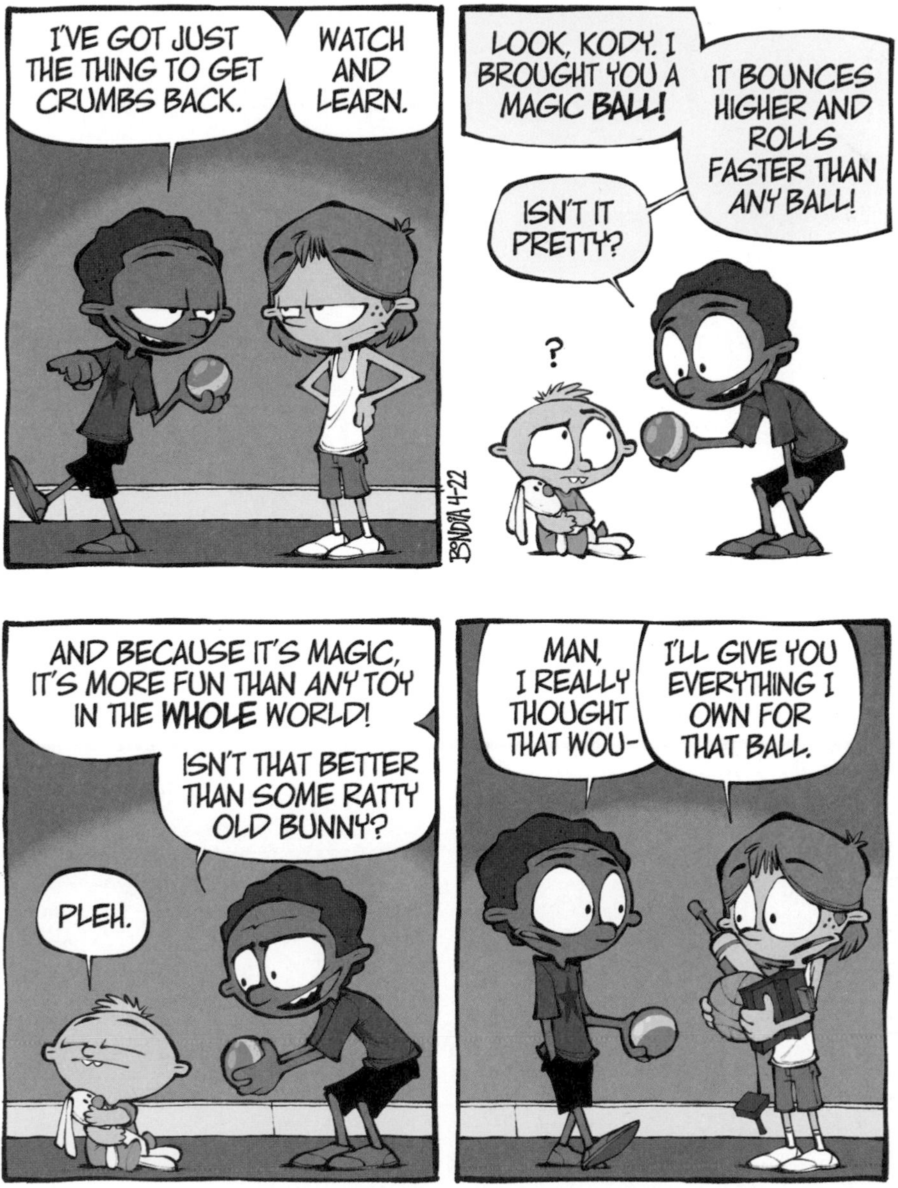
I'VE GOT JUST THE THING TO GET CRUMBS BACK.
WATCH AND LEARN.
BONDIA 4-22
LOOK, KODY. I BROUGHT YOU A MAGIC BALL!
IT BOUNCES HIGHER AND ROLLS FASTER THAN ANY BALL!
ISN'T IT PRETTY?
?
AND BECAUSE IT'S MAGIC, IT'S MORE FUN THAN ANY TOY IN THE WHOLE WORLD!
ISN'T THAT BETTER THAN SOME RATTY OLD BUNNY?
PLEH.
MAN, I REALLY THOUGHT THAT WOU-
I'LL GIVE YOU EVERYTHING I OWN FOR THAT BALL.

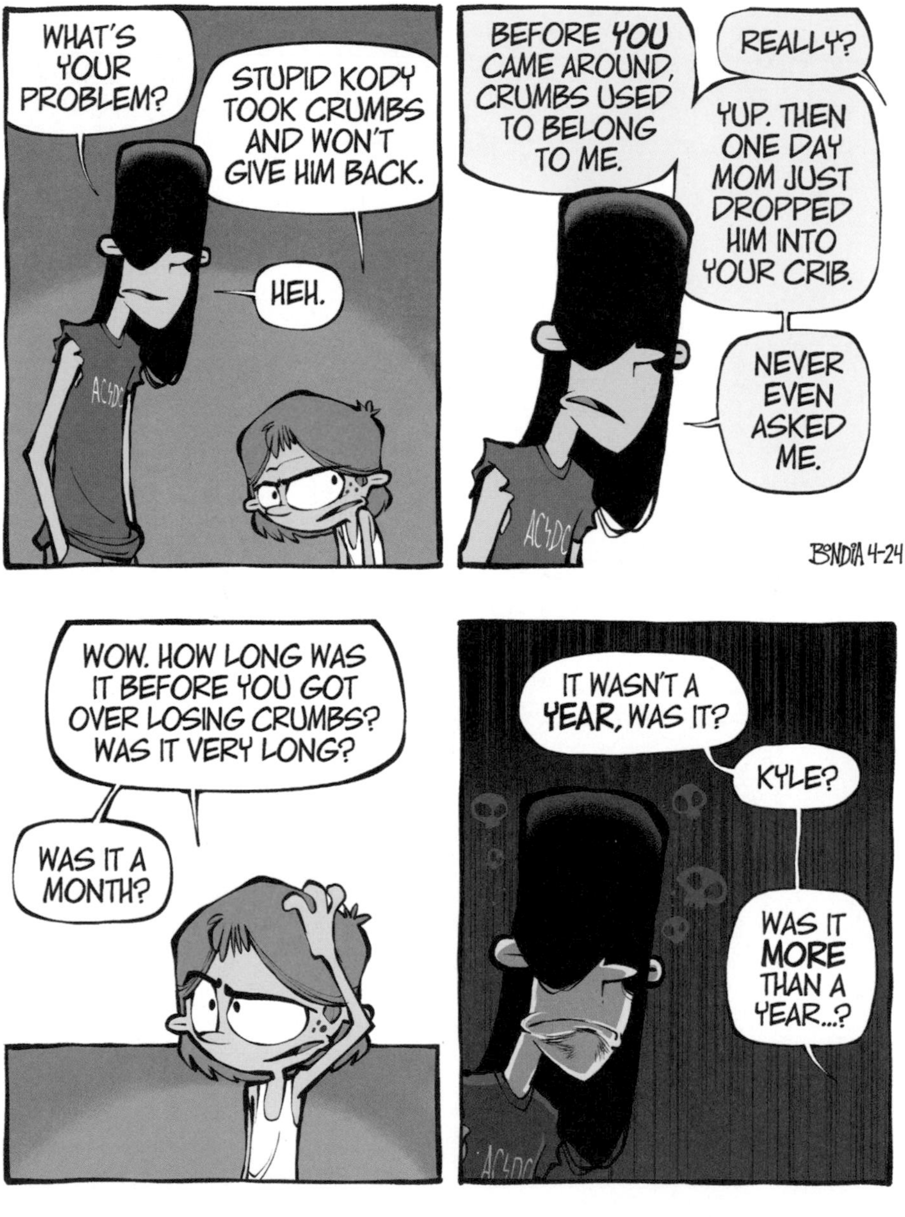
WHAT'S YOUR PROBLEM?
STUPID KODY TOOK CRUMBS AND WON'T GIVE HIM BACK.
HEH.
ACDC
BEFORE YOU CAME AROUND, CRUMBS USED TO BELONG TO ME.
REALLY?
YUP. THEN ONE DAY MOM JUST DROPPED HIM INTO YOUR CRIB.
NEVER EVEN ASKED ME.
BONDIA 4-24
WOW. HOW LONG WAS IT BEFORE YOU GOT OVER LOSING CRUMBS? WAS IT VERY LONG?
WAS IT A MONTH?
IT WASN'T A YEAR, WAS IT?
KYLE?
WAS IT MORE THAN A YEAR...?

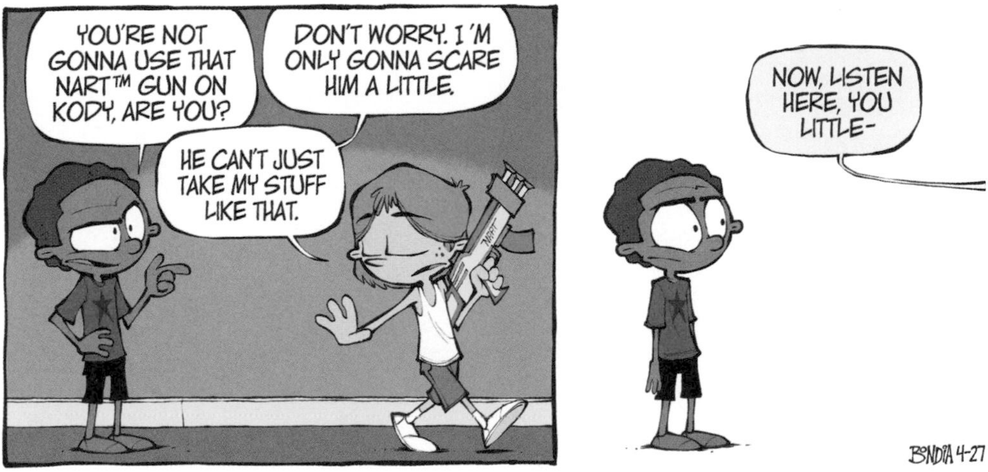
YOU'RE NOT GONNA USE THAT NART™ GUN ON KODY, ARE YOU?
DON'T WORRY. I'M ONLY GONNA SCARE HIM A LITTLE.
HE CAN'T JUST TAKE MY STUFF LIKE THAT.
NOW, LISTEN HERE, YOU LITTLE-
BONDIA 4-27

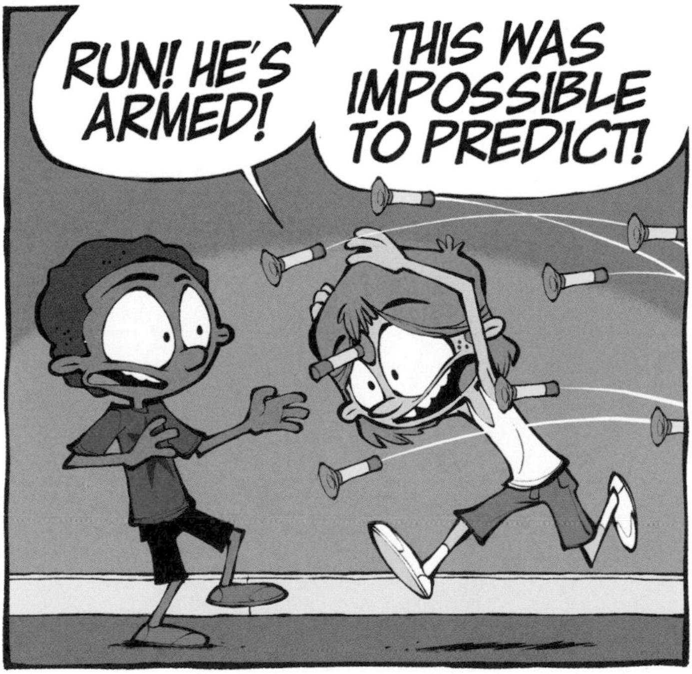
RUN! HE'S ARMED!
THIS WAS IMPOSSIBLE TO PREDICT!

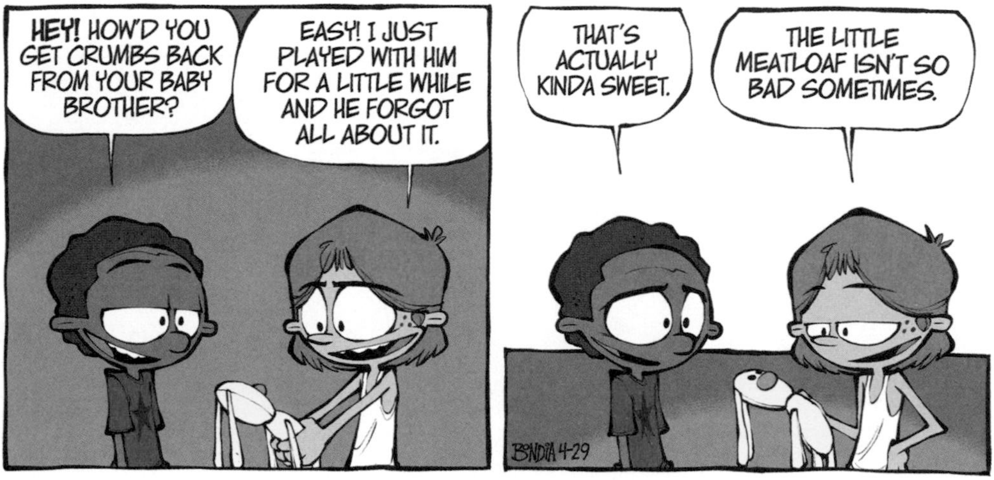
HEY! HOW'D YOU GET CRUMBS BACK FROM YOUR BABY BROTHER?
EASY! I JUST PLAYED WITH HIM FOR A LITTLE WHILE AND HE FORGOT ALL ABOUT IT.
THAT'S ACTUALLY KINDA SWEET.
THE LITTLE MEATLOAF ISN'T SO BAD SOMETIMES.
BONDIA 4-29

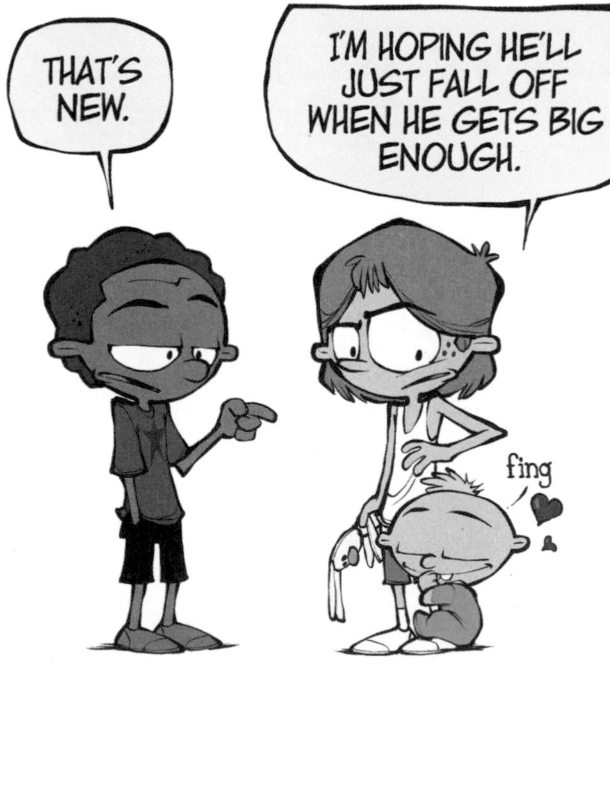
THAT'S NEW.
I'M HOPING HE'LL JUST FALL OFF WHEN HE GETS BIG ENOUGH.
fing

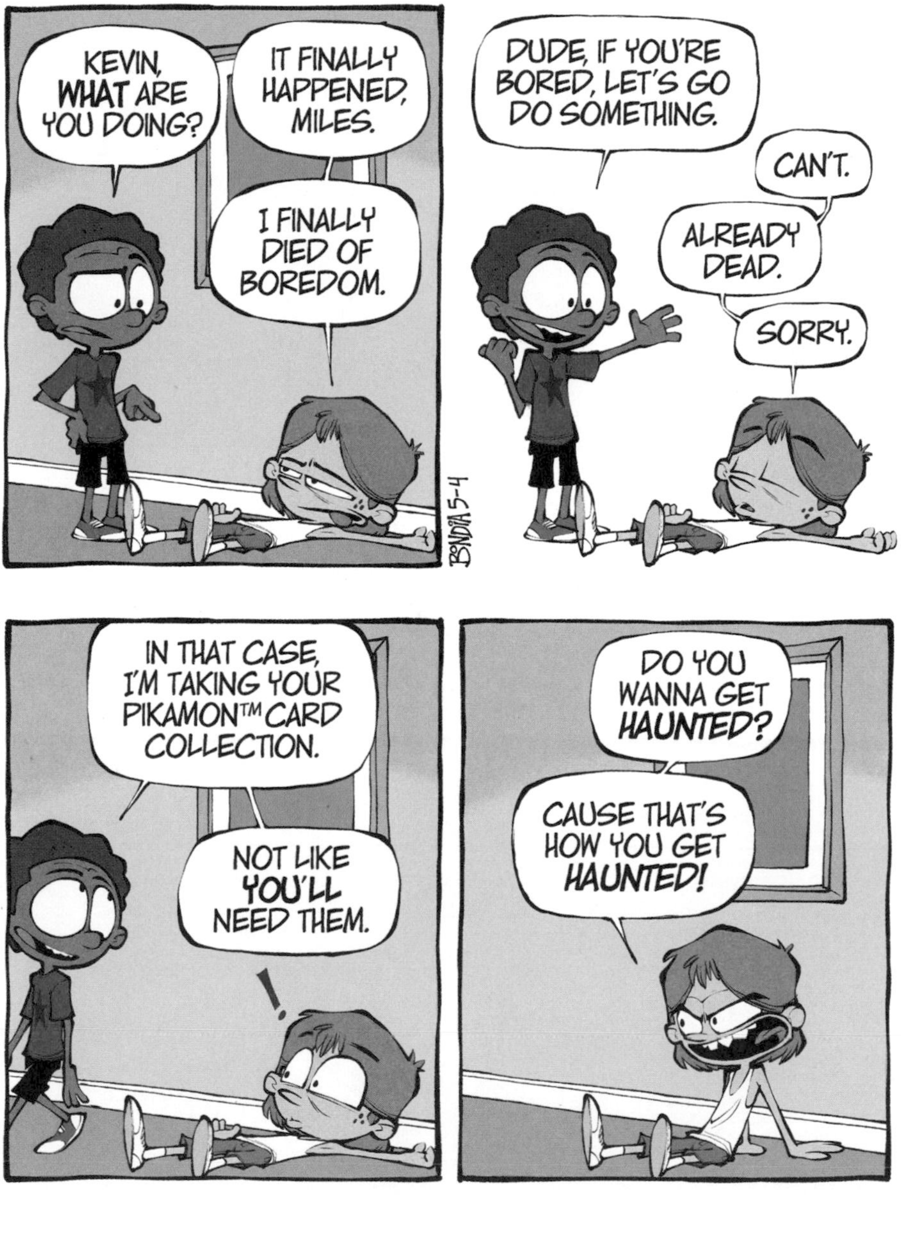
KEVIN, **WHAT** ARE YOU DOING?
IT FINALLY HAPPENED, MILES.
I FINALLY DIED OF BOREDOM.
BONDIA 5-4
DUDE, IF YOU'RE BORED, LET'S GO DO SOMETHING.
CAN'T.
ALREADY DEAD.
SORRY.
IN THAT CASE, I'M TAKING YOUR PIKAMON™ CARD COLLECTION.
NOT LIKE **YOU'LL** NEED THEM.
!
DO YOU WANNA GET **HAUNTED?**
CAUSE THAT'S HOW YOU GET **HAUNTED!**

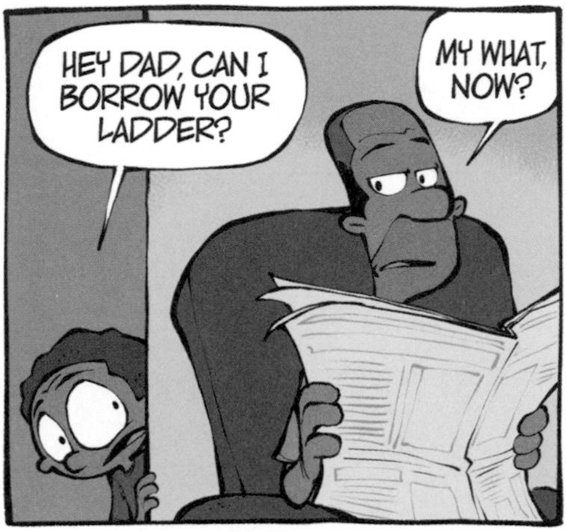
HEY DAD, CAN I BORROW YOUR LADDER?
MY WHAT, NOW?

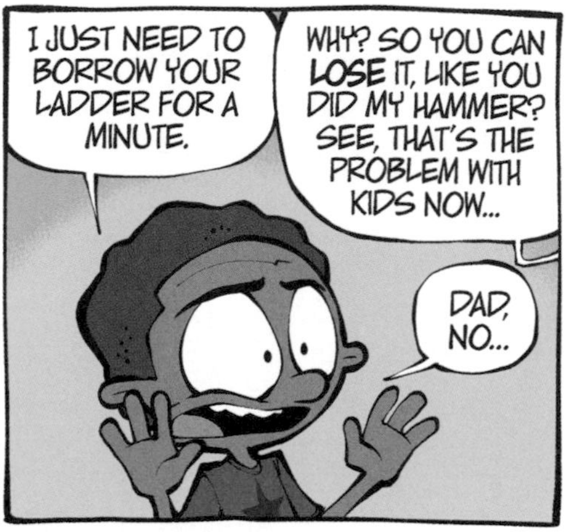
I JUST NEED TO BORROW YOUR LADDER FOR A MINUTE.
WHY? SO YOU CAN **LOSE** IT, LIKE YOU DID MY HAMMER? SEE, THAT'S THE PROBLEM WITH KIDS NOW...
DAD, NO...

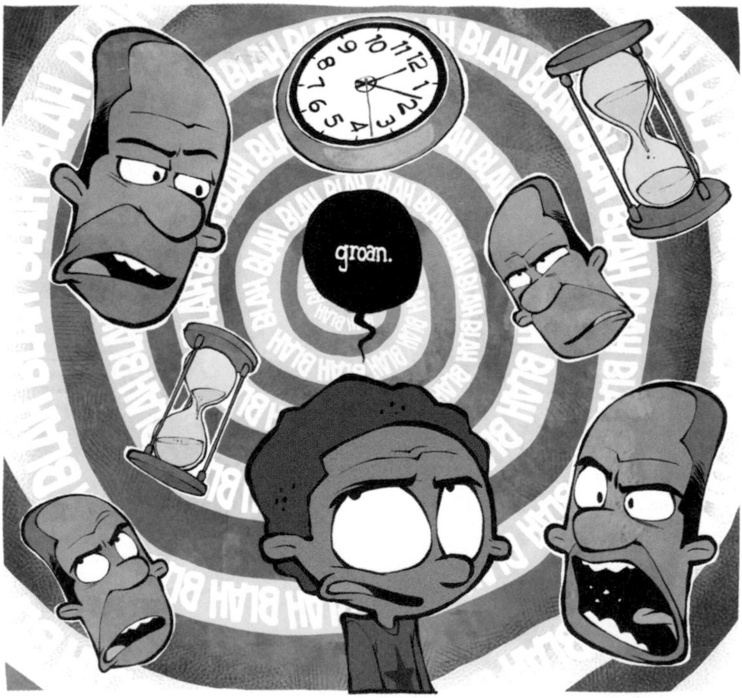
groan.

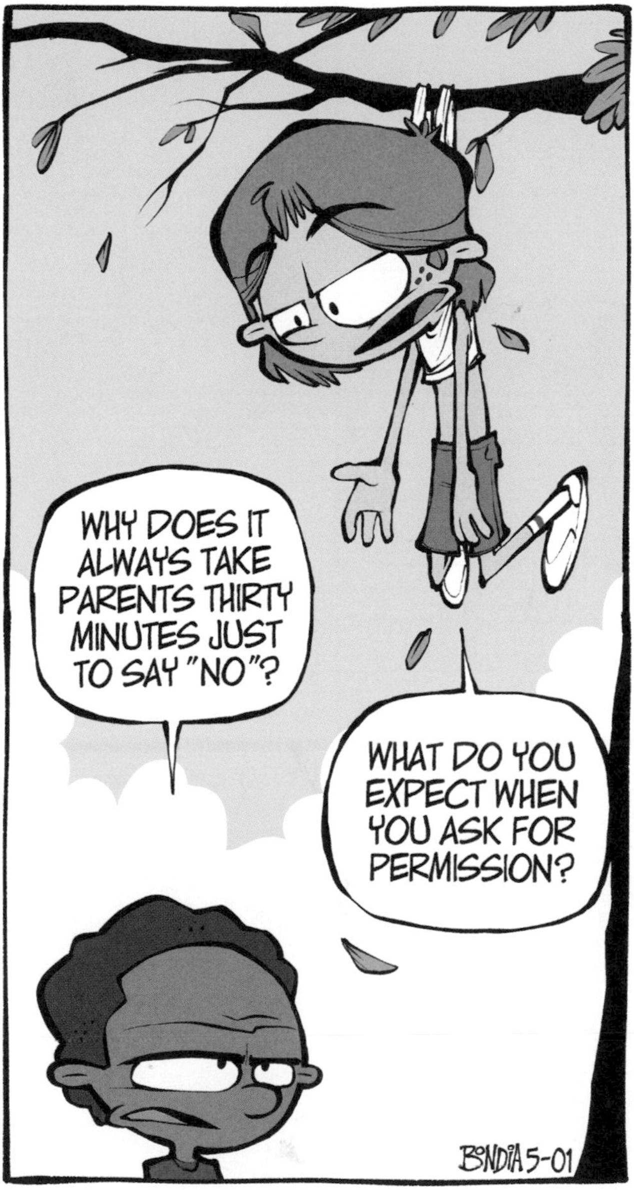
WHY DOES IT ALWAYS TAKE PARENTS THIRTY MINUTES JUST TO SAY "NO"?
WHAT DO YOU EXPECT WHEN YOU ASK FOR PERMISSION?
BONDIA 5-01

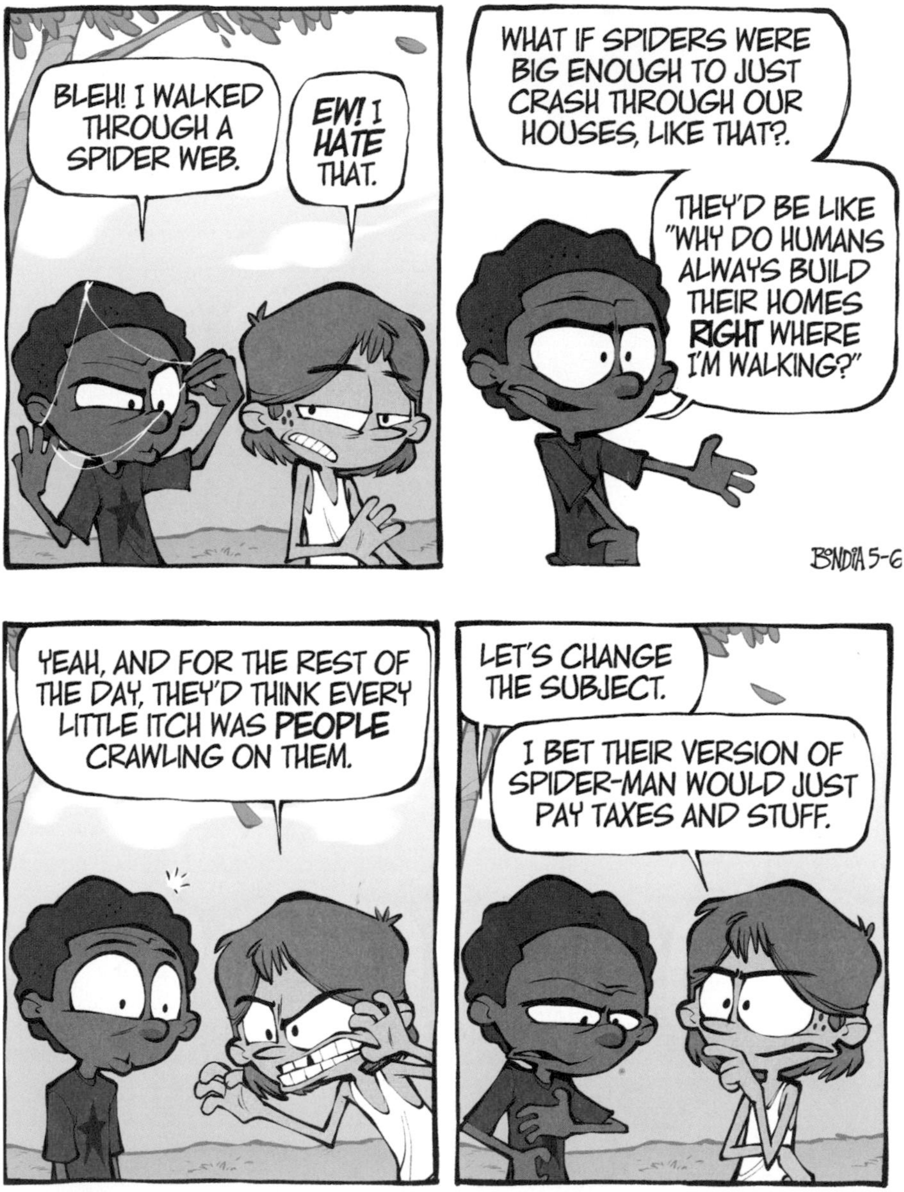
BLEH! I WALKED THROUGH A SPIDER WEB.
EW! I HATE THAT.
WHAT IF SPIDERS WERE BIG ENOUGH TO JUST CRASH THROUGH OUR HOUSES, LIKE THAT?.
THEY'D BE LIKE "WHY DO HUMANS ALWAYS BUILD THEIR HOMES RIGHT WHERE I'M WALKING?"
BONDIA 5-6
YEAH, AND FOR THE REST OF THE DAY, THEY'D THINK EVERY LITTLE ITCH WAS PEOPLE CRAWLING ON THEM.
LET'S CHANGE THE SUBJECT.
I BET THEIR VERSION OF SPIDER-MAN WOULD JUST PAY TAXES AND STUFF.

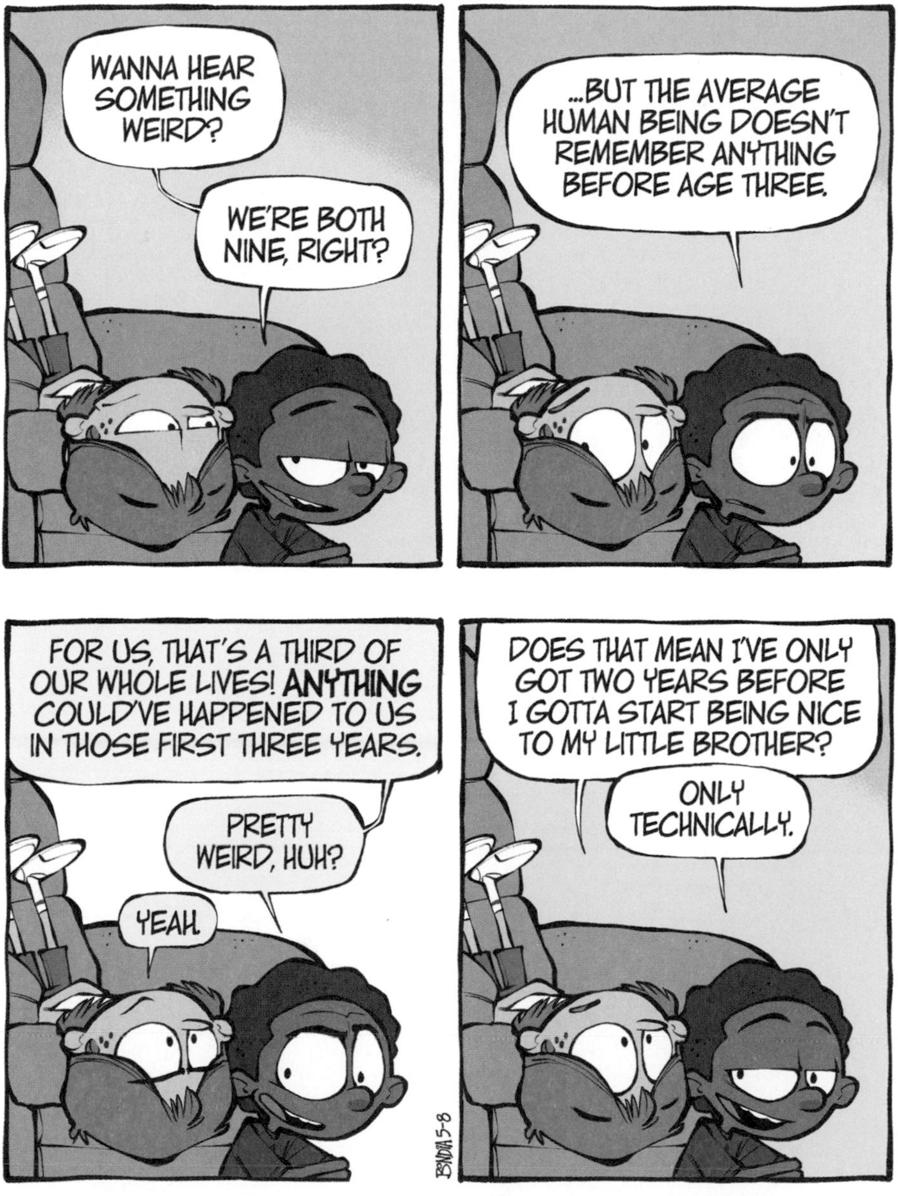
WANNA HEAR SOMETHING WEIRD?
WE'RE BOTH NINE, RIGHT?
...BUT THE AVERAGE HUMAN BEING DOESN'T REMEMBER ANYTHING BEFORE AGE THREE.
FOR US, THAT'S A THIRD OF OUR WHOLE LIVES! **ANYTHING** COULD'VE HAPPENED TO US IN THOSE FIRST THREE YEARS.
PRETTY WEIRD, HUH?
YEAH.
DOES THAT MEAN I'VE ONLY GOT TWO YEARS BEFORE I GOTTA START BEING NICE TO MY LITTLE BROTHER?
ONLY TECHNICALLY.

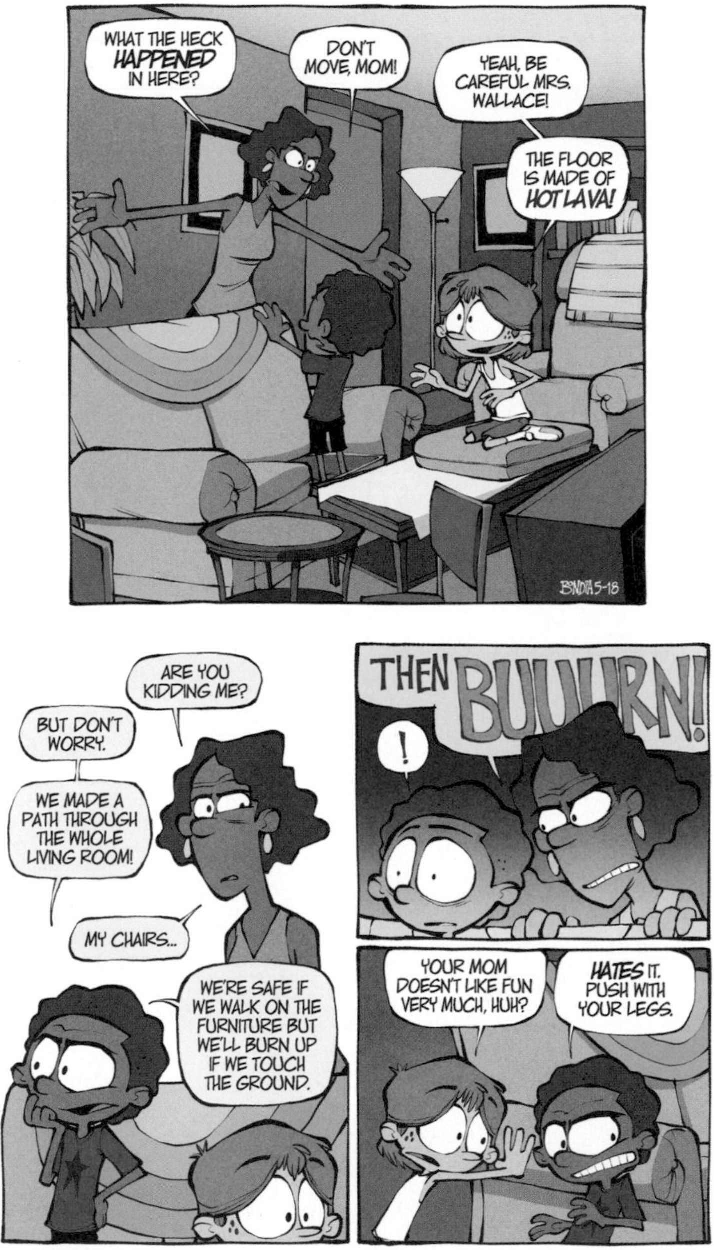
WHAT THE HECK HAPPENED IN HERE?
DON'T MOVE, MOM!
YEAH, BE CAREFUL MRS. WALLACE!
THE FLOOR IS MADE OF HOT LAVA!
BUT DON'T WORRY.
WE MADE A PATH THROUGH THE WHOLE LIVING ROOM!
ARE YOU KIDDING ME?
MY CHAIRS...
WE'RE SAFE IF WE WALK ON THE FURNITURE BUT WE'LL BURN UP IF WE TOUCH THE GROUND.
THEN BUUURN!
!
YOUR MOM DOESN'T LIKE FUN VERY MUCH, HUH?
HATES IT. PUSH WITH YOUR LEGS.

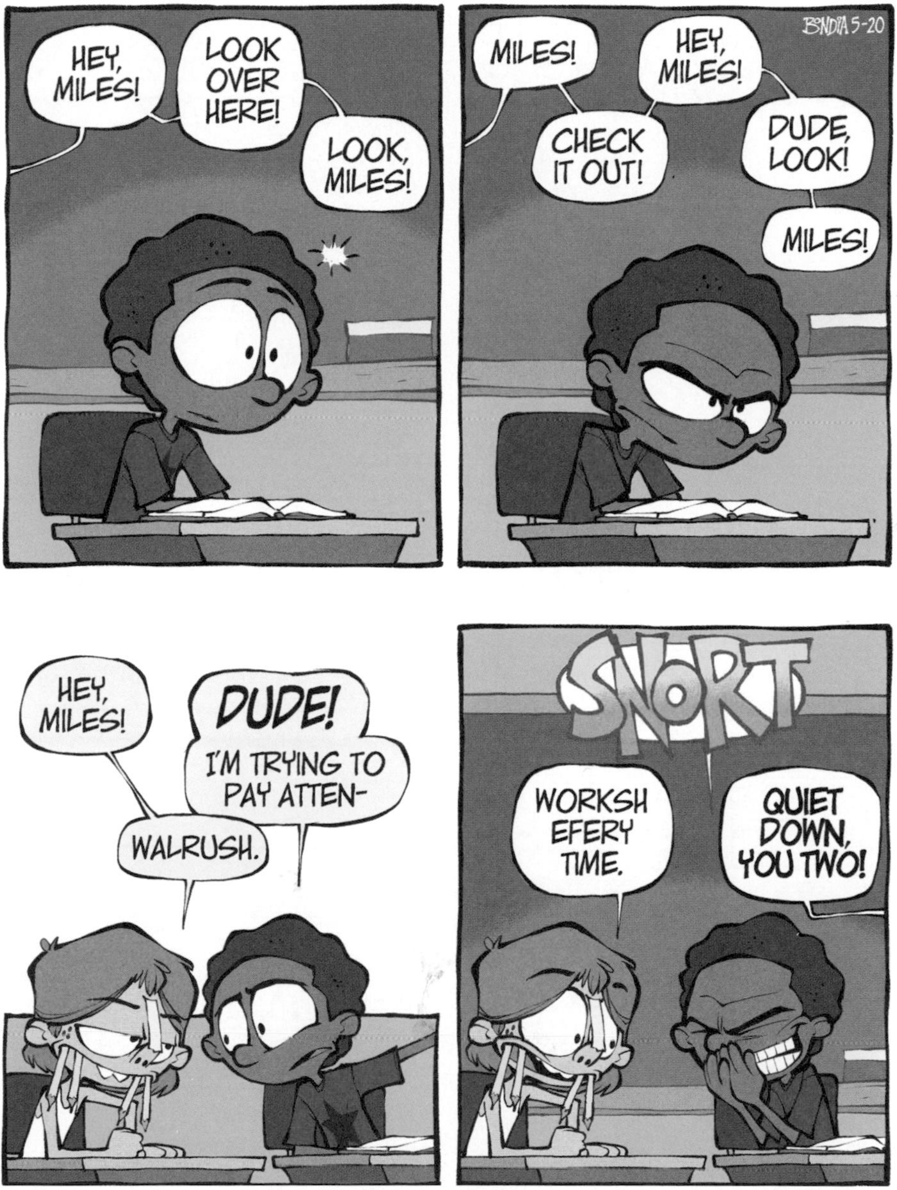

HEY, MILES!
LOOK OVER HERE!
LOOK, MILES!
BONDIA 5-20
MILES!
HEY, MILES!
CHECK IT OUT!
DUDE, LOOK!
MILES!
HEY, MILES!
DUDE! I'M TRYING TO PAY ATTEN-
WALRUSH.
SNORT
WORKSH EFERY TIME.
QUIET DOWN, YOU TWO!

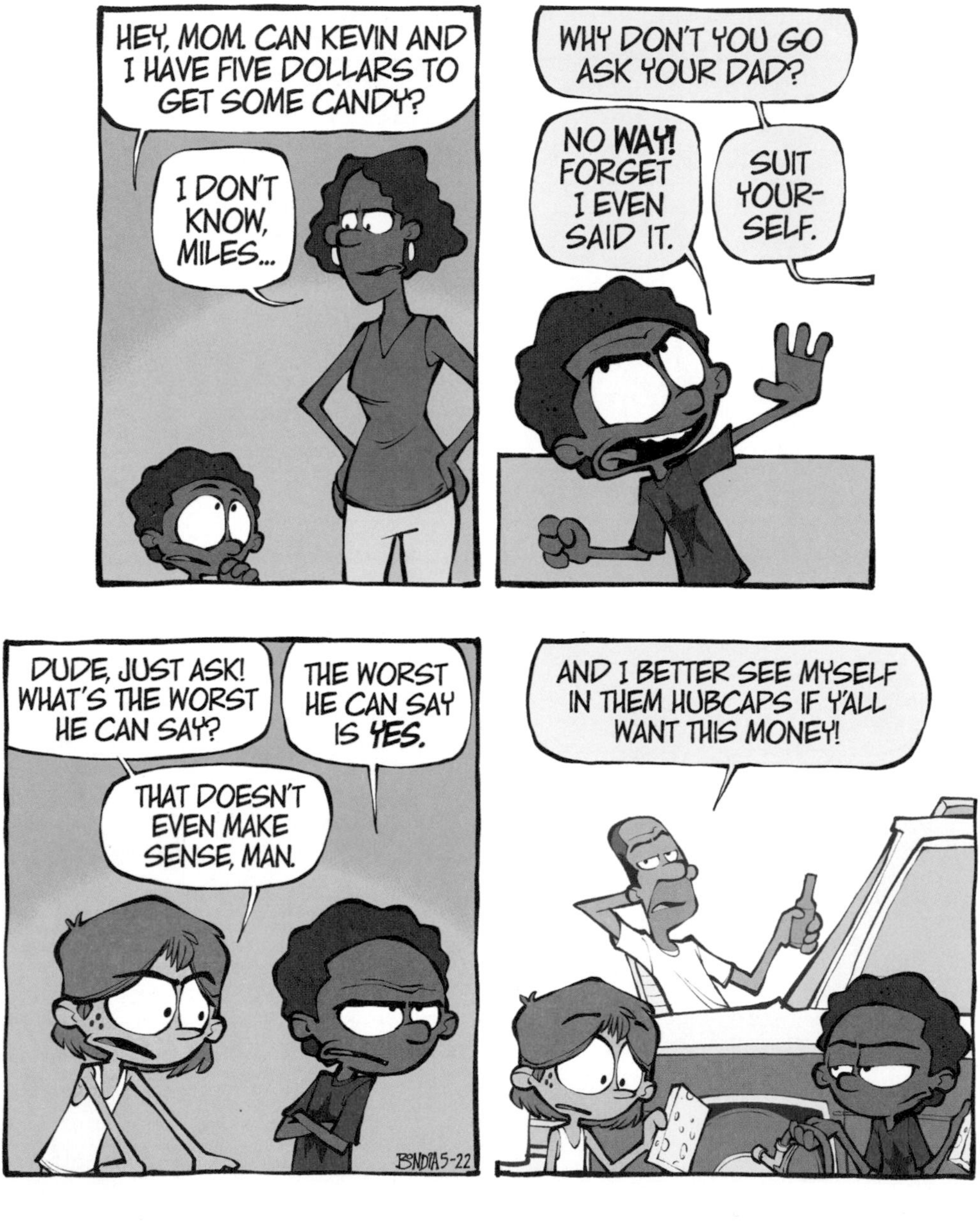
HEY, MOM. CAN KEVIN AND I HAVE FIVE DOLLARS TO GET SOME CANDY?
I DON'T KNOW, MILES...
WHY DON'T YOU GO ASK YOUR DAD?
NO WAY! FORGET I EVEN SAID IT.
SUIT YOURSELF.
DUDE, JUST ASK! WHAT'S THE WORST HE CAN SAY?
THAT DOESN'T EVEN MAKE SENSE, MAN.
THE WORST HE CAN SAY IS YES.
BONDIA 5-22
AND I BETTER SEE MYSELF IN THEM HUBCAPS IF Y'ALL WANT THIS MONEY!

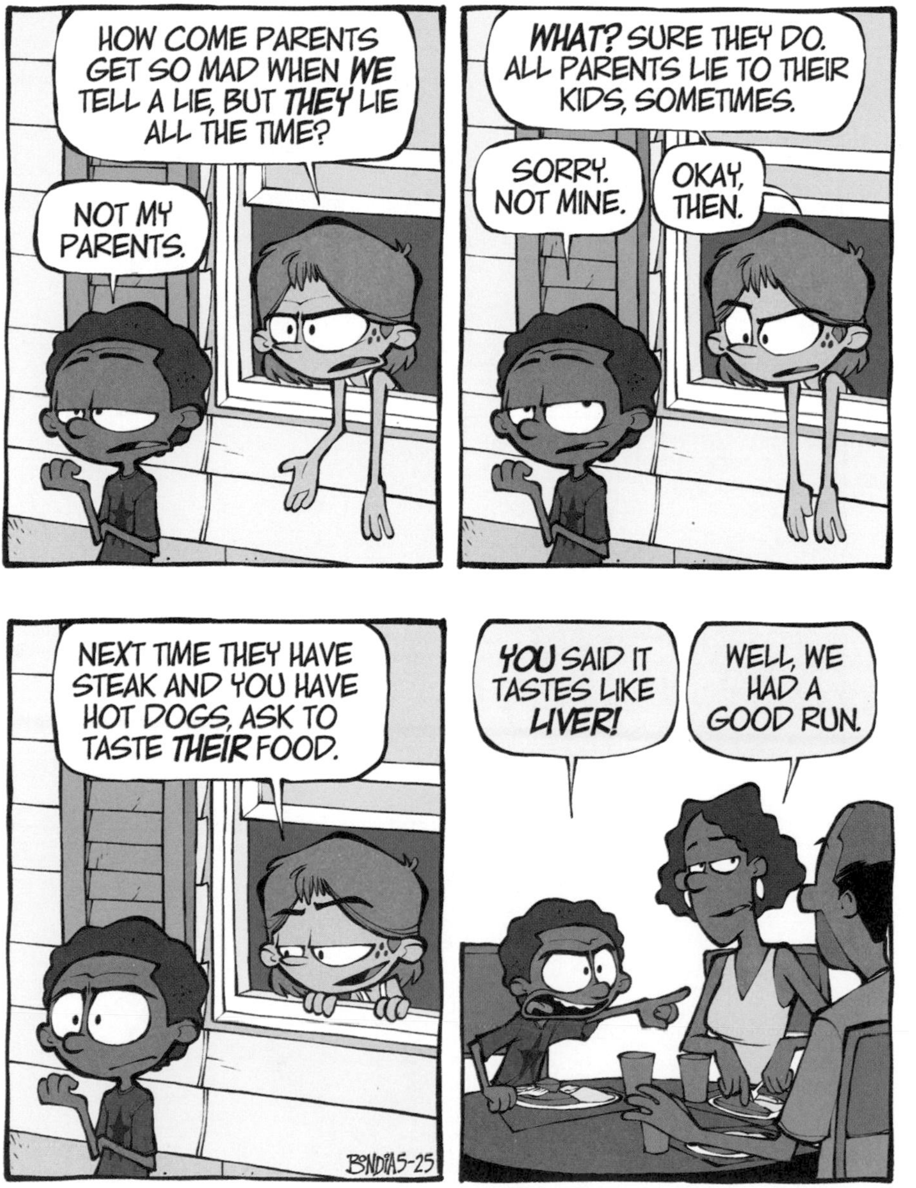
HOW COME PARENTS GET SO MAD WHEN WE TELL A LIE, BUT THEY LIE ALL THE TIME?
NOT MY PARENTS.
WHAT? SURE THEY DO. ALL PARENTS LIE TO THEIR KIDS, SOMETIMES.
SORRY. NOT MINE.
OKAY, THEN.
NEXT TIME THEY HAVE STEAK AND YOU HAVE HOT DOGS, ASK TO TASTE THEIR FOOD.
BONDIA 5-25
YOU SAID IT TASTES LIKE LIVER!
WELL, WE HAD A GOOD RUN.

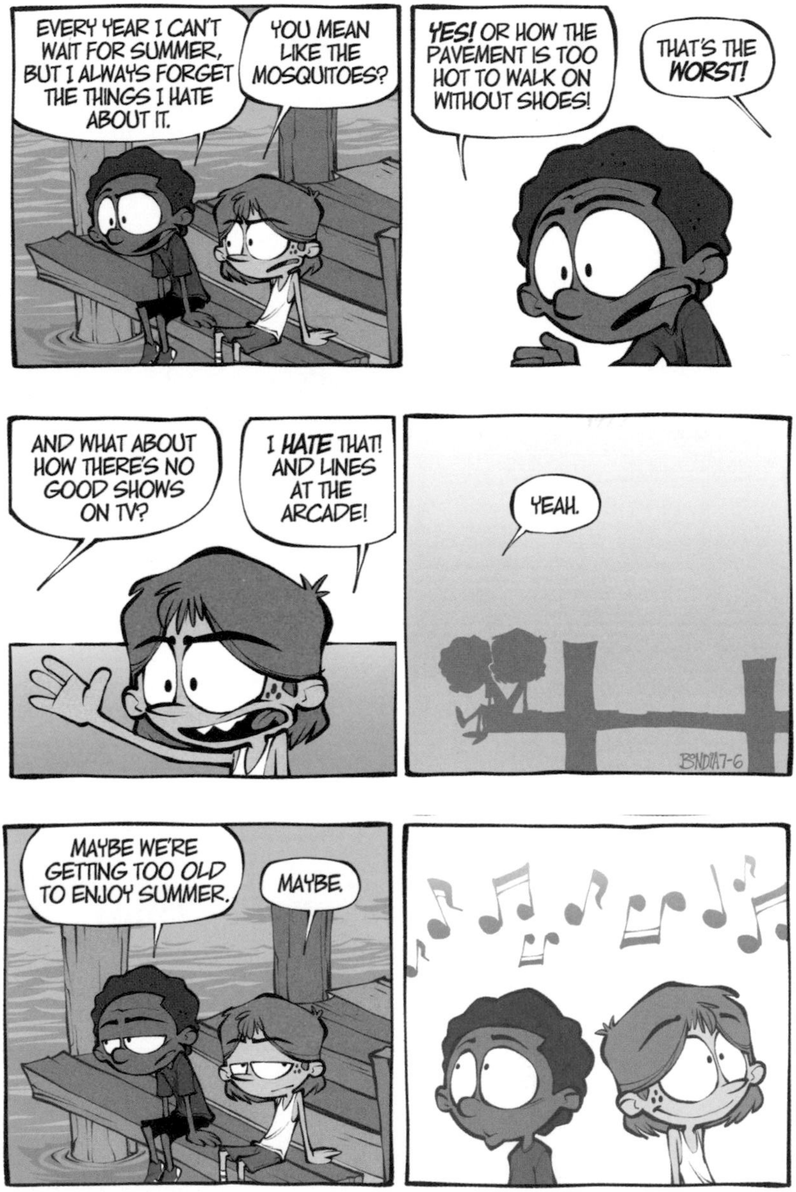
EVERY YEAR I CAN'T WAIT FOR SUMMER, BUT I ALWAYS FORGET THE THINGS I HATE ABOUT IT.
YOU MEAN LIKE THE MOSQUITOES?
YES! OR HOW THE PAVEMENT IS TOO HOT TO WALK ON WITHOUT SHOES!
THAT'S THE WORST!
AND WHAT ABOUT HOW THERE'S NO GOOD SHOWS ON TV?
I HATE THAT! AND LINES AT THE ARCADE!
YEAH.
BSNDRA7-6
MAYBE WE'RE GETTING TOO OLD TO ENJOY SUMMER.
MAYBE.

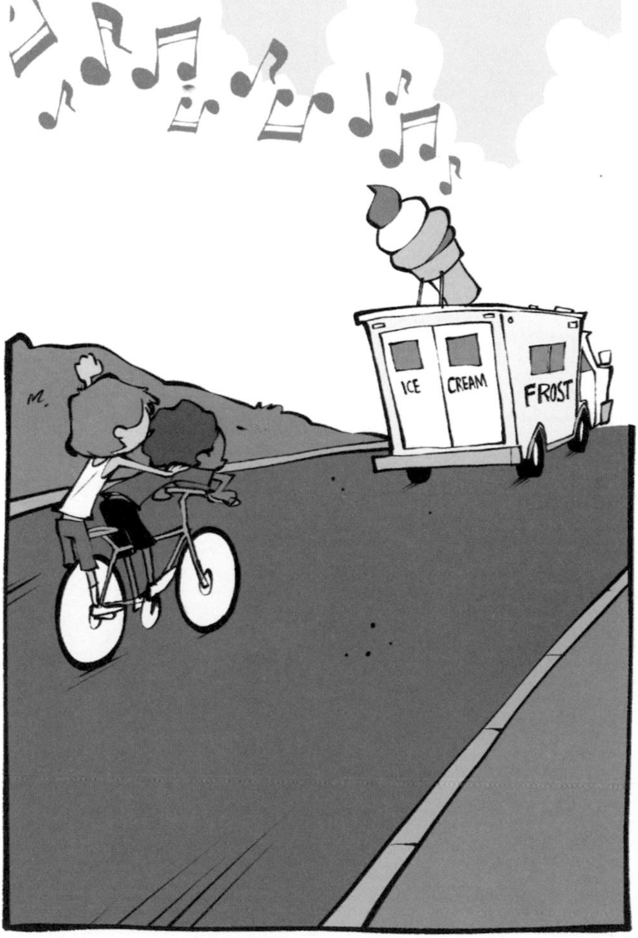
ICE
CREAM
FROST

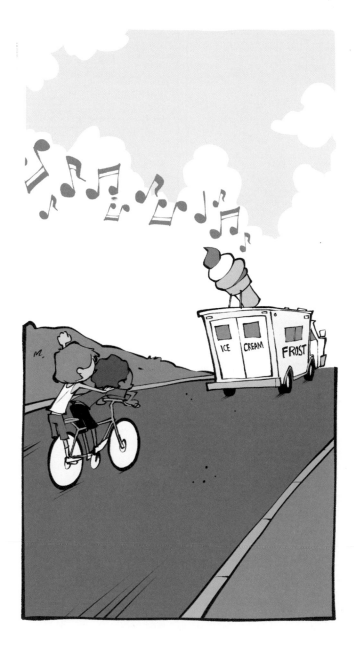

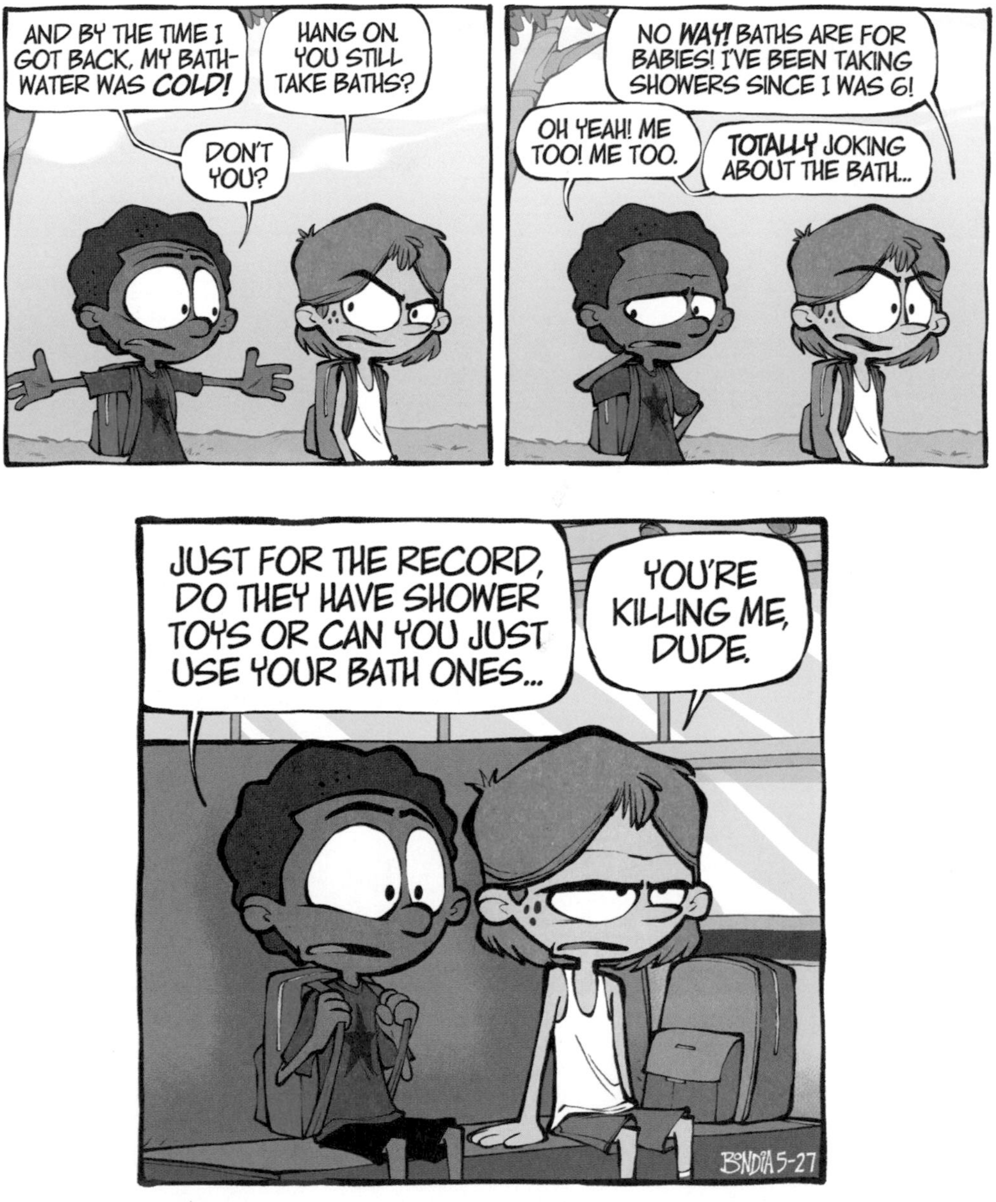
AND BY THE TIME I GOT BACK, MY BATH-WATER WAS COLD!
HANG ON. YOU STILL TAKE BATHS?
DON'T YOU?
NO WAY! BATHS ARE FOR BABIES! I'VE BEEN TAKING SHOWERS SINCE I WAS 6!
OH YEAH! ME TOO! ME TOO.
TOTALLY JOKING ABOUT THE BATH...
JUST FOR THE RECORD, DO THEY HAVE SHOWER TOYS OR CAN YOU JUST USE YOUR BATH ONES...
YOU'RE KILLING ME, DUDE.
BONDIA 5-27

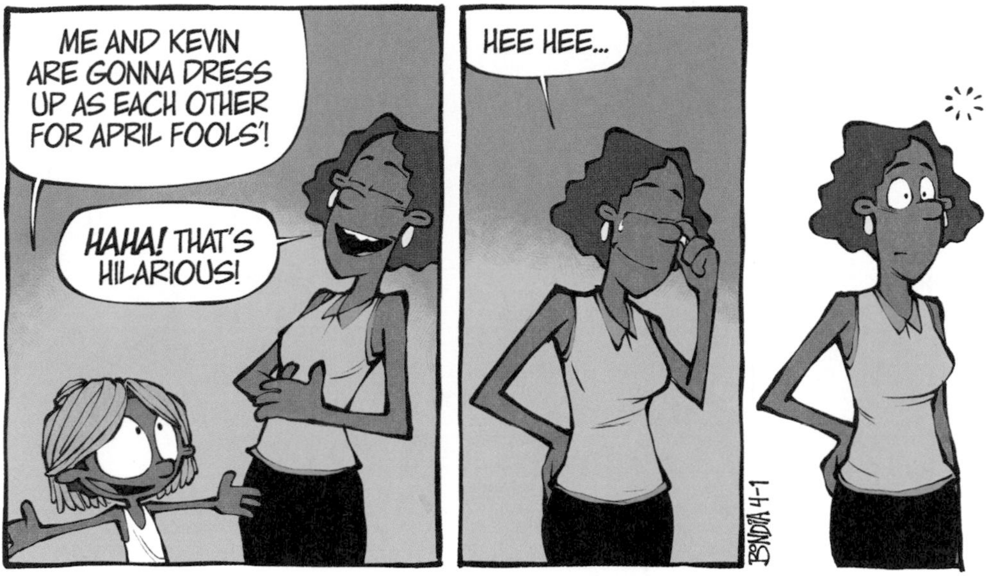
ME AND KEVIN ARE GONNA DRESS UP AS EACH OTHER FOR APRIL FOOLS'!
HAHA! THAT'S HILARIOUS!
HEE HEE...
BONDIA 4-1

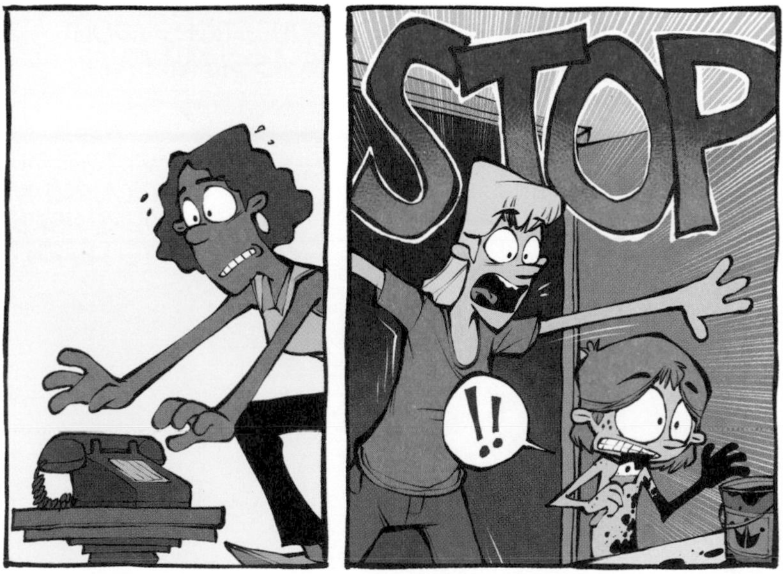
STOP
!!

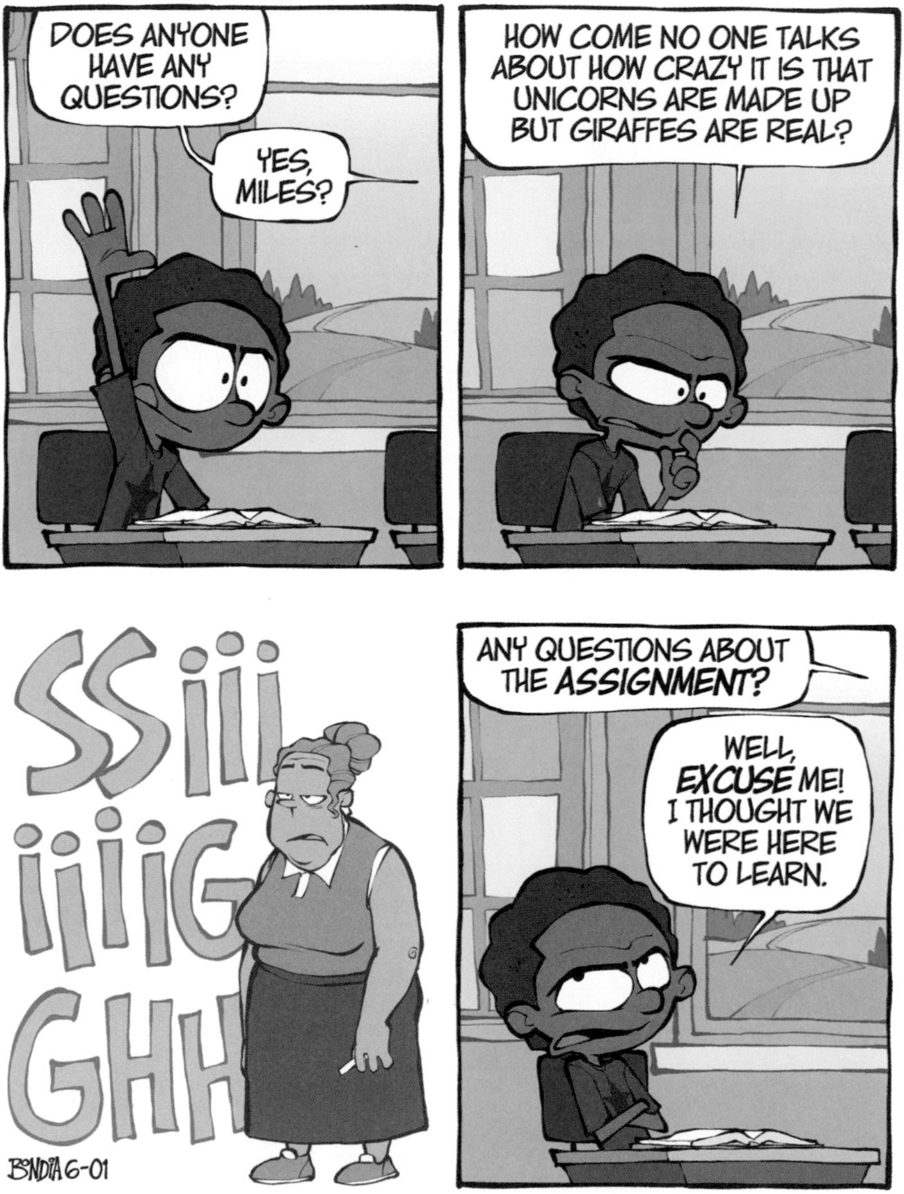
DOES ANYONE HAVE ANY QUESTIONS?
YES, MILES?
HOW COME NO ONE TALKS ABOUT HOW CRAZY IT IS THAT UNICORNS ARE MADE UP BUT GIRAFFES ARE REAL?
SSiii iiiiG GHH
BONDIA 6-01
ANY QUESTIONS ABOUT THE ***ASSIGNMENT***?
WELL, ***EXCUSE*** ME! I THOUGHT WE WERE HERE TO LEARN.

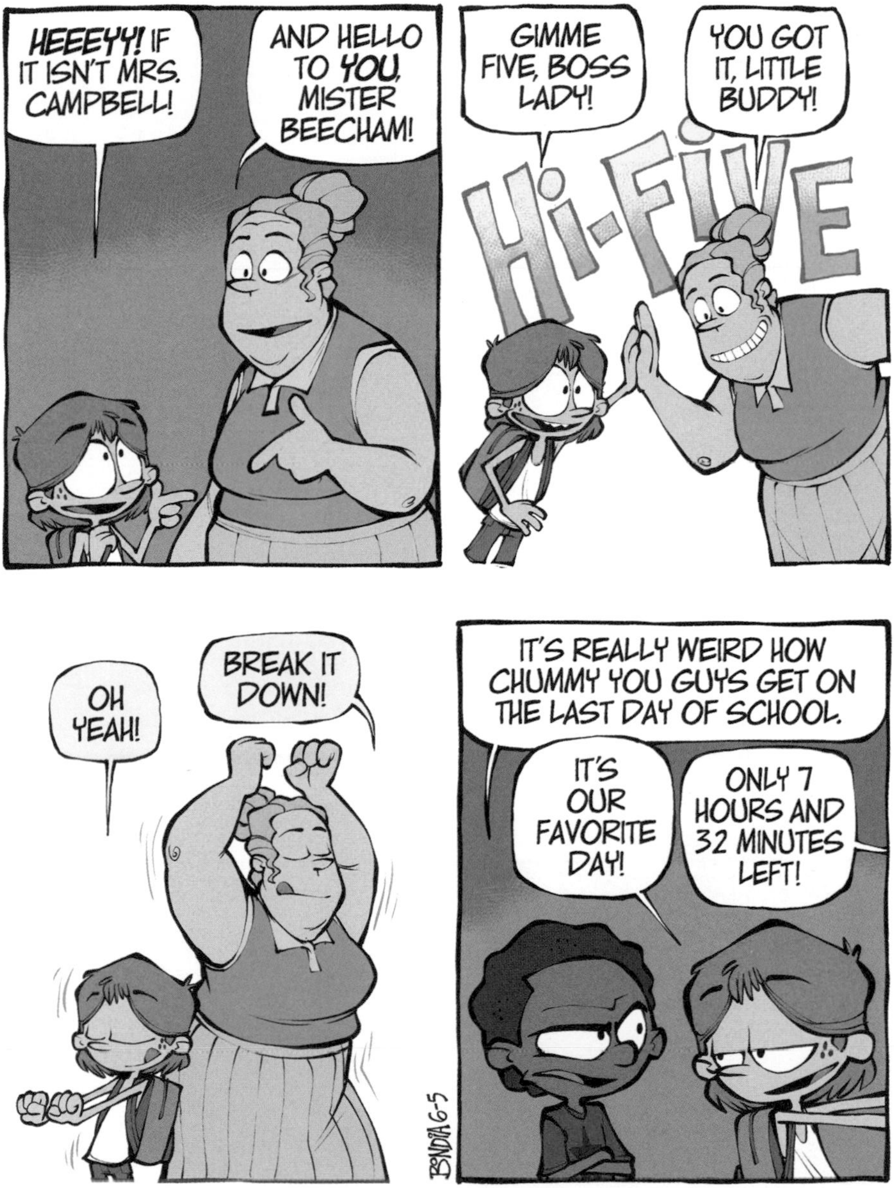
HEEEYY! IF IT ISN'T MRS. CAMPBELL!
AND HELLO TO YOU, MISTER BEECHAM!
GIMME FIVE, BOSS LADY!
YOU GOT IT, LITTLE BUDDY!
HI-FIVE
OH YEAH!
BREAK IT DOWN!
IT'S REALLY WEIRD HOW CHUMMY YOU GUYS GET ON THE LAST DAY OF SCHOOL.
IT'S OUR FAVORITE DAY!
ONLY 7 HOURS AND 32 MINUTES LEFT!

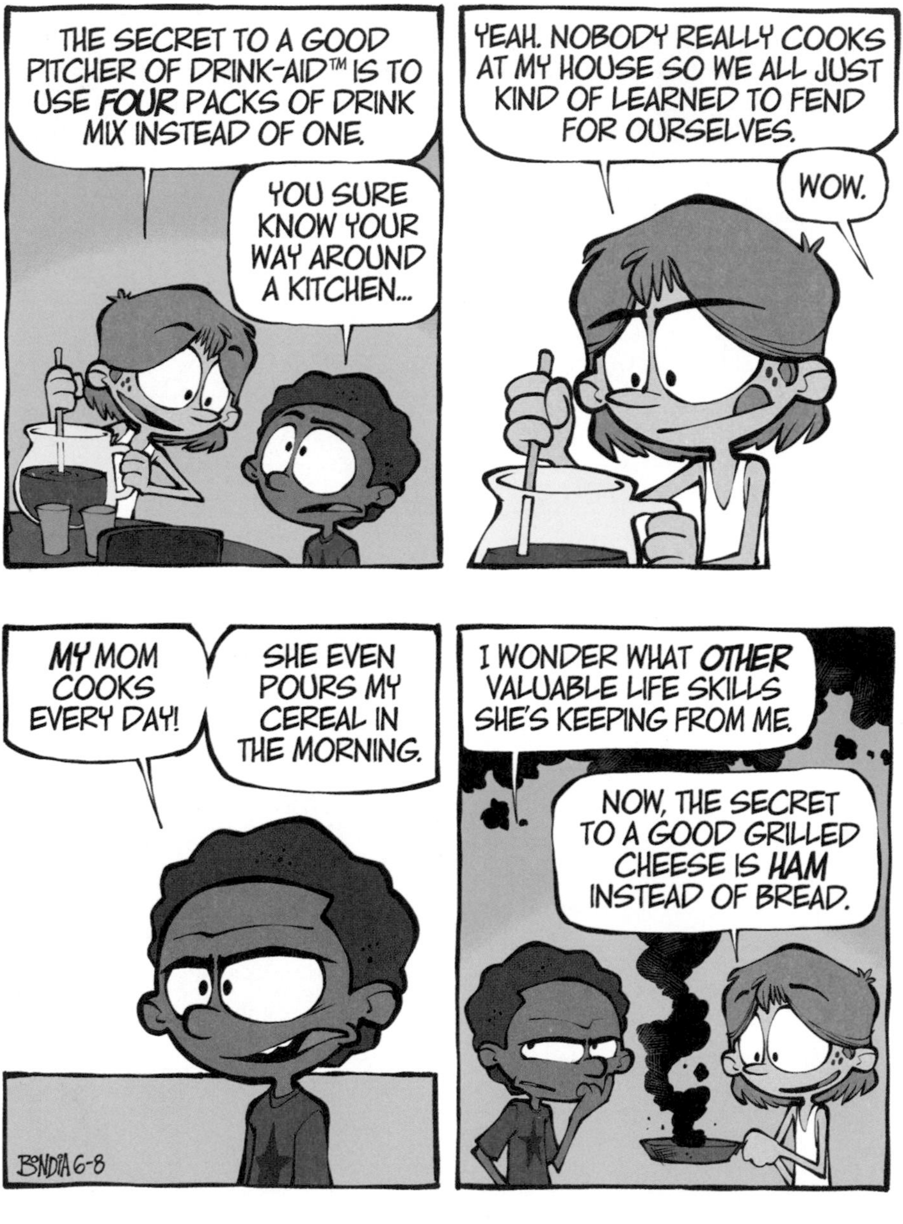
THE SECRET TO A GOOD PITCHER OF DRINK-AID™ IS TO USE FOUR PACKS OF DRINK MIX INSTEAD OF ONE.
YOU SURE KNOW YOUR WAY AROUND A KITCHEN...
YEAH. NOBODY REALLY COOKS AT MY HOUSE SO WE ALL JUST KIND OF LEARNED TO FEND FOR OURSELVES.
WOW.
MY MOM COOKS EVERY DAY!
SHE EVEN POURS MY CEREAL IN THE MORNING.
BONDIA 6-8
I WONDER WHAT OTHER VALUABLE LIFE SKILLS SHE'S KEEPING FROM ME.
NOW, THE SECRET TO A GOOD GRILLED CHEESE IS HAM INSTEAD OF BREAD.

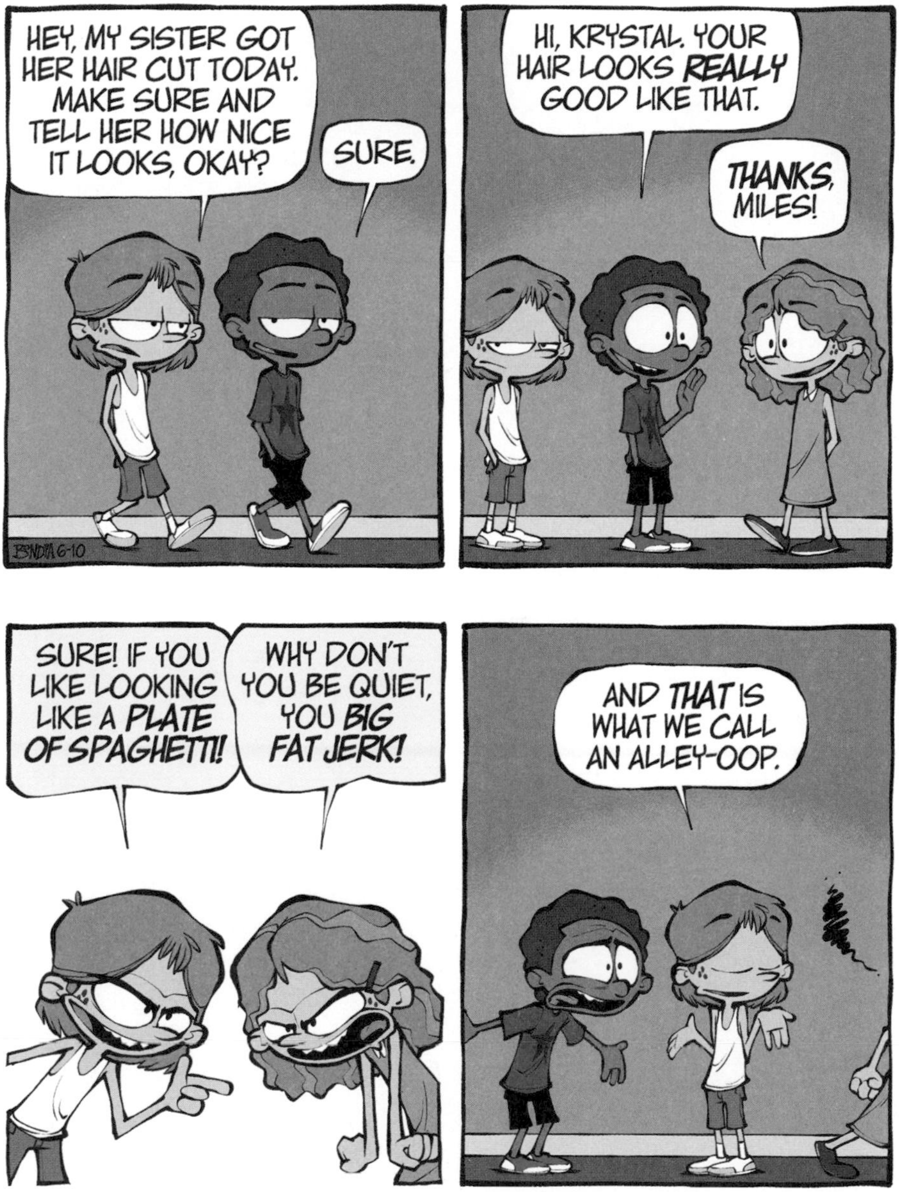
HEY, MY SISTER GOT HER HAIR CUT TODAY. MAKE SURE AND TELL HER HOW NICE IT LOOKS, OKAY?
SURE.
HI, KRYSTAL. YOUR HAIR LOOKS REALLY GOOD LIKE THAT.
THANKS, MILES!
SURE! IF YOU LIKE LOOKING LIKE A PLATE OF SPAGHETTI!
WHY DON'T YOU BE QUIET, YOU BIG FAT JERK!
AND THAT IS WHAT WE CALL AN ALLEY-OOP.

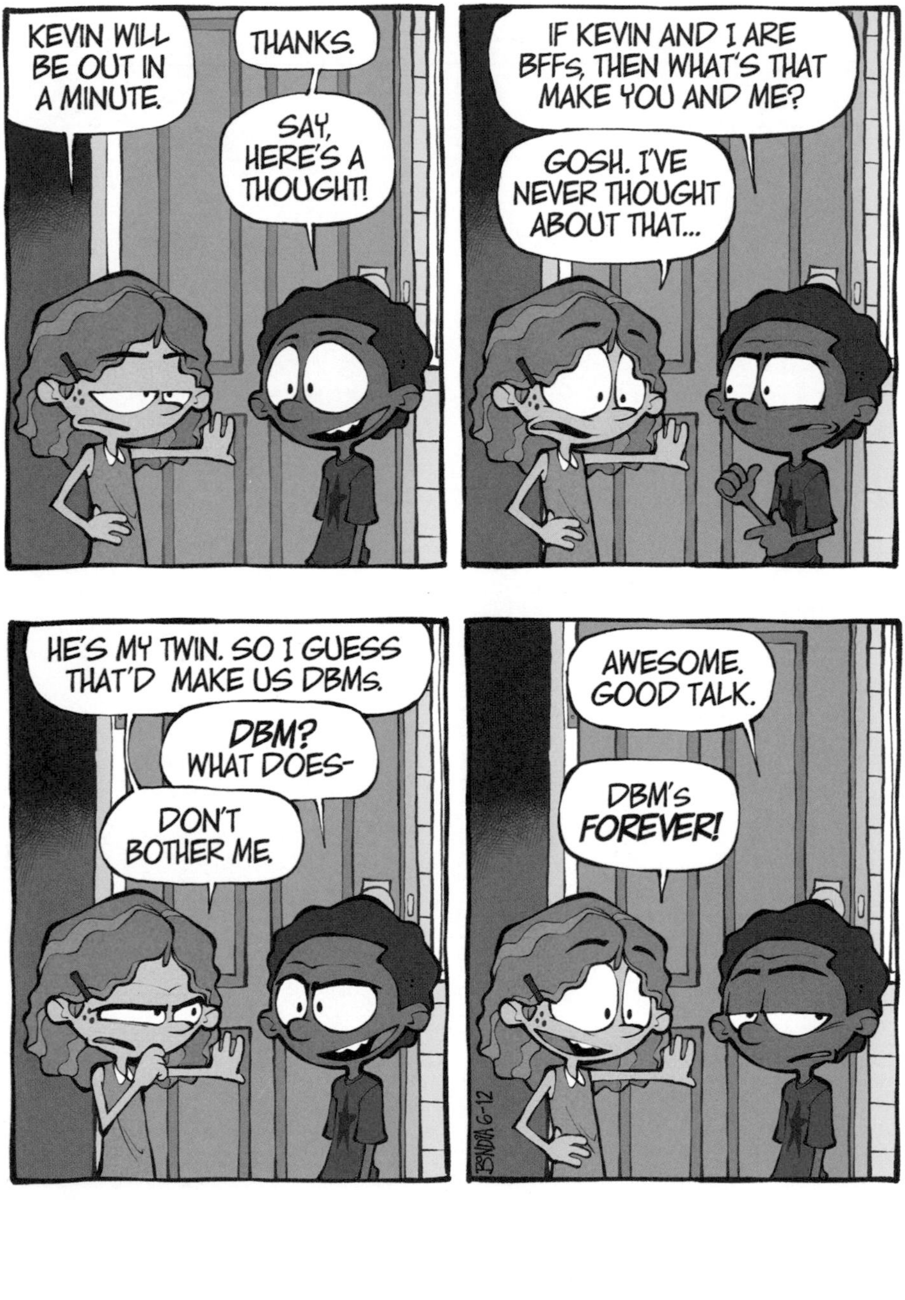
KEVIN WILL BE OUT IN A MINUTE.
THANKS.
SAY, HERE'S A THOUGHT!
IF KEVIN AND I ARE BFFs, THEN WHAT'S THAT MAKE YOU AND ME?
GOSH. I'VE NEVER THOUGHT ABOUT THAT...
HE'S MY TWIN. SO I GUESS THAT'D MAKE US DBMs.
DBM? WHAT DOES-
DON'T BOTHER ME.
AWESOME. GOOD TALK.
DBM's FOREVER!
BINDIA 6-12

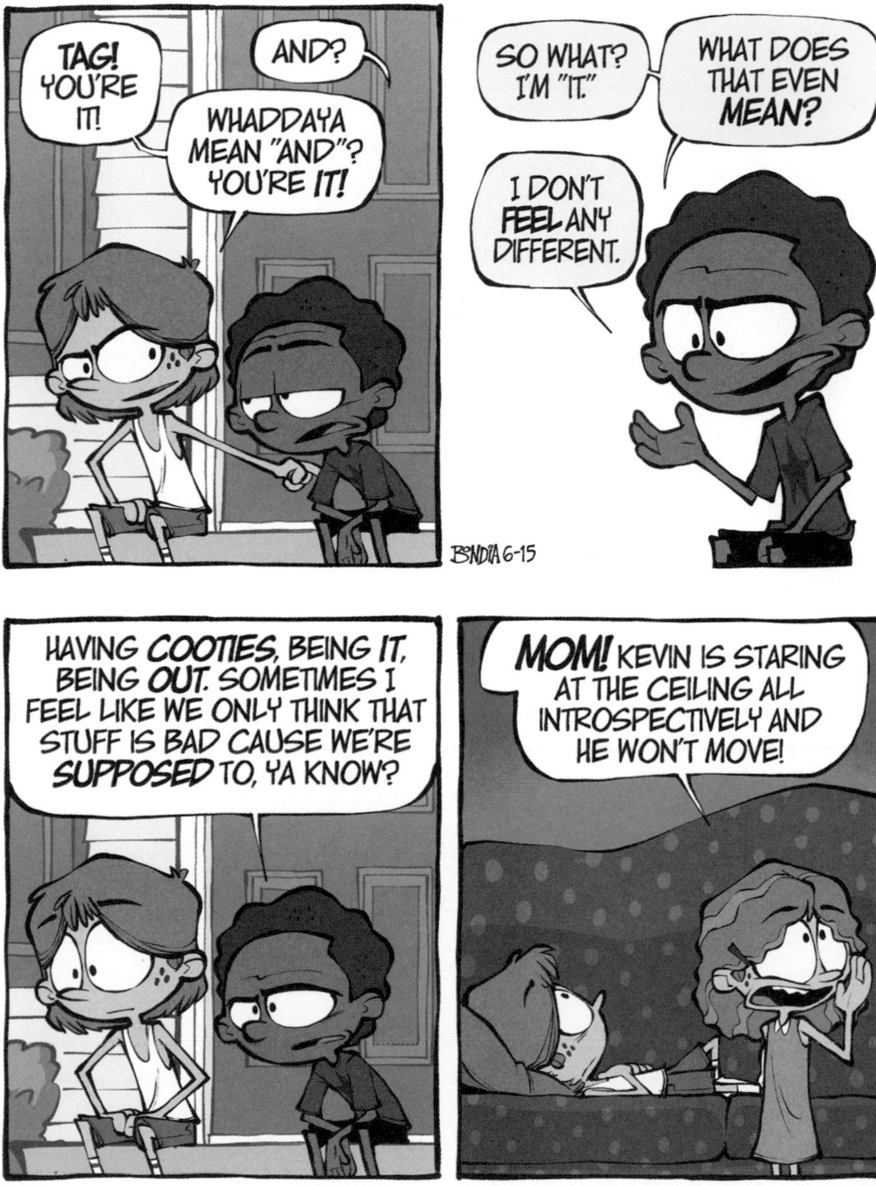
TAG! YOU'RE IT!
AND?
WHADDAYA MEAN "AND"? YOU'RE IT!
SO WHAT? I'M "IT."
WHAT DOES THAT EVEN MEAN?
I DON'T FEEL ANY DIFFERENT.
BONDIA 6-15
HAVING COOTIES, BEING IT, BEING OUT. SOMETIMES I FEEL LIKE WE ONLY THINK THAT STUFF IS BAD CAUSE WE'RE SUPPOSED TO, YA KNOW?
MOM! KEVIN IS STARING AT THE CEILING ALL INTROSPECTIVELY AND HE WON'T MOVE!

BONDIA 6-19

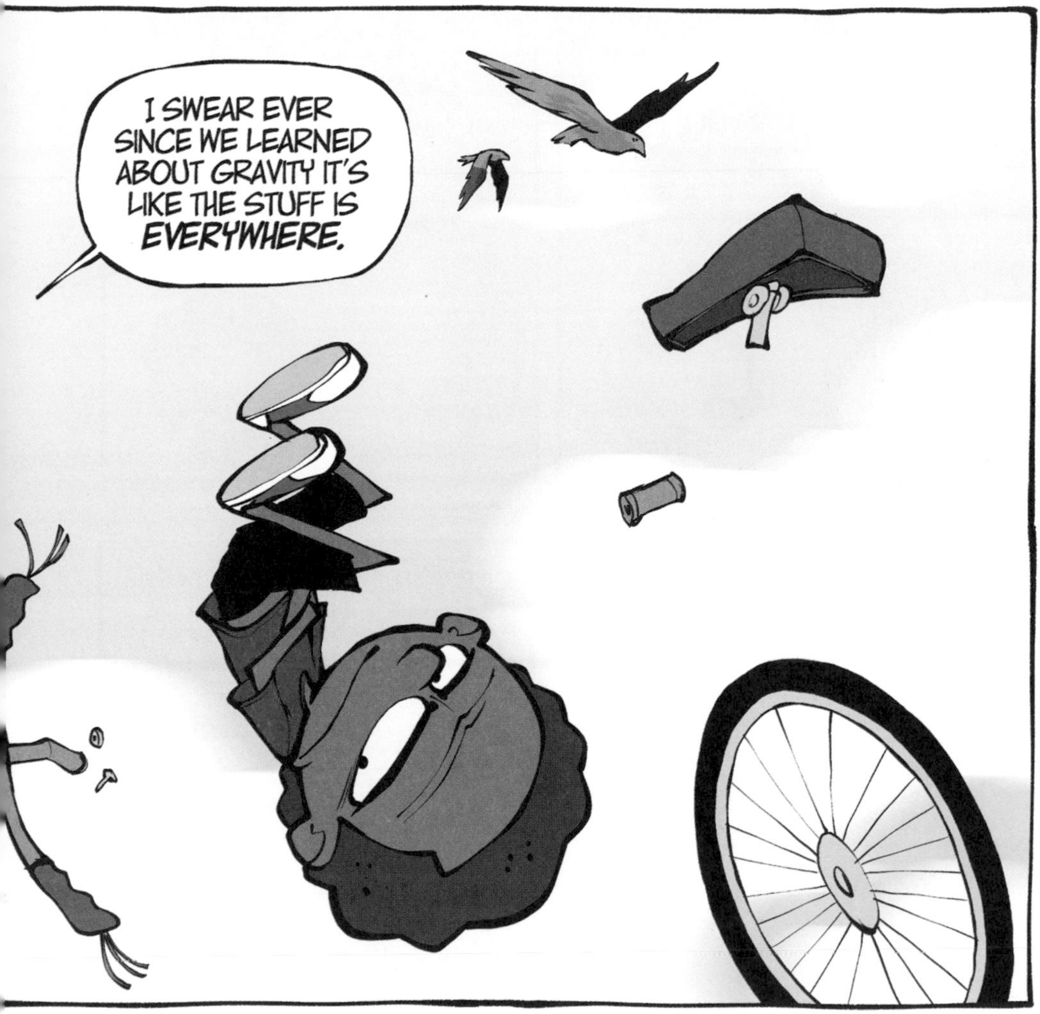
I SWEAR EVER SINCE WE LEARNED ABOUT GRAVITY IT'S LIKE THE STUFF IS *EVERYWHERE.*

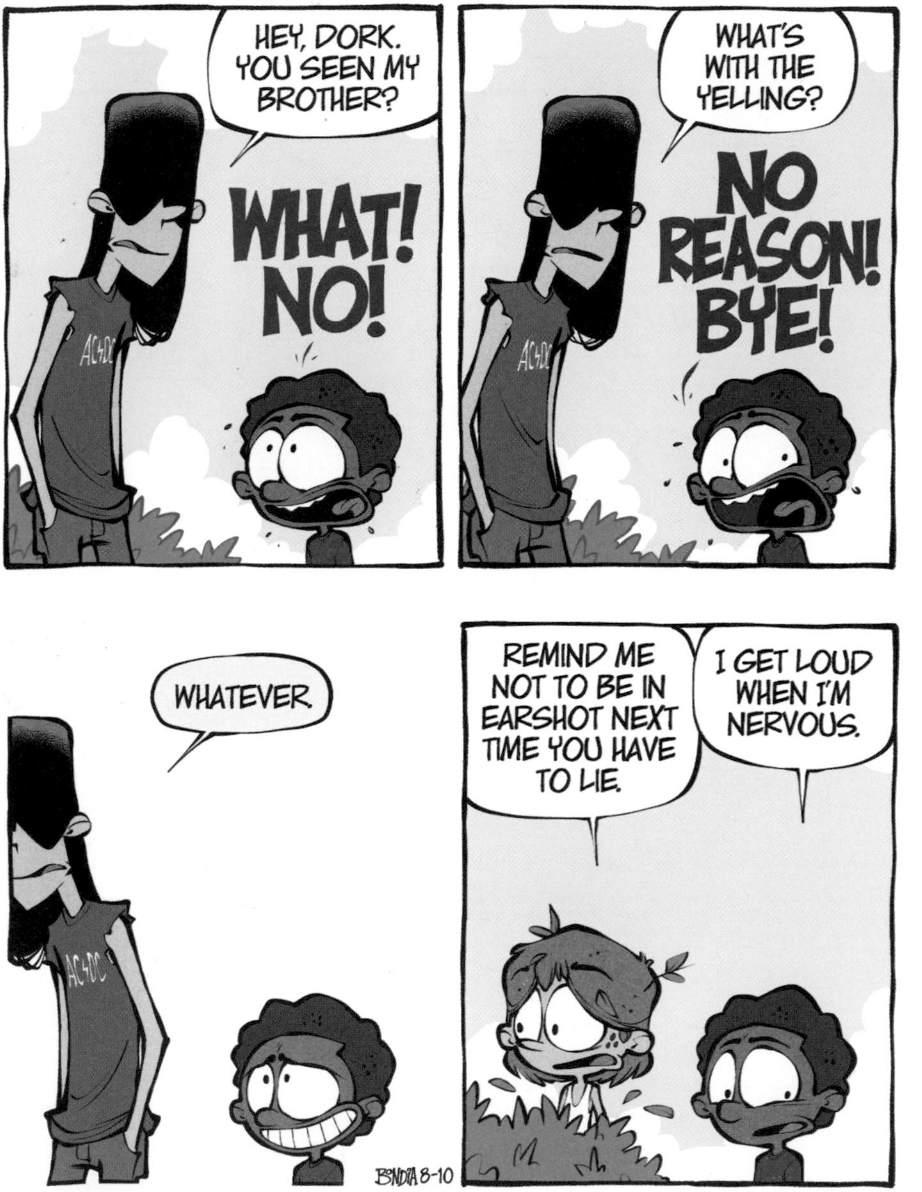
HEY, DORK. YOU SEEN MY BROTHER?
WHAT! NO!
WHAT'S WITH THE YELLING?
NO REASON! BYE!
WHATEVER.
REMIND ME NOT TO BE IN EARSHOT NEXT TIME YOU HAVE TO LIE.
I GET LOUD WHEN I'M NERVOUS.

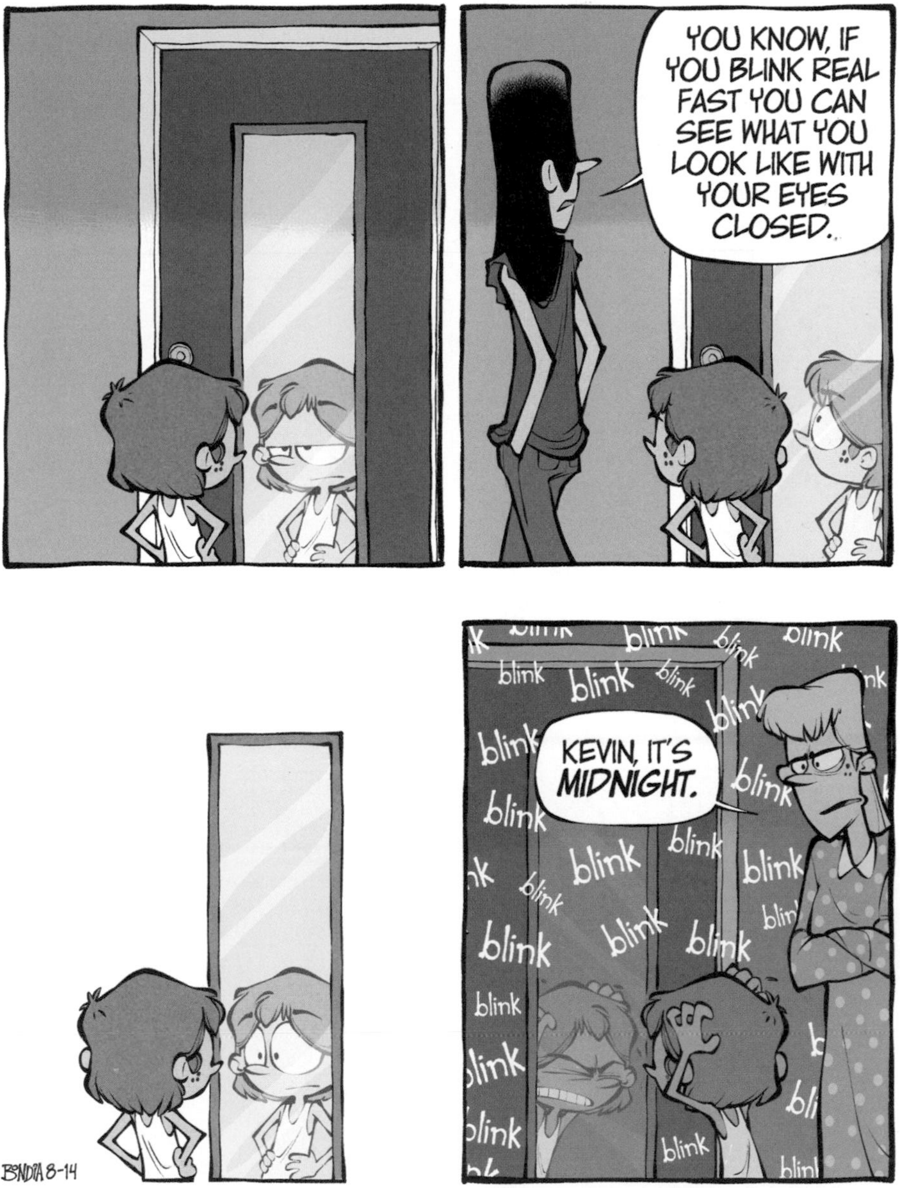
YOU KNOW, IF YOU BLINK REAL FAST YOU CAN SEE WHAT YOU LOOK LIKE WITH YOUR EYES CLOSED.
KEVIN, IT'S **MIDNIGHT.**
blink

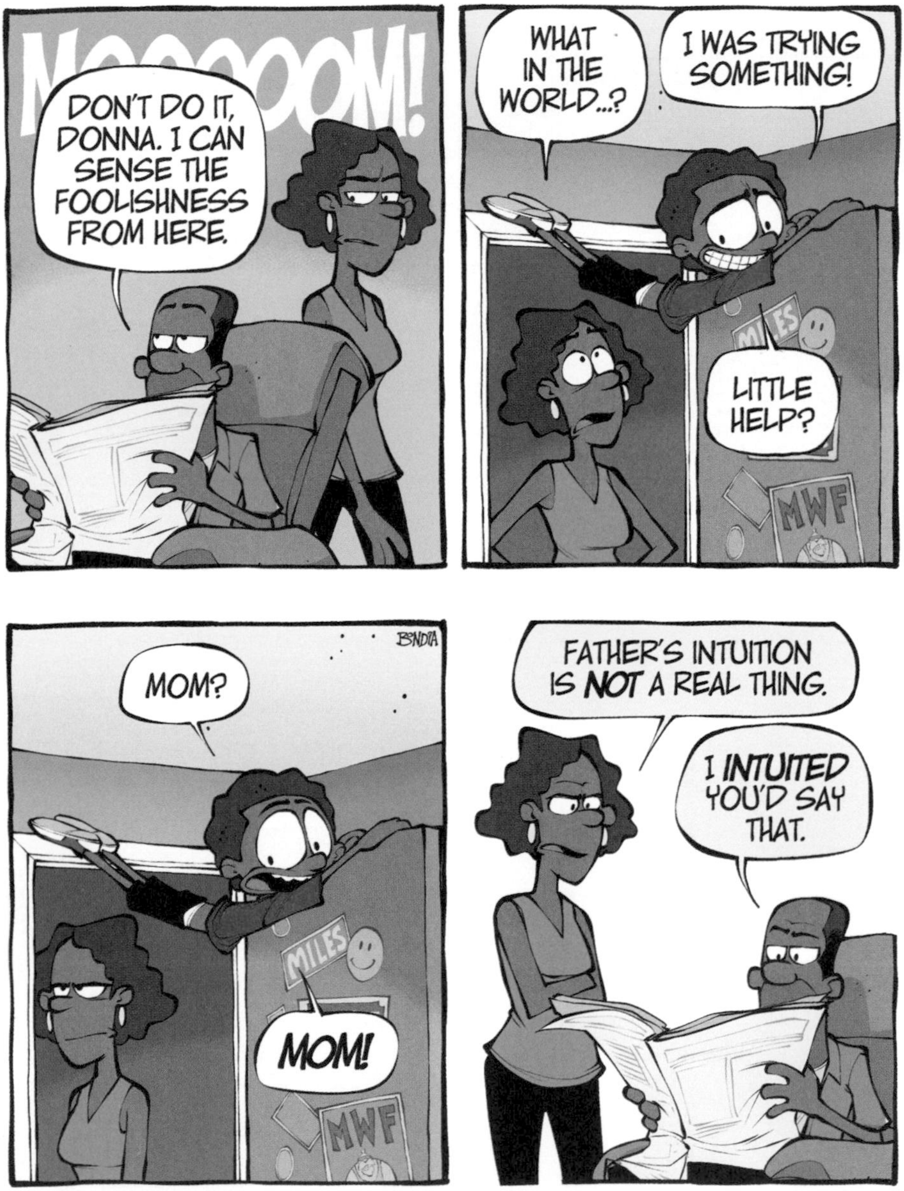
DON'T DO IT, DONNA. I CAN SENSE THE FOOLISHNESS FROM HERE.
WHAT IN THE WORLD...?
I WAS TRYING SOMETHING!
LITTLE HELP?
MILES
MWF
MOM?
MOM!
MILES
MWF
FATHER'S INTUITION IS **NOT** A REAL THING.
I **INTUITED** YOU'D SAY THAT.

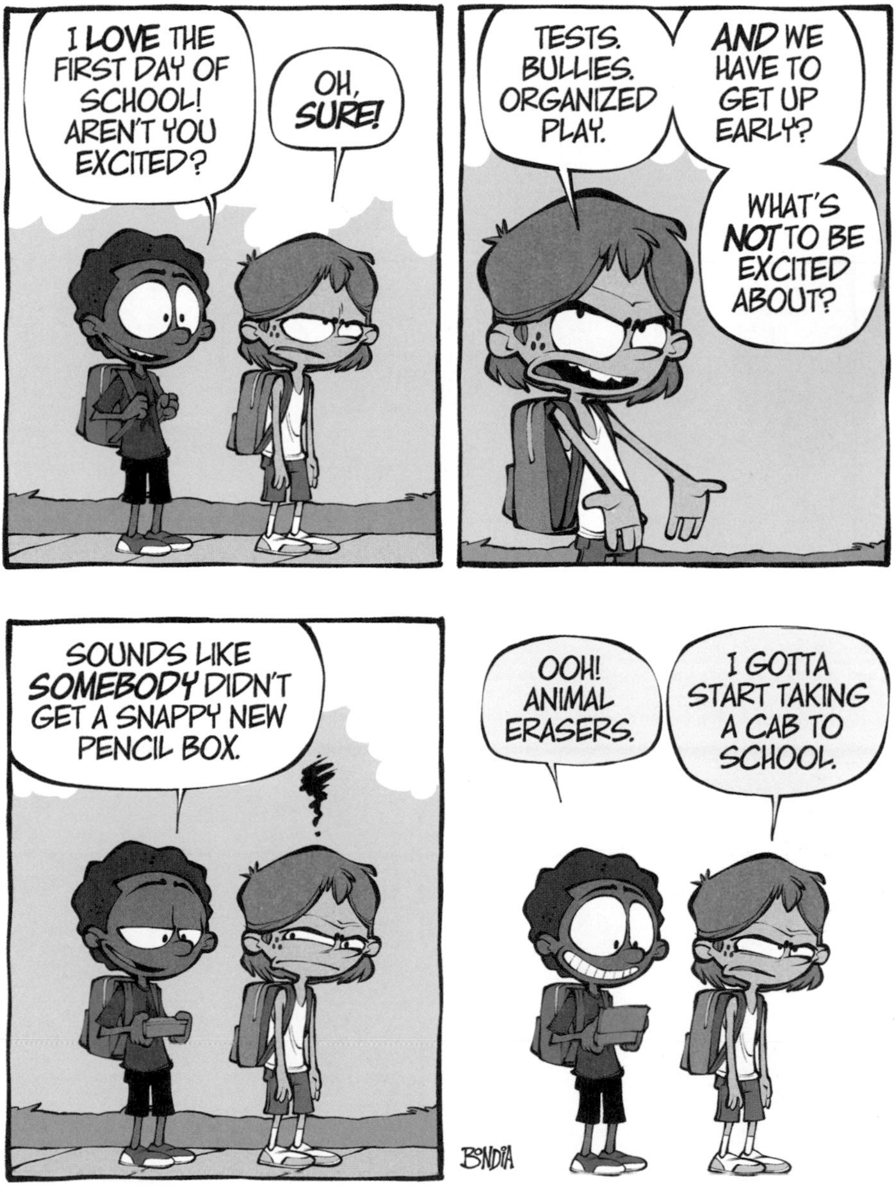
I LOVE THE FIRST DAY OF SCHOOL! AREN'T YOU EXCITED?
OH, SURE!
TESTS. BULLIES. ORGANIZED PLAY.
AND WE HAVE TO GET UP EARLY?
WHAT'S NOT TO BE EXCITED ABOUT?
SOUNDS LIKE SOMEBODY DIDN'T GET A SNAPPY NEW PENCIL BOX.
OOH! ANIMAL ERASERS.
I GOTTA START TAKING A CAB TO SCHOOL.
BONDIA

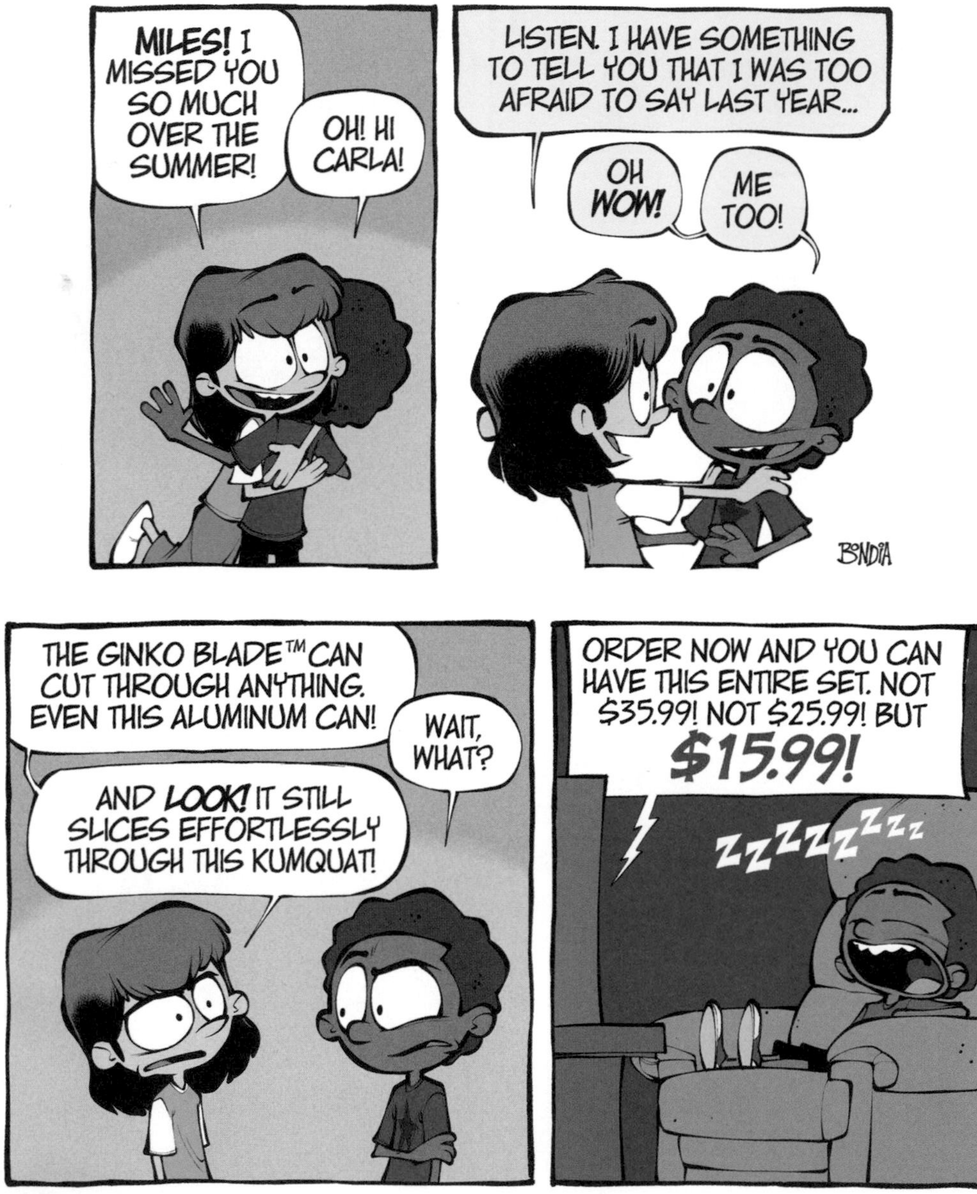
MILES! I MISSED YOU SO MUCH OVER THE SUMMER!
OH! HI CARLA!
LISTEN. I HAVE SOMETHING TO TELL YOU THAT I WAS TOO AFRAID TO SAY LAST YEAR...
OH WOW!
ME TOO!
BONDIA
THE GINKO BLADE™ CAN CUT THROUGH ANYTHING. EVEN THIS ALUMINUM CAN!
AND LOOK! IT STILL SLICES EFFORTLESSLY THROUGH THIS KUMQUAT!
WAIT, WHAT?
ORDER NOW AND YOU CAN HAVE THIS ENTIRE SET. NOT $35.99! NOT $25.99! BUT $15.99!
ZZZZZZZZZ

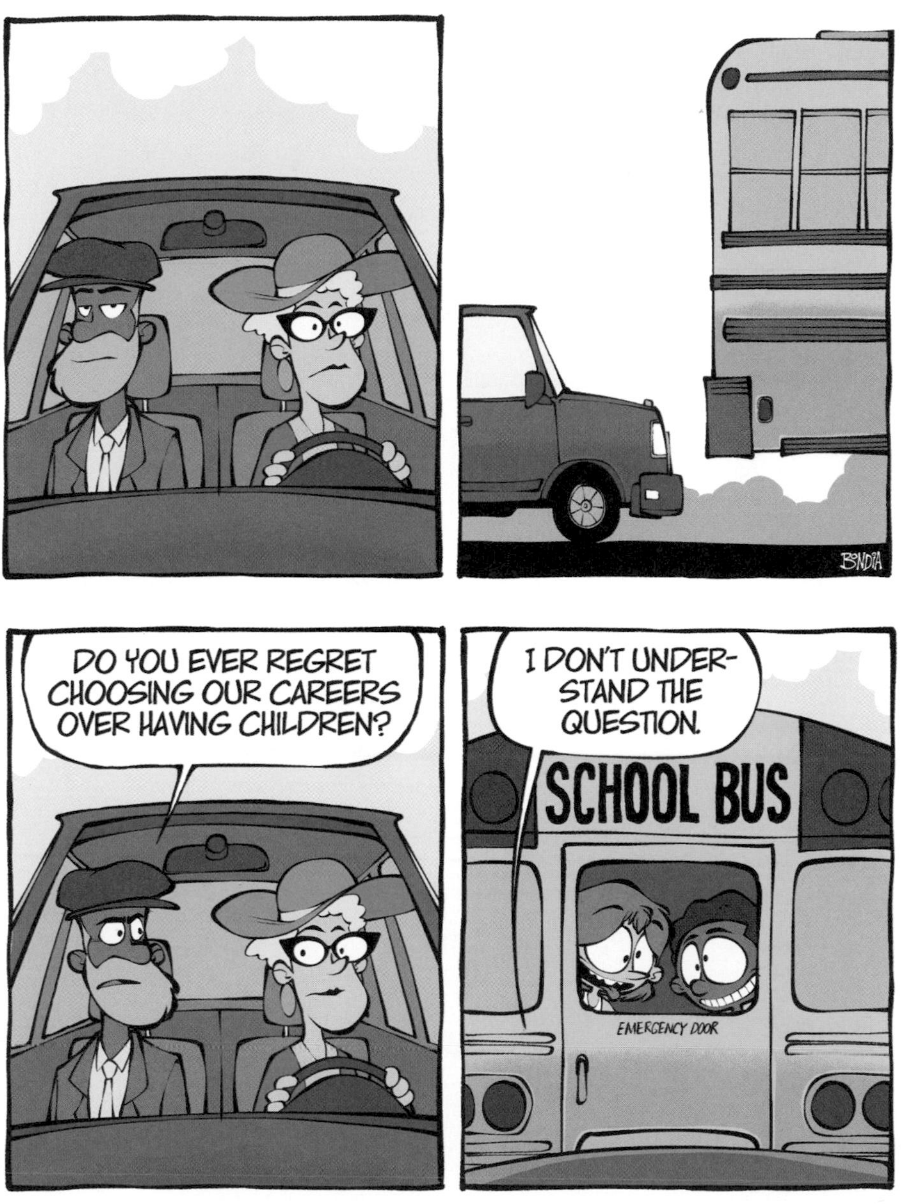
BONDIA
DO YOU EVER REGRET CHOOSING OUR CAREERS OVER HAVING CHILDREN?
I DON'T UNDER-STAND THE QUESTION.
SCHOOL BUS
EMERGENCY DOOR

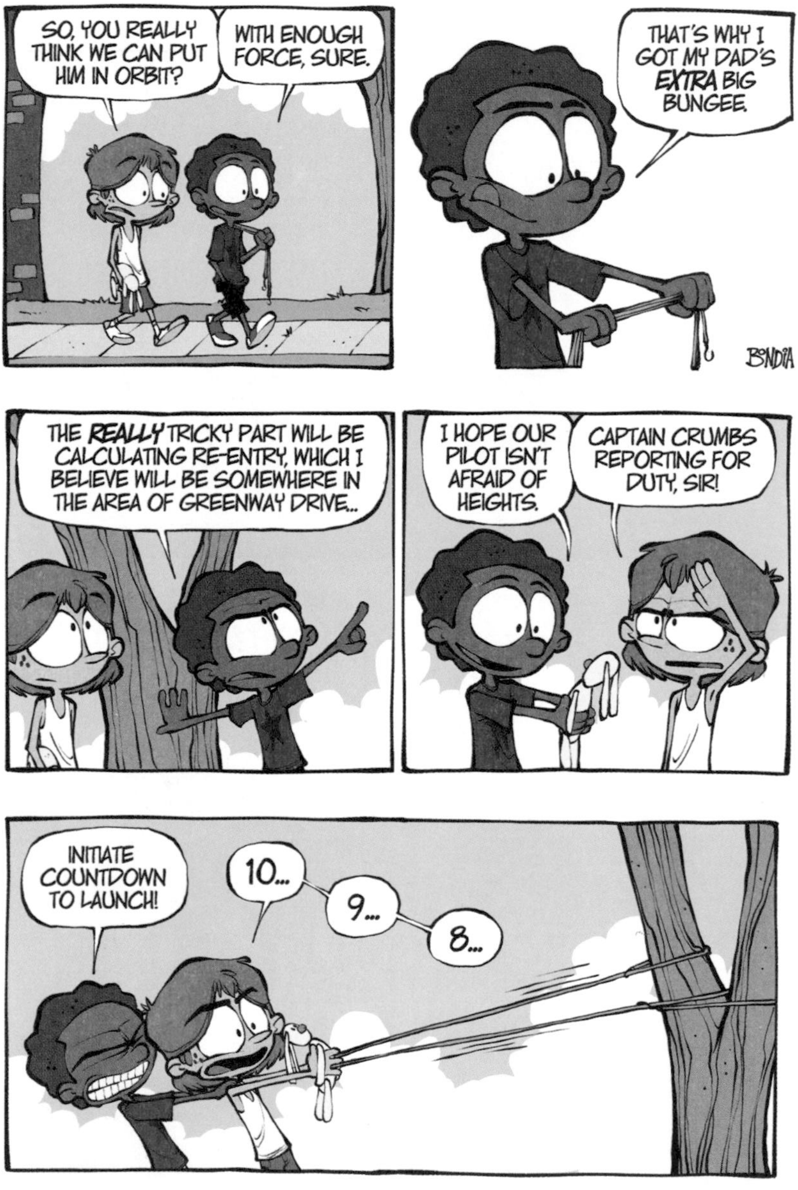
SO, YOU REALLY THINK WE CAN PUT HIM IN ORBIT?
WITH ENOUGH FORCE, SURE.
THAT'S WHY I GOT MY DAD'S *EXTRA* BIG BUNGEE.
BONDIA
THE *REALLY* TRICKY PART WILL BE CALCULATING RE-ENTRY, WHICH I BELIEVE WILL BE SOMEWHERE IN THE AREA OF GREENWAY DRIVE...
I HOPE OUR PILOT ISN'T AFRAID OF HEIGHTS.
CAPTAIN CRUMBS REPORTING FOR DUTY, SIR!
INITIATE COUNTDOWN TO LAUNCH!
10...
9...
8...

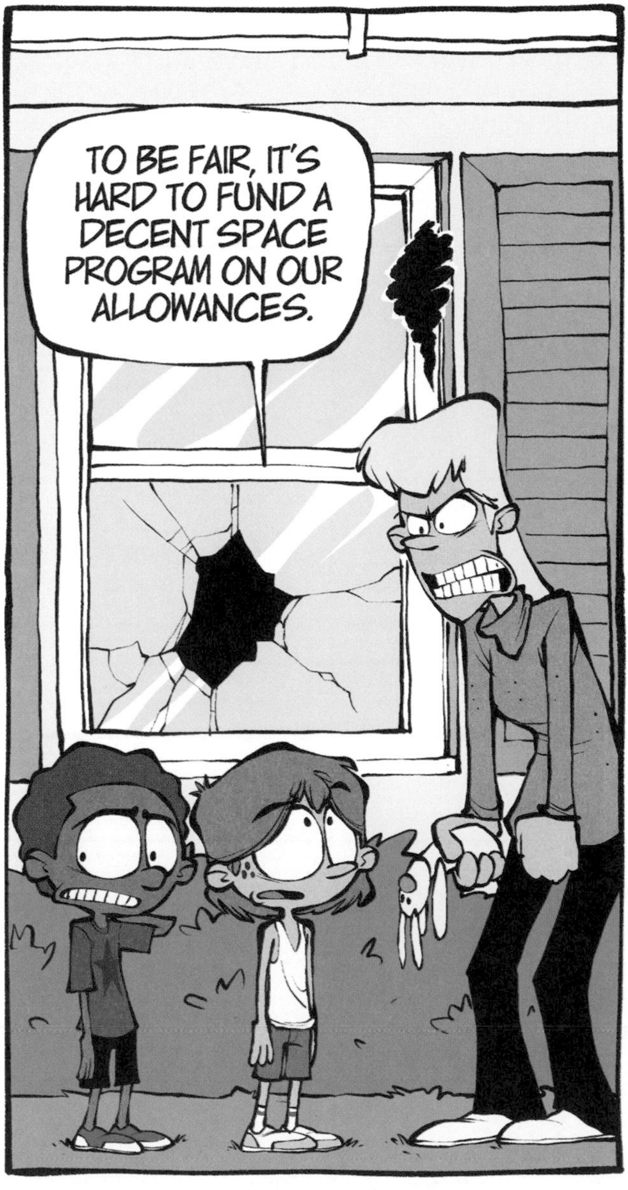
TO BE FAIR, IT'S HARD TO FUND A DECENT SPACE PROGRAM ON OUR ALLOWANCES.

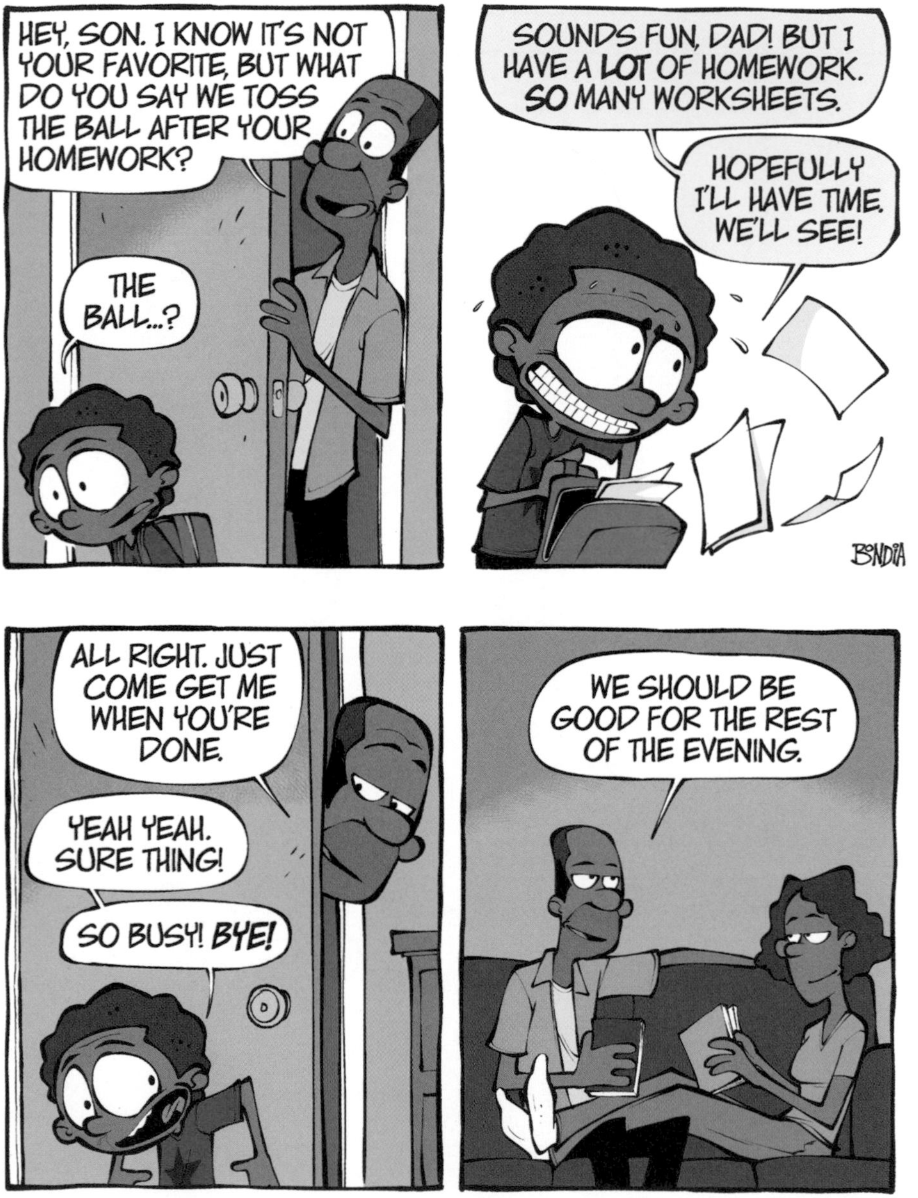
HEY, SON. I KNOW IT'S NOT YOUR FAVORITE, BUT WHAT DO YOU SAY WE TOSS THE BALL AFTER YOUR HOMEWORK?
THE BALL...?
SOUNDS FUN, DAD! BUT I HAVE A **LOT** OF HOMEWORK. **SO** MANY WORKSHEETS.
HOPEFULLY I'LL HAVE TIME. WE'LL SEE!
BONDIA
ALL RIGHT. JUST COME GET ME WHEN YOU'RE DONE.
YEAH YEAH. SURE THING!
SO BUSY! ***BYE!***
WE SHOULD BE GOOD FOR THE REST OF THE EVENING.

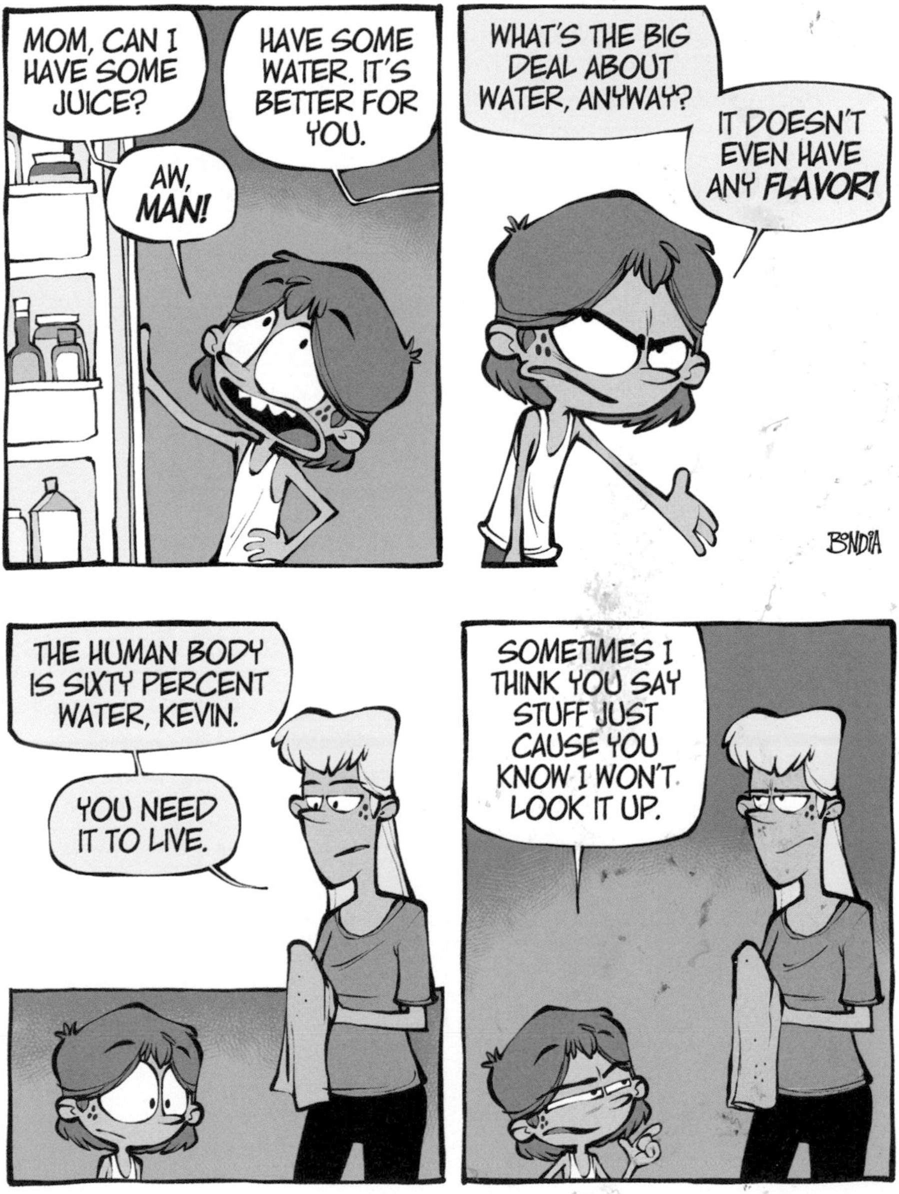
MOM, CAN I HAVE SOME JUICE?
HAVE SOME WATER. IT'S BETTER FOR YOU.
AW, MAN!
WHAT'S THE BIG DEAL ABOUT WATER, ANYWAY?
IT DOESN'T EVEN HAVE ANY FLAVOR!
BONDIA
THE HUMAN BODY IS SIXTY PERCENT WATER, KEVIN.
YOU NEED IT TO LIVE.
SOMETIMES I THINK YOU SAY STUFF JUST CAUSE YOU KNOW I WON'T LOOK IT UP.

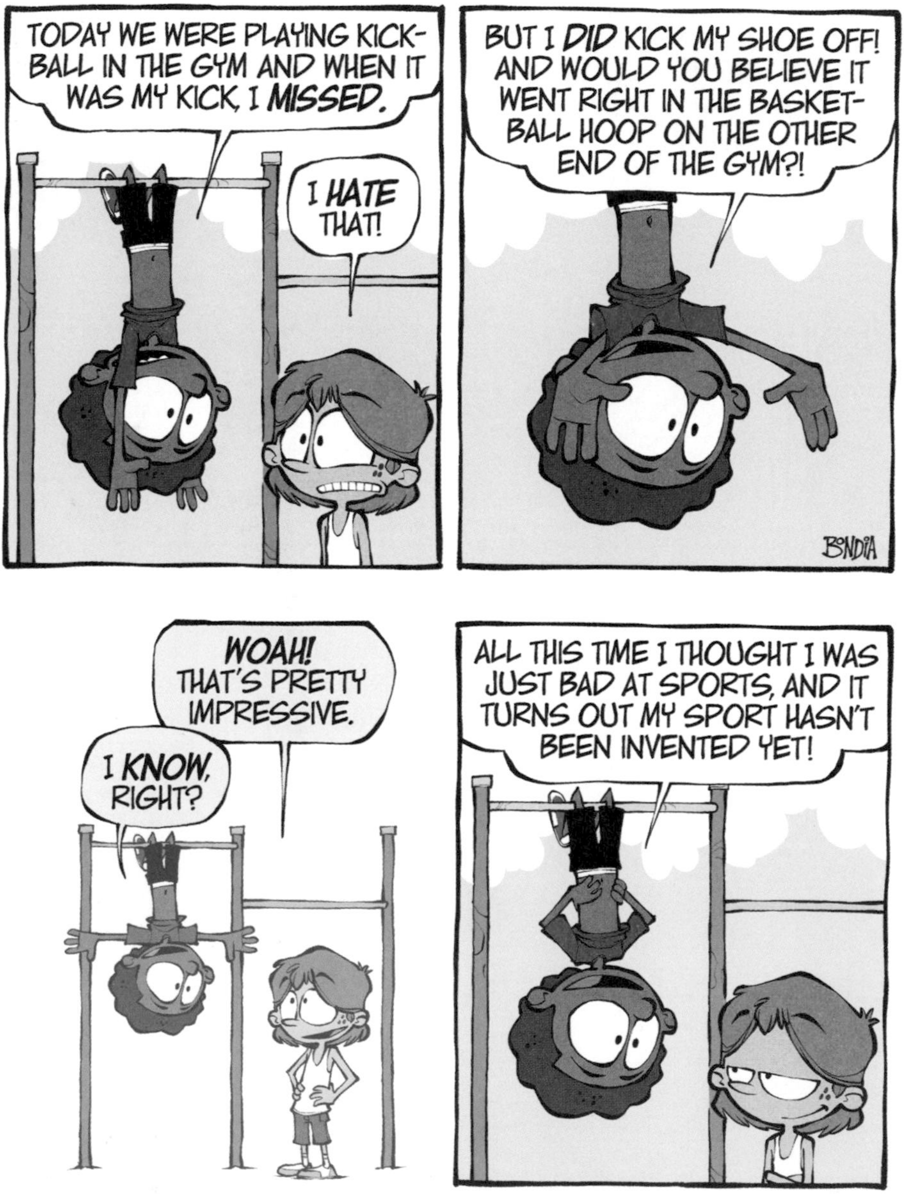
TODAY WE WERE PLAYING KICK-BALL IN THE GYM AND WHEN IT WAS MY KICK, I MISSED.
I HATE THAT!
BUT I DID KICK MY SHOE OFF! AND WOULD YOU BELIEVE IT WENT RIGHT IN THE BASKET-BALL HOOP ON THE OTHER END OF THE GYM?!
BONDIA
WOAH! THAT'S PRETTY IMPRESSIVE.
I KNOW, RIGHT?
ALL THIS TIME I THOUGHT I WAS JUST BAD AT SPORTS, AND IT TURNS OUT MY SPORT HASN'T BEEN INVENTED YET!

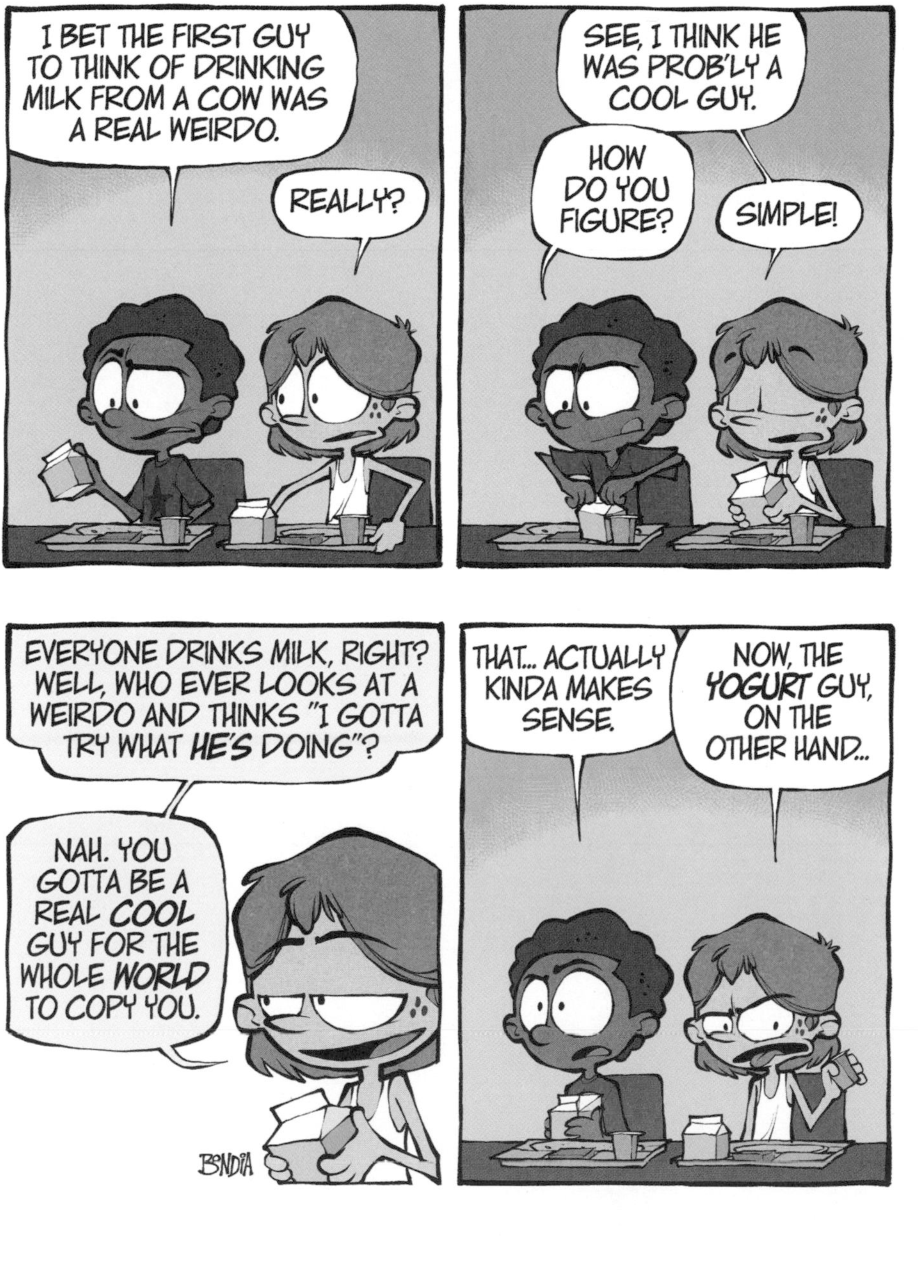
I BET THE FIRST GUY TO THINK OF DRINKING MILK FROM A COW WAS A REAL WEIRDO.
REALLY?
SEE, I THINK HE WAS PROB'LY A COOL GUY.
HOW DO YOU FIGURE?
SIMPLE!
EVERYONE DRINKS MILK, RIGHT? WELL, WHO EVER LOOKS AT A WEIRDO AND THINKS "I GOTTA TRY WHAT *HE'S* DOING"?
NAH. YOU GOTTA BE A REAL *COOL* GUY FOR THE WHOLE *WORLD* TO COPY YOU.
BSNDIA
THAT... ACTUALLY KINDA MAKES SENSE.
NOW, THE *YOGURT* GUY, ON THE OTHER HAND...

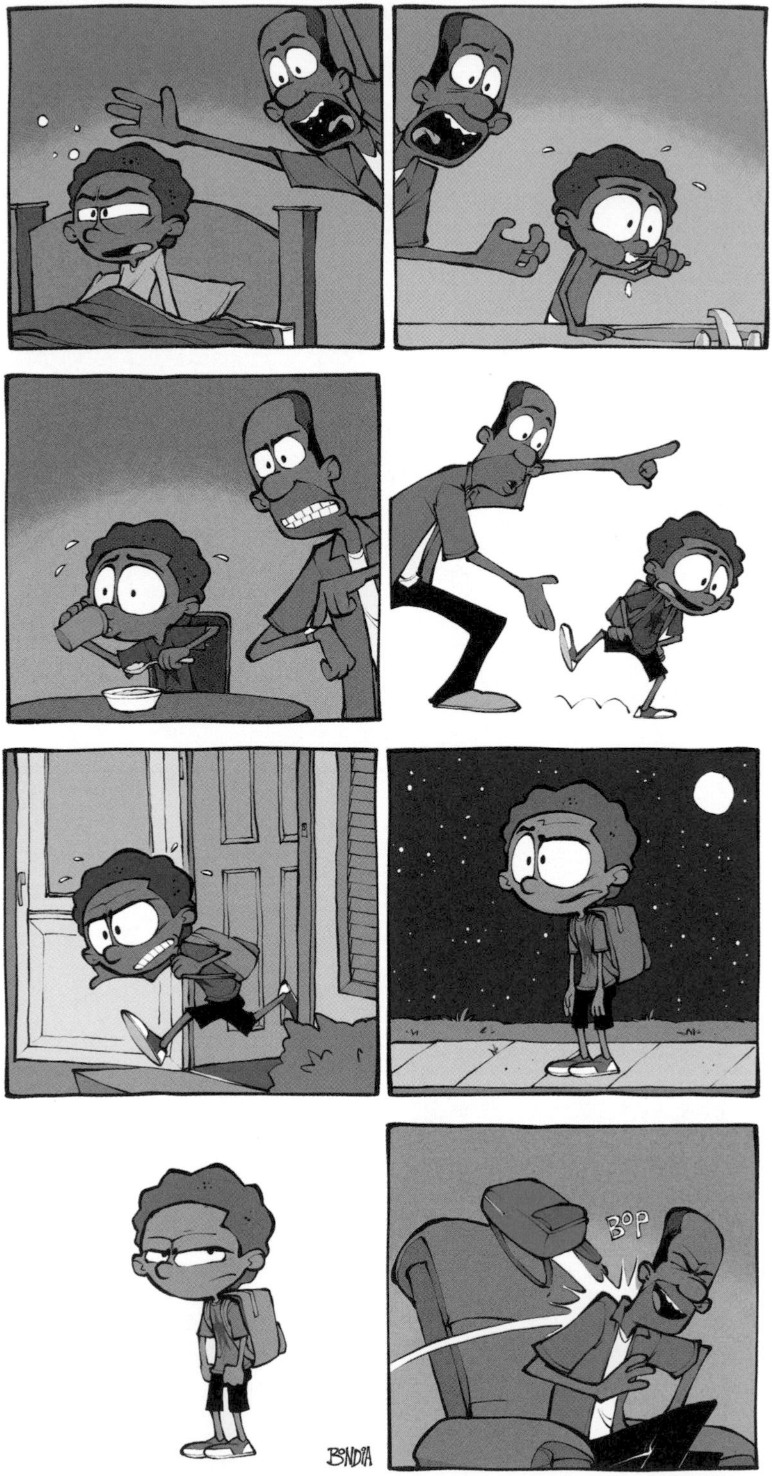
BOP
BONDIA

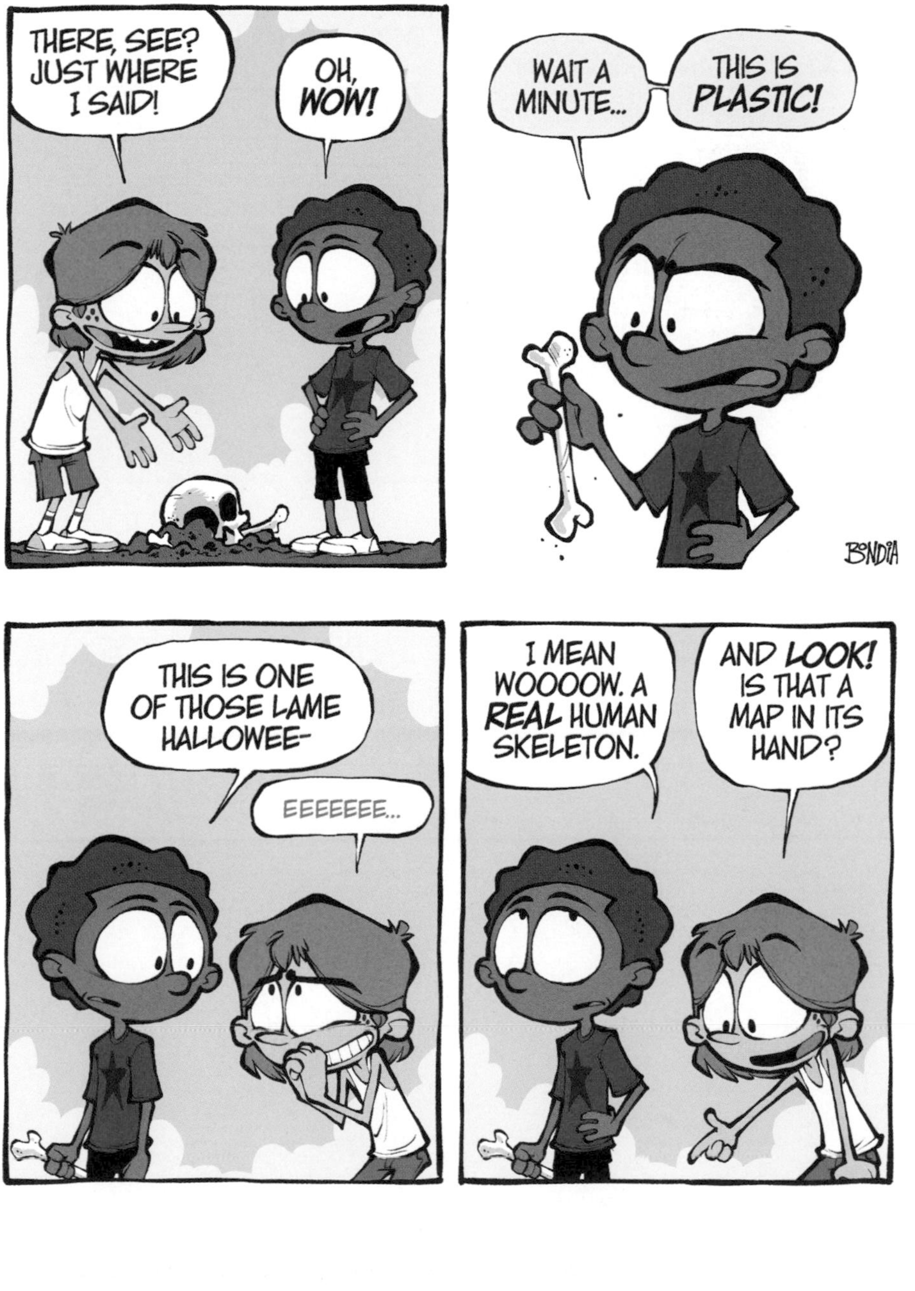
THERE, SEE? JUST WHERE I SAID!
OH, **WOW!**
WAIT A MINUTE...
THIS IS **PLASTIC!**
BONDIA
THIS IS ONE OF THOSE LAME HALLOWEE-
EEEEEEE...
I MEAN WOOOOW. A **REAL** HUMAN SKELETON.
AND **LOOK!** IS THAT A MAP IN ITS HAND?

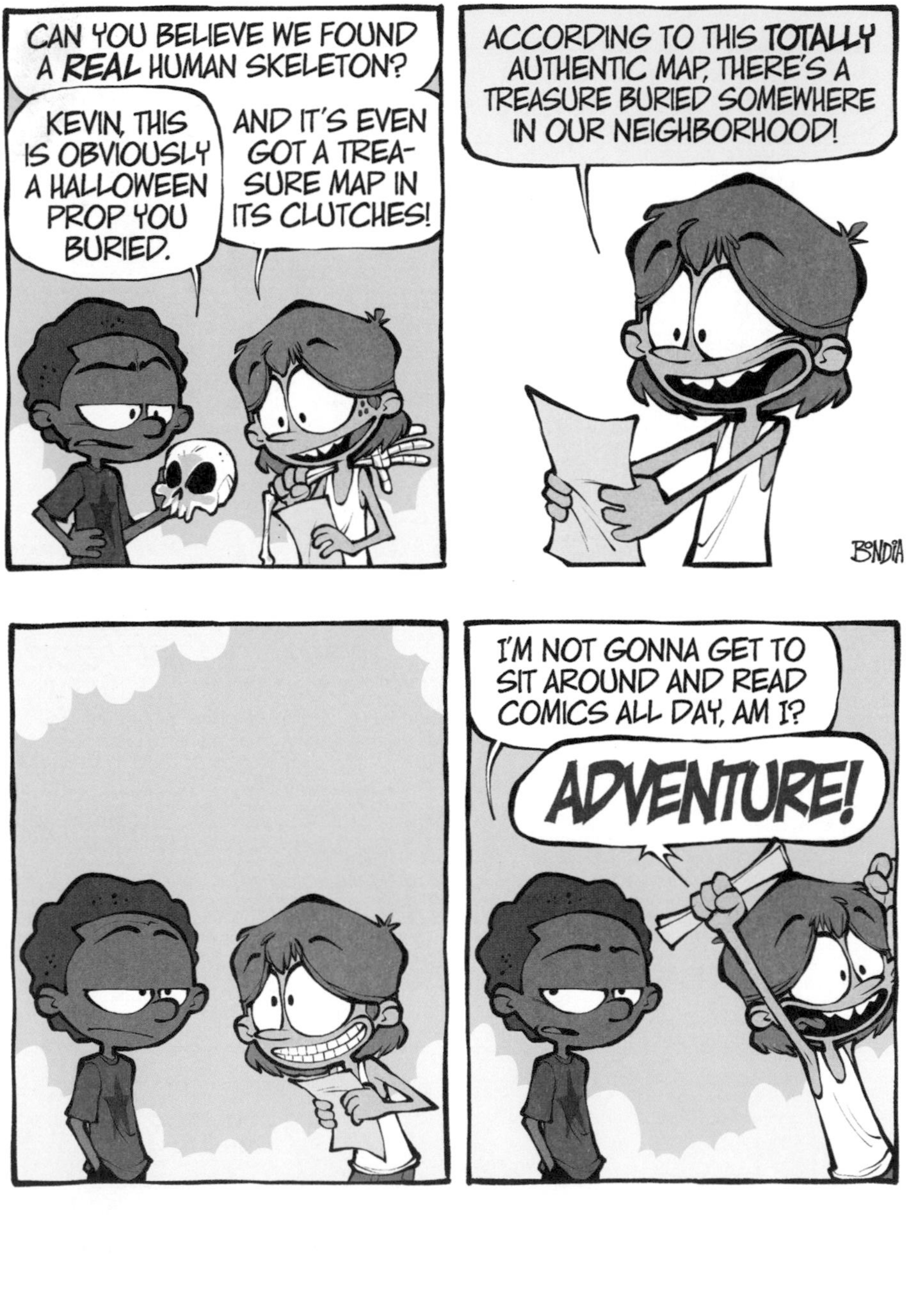
CAN YOU BELIEVE WE FOUND A REAL HUMAN SKELETON?
KEVIN, THIS IS OBVIOUSLY A HALLOWEEN PROP YOU BURIED.
AND IT'S EVEN GOT A TREASURE MAP IN ITS CLUTCHES!
ACCORDING TO THIS TOTALLY AUTHENTIC MAP, THERE'S A TREASURE BURIED SOMEWHERE IN OUR NEIGHBORHOOD!
BONDIA
I'M NOT GONNA GET TO SIT AROUND AND READ COMICS ALL DAY, AM I?
ADVENTURE!

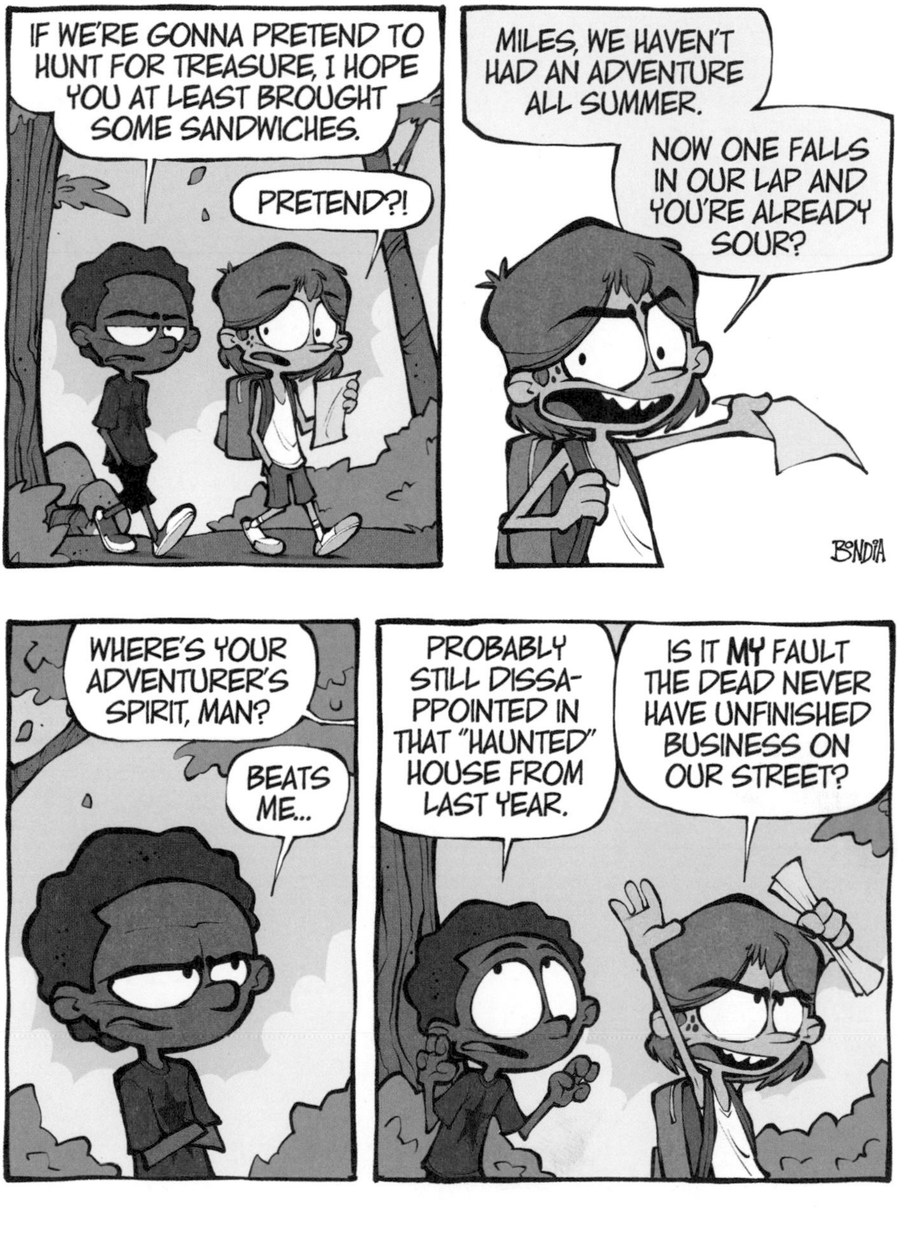
IF WE'RE GONNA PRETEND TO HUNT FOR TREASURE, I HOPE YOU AT LEAST BROUGHT SOME SANDWICHES.
PRETEND?!
MILES, WE HAVEN'T HAD AN ADVENTURE ALL SUMMER.
NOW ONE FALLS IN OUR LAP AND YOU'RE ALREADY SOUR?
BONDIA
WHERE'S YOUR ADVENTURER'S SPIRIT, MAN?
BEATS ME...
PROBABLY STILL DISSA-PPOINTED IN THAT "HAUNTED" HOUSE FROM LAST YEAR.
IS IT MY FAULT THE DEAD NEVER HAVE UNFINISHED BUSINESS ON OUR STREET?

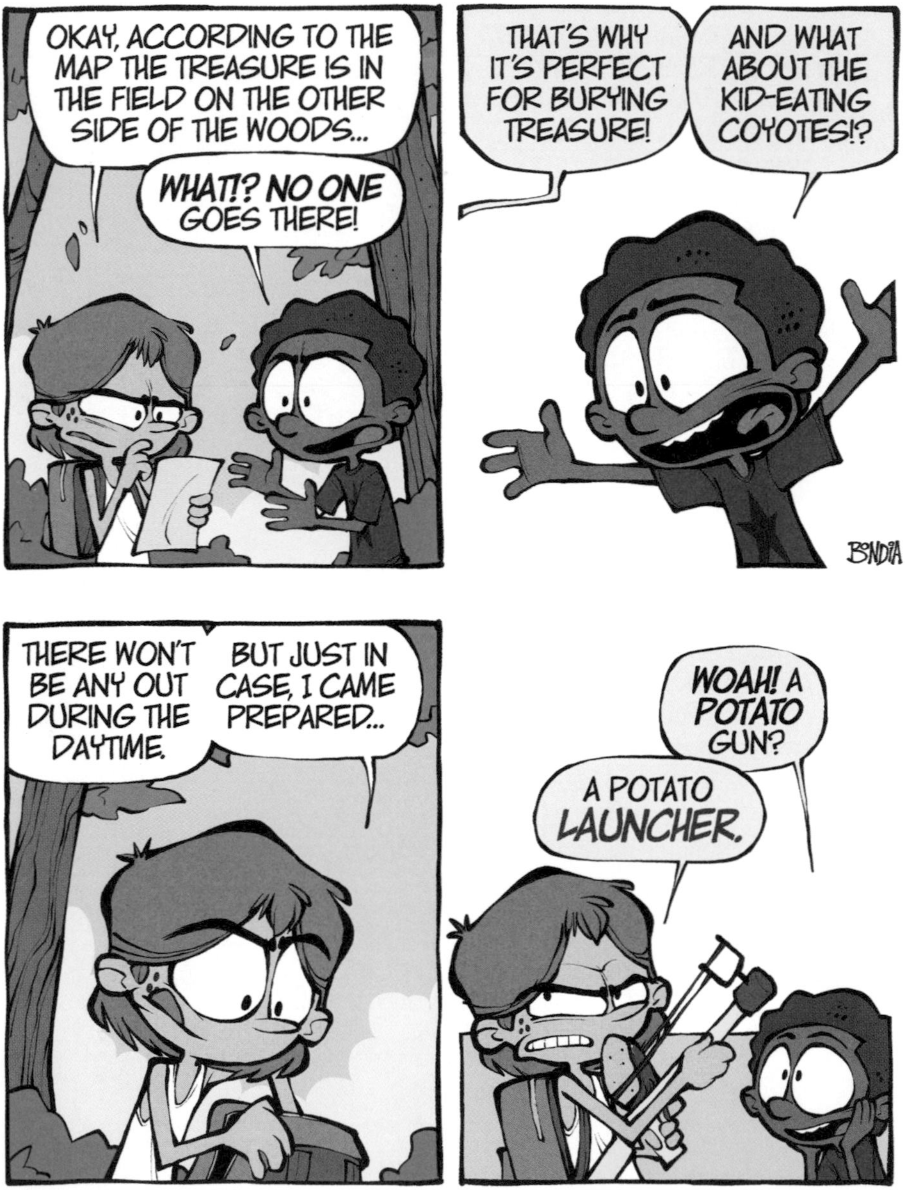
OKAY, ACCORDING TO THE MAP THE TREASURE IS IN THE FIELD ON THE OTHER SIDE OF THE WOODS...
WHAT!? NO ONE GOES THERE!
THAT'S WHY IT'S PERFECT FOR BURYING TREASURE!
AND WHAT ABOUT THE KID-EATING COYOTES!?
BONDIA
THERE WON'T BE ANY OUT DURING THE DAYTIME.
BUT JUST IN CASE, I CAME PREPARED...
WOAH! A POTATO GUN?
A POTATO LAUNCHER.

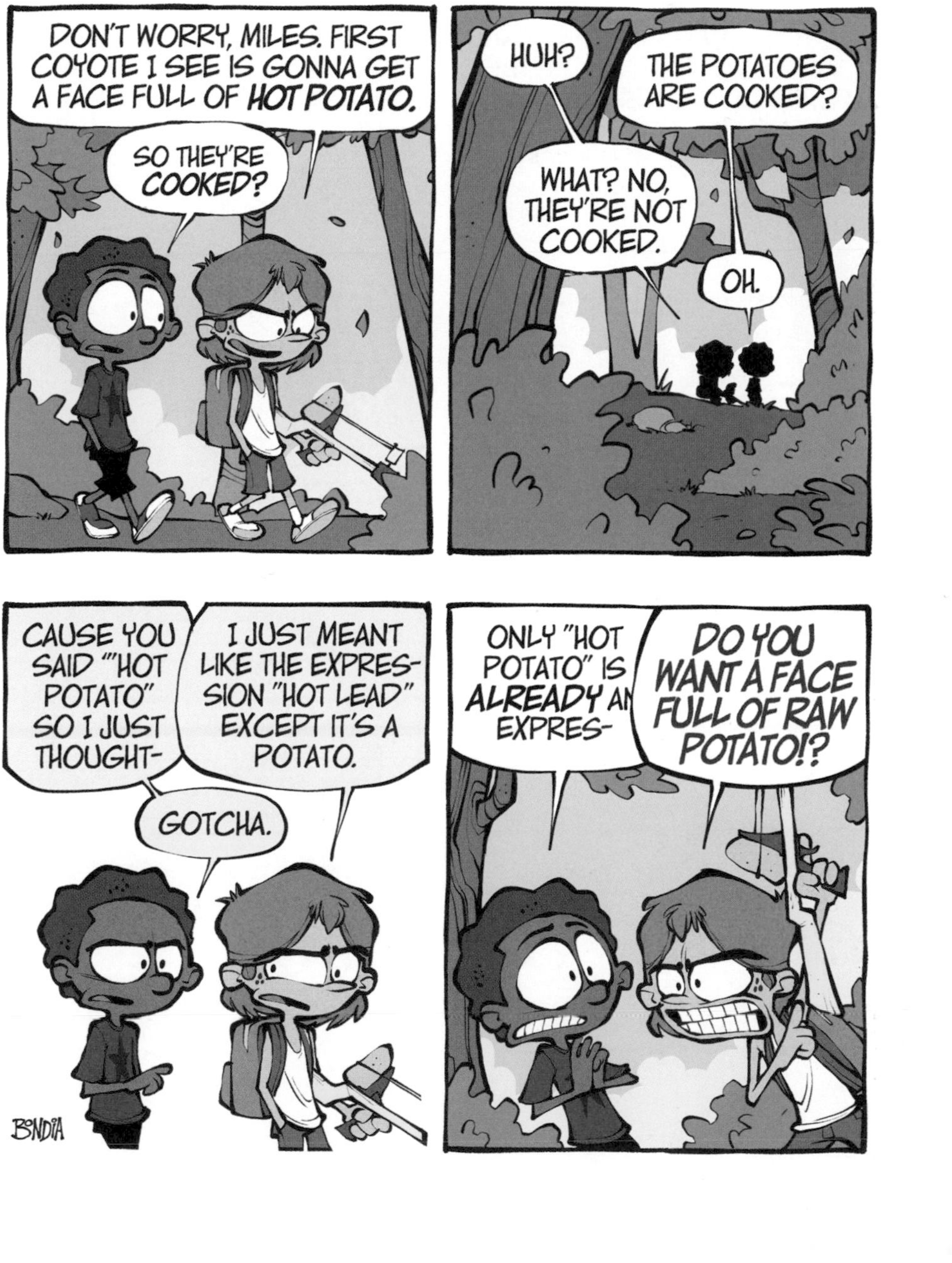
DON'T WORRY, MILES. FIRST COYOTE I SEE IS GONNA GET A FACE FULL OF **HOT POTATO.**
SO THEY'RE ***COOKED?***
HUH?
THE POTATOES ARE COOKED?
WHAT? NO, THEY'RE NOT COOKED.
OH.
CAUSE YOU SAID ""HOT POTATO" SO I JUST THOUGHT-
I JUST MEANT LIKE THE EXPRES-SION "HOT LEAD" EXCEPT IT'S A POTATO.
GOTCHA.
BONDIA
ONLY "HOT POTATO" IS ***ALREADY*** AN EXPRES-
DO YOU WANT A FACE FULL OF RAW POTATO!?

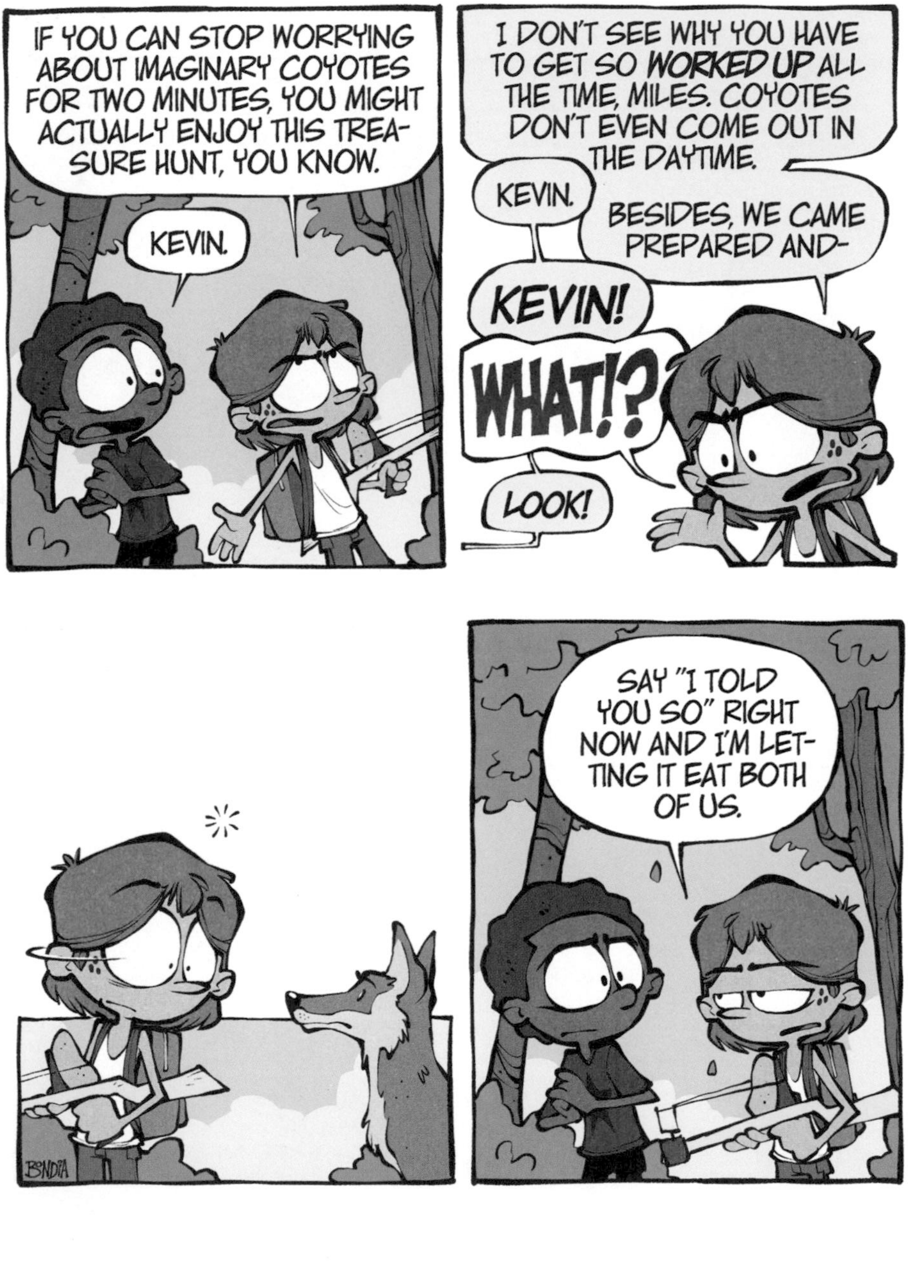
IF YOU CAN STOP WORRYING ABOUT IMAGINARY COYOTES FOR TWO MINUTES, YOU MIGHT ACTUALLY ENJOY THIS TREA-SURE HUNT, YOU KNOW.
KEVIN.
I DON'T SEE WHY YOU HAVE TO GET SO WORKED UP ALL THE TIME, MILES. COYOTES DON'T EVEN COME OUT IN THE DAYTIME.
KEVIN.
BESIDES, WE CAME PREPARED AND-
KEVIN!
WHAT!?
LOOK!
SAY "I TOLD YOU SO" RIGHT NOW AND I'M LET-TING IT EAT BOTH OF US.
BENDIA

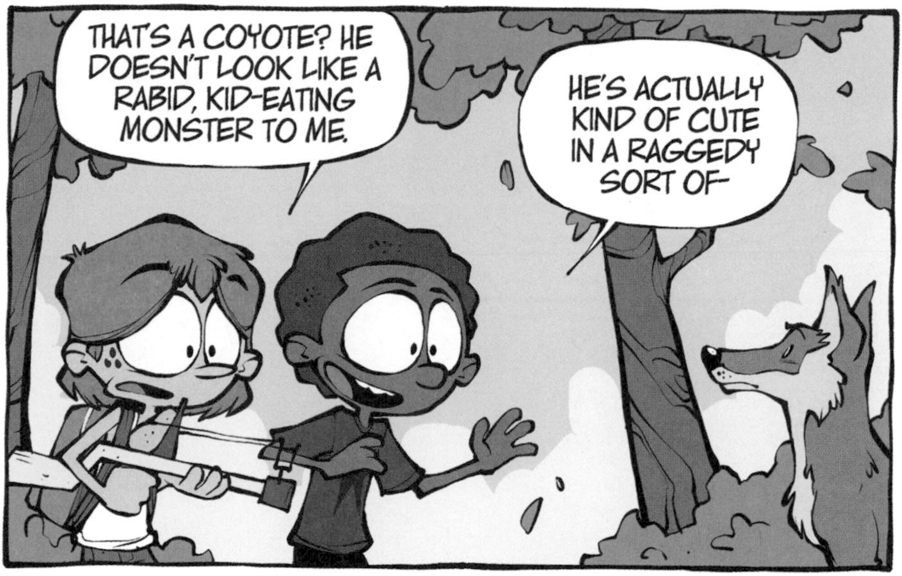
THAT'S A COYOTE? HE DOESN'T LOOK LIKE A RABID, KID-EATING MONSTER TO ME.
HE'S ACTUALLY KIND OF CUTE IN A RAGGEDY SORT OF-

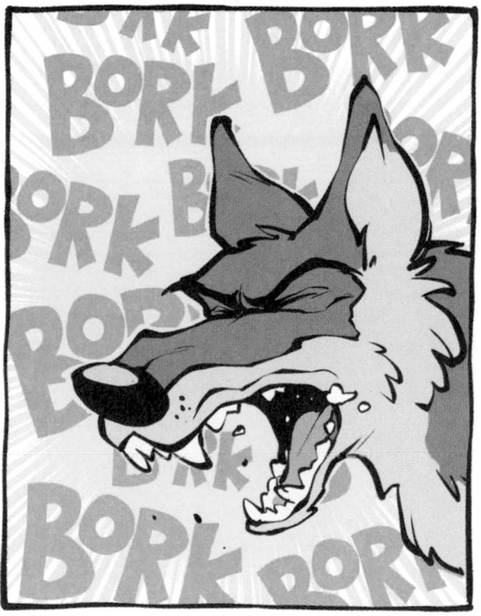
BORK BORK BORK BORK BORK BORK
BONDIA

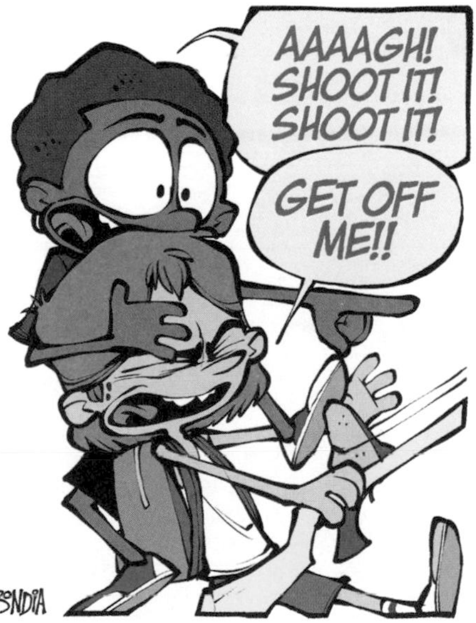
AAAAGH! SHOOT IT! SHOOT IT!
GET OFF ME!!

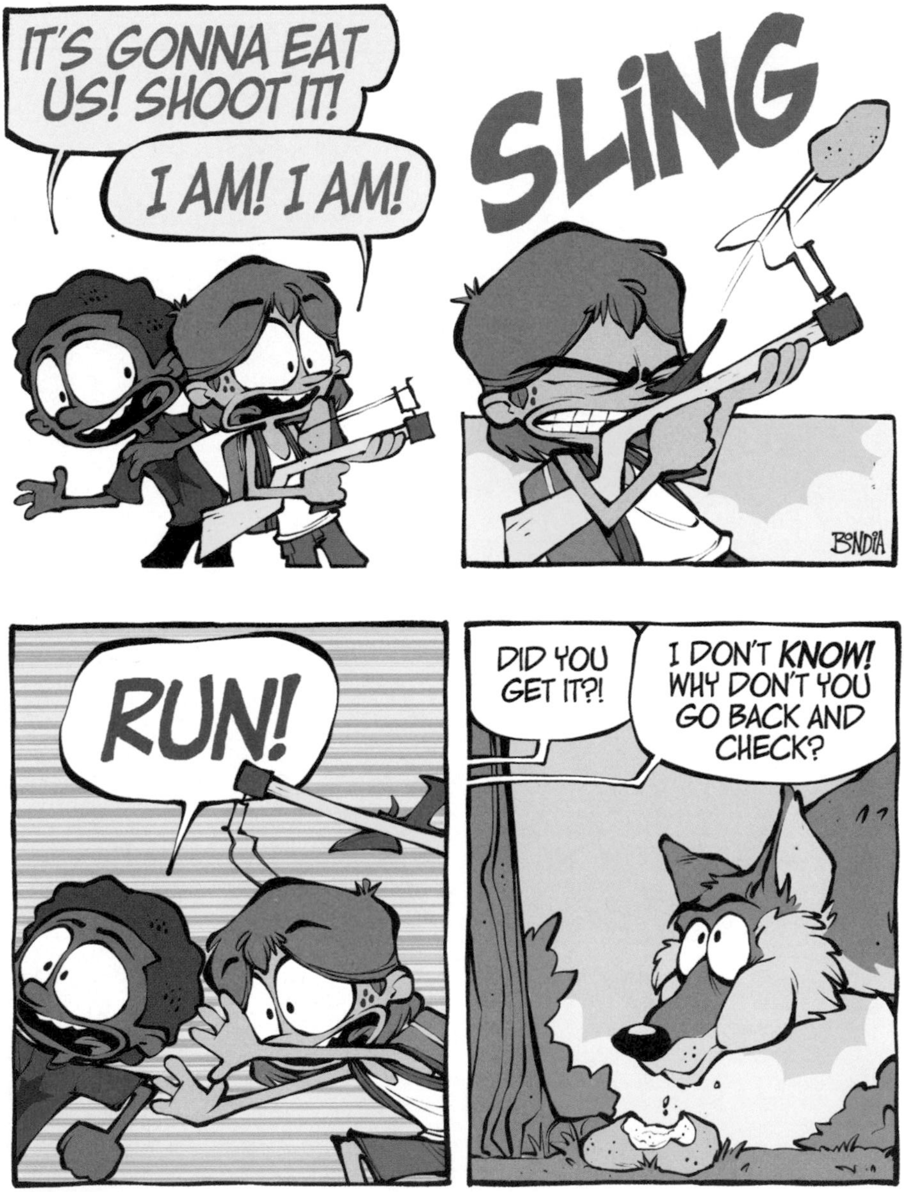
IT'S GONNA EAT US! SHOOT IT!
I AM! I AM!
SLING
BONDIA
RUN!
DID YOU GET IT?!
I DON'T KNOW! WHY DON'T YOU GO BACK AND CHECK?

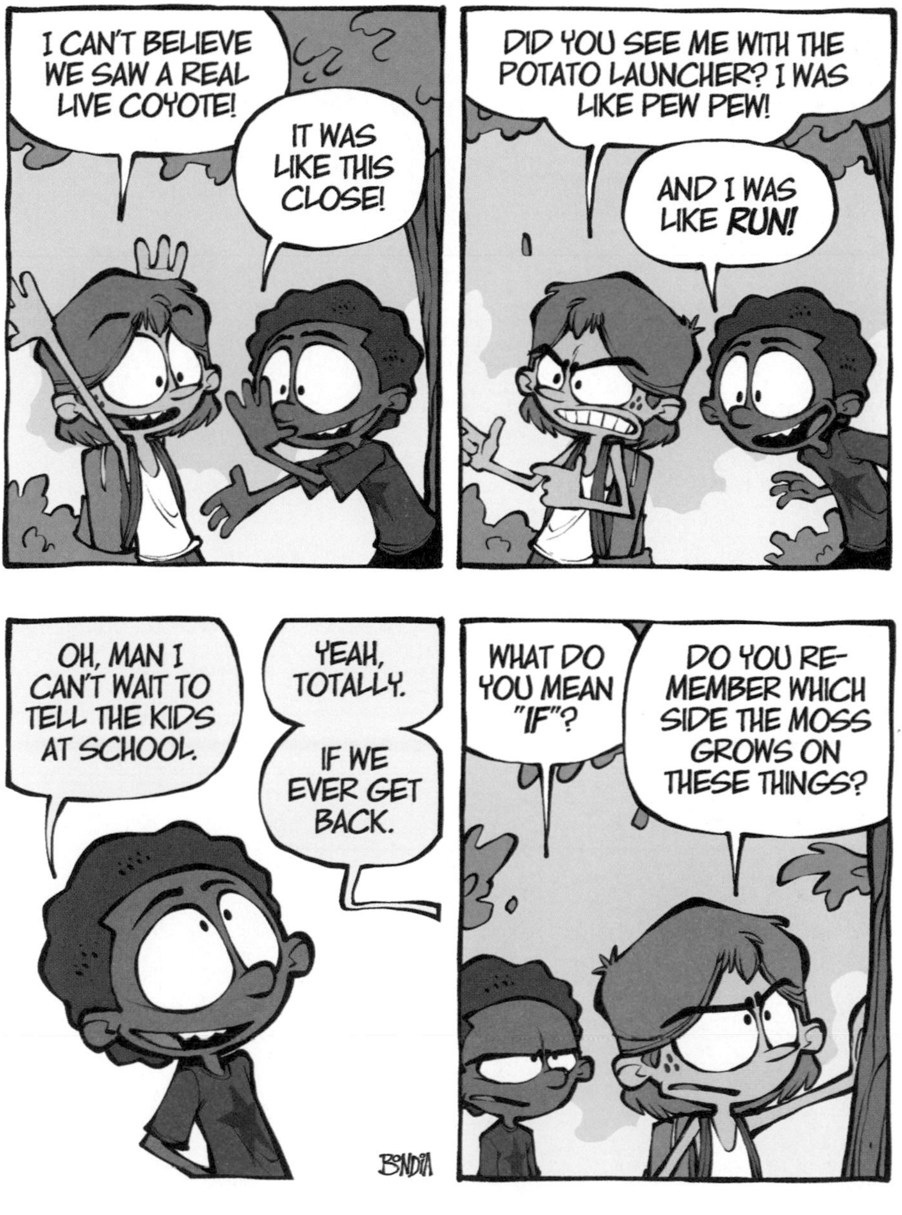
I CAN'T BELIEVE WE SAW A REAL LIVE COYOTE!
IT WAS LIKE THIS CLOSE!
DID YOU SEE ME WITH THE POTATO LAUNCHER? I WAS LIKE PEW PEW!
AND I WAS LIKE RUN!
OH, MAN I CAN'T WAIT TO TELL THE KIDS AT SCHOOL.
YEAH, TOTALLY.
IF WE EVER GET BACK.
WHAT DO YOU MEAN "IF"?
DO YOU RE-MEMBER WHICH SIDE THE MOSS GROWS ON THESE THINGS?
BONDIA

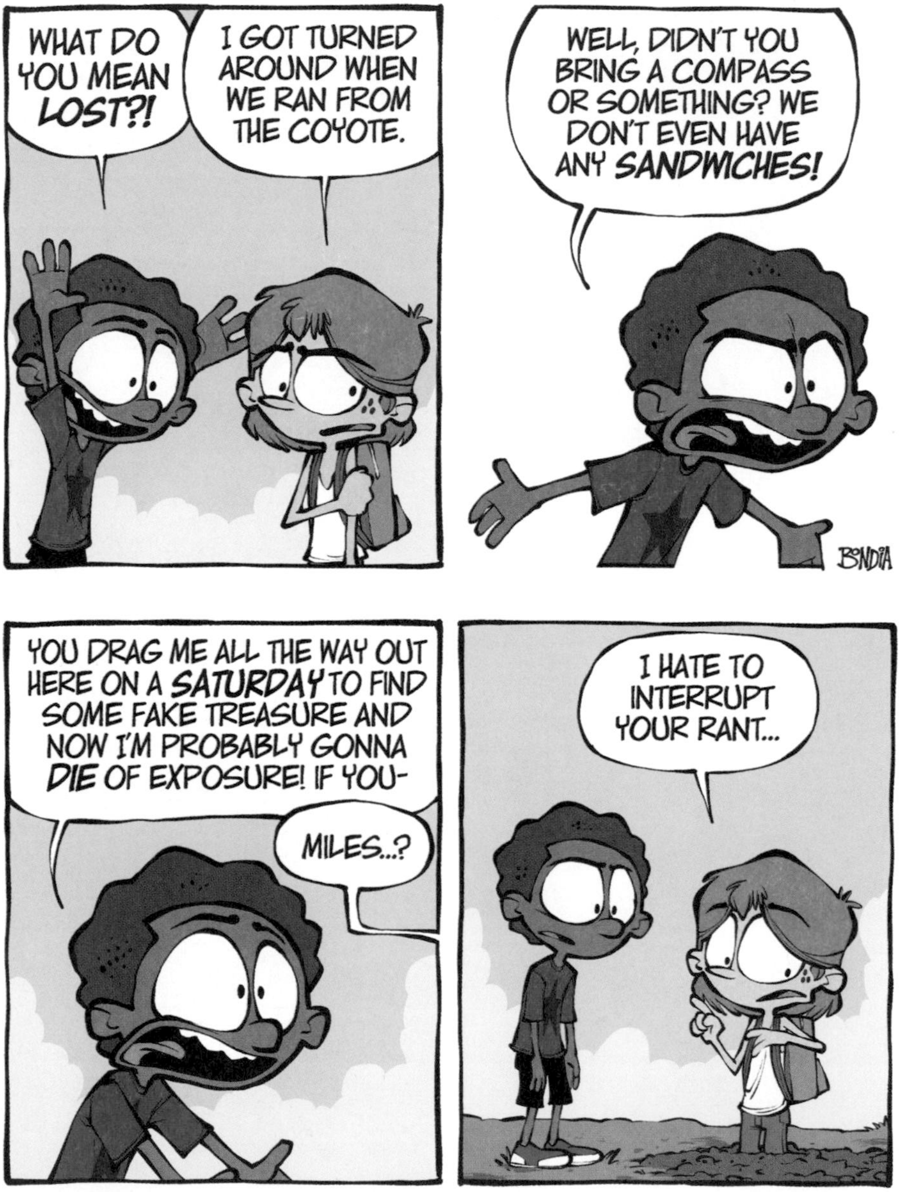
WHAT DO YOU MEAN LOST?!
I GOT TURNED AROUND WHEN WE RAN FROM THE COYOTE.
WELL, DIDN'T YOU BRING A COMPASS OR SOMETHING? WE DON'T EVEN HAVE ANY SANDWICHES!
BONDIA
YOU DRAG ME ALL THE WAY OUT HERE ON A SATURDAY TO FIND SOME FAKE TREASURE AND NOW I'M PROBABLY GONNA DIE OF EXPOSURE! IF YOU-
MILES...?
I HATE TO INTERRUPT YOUR RANT...

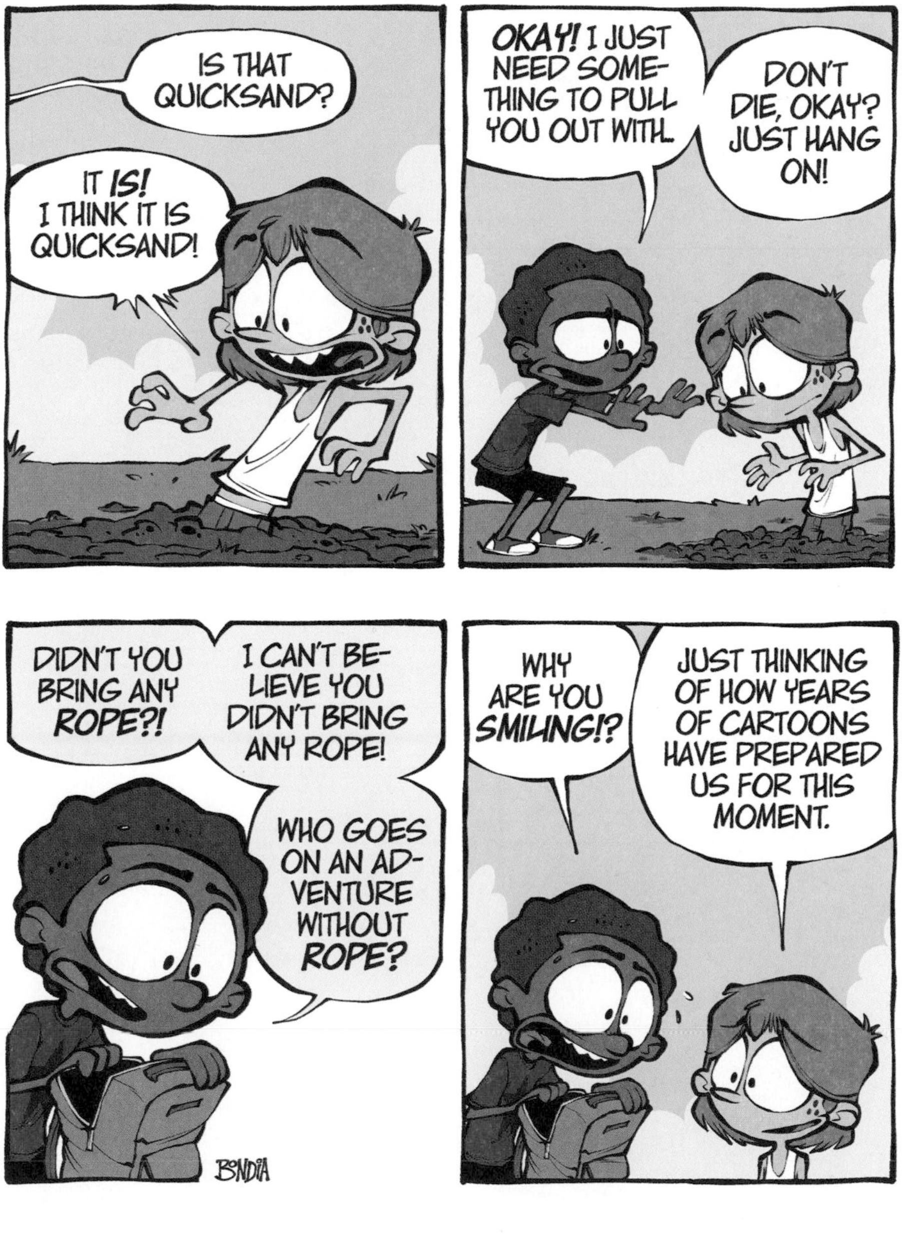
IS THAT QUICKSAND?
IT IS! I THINK IT IS QUICKSAND!
OKAY! I JUST NEED SOMETHING TO PULL YOU OUT WITH.
DON'T DIE, OKAY? JUST HANG ON!
DIDN'T YOU BRING ANY ROPE?!
I CAN'T BELIEVE YOU DIDN'T BRING ANY ROPE!
WHO GOES ON AN ADVENTURE WITHOUT ROPE?
BONDIA
WHY ARE YOU SMILING!?
JUST THINKING OF HOW YEARS OF CARTOONS HAVE PREPARED US FOR THIS MOMENT.

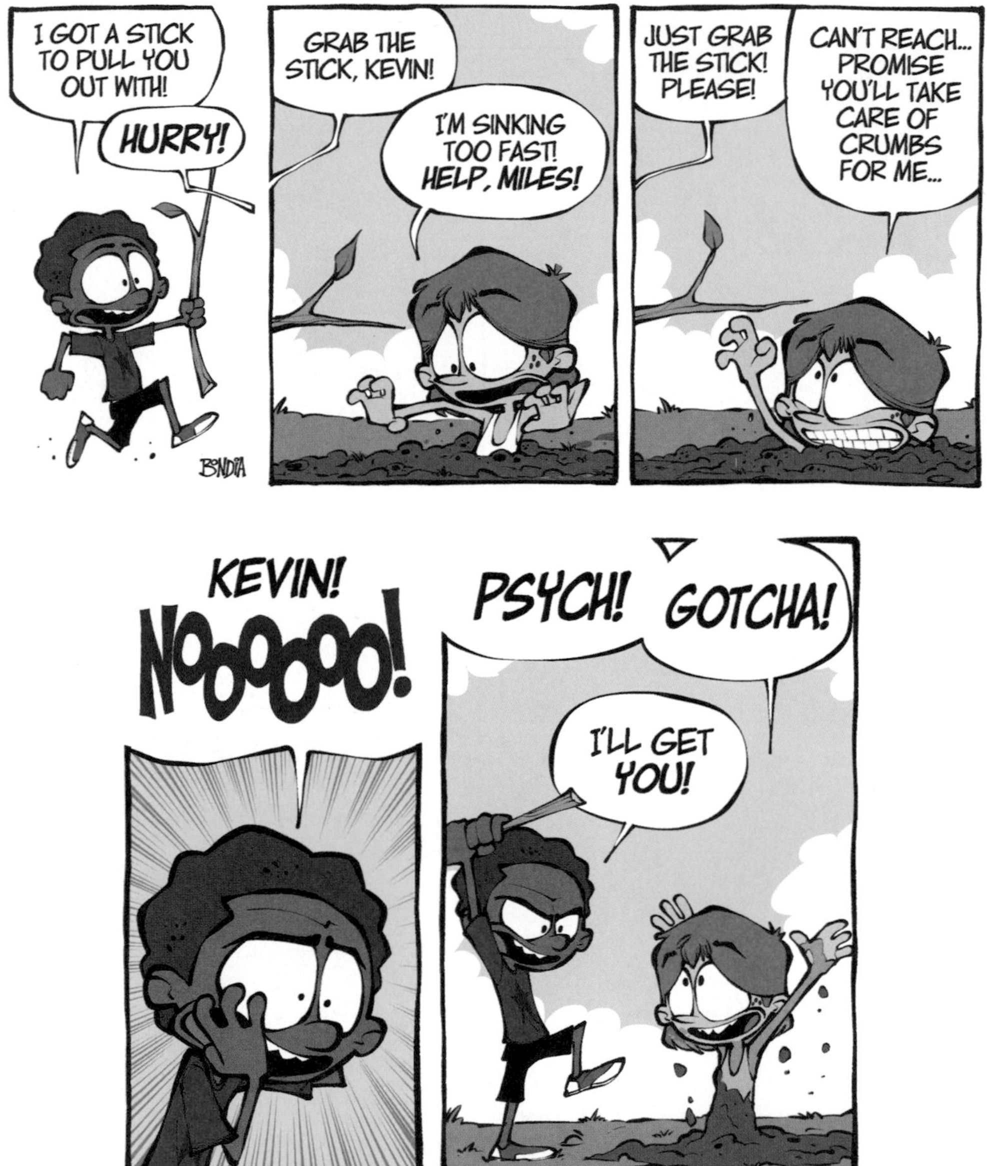
I GOT A STICK TO PULL YOU OUT WITH!
HURRY!
BONDIA
GRAB THE STICK, KEVIN!
I'M SINKING TOO FAST! HELP, MILES!
JUST GRAB THE STICK! PLEASE!
CAN'T REACH... PROMISE YOU'LL TAKE CARE OF CRUMBS FOR ME...
KEVIN!
NOOOOOO!
PSYCH!
GOTCHA!
I'LL GET YOU!

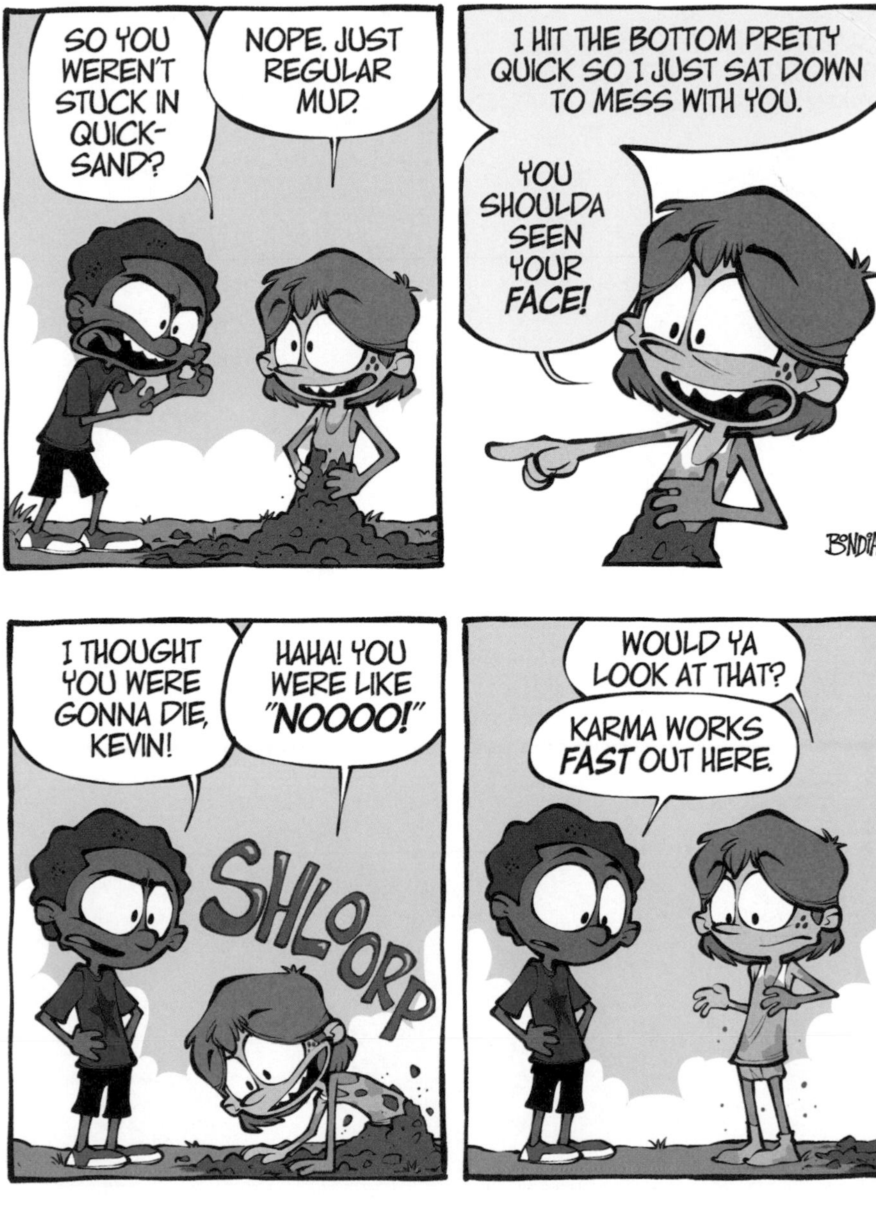

SO YOU WEREN'T STUCK IN QUICK-SAND?
NOPE. JUST REGULAR MUD.
I HIT THE BOTTOM PRETTY QUICK SO I JUST SAT DOWN TO MESS WITH YOU.
YOU SHOULDA SEEN YOUR FACE!
BONDIA
I THOUGHT YOU WERE GONNA DIE, KEVIN!
HAHA! YOU WERE LIKE "NOOOO!"
SHLOORP
WOULD YA LOOK AT THAT?
KARMA WORKS FAST OUT HERE.

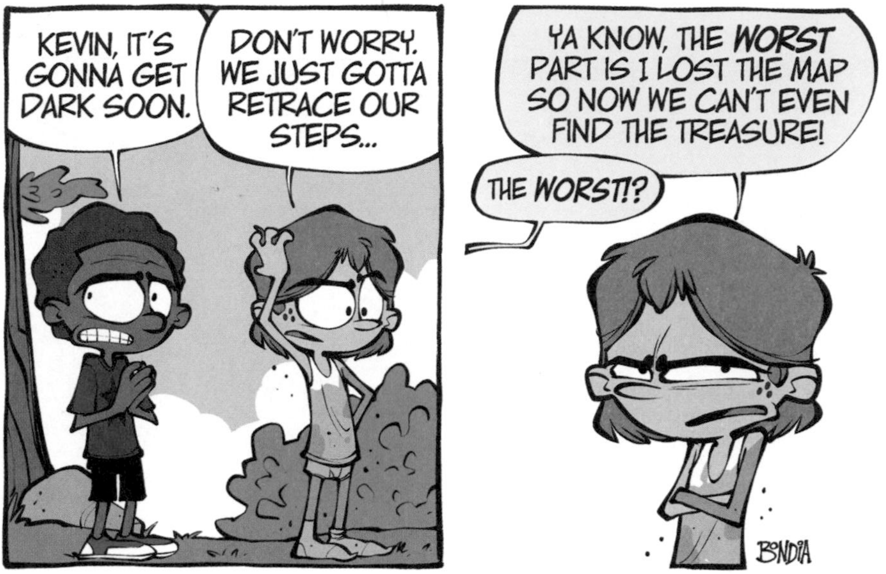
KEVIN, IT'S GONNA GET DARK SOON.
DON'T WORRY. WE JUST GOTTA RETRACE OUR STEPS...
YA KNOW, THE **WORST** PART IS I LOST THE MAP SO NOW WE CAN'T EVEN FIND THE TREASURE!
THE **WORST!?**

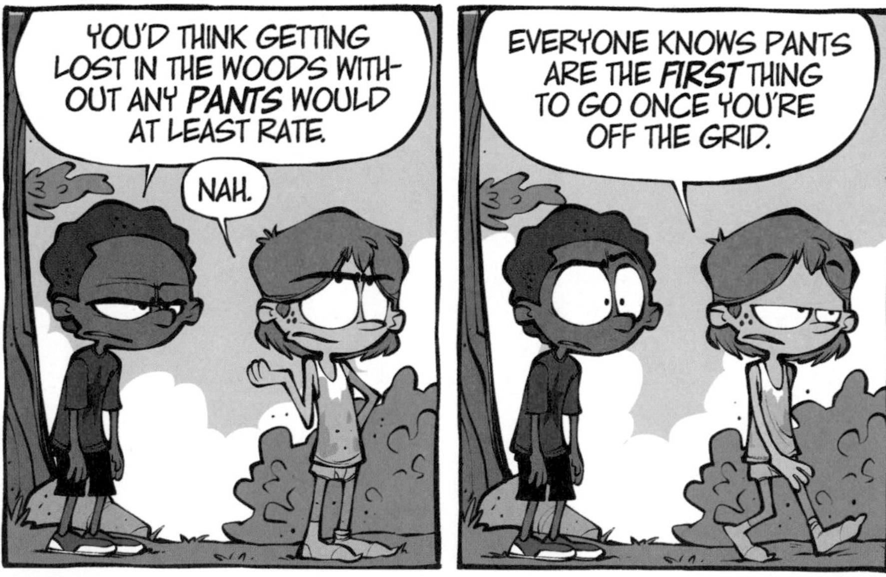
YOU'D THINK GETTING LOST IN THE WOODS WITH-OUT ANY **PANTS** WOULD AT LEAST RATE.
NAH.
EVERYONE KNOWS PANTS ARE THE **FIRST** THING TO GO ONCE YOU'RE OFF THE GRID.

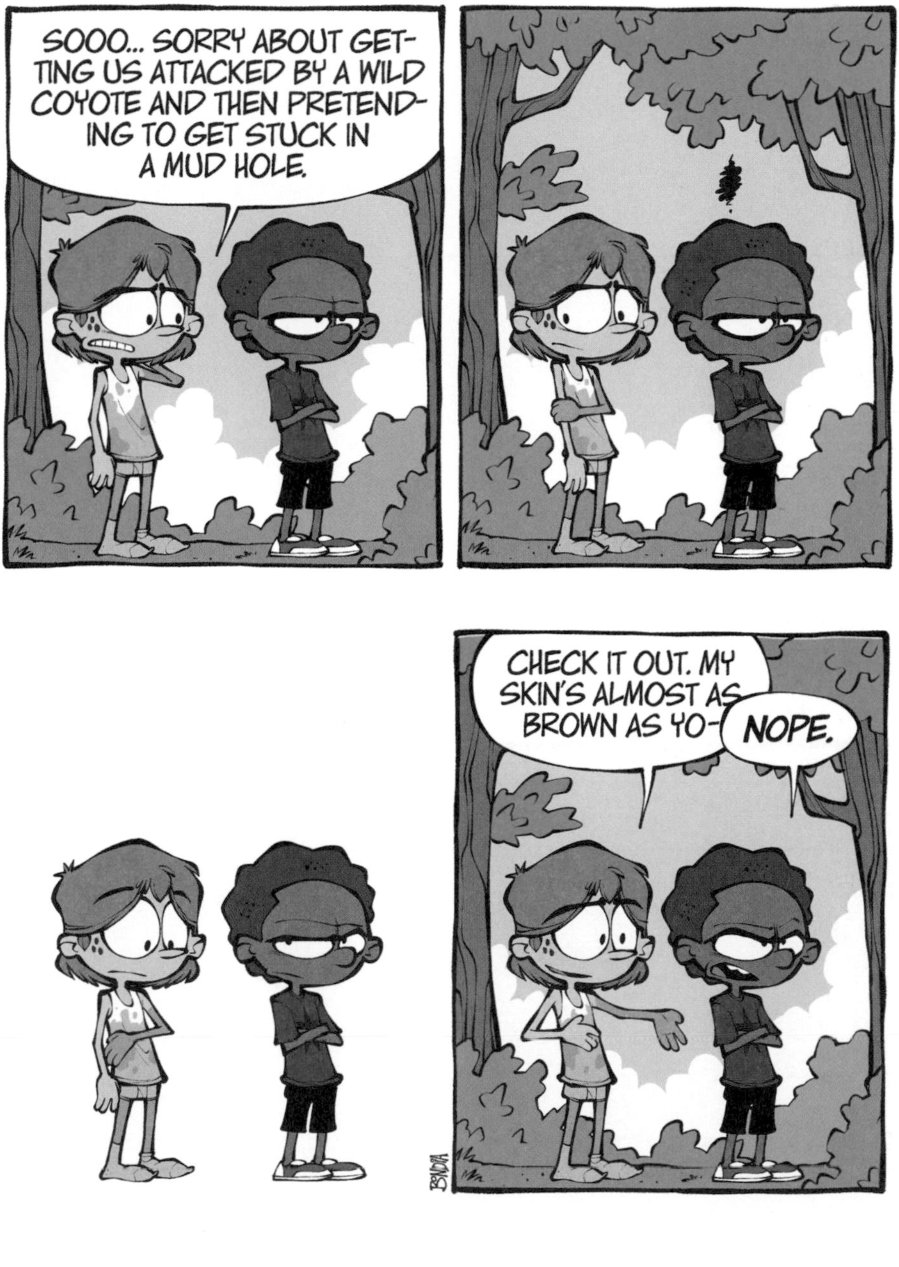
SOOO... SORRY ABOUT GETTING US ATTACKED BY A WILD COYOTE AND THEN PRETENDING TO GET STUCK IN A MUD HOLE.
CHECK IT OUT. MY SKIN'S ALMOST AS BROWN AS YO-
NOPE.

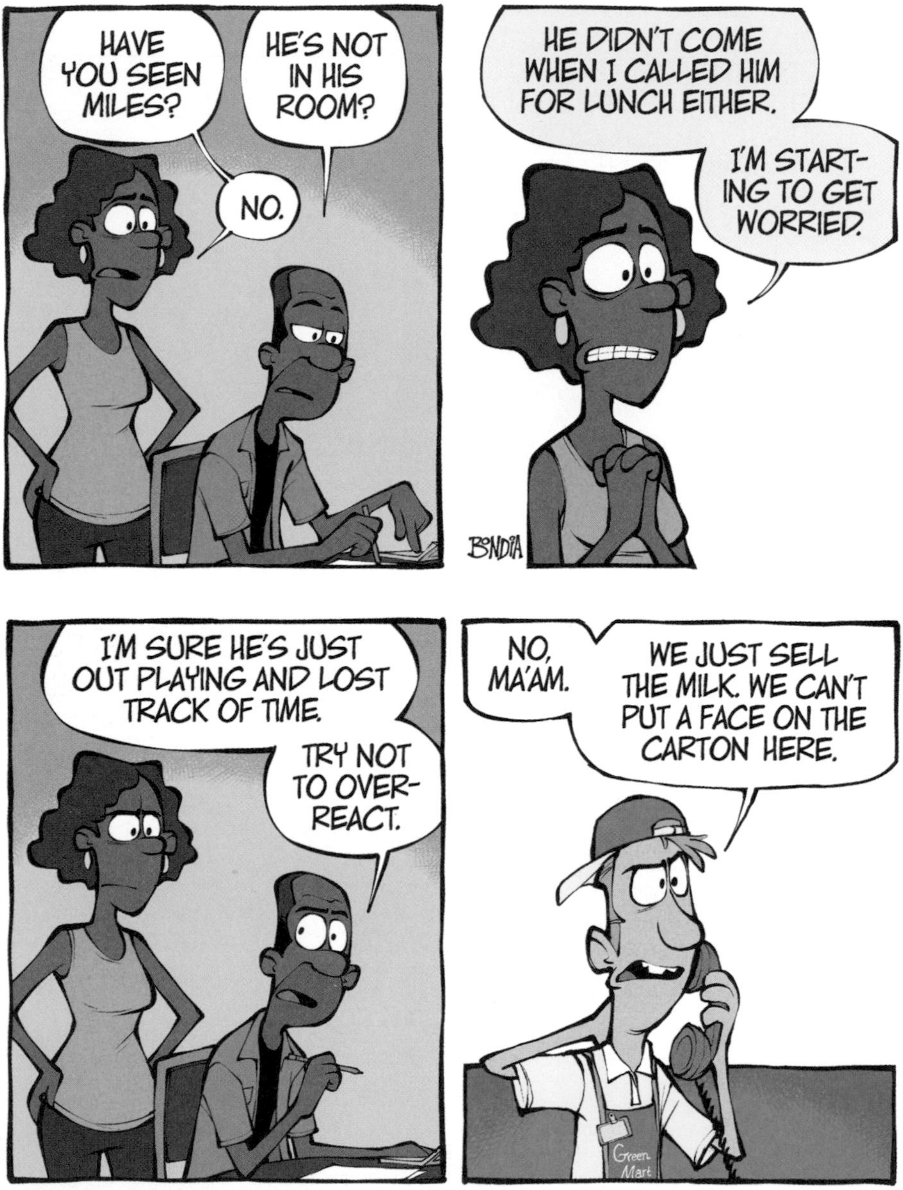
HAVE YOU SEEN MILES?
HE'S NOT IN HIS ROOM?
NO.
BONDIA
HE DIDN'T COME WHEN I CALLED HIM FOR LUNCH EITHER.
I'M STARTING TO GET WORRIED.
I'M SURE HE'S JUST OUT PLAYING AND LOST TRACK OF TIME.
TRY NOT TO OVER-REACT.
NO, MA'AM.
WE JUST SELL THE MILK. WE CAN'T PUT A FACE ON THE CARTON HERE.
Green Mart

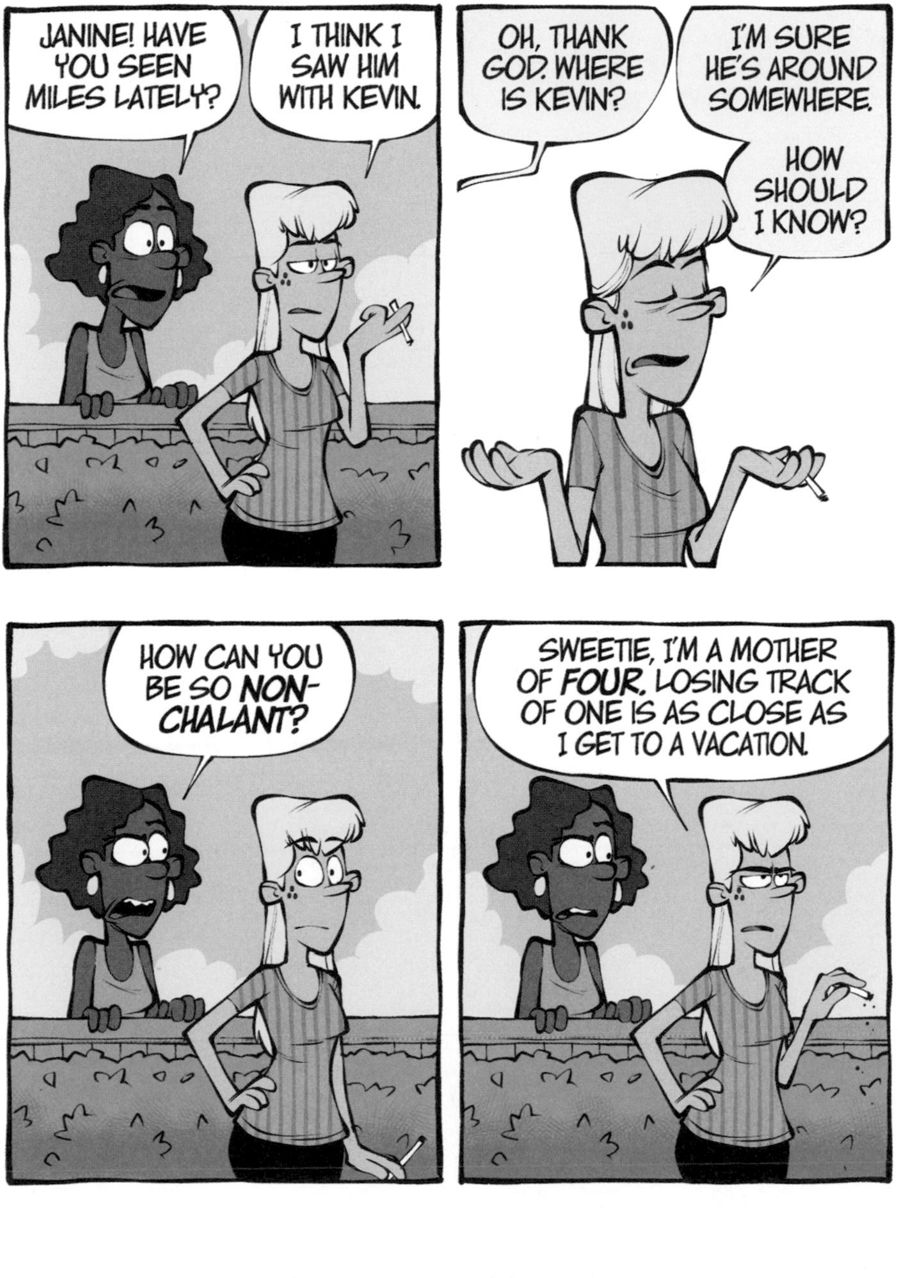
JANINE! HAVE YOU SEEN MILES LATELY?
I THINK I SAW HIM WITH KEVIN.
OH, THANK GOD. WHERE IS KEVIN?
I'M SURE HE'S AROUND SOMEWHERE.
HOW SHOULD I KNOW?
HOW CAN YOU BE SO NON-CHALANT?
SWEETIE, I'M A MOTHER OF FOUR. LOSING TRACK OF ONE IS AS CLOSE AS I GET TO A VACATION.

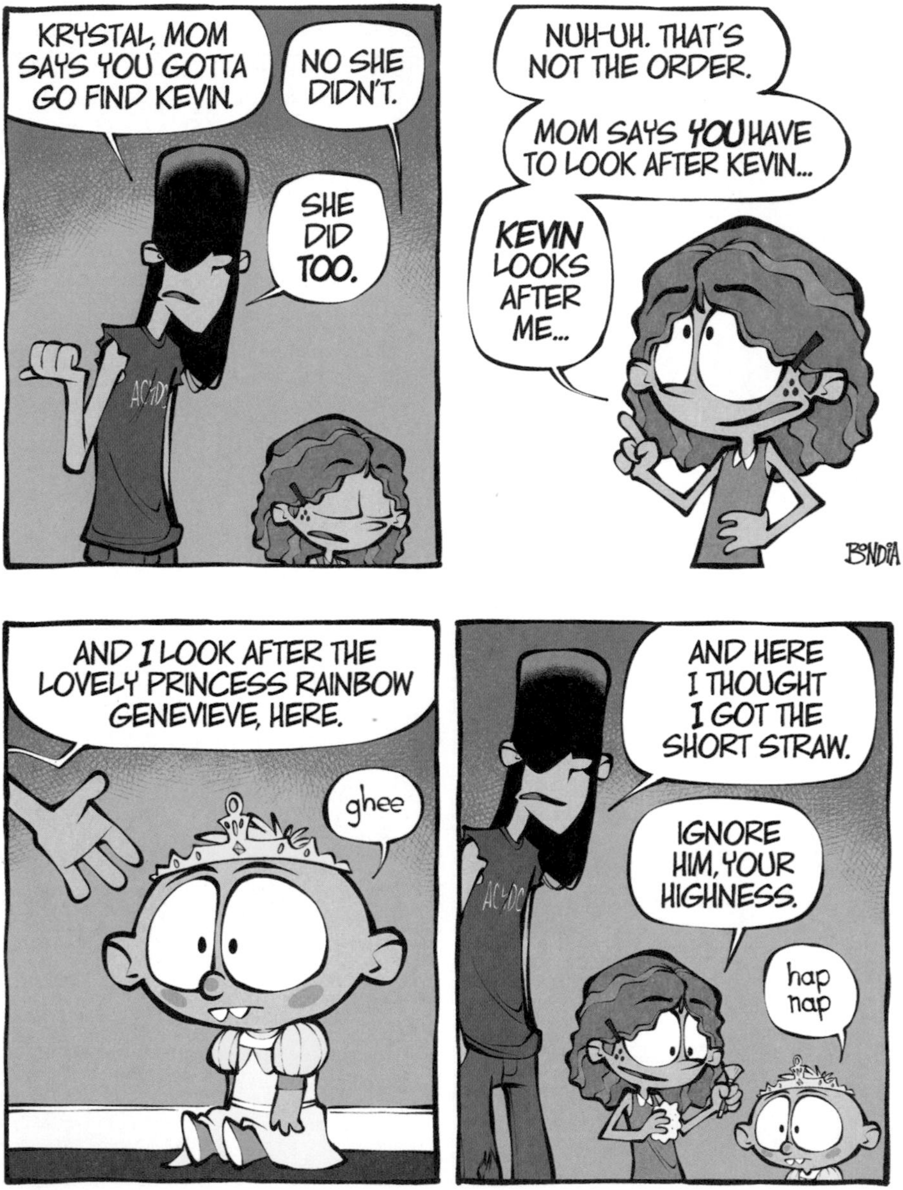
KRYSTAL, MOM SAYS YOU GOTTA GO FIND KEVIN.
NO SHE DIDN'T.
SHE DID TOO.
AC/DC
NUH-UH. THAT'S NOT THE ORDER.
MOM SAYS YOU HAVE TO LOOK AFTER KEVIN...
KEVIN LOOKS AFTER ME...
BONDIA
AND I LOOK AFTER THE LOVELY PRINCESS RAINBOW GENEVIEVE, HERE.
ghee
AND HERE I THOUGHT I GOT THE SHORT STRAW.
IGNORE HIM, YOUR HIGHNESS.
hap nap

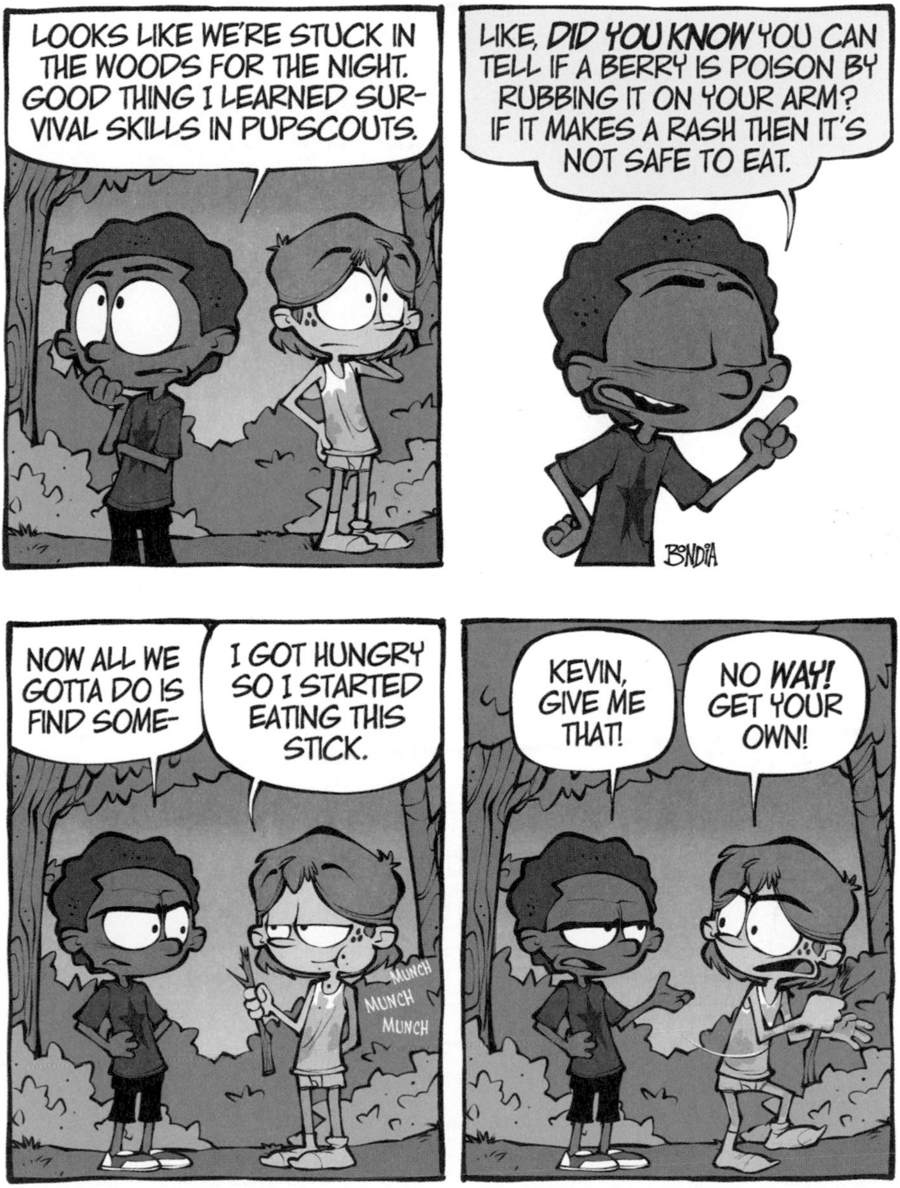
LOOKS LIKE WE'RE STUCK IN THE WOODS FOR THE NIGHT. GOOD THING I LEARNED SURVIVAL SKILLS IN PUPSCOUTS.
LIKE, DID YOU KNOW YOU CAN TELL IF A BERRY IS POISON BY RUBBING IT ON YOUR ARM? IF IT MAKES A RASH THEN IT'S NOT SAFE TO EAT.
BONDIA
NOW ALL WE GOTTA DO IS FIND SOME-
I GOT HUNGRY SO I STARTED EATING THIS STICK.
MUNCH
MUNCH
MUNCH
KEVIN, GIVE ME THAT!
NO WAY! GET YOUR OWN!

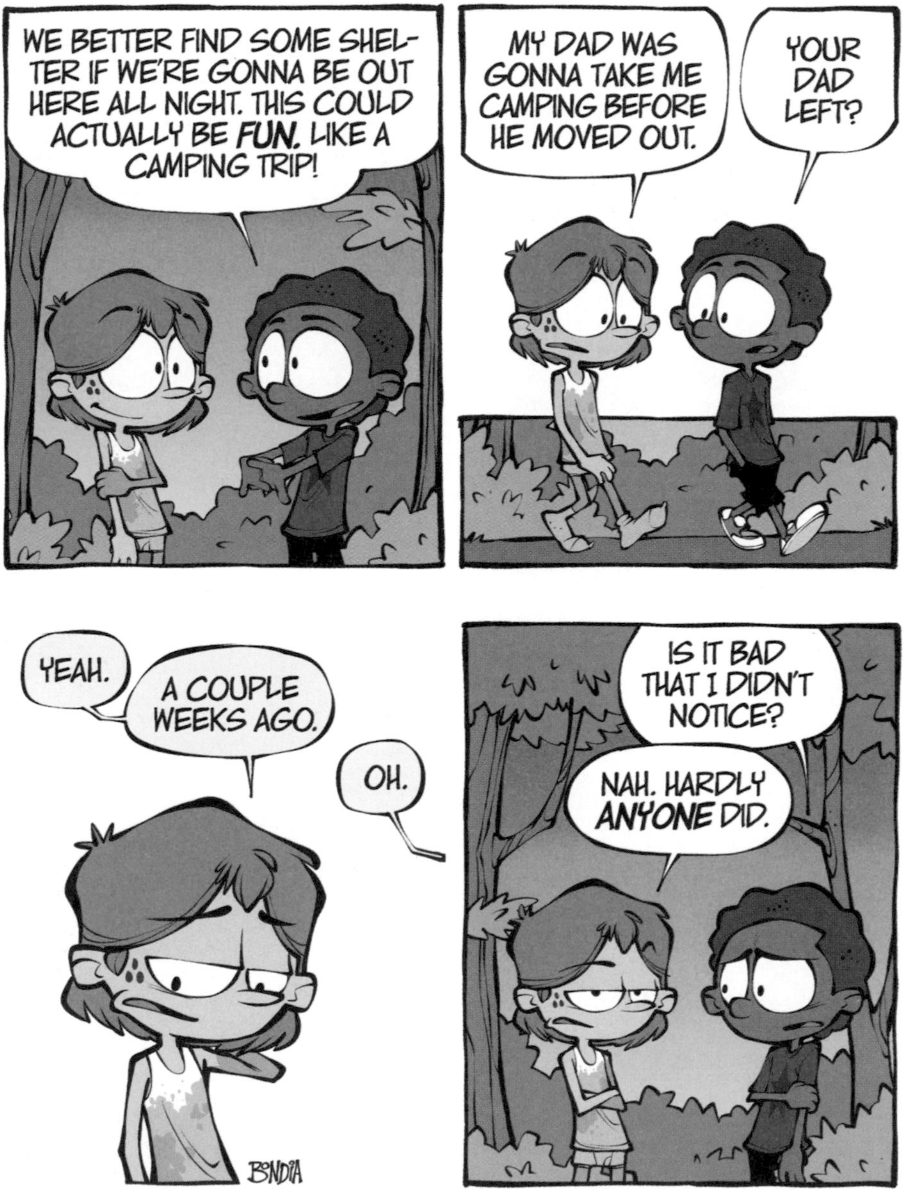
WE BETTER FIND SOME SHEL-TER IF WE'RE GONNA BE OUT HERE ALL NIGHT. THIS COULD ACTUALLY BE FUN. LIKE A CAMPING TRIP!
MY DAD WAS GONNA TAKE ME CAMPING BEFORE HE MOVED OUT.
YOUR DAD LEFT?
YEAH.
A COUPLE WEEKS AGO.
OH.
BONDIA
IS IT BAD THAT I DIDN'T NOTICE?
NAH. HARDLY ANYONE DID.

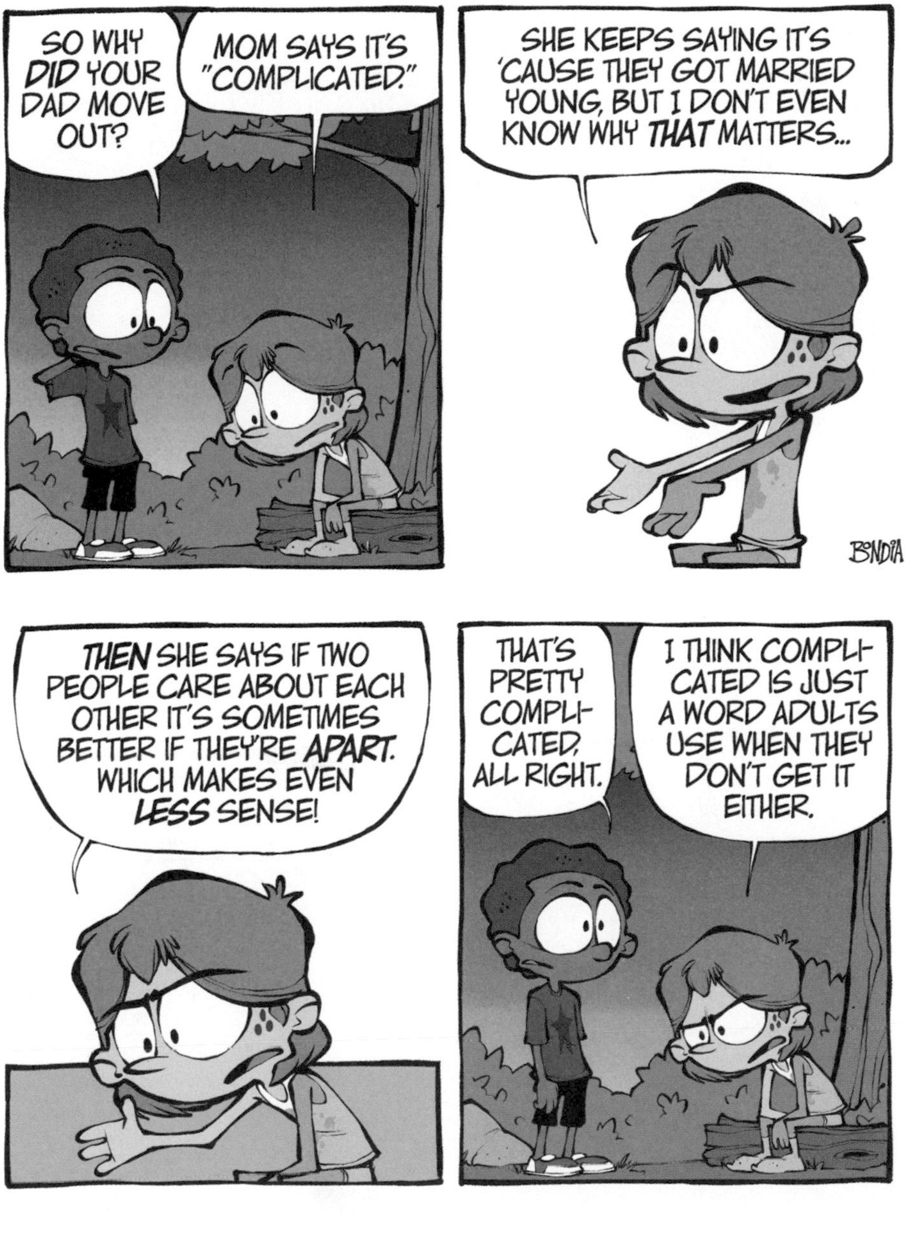
SO WHY DID YOUR DAD MOVE OUT?
MOM SAYS IT'S "COMPLICATED."
SHE KEEPS SAYING IT'S 'CAUSE THEY GOT MARRIED YOUNG, BUT I DON'T EVEN KNOW WHY THAT MATTERS...
BONDIA
THEN SHE SAYS IF TWO PEOPLE CARE ABOUT EACH OTHER IT'S SOMETIMES BETTER IF THEY'RE APART. WHICH MAKES EVEN LESS SENSE!
THAT'S PRETTY COMPLI-CATED, ALL RIGHT.
I THINK COMPLI-CATED IS JUST A WORD ADULTS USE WHEN THEY DON'T GET IT EITHER.

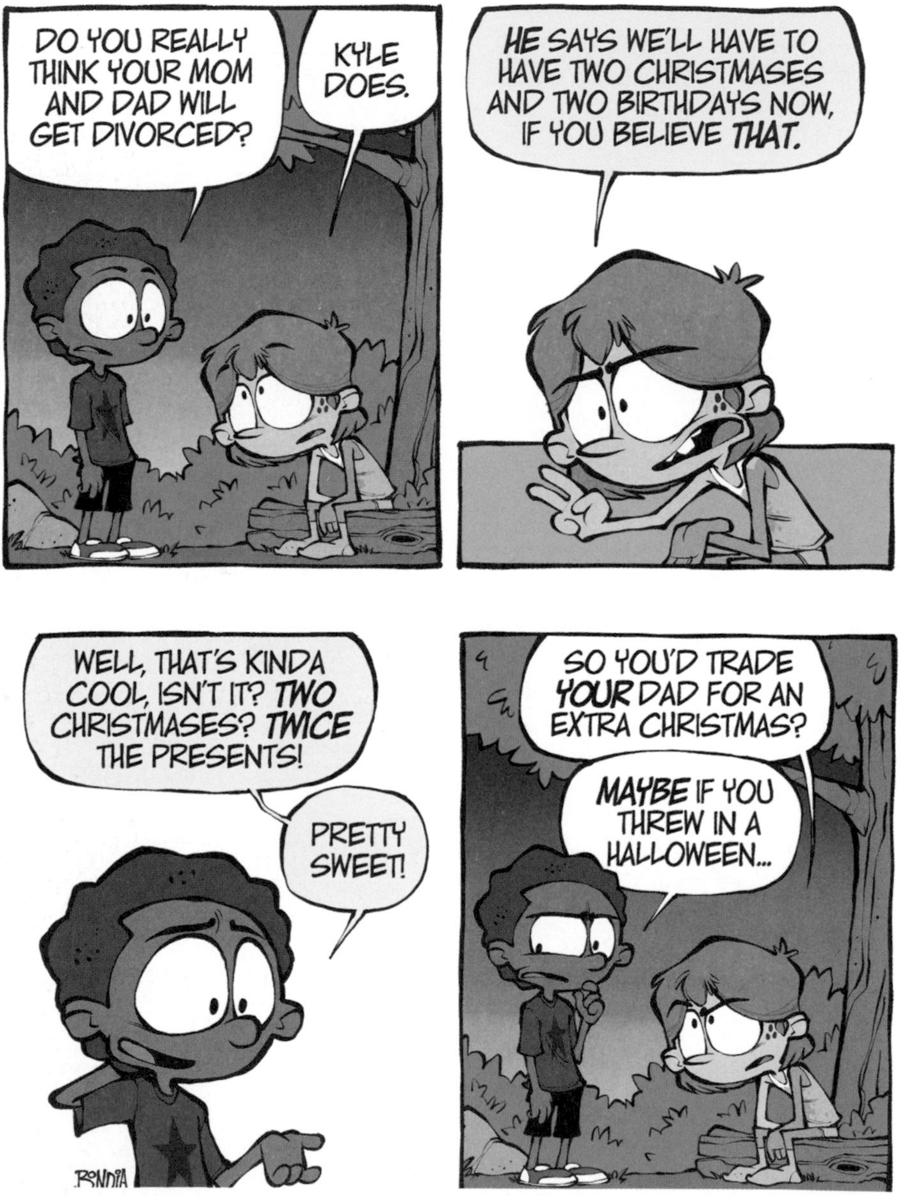
DO YOU REALLY THINK YOUR MOM AND DAD WILL GET DIVORCED?
KYLE DOES.
HE SAYS WE'LL HAVE TO HAVE TWO CHRISTMASES AND TWO BIRTHDAYS NOW, IF YOU BELIEVE THAT.
WELL, THAT'S KINDA COOL, ISN'T IT? TWO CHRISTMASES? TWICE THE PRESENTS!
PRETTY SWEET!
RONDIA
SO YOU'D TRADE YOUR DAD FOR AN EXTRA CHRISTMAS?
MAYBE IF YOU THREW IN A HALLOWEEN...

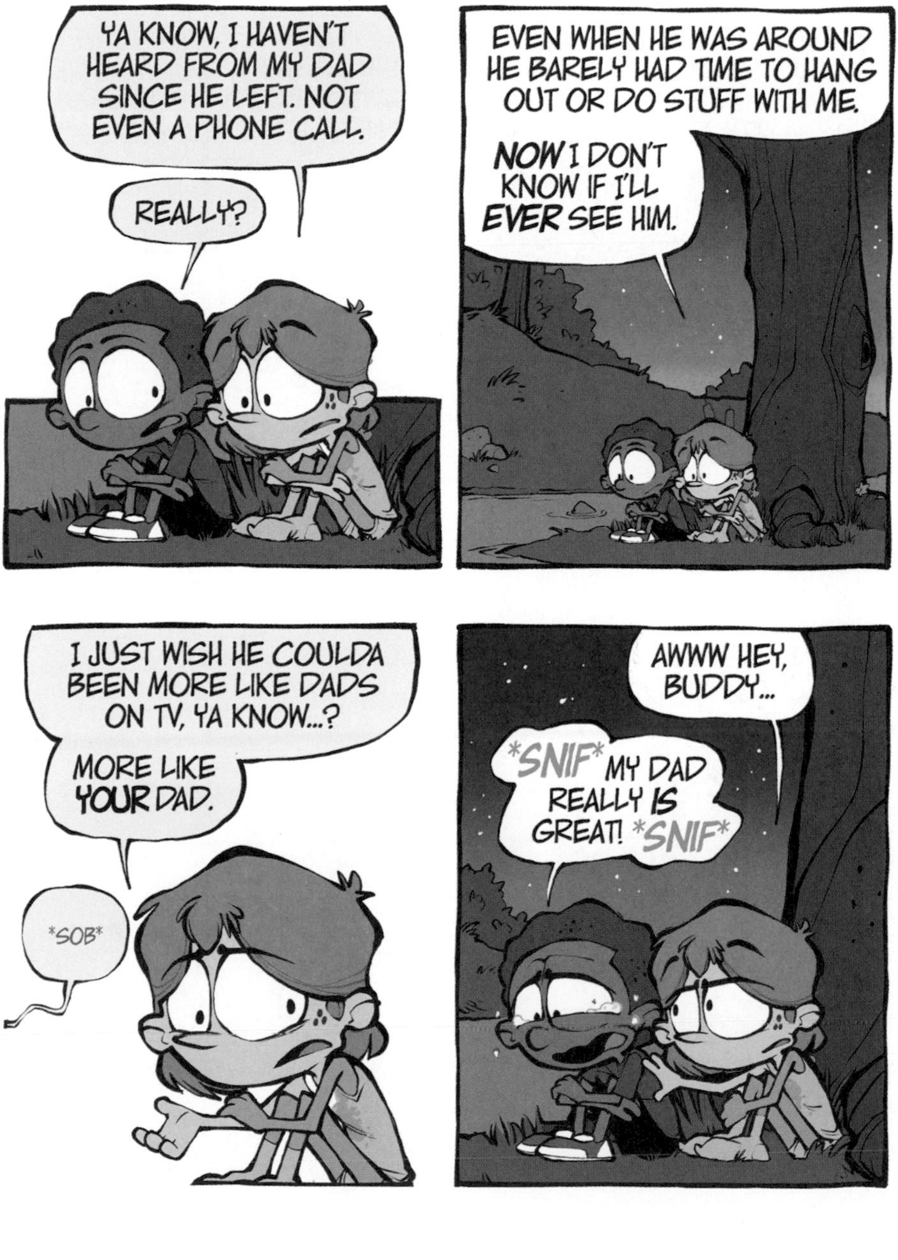
YA KNOW, I HAVEN'T HEARD FROM MY DAD SINCE HE LEFT. NOT EVEN A PHONE CALL.
REALLY?
EVEN WHEN HE WAS AROUND HE BARELY HAD TIME TO HANG OUT OR DO STUFF WITH ME.
NOW I DON'T KNOW IF I'LL EVER SEE HIM.
I JUST WISH HE COULDA BEEN MORE LIKE DADS ON TV, YA KNOW...?
MORE LIKE YOUR DAD.
SOB
AWWW HEY, BUDDY...
SNIF MY DAD REALLY IS GREAT! *SNIF*

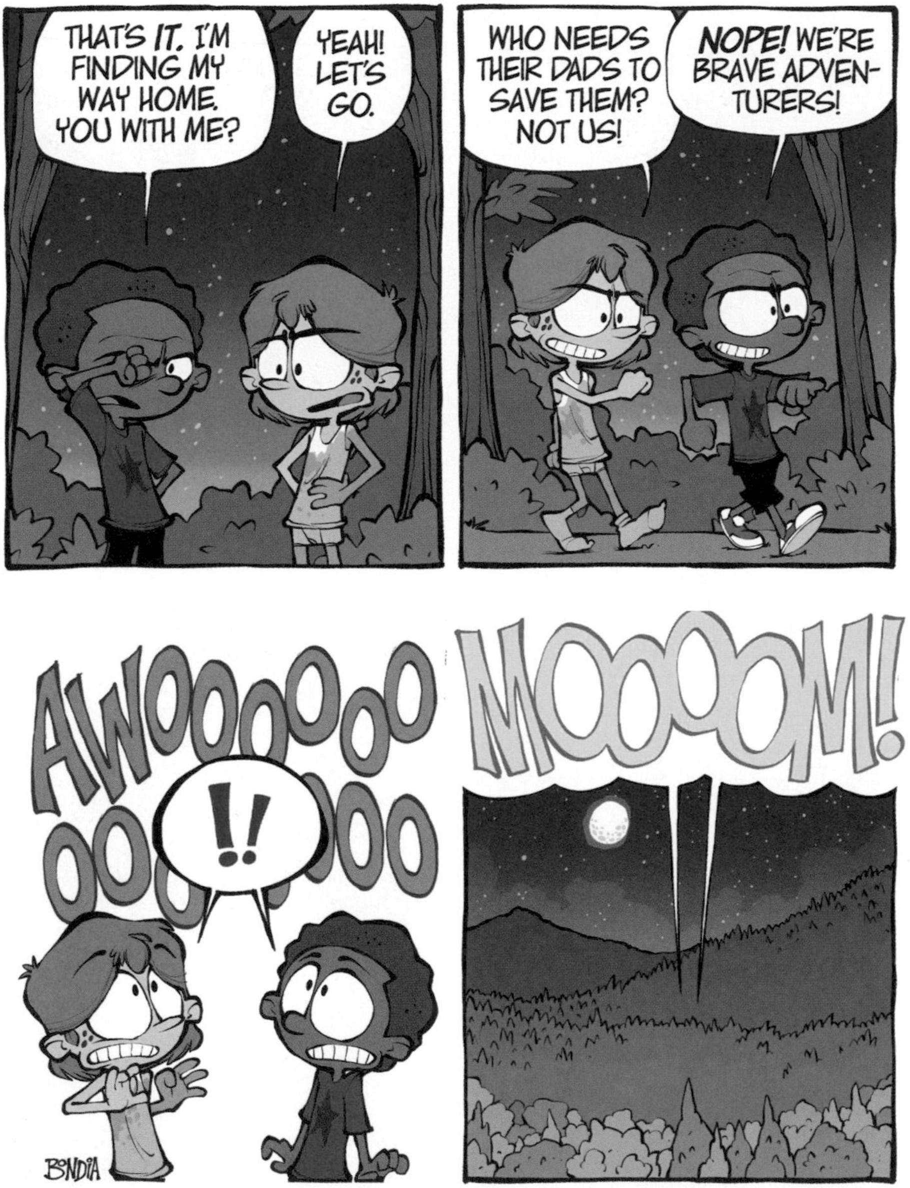
THAT'S *IT.* I'M FINDING MY WAY HOME. YOU WITH ME?
YEAH! LET'S GO.
WHO NEEDS THEIR DADS TO SAVE THEM? NOT US!
NOPE! WE'RE BRAVE ADVEN-TURERS!
AWOOOOOOO
OOO OOOO
!!
MOOOOM!
BONDIA

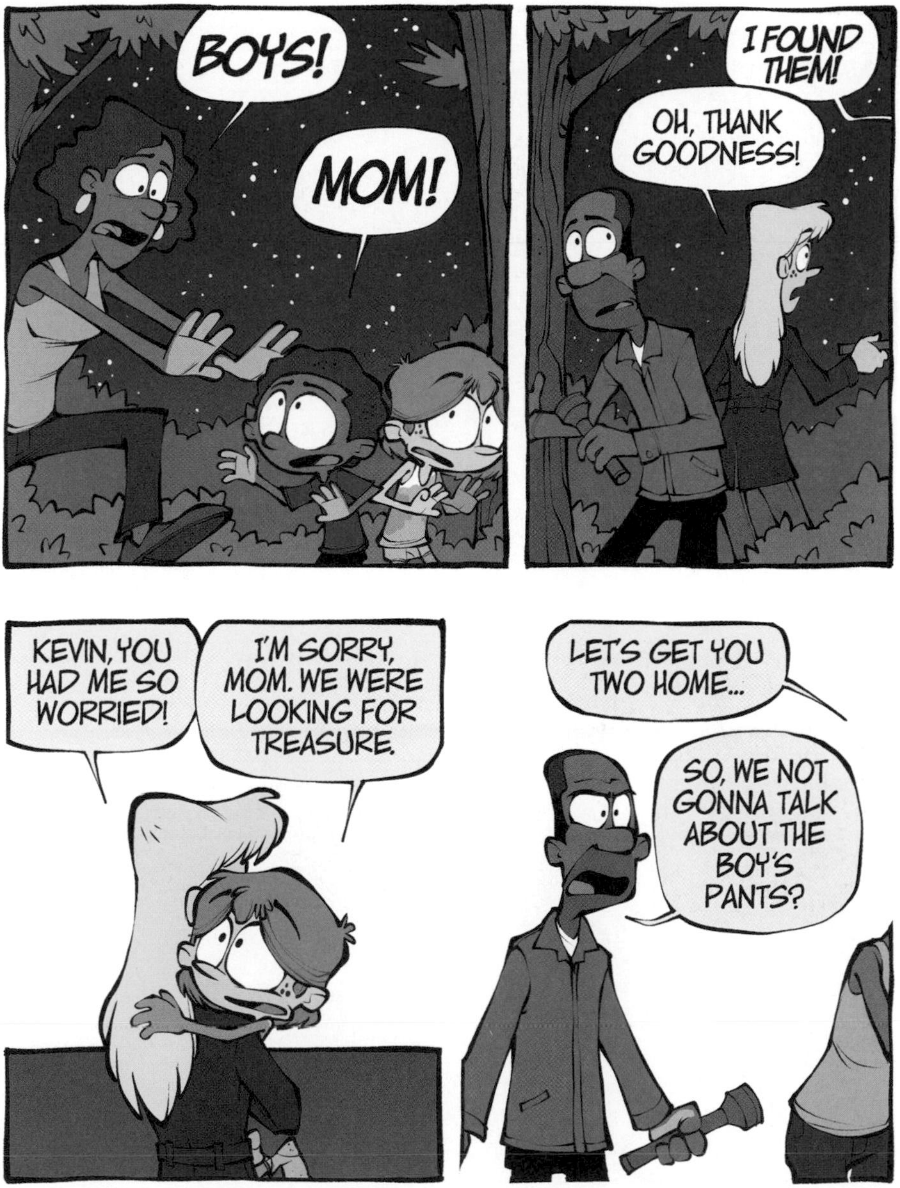
BOYS!
MOM!
I FOUND THEM!
OH, THANK GOODNESS!
KEVIN, YOU HAD ME SO WORRIED!
I'M SORRY, MOM. WE WERE LOOKING FOR TREASURE.
LET'S GET YOU TWO HOME...
SO, WE NOT GONNA TALK ABOUT THE BOY'S PANTS?

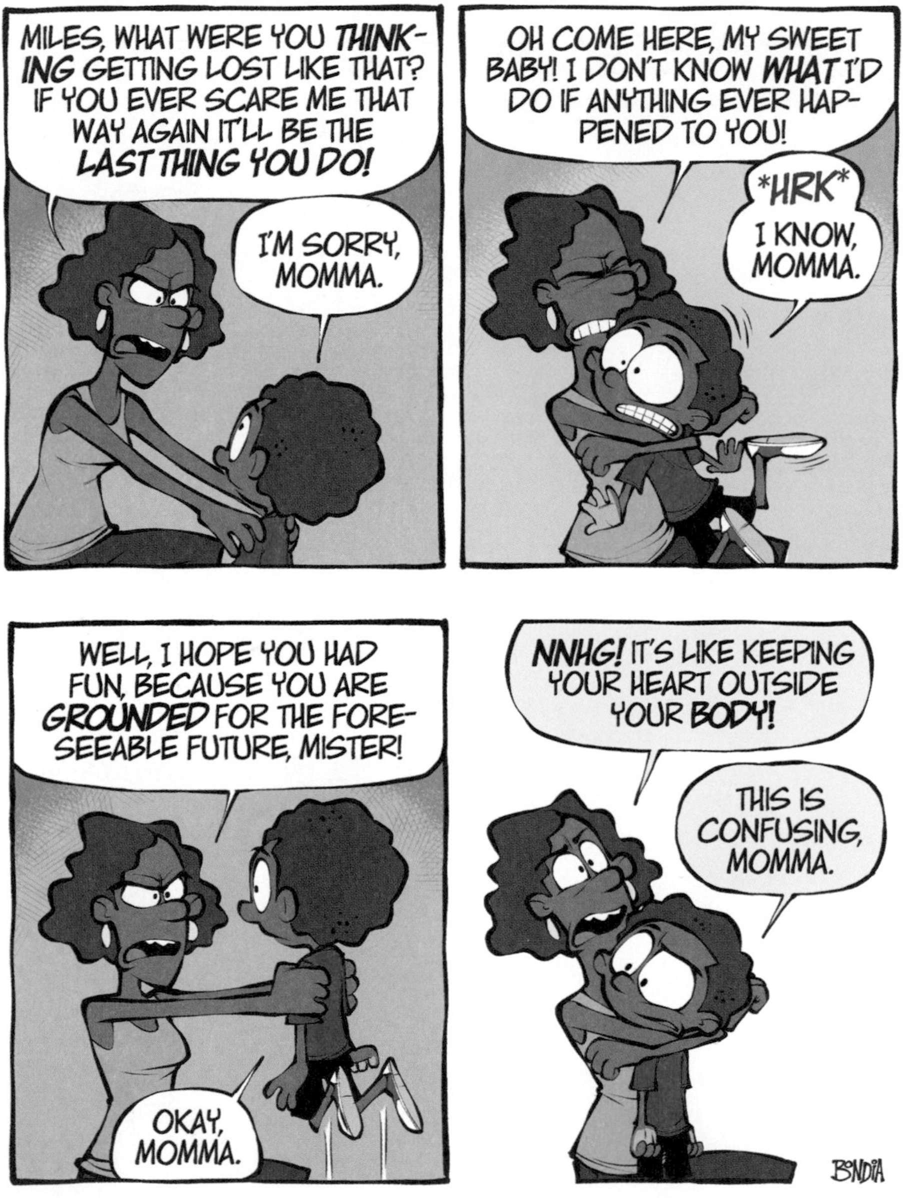
MILES, WHAT WERE YOU THINKING GETTING LOST LIKE THAT? IF YOU EVER SCARE ME THAT WAY AGAIN IT'LL BE THE LAST THING YOU DO!
I'M SORRY, MOMMA.
OH COME HERE, MY SWEET BABY! I DON'T KNOW WHAT I'D DO IF ANYTHING EVER HAPPENED TO YOU!
HRK
I KNOW, MOMMA.
WELL, I HOPE YOU HAD FUN, BECAUSE YOU ARE GROUNDED FOR THE FORESEEABLE FUTURE, MISTER!
OKAY, MOMMA.
NNHG! IT'S LIKE KEEPING YOUR HEART OUTSIDE YOUR BODY!
THIS IS CONFUSING, MOMMA.
BONDIA

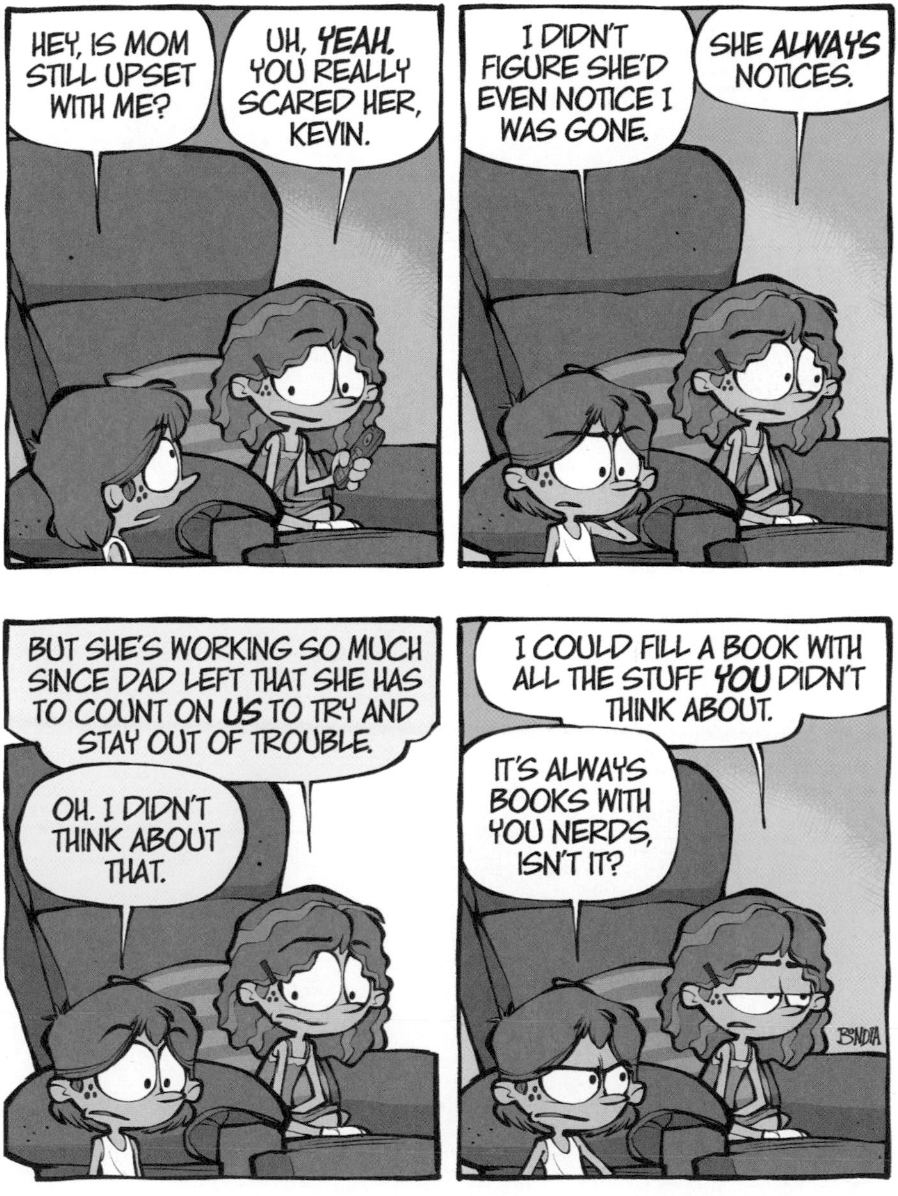

HEY, IS MOM STILL UPSET WITH ME?
UH, *YEAH.* YOU REALLY SCARED HER, KEVIN.
I DIDN'T FIGURE SHE'D EVEN NOTICE I WAS GONE.
SHE *ALWAYS* NOTICES.
BUT SHE'S WORKING SO MUCH SINCE DAD LEFT THAT SHE HAS TO COUNT ON *US* TO TRY AND STAY OUT OF TROUBLE.
OH. I DIDN'T THINK ABOUT THAT.
I COULD FILL A BOOK WITH ALL THE STUFF *YOU* DIDN'T THINK ABOUT.
IT'S ALWAYS BOOKS WITH YOU NERDS, ISN'T IT?
BONDIA

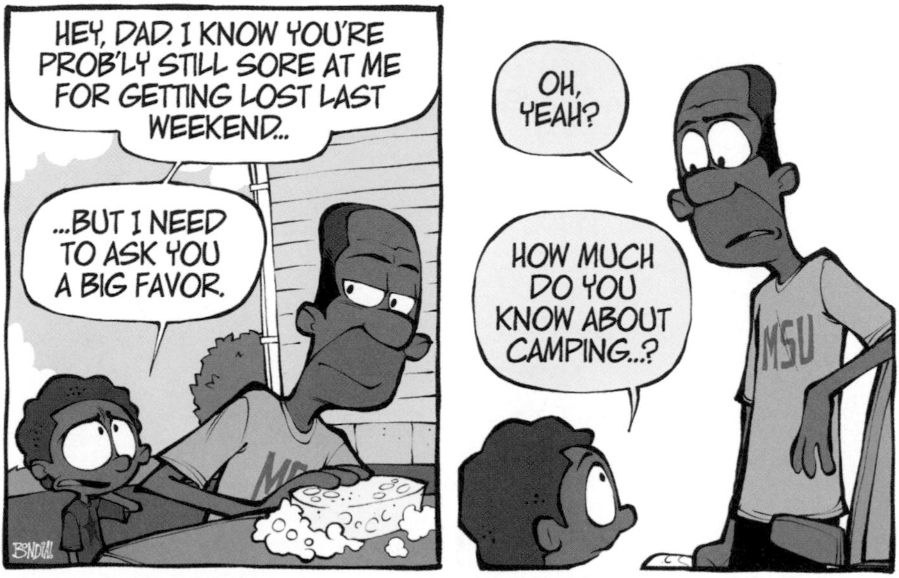
HEY, DAD. I KNOW YOU'RE PROB'LY STILL SORE AT ME FOR GETTING LOST LAST WEEKEND...
...BUT I NEED TO ASK YOU A BIG FAVOR.
OH, YEAH?
HOW MUCH DO YOU KNOW ABOUT CAMPING...?

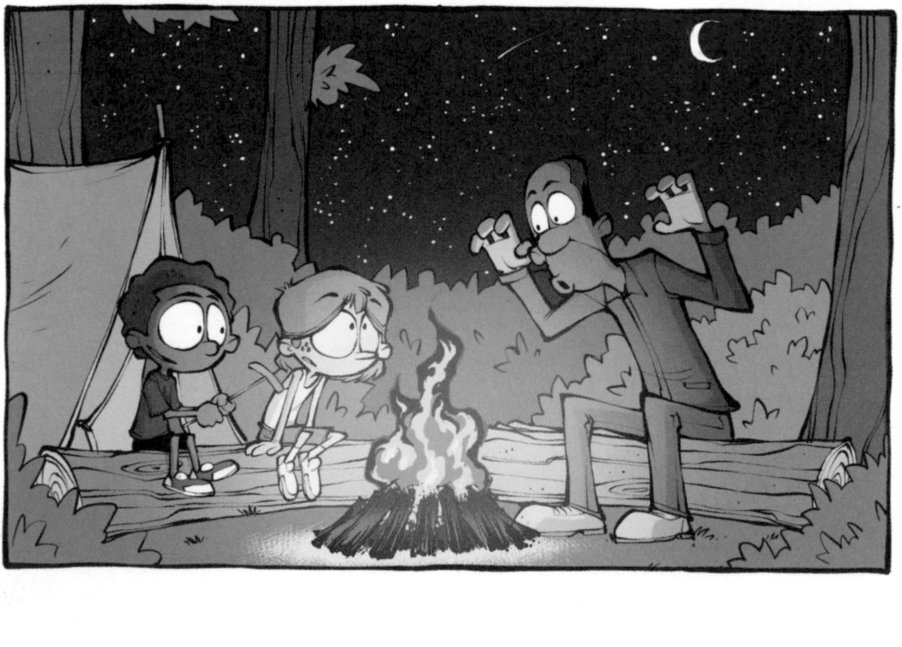

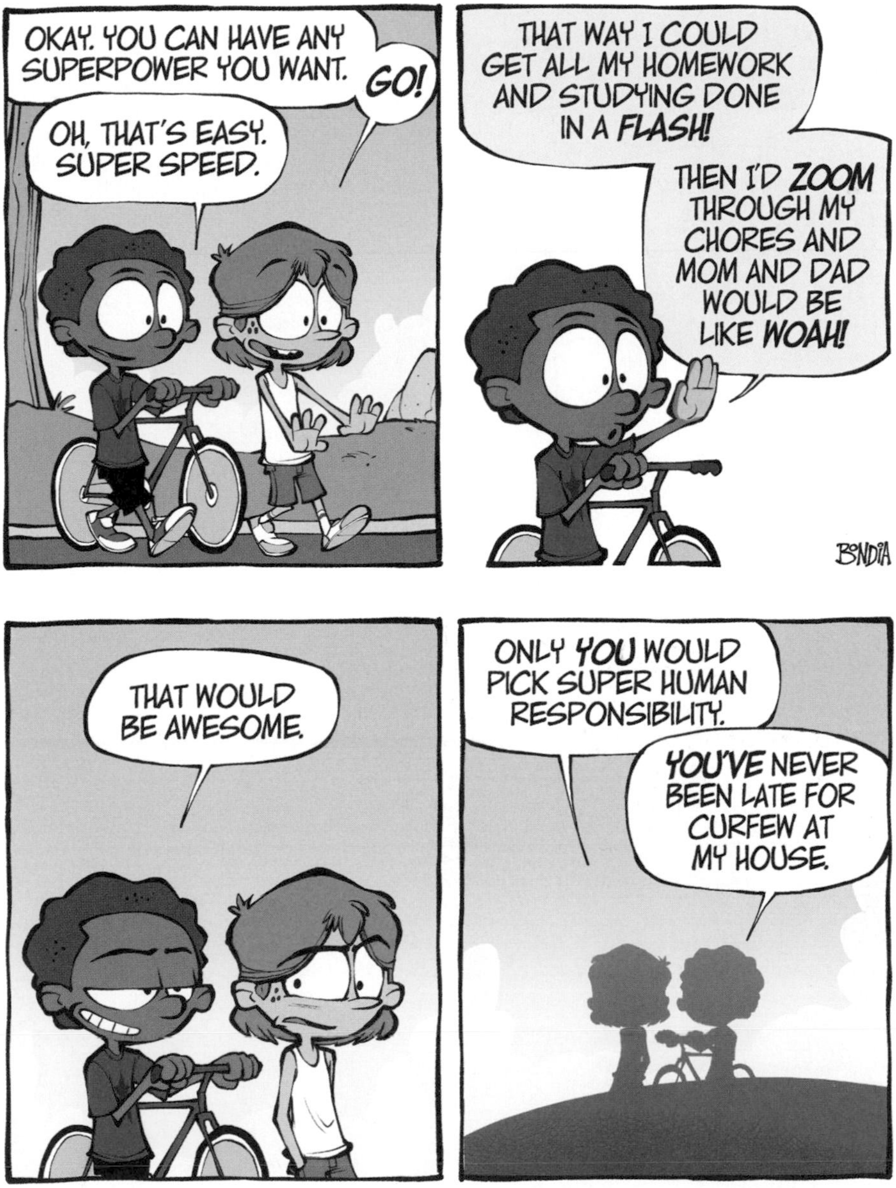
OKAY. YOU CAN HAVE ANY SUPERPOWER YOU WANT.
GO!
OH, THAT'S EASY. SUPER SPEED.
THAT WAY I COULD GET ALL MY HOMEWORK AND STUDYING DONE IN A FLASH!
THEN I'D ZOOM THROUGH MY CHORES AND MOM AND DAD WOULD BE LIKE WOAH!
BONDIA
THAT WOULD BE AWESOME.
ONLY YOU WOULD PICK SUPER HUMAN RESPONSIBILITY.
YOU'VE NEVER BEEN LATE FOR CURFEW AT MY HOUSE.

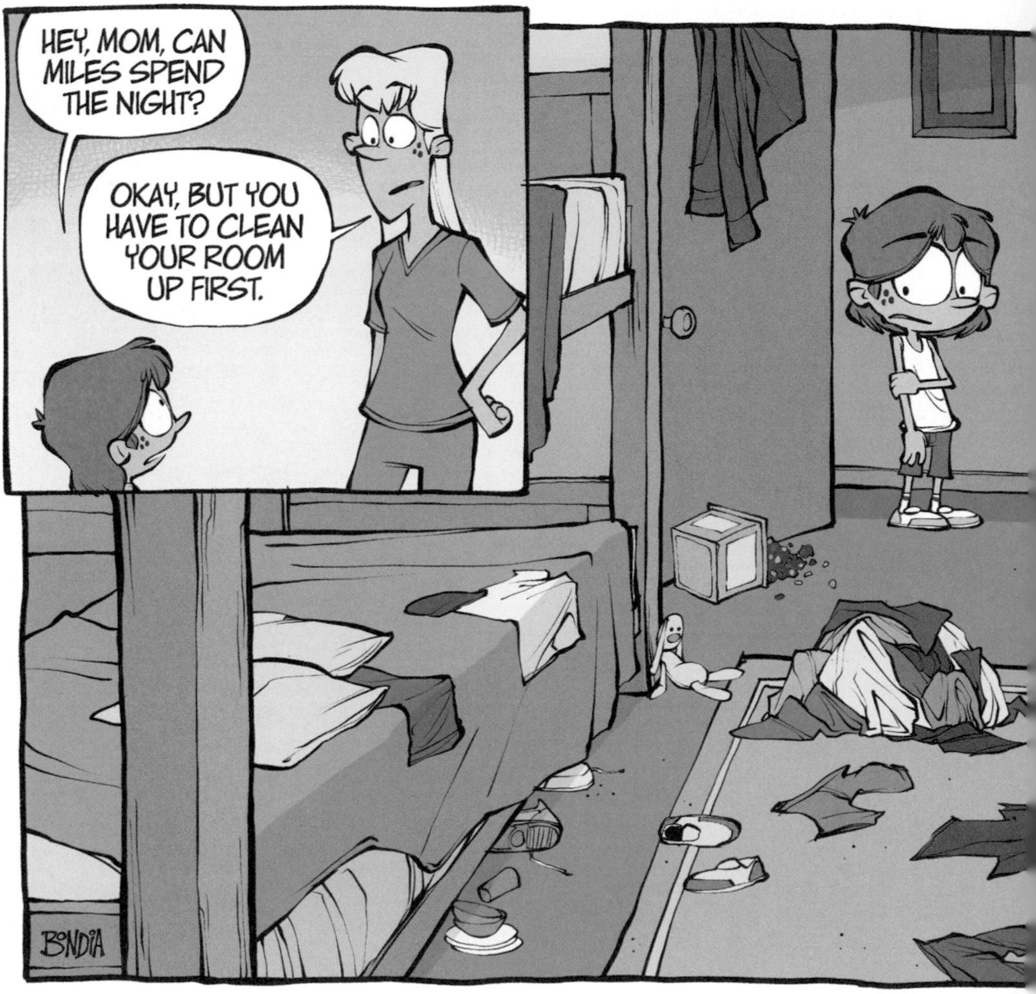
HEY, MOM, CAN MILES SPEND THE NIGHT?
OKAY, BUT YOU HAVE TO CLEAN YOUR ROOM UP FIRST.
BONDIA

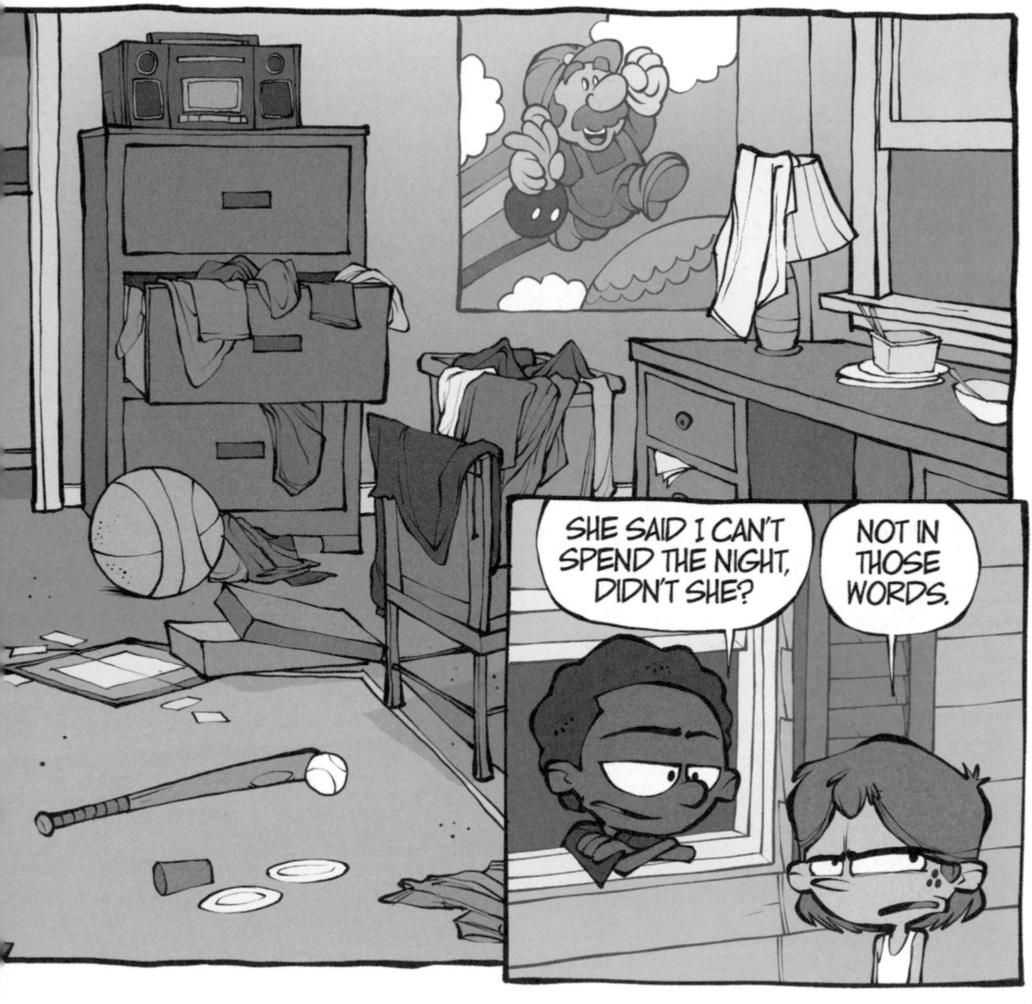
SHE SAID I CAN'T SPEND THE NIGHT, DIDN'T SHE?
NOT IN THOSE WORDS.

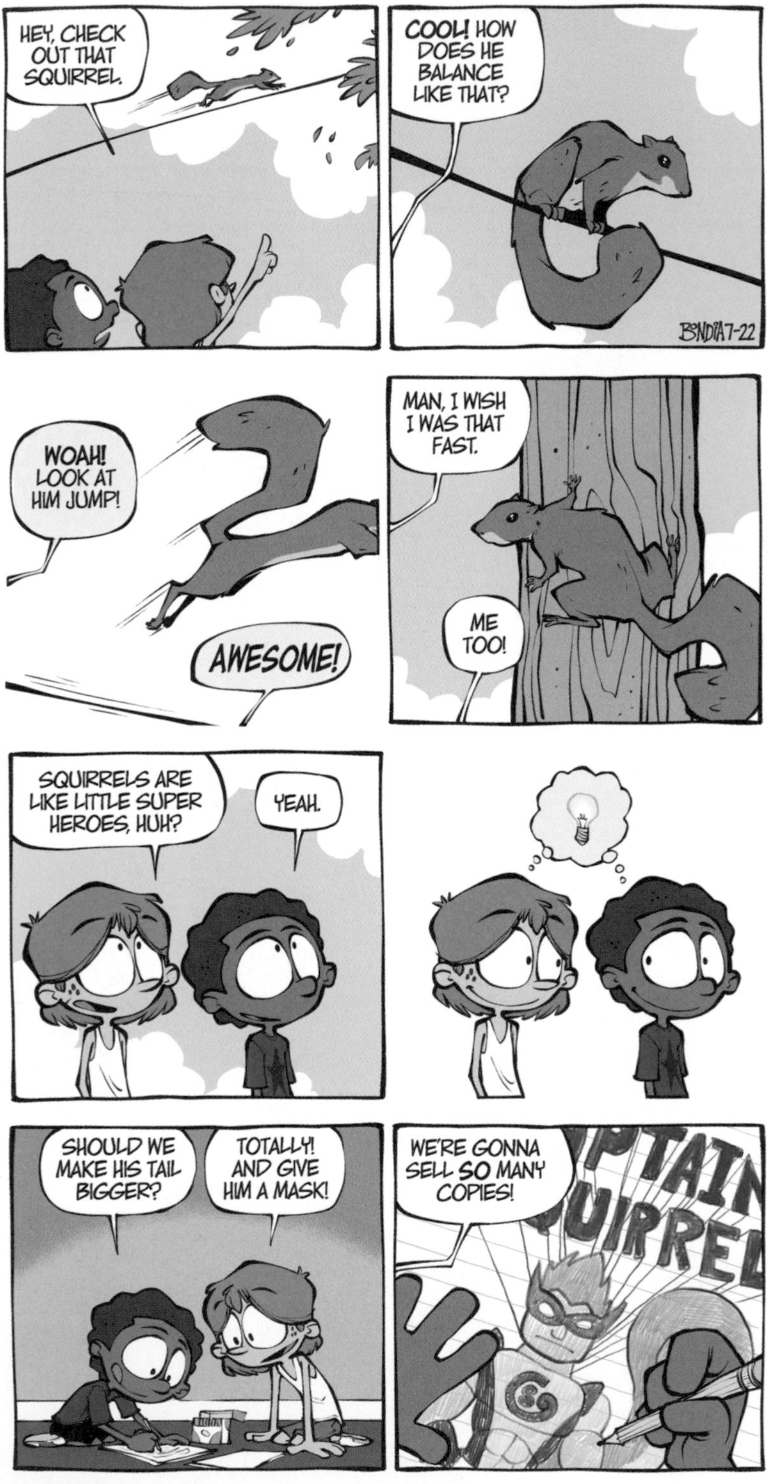
HEY, CHECK OUT THAT SQUIRREL.
COOL! HOW DOES HE BALANCE LIKE THAT?
BONDIA 7-22
WOAH! LOOK AT HIM JUMP!
AWESOME!
MAN, I WISH I WAS THAT FAST.
ME TOO!
SQUIRRELS ARE LIKE LITTLE SUPER HEROES, HUH?
YEAH.
SHOULD WE MAKE HIS TAIL BIGGER?
TOTALLY! AND GIVE HIM A MASK!
WE'RE GONNA SELL SO MANY COPIES!

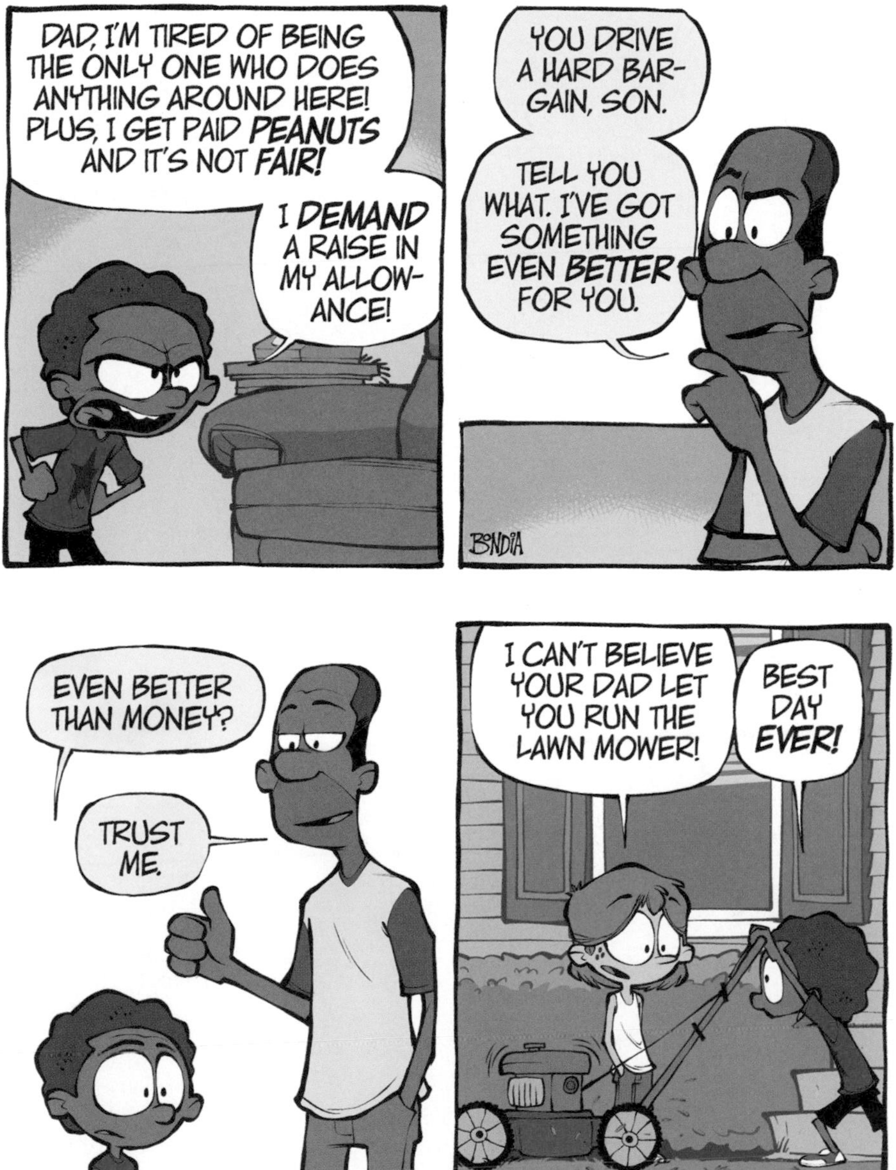
DAD, I'M TIRED OF BEING THE ONLY ONE WHO DOES ANYTHING AROUND HERE! PLUS, I GET PAID PEANUTS AND IT'S NOT FAIR!
I DEMAND A RAISE IN MY ALLOWANCE!
YOU DRIVE A HARD BARGAIN, SON.
TELL YOU WHAT. I'VE GOT SOMETHING EVEN BETTER FOR YOU.
BONDIA
EVEN BETTER THAN MONEY?
TRUST ME.
I CAN'T BELIEVE YOUR DAD LET YOU RUN THE LAWN MOWER!
BEST DAY EVER!

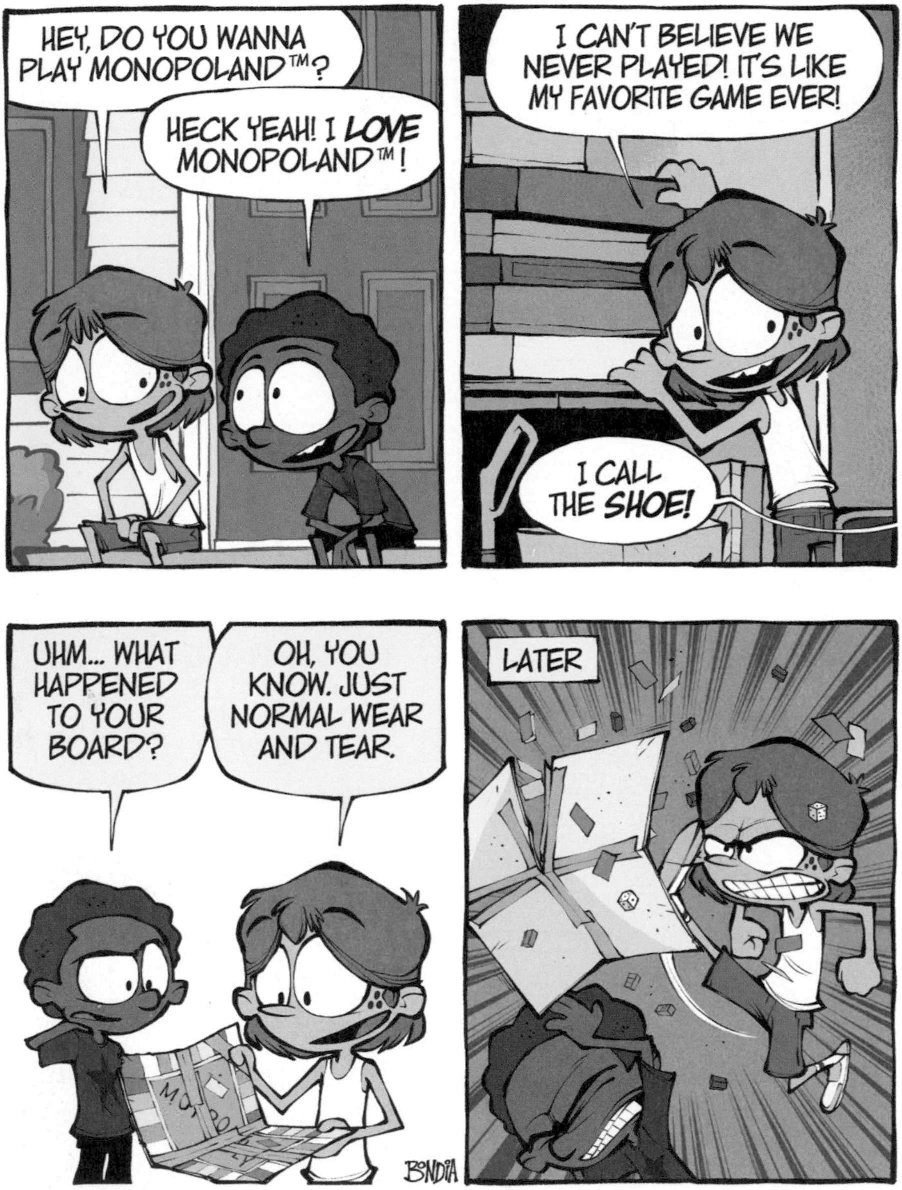
HEY, DO YOU WANNA PLAY MONOPOLAND™?
HECK YEAH! I LOVE MONOPOLAND™!
I CAN'T BELIEVE WE NEVER PLAYED! IT'S LIKE MY FAVORITE GAME EVER!
I CALL THE SHOE!
UHM... WHAT HAPPENED TO YOUR BOARD?
OH, YOU KNOW. JUST NORMAL WEAR AND TEAR.
LATER
BONDIA

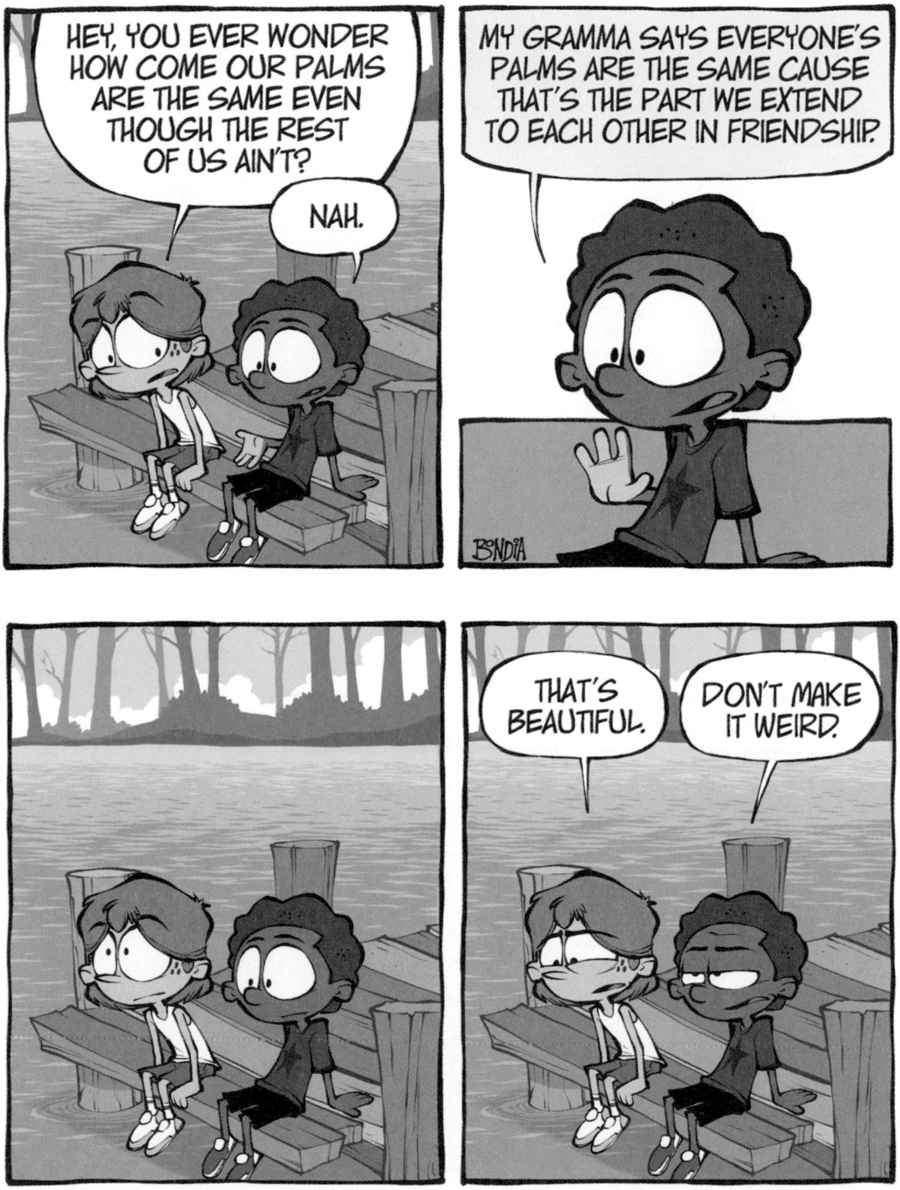
HEY, YOU EVER WONDER HOW COME OUR PALMS ARE THE SAME EVEN THOUGH THE REST OF US AIN'T?
NAH.
MY GRAMMA SAYS EVERYONE'S PALMS ARE THE SAME CAUSE THAT'S THE PART WE EXTEND TO EACH OTHER IN FRIENDSHIP.
BONDIA
THAT'S BEAUTIFUL.
DON'T MAKE IT WEIRD.

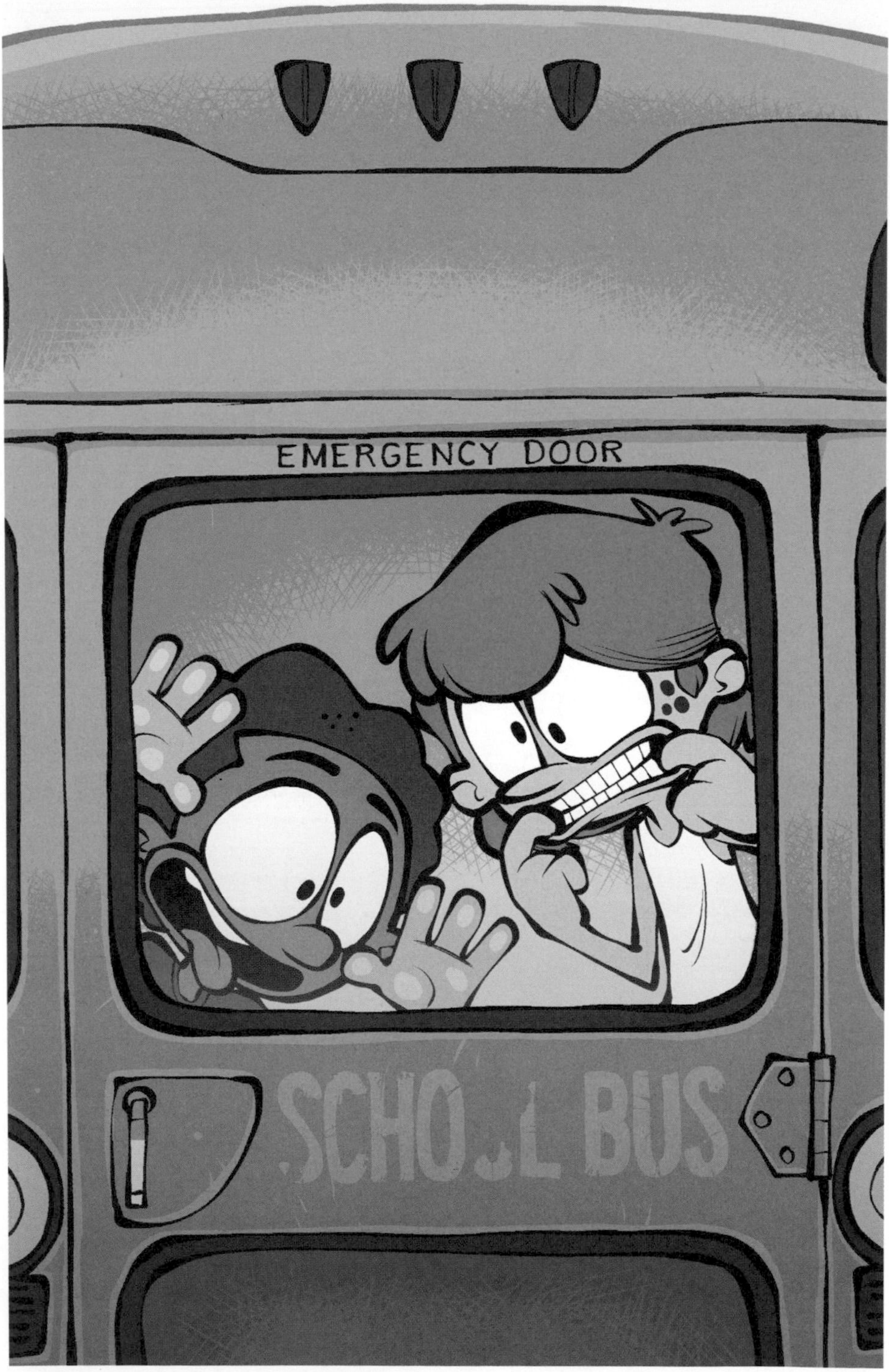
EMERGENCY DOOR
SCHO L BUS

Andrews McMeel Publishing
a division of Andrews McMeel Universal
1130 Walnut Street, Kansas City, Missouri 64106

www.andrewsmcmeel.com

22 23 24 25 26 SDB 10 9 8 7 6 5 4 3 2 1

ISBN: 978-1-5248-7555-8

Library of Congress Control Number: 2022933529

Made by:
King Yip (Dongguan) Printing & Packaging Factory Ltd.
Address and location of production:
Daning Administrative District, Humen Town
Dongguan Guangdong, China 523930
1st Printing — 6/6/22

ATTENTION: SCHOOLS AND BUSINESSES

Andrews McMeel books are available at quantity discounts with bulk purchase for educational, business, or sales promotional use. For information, please e-mail the Andrews McMeel Publishing Special Sales Department: specialsales@amuniversal.com.

Look for these books!

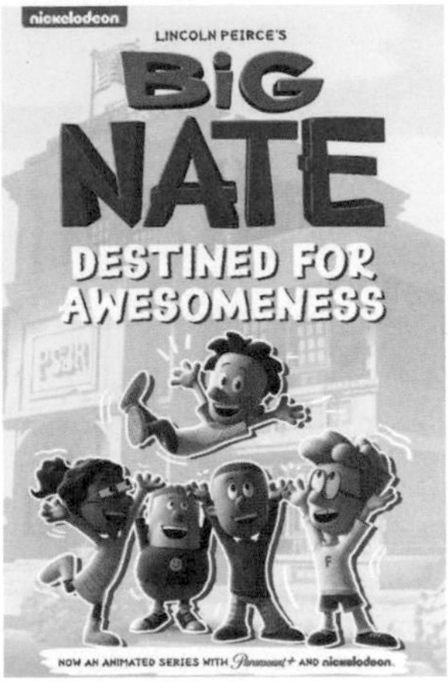
nickelodeon
LINCOLN PEIRCE'S
BIG NATE
DESTINED FOR AWESOMENESS
NOW AN ANIMATED SERIES WITH Paramount+ AND nickelodeon.

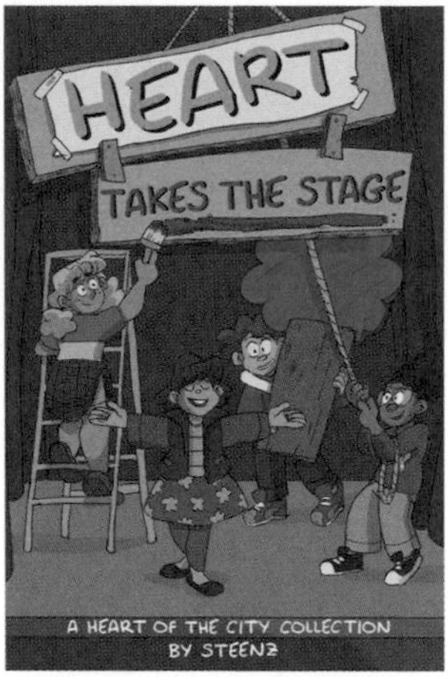
HEART
TAKES THE STAGE
A HEART OF THE CITY COLLECTION
BY STEENZ

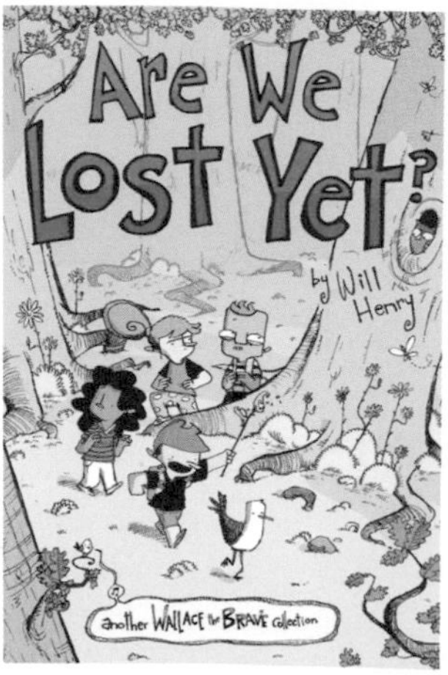
Are We Lost Yet?
by Will Henry
another WALLACE the BRAVE collection

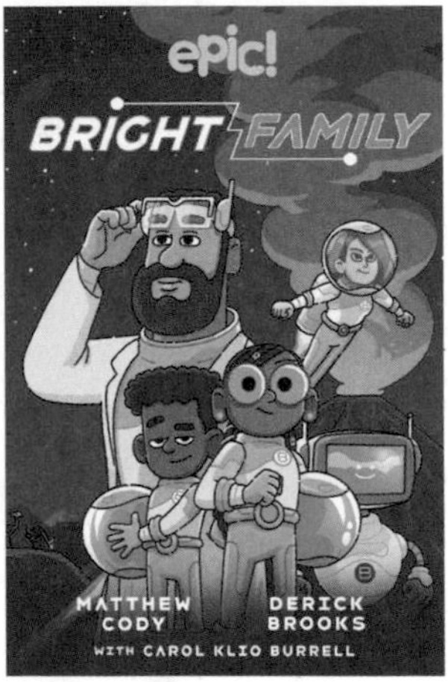
epic!
BRIGHT FAMILY
MATTHEW CODY
DERICK BROOKS
WITH CAROL KLIO BURRELL

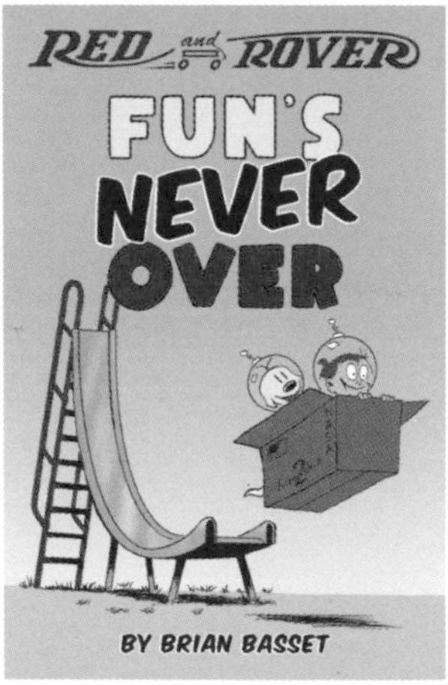
RED and ROVER
FUN'S NEVER OVER
BY BRIAN BASSET

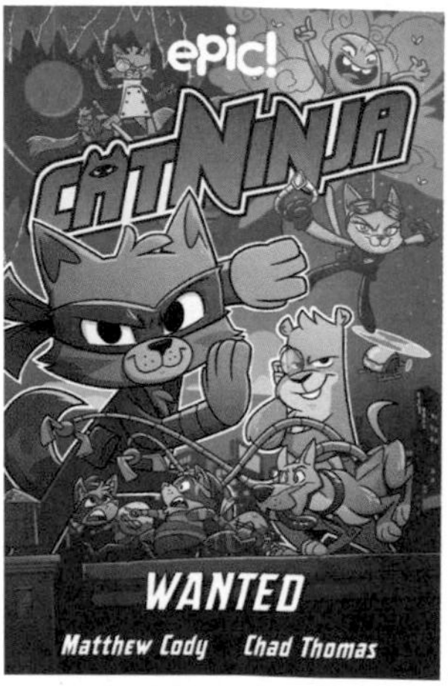
epic!
CAT NINJA
WANTED
Matthew Cody
Chad Thomas

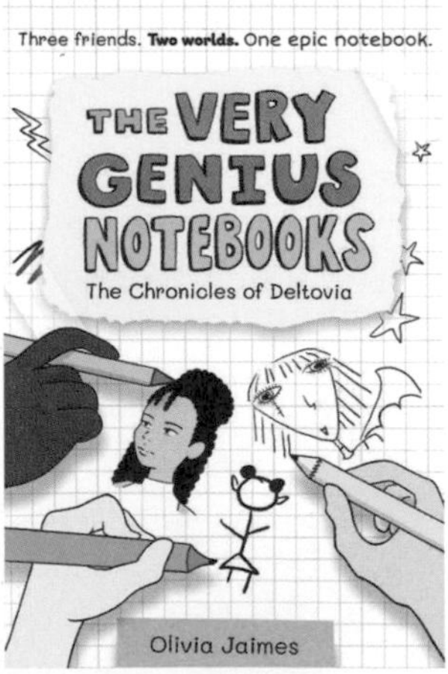
Three friends. Two worlds. One epic notebook.
THE VERY GENIUS NOTEBOOKS
The Chronicles of Deltovia
Olivia Jaimes

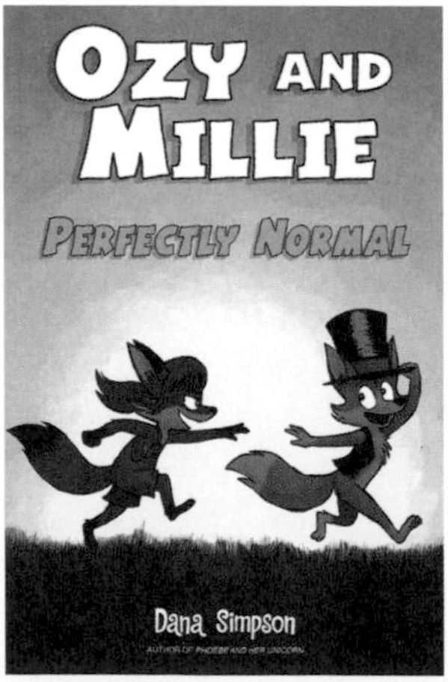
OZY AND MILLIE
PERFECTLY NORMAL
Dana Simpson

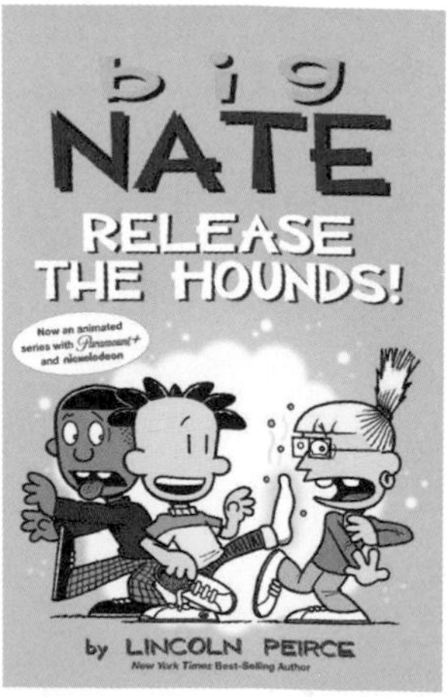
big NATE
RELEASE THE HOUNDS!
Now an animated series with Paramount+ and nickelodeon
by LINCOLN PEIRCE
New York Times Best-Selling Author